A Gift from Woolworths

Elaine Everest was born and brought up in north-west Kent, where her books are set, and has written widely for women's magazines – both short stories and features – as well as fiction and non-fiction books for the past twenty-one years. Successful in writing competitions she was shortlisted in The Harry Bowling Prize and was BBC Radio Kent Short Story Writer of the Year in 2003.

A qualified tutor, she runs The Write Place creative writing school in Hextable, Kent. Elaine lives with her husband, Michael, and their Polish Lowland Sheepdog, Henry, in Swanley, Kent. *A Gift from Woolworths* is the fifth book in her Woolworths series.

You can say hello to Elaine on
Twitter @ElaineEverest or
Facebook at www.facebook.com/ElaineEverestAuthor

Praise for Elaine Everest

'Heart-warming . . . a must-read'
Woman's Own

'A warm, tender tale of friendship and love'
Milly Johnson

'A lovely read'
Bella

'Elaine brings the heyday of the iconic
high-street giant to life in her charming novel'
S Magazine

Also by Elaine Everest

The Woolworths Girls
The Butlins Girls
Christmas at Woolworths
Wartime at Woolworths

Ebook novella
Carols at Woolworths

Elaine Everest

A Gift from Woolworths

PAN BOOKS

First published 2018 by Pan Books
an imprint of Pan Macmillan
20 New Wharf Road, London N1 9RR
Associated companies throughout the world
www.panmacmillan.com

ISBN 978-1-5098-9252-5

3 5 7 9 8 6 4 2

A CIP catalogue record for this book is available from the British Library.

Typeset by Palimpsest Book Production Ltd, Falkirk, Stirlingshire
Printed and bound by CPI Group (UK) Ltd, Croydon, CR0 4YY

Visit www.panmacmillan.com to read more about all our books
and to buy them. You will also find features, author interviews and
news of any author events, and you can sign up for e-newsletters
so that you're always first to hear about our new releases.

*For the many readers who have taken
my girls to their hearts x*

Prologue

~

December 1945

Betty Billington stared at the tall bowed windows of the Erith branch of Woolworths. Even now, with the war over, she could see marks where the crisscross of sticky tape had covered the glass to save the windows from the blast of exploding bombs. She'd need to have a word with the cleaning staff, as standards seemed to have slipped.

A Christmas tree displayed in one of the windows, adorned with paper chains more a faded pink colour than red, no doubt due to the winter sunshine, glinted brightly even though the air was crisp and cold. Betty tutted as she leant her head sideways: no, that tree was not standing straight. Whatever had become of her cherished store?

Pushing open the heavy wood-framed door, Betty joined the busy throng of shoppers pushing and shoving their way to the counters. The store would be closing soon and even now customers were keen to make purchases. There was still two weeks to Christmas Day, the first peacetime Christmas since 1938, which now seemed so long ago that it was hard to remember. Betty knew she should be happy and gay, but her heart felt heavy and sad.

'Cheer up, love, it might not 'appen,' a cheeky man said as he passed her by. The problem was that it already had, Betty thought to herself as she headed towards the staircase that would take her up to the private staff area.

'Betty, we're in here,' Freda called out, popping her head round the door of the canteen. 'Come and take a look at what Sarah has done.'

Betty gave the young woman a nod and followed her into the large room. Just inside the door she stopped and gasped. 'You've certainly transformed the room – well done, Sarah,' she said, looking at the brightly coloured table covers, and bunting looped along the walls. 'Where did all this come from?'

'It was a case of beg, steal or borrow. These came from Nan's loft. They were made for the VE celebrations. I wanted to brighten up the canteen for the old soldiers' party, but they don't seem very festive,' she added wistfully.

Betty gazed at the red, white and blue bunting fluttering in the slight breeze of the open window in the kitchen area. 'You've done a good job, Sarah. Well done indeed.' She gave her friend a weak smile, but Sarah simply nodded her head and went off to direct staff who were moving a piano into the corner of the room.

'Cup of tea, Mrs Billington?' Maureen Gilbert called from the counter, where she was lining up row upon row of green cups and saucers.

'Here, let me help you,' Betty said as she hurried over. 'Bless you, there's no need. We have everything in hand. Why don't you take a cuppa and one of my iced buns, and rest your feet? You must be run ragged at the moment.'

Betty nodded and took the plate Maureen was holding out. 'I must admit I've been rather busy lately.'

'That's the ticket,' Maureen said absent-mindedly, as she turned to call out instructions to a woman who was washing up in a stone sink. 'It's time to change that water, Mavis. The cups will be coming out dirtier than they went in.'

Betty looked round the room as she nibbled on the cake. Perhaps she could help someone else? Maisie was teetering on a wooden chair, pinning the last of the bunting to a window frame. As Betty moved to help hold the chair she was beaten to it by a young warehouseman in a Woolworth brown overall. 'It's all right, love, I'll get this,' he said as he pushed in front of Betty to get to the chair. She could see he was more interested in Maisie's long stocking-clad legs than in helping with the task of pinning up bunting, and was about to reprimand him for talking to her as he had when she realized the lad had no idea who she was.

Feeling surplus to requirements, Betty headed towards the door. She'd take a walk round the shop floor. The bells had just rung to alert staff and customers that the store was about to close. This was always the time she liked best, when the busy Woolworths store fell quiet as the staff covered the counters and headed towards the stairs to the private area to collect their coats before going home. Today being the annual old soldiers' party, some of the girls would be staying on to help out. It was always a joyful affair, and Betty had yet to miss one in all the years she'd worked for Woolworths.

'Excuse me, ducks, you shouldn't be in the shop now, we're closing up for the night,' a shop assistant called out to her. 'You'd best get cracking or you'll be locked in and have to join us for the party,' she giggled as she looped her arm through a fellow worker's and headed to the door marked 'staff only'.

Betty frowned. 'You don't understand . . . I'm Mrs Betty Billington . . .'

One of the girls nudged the other and sniggered. 'You could be Charlie's Aunt for all I care, but the shop's closed and you shouldn't be in here.'

Betty nodded, feeling old and tired, watching as the young women disappeared through the door. The lights had been dimmed, and apart from a warehouseman jangling a bunch of keys as he chatted to a young shop assistant standing by a side door, Betty was alone.

She slowly walked the length of the store. Stopping to look at a cracked glass tile that decorated one of the pillars between the counters, she smiled to herself, remembering the first air raid. They'd hurried shoppers and staff down to the cellars, only just making it in time before the whole building shook as a bomb exploded close to the riverside docks. A few broken windows and patches of plaster coming down from the ceiling in an upstairs storeroom had been the only damage, apart from this crack. She ran her finger across the scar. We all carry our scars from this war, she thought as she strolled on, deep in thought, before stopping at the end of a counter in the middle of the store. She struggled with her memories and smiled as she recalled the day her friend Sarah had received a proposal of marriage on this very spot. It had been such a joyous day, and so long ago . . .

'Betty . . . ? Thank goodness. We thought you'd gone home,' Freda said as she hurried across the shop floor, followed by Sarah and Maisie.

'Reliving memories of good times and bad,' she said as the girls hugged her.

'Blimey, we've 'ad a right old time here, 'aven't we?' Maisie said as she looked around her. 'Mind you, it's a bit on the creepy side wiv only a few lights on,' she added. 'Some of the staff say Woolies is haunted.'

Freda shuddered. 'Please don't talk about ghosts. It gives me the creeps. What do you think, Sarah?'

Sarah Gilbert put her arm round the youngest of her friends. 'It's just an old building, and old buildings hold many memories. Well, that's what my nan always says. There's nothing to be afraid of. We should be happy that the war is over and we're all looking forward to our first Christmas in peacetime.'

'You should remember that as well,' Maisie said. 'You've been as miserable as sin these past weeks. It's time you pinned a smile on yer face and looked forward to the future, Sarah.'

Sarah ignored the comment. 'Come on, we'd best be cracking on or our guests will be here before we've finished preparing their welcome. Are you coming upstairs, Betty?' she asked as they made a move towards the staff door.

'I'll be with you shortly,' Betty said, as she thought about the girls' words. What did she have to look forward to? Her life had changed immeasurably in the past year, and in ways that she wasn't enjoying as she should. She gazed around the dimly lit store, taking in the polished wood counters covered up for the night, and breathed in the faint aroma of lavender floor polish. Apart from the wounds of war, Woolies was carrying on as usual. She wished she could say the same for herself. Yes, she was a lucky woman in so many ways, but she so missed her old life and her chums. Her future felt bleak, and she couldn't help feeling she had somehow taken the wrong path in life. 'You're a fool, Betty Billington, a bloody, bloody fool,' she muttered to herself. 'And there's no way of going back to the life you loved.'

1

February 1945

'Come on, lovey, you can't give up now,' Maisie urged her friend Sarah.

Sarah flopped back against the pillow and took a shuddering breath. 'Why is it taking so long? Georgina was with us in a couple of hours. Do you . . . do you think there's something wrong?' She asked, as another pain took hold and she gripped Maisie's hand so tightly both women's fingers turned white.

There was a quiet tap on the bedroom door and Ruby entered. 'How's my favourite granddaughter doing?' she asked with a concerned look towards Maisie, who was rubbing her hand to bring some life back into it.

'I think there's something wrong,' Sarah whispered. 'Nan, I'm going to lose the baby,' she added as large tears dripped onto her cheeks. 'Please help me.'

'Now what's all this about?' Ruby fussed, as she dipped a flannel into a bowl of cold water and wrung it out before wiping Sarah's face and bending close to give her cheek a kiss. 'What you could do with is to get yourself up on your feet and have a little walk around. Lying on your back never did any good to no one. Why, your dad popped out like a bullet out of a gun after I took meself off for a brisk walk round the town. It frightened your granddad when your dad appeared before the midwife did, I can tell you. I think I'll change your sheets as well. They're all a tangle where you've been tossing and turning. Maisie, you help her to her feet while I go get some fresh sheets from Maureen downstairs and put the kettle on. I don't know about you, but I could do with a strong, hot cup of tea with a couple of sugars in it. All this waiting for a baby to arrive fair whacks me out,' she added, giving Sarah a grin as she wiped a stray hair from her forehead and gave Maisie a discreet nudge to follow her out of the door.

'I'll collect the sheets for you,' Maisie said by way of an excuse to leave the room. 'I'll be back before you know it,' she added as she noticed Sarah's worried look. 'It's a shame we don't 'ave an air raid, cos we could all get into yer nan's shelter and repeat what 'appened when Georgina came into the world.'

'No fear,' Sarah tried to laugh, thinking back to her first child's appearance during an air raid. 'I'd not wish Hitler sending his bombers for all the tea in China,' she said as she struggled to sit up.

'Stay there until I get back, then I'll give you a hand,' Maisie said, trying to keep a cheerful grin on her face. 'I'll see if there's a slice of Maureen's seed cake ter go with that cuppa. I don't know about you but I'm starving.'

Maisie hurried down the narrow, steep stairs of Maureen Gilbert's house into the front room, where Ruby carefully closed the door. 'Truth be told, I'm starting to get worried,' she said to the two women in the room.

'Oh dear, I do wish I could do more,' Sarah's mother-in-law said from where she was sitting in a cosy armchair. 'I'll be glad when I'm well enough to get up and around properly. It's so frustrating.'

'You're not ter worry, Maureen,' Maisie said. 'You do more than enough as it is. It's not been ten weeks since the accident. If you go being daft now, you'll end up back in hospital, and then where would we be?'

The three women fell silent as they thought of the V2 rocket that had landed on the Woolworths store in New Cross and killed so many adults and children. Amongst them had been Sarah's mother, Irene.

Maisie looked up to the ceiling above, where Sarah was trying to bring her second child into the world; a child that would never meet one of its grandmothers. 'Where the hell has that midwife got ter? She's been gone hours.'

Maureen leant over and switched off the wireless, giving a shudder as she did so. 'There's us here wanting to bring one child into the world while our own air force are murdering young kiddies over in Dresden. It makes you think, doesn't it?'

'It's war, Maureen, and we need to bring it ter an end before too many more people get killed. What the RAF is doing may seem wrong, but the boot could so easily be on the other foot.'

Ruby looked sad. 'I'd like to go over there and bump off that bloody Hitler.'

'At least my Alan's not flying over to Germany with those bombs in a plane,' Maureen added.

Maisie raised her pencilled eyebrows. She knew that Alan Gilbert was training the pilots who would no doubt be playing a large part in what was being relayed by the newsreader on the wireless.

They all jumped at a sharp tap on the front door behind them. Maureen's home was a cosy two-up, two-down and the front room led straight onto Crayford Road, with just a small scrap of garden between the house and pavement.

'P'raps it's the midwife,' Maisie said as she quickly pulled back the curtain that covered the door and swung it open onto a sharp, cold morning. She was dismayed to see a young lad shivering on the doorstep and cuffing his nose with the back of his hand.

'Nurse Rose asked me to bring this to you, missus,' he said, shoving a piece of paper into her hand and backing away to where a group of his mates were waiting.

'Hang on a minute,' Maisie said as she read the few words before reaching for her handbag, which lay on the arm of the one empty armchair. 'Here, 'ave this fer being a good kid. But I want you ter go back ter the nurse and tell her that Mrs Gilbert is not doing well, and we are going ter call the doctor. Do you understand me?'

The boy nodded his head solemnly as his eyes grew wider. 'Is she going to die, Missus?'

'Not if we can 'elp it. Now, hurry up and deliver the message. And don't stop ter play on the way,' she added sternly, closing the door on the cold day.

'I take it she's held up somewhere?' Ruby asked as she came downstairs to see what the commotion was about.

'Yes, she's over the other side of town and will be

another hour at least. I'm going ter run over ter the doctor's house and get some 'elp. The poor girl's exhausted and I don't like the look of her one little bit.'

'No, I'll go,' Ruby said, pulling Maisie away from the door. 'You'll be more help upstairs until the doctor arrives, what with not long having kids yourself. I know I'll go all soft on her and be of no use at all. I think she's giving up after what happened to her mum. I want you to tell her what you told me . . .'

'But I've not told another living soul, not even me old man.'

'It could help Sarah get her fighting spirit back,' Ruby said, as the two women stood looking at each other.

'I wish I knew what the pair of you were going on about,' Maureen said. 'But while you are doing all that, I can at least put the kettle on and make some hot tea,' she went on, slowly pulling herself onto her feet and leaning heavily on a walking stick. 'Did I hear you wanted some clean sheets?'

Maisie gave Maureen a quick hug. 'I'll get the sheets, and as fer the other thing, I'll fill you in about it later.'

Racing back up the stairs, Maisie charged into the bedroom that Sarah shared with her husband, Alan, when he was home and off duty. She threw back the curtain and blinked. 'It's going ter be a beautiful day, and even more beautiful as by the end of it we'll have another baby in the family,' she grinned at Sarah.

'There's something wrong, isn't there?' Sarah half whispered as she took a deep breath and then shuddered. 'It was nothing like this when I had Georgina. Will you do something for me, Maisie?'

'Whatever you want me ter do you've only ter shout,' Maisie said as she sat down by her friend's side. 'If it's tea you're after Maureen's got the kettle on right now. She'll be shouting "tea up" before we know it.'

'No . . . I want you to get Alan before it's too late. I don't think I'm going to be here for much longer.'

'Don't talk so bloody daft,' Maisie said as she squeezed Sarah's arm. 'I felt the same as you when I had the twins. Imagine that? I had twice as much work ter do as you.'

'Did you feel as though you were dying?' Sarah asked, looking her friend directly in the eyes. 'Did you?'

Maisie sighed. The time had come to tell her friend something she had not planned to share with a living soul; that was, until Ruby wheedled it out of her. 'Ter be honest, I thought it would never end. I lost all sense of time and just wanted ter sleep and never wake up.'

Sarah winced before nodding her head. 'Then you know . . .'

Maisie nodded her head. 'I do, but there is something else. Sarah, something happened on the day I was in labour with the twins. You may think me daft, but I swear yer mum was sitting in the hospital urging me not ter give up. She was really annoying. I remember giving her a few choice words and telling her ter sod off, but she just wouldn't go away.'

Sarah rubbed her eyes and stared at her friend. 'But . . . but Mum died the day you had the twins. If you are trying to make me laugh, it isn't working. This isn't funny, Maisie. It's not funny at all.'

Maisie took her friend's hand and gripped it tight. 'I swear ter you, I'm not joking. I was tired ter the bone. So tired I just wanted ter give up, and didn't care about the consequences. I wasn't bothered about Ruby, Bessie or Claudette. Come ter that, I didn't care if I ever saw David again, either. I just wanted it all ter stop so I could go ter sleep and never wake up. It was then that Irene came and sat by me side. You know how we never really saw eye ter eye, and I never cared much for her posh ways. Well, we had a right old ding-dong, and she just kept telling me ter get on wiv it and give birth, as I was needed ter take care of you. I told her that you had Alan and yer family in yer corner, and you weren't short of supporters, so she could go and bugger off for all I cared. She told me she would once I saw sense. I was that annoyed with her, I gave it all I'd got ter deliver those little ones. By heck I'd show her, I thought ter meself. It was the next day that David told me about the V2 rocket, and that yer mum 'adn't survived. I didn't know what ter think,' Maisie added, reaching for her cigarettes with shaking hands, then thought better of lighting up.

Sarah closed her eyes and took a deep breath. She felt so far removed from the world around her; a world that no longer included her mum. In the weeks since she'd heard the news of so many poor souls losing their lives when a V2 rocket had landed on a Woolworths store in southeast London, she'd done her best to blot out anything not remotely close to her family. Instead she'd kept her daughter close to her and insisted Alan stay by her side, although he'd returned to his work with the RAF regardless of her insistence. If anything were to happen, then they'd either survive together or perish together. No one would be left to feel this empty nagging that had eaten away at her soul since that fateful day in November 1944. Her thoughts were blotted out for a while until a pain so intense she thought it would rip her insides out subsided and the sweat that drenched her body, and stung her eyes through her closed lids, was wiped away by someone close by. She felt peace flow through her, but knew that from somewhere deep inside the pain and devastation of what had happened would join forces with the child waiting to be born, and she'd be dragged back to face the past and her future – a future without her mum.

'This way,' Ruby said as she ushered the ageing doctor up the stairs ahead of her, trying at the same time to fight the urge to gasp for air. Some things were just too important to stop and think about breathing. 'She's been like this for most of the night now, and as her first kiddie came so quick like, we thought it best to call you. I'm sorry to have interrupted your breakfast,' she added, noticing the toast crumbs in the doctor's bushy beard.

'I'm not surprised at all, considering Mrs Gilbert's distress after losing her mother. Some women are prone to melancholy, and this will be having an effect on her giving birth,' he said over his shoulder as he reached the top of the staircase and entered the bedroom.

Ruby frowned. She'd heard some things in her time, but this took the biscuit. Usually a baby came into the world regardless of what was happening on the outside. She had no time for fanciful words. She'd be keeping an eye on this man and his Victorian attitude.

'She's been out for the count almost since you left,' Maisie whispered to Ruby as the older woman stood by her side just inside the bedroom door. 'I'm not sure she understood what I told her about Irene, so I don't think it will give her any great comfort. Who's this chap?' She nodded to where the doctor had pulled back the sheets and was starting to prod Sarah's stomach and mutter to himself.

'It's Doctor Gregg's father. He came out of retirement when his son joined the army. I've not had much call to visit him, but I've heard he can be rough-handed and a little old-fashioned in his attitude,' Ruby whispered.

'Will you two women stop your infernal yapping,' the doctor growled without turning round. 'Now, one of you go and put the kettle on.'

'What are you going ter do?' Maisie asked somewhat fearfully. She knew some of what went on in hospitals, and didn't wish to see any of it happening in her best friend's bedroom.

'I would like a cup of tea, if it's not too much bother?' He glared back at Maisie through bushy eyebrows that seemed to have a life of their own. 'This woman disturbed my meal with her panicking.'

'What about Sarah . . . I mean Mrs Gilbert?'

The doctor shrugged his shoulders as he snapped closed the brown leather case he'd left on the bottom of the bed. 'Hysteria. The woman has got herself into a hysterical state for nothing. I suggest a cold bed bath will bring her to her senses and speed up the delivery of the child. Now, lead me down to this cup of tea please.'

As the doctor followed an extremely worried Ruby back downstairs, Maisie went over to Sarah and straightened her nightgown before pulling up the bedclothes.

'Don't listen ter the silly bugger, Sarah. I promised yer mum I'd take care of you, and take care of you I will.'

Sarah's eyelids fluttered for a moment before she muttered her mum's name and fell back into a fitful sleep.

Maisie wiped a fresh sheen of sweat from her friend's hot face as Ruby reappeared. 'That was quick.'

Ruby was red in the face, and it wasn't from climbing the staircase. 'I gave him his money and showed him the door. God help any woman who goes to him with a problem. The man's an idiot,' she said, leaning down to peer closely at her granddaughter.

'I'm going ter pop out and make a telephone call ter the Hainault maternity home. Hopefully the doctor who saw me through the birth of the twins will be there and can give us some advice. I'd rather do that before calling for an ambulance that would take her straight ter the cottage hospital. Knowing our luck, old Doctor Gregg will be on duty up there too, and I won't be responsible fer me actions. Sarah may be upset about her mum's death, but she's not one fer hysteria. There's something wrong, and I'm not going ter stand by and watch me friend and her baby die.'

Gwyneth Jackson knocked on the door of the Woolworths manager's office, and entered when she heard her boss respond.

Betty Billington looked up and smiled at the pretty, dark-haired Welshwoman and indicated for her to take a seat. 'Good morning, Gwyneth. I hope you bring good news about Sarah?'

'Sadly not. I popped into Maureen's house on my way to work, and she was most upset. Sarah's having a bad time of things and has been taken up to the Hainault in an ambulance. Ruby and Maisie have gone up there and have promised to let us know as soon as possible. I pray she will be all right.'

'My goodness,' Betty exclaimed. 'Who'd have thought that would happen? Why, she gave birth to her Georgina with such ease, even if the circumstances were a little unusual.'

Gwyneth smiled. She hadn't been living in Erith when Sarah had her first child back in 1940, but from all accounts it had been rather unusual to say the least. 'Who knows how these things turn out. I just pray that Sarah will soon have her new baby in her arms, and can look forward to a happier future.'

'I agree. It was such a shock to lose Irene like that. We got on quite well. I for one will miss her.'

Gwyneth nodded her head, but kept quiet. She'd found Irene Caselton to be a daunting woman, who looked down on her for being a simple shop girl who'd been Ruby Caselton's lodger before marrying the local police sergeant. On the other hand, Irene's husband, George, was a delightful man with no airs or graces at all. Thank goodness Sarah had turned out to be more like her dad. 'She was an admirable woman,' was all she could think to say out loud.

Betty allowed a small smile to cross her face. She could see that Gwyneth had struggled with her words. 'Now, do tell me who is looking after all the little ones while Sarah and Maisie are busy elsewhere?'

Gwyneth chuckled. 'Georgina is with her granddad George, which will help keep her mind off things. Bob volunteered, or I should say Ruby sent him, to help David with his brood. He's up at Maisie's house, as they have a telephone. I hope you don't mind but I've asked them to keep us informed if anything should happen?'

'Good grief, of course I don't mind. The Caseltons and Gilberts, and now the Jacksons,' Betty added, acknowledging Gwyneth's married status, 'are very much part of my own extended family. I have no idea what I'd do without you all. Especially now,' she smiled, placing a hand on her stomach, which was covered by a floral smock she wore with her smart tweed work suit. 'Sarah and Alan are our main priority right now. Speaking of which . . . ?'

'David has notified Alan's commanding officer of the situation. Thank goodness Alan isn't seeing action at the moment, and they will do all they can to keep him informed of any news.'

Betty nodded her head. She knew Sarah told everyone that Alan taught new intakes how to fly, but secretly she wondered if this was a smokescreen to keep his pregnant wife from worrying.

'Good, I think that accounts for all the family and friends.'

Gwyneth frowned; surely Betty hadn't forgotten . . . 'What about Freda?'

Betty clapped her hand to her mouth in horror. 'How could I have forgotten Freda? Why, those girls are like the three musketeers.' She glanced at the staff rota pinned to the wall. 'She's not due in work until late afternoon. She has a shift with the Fire Service. They've been at sixes and sevens since the fire station was bombed, and they've moved premises. Perhaps I should make a call to the fire station and ask them to let Freda know of developments?'

'If you like I could run over there now, before I start my duties here?'

'That would make sense. Thank you, Gwyneth,' Betty said, and all at once the discussion became one of employer and employees rather than women who shared the companionship of the same friends. 'Please tell Freda not to rush into work until she is ready. We can easily rearrange the rota so she completes her hours for this week.'

Gwyneth agreed. It often amazed her how Betty could be a friend one moment, laughing and joking at a family celebration, and then the next she was the level-headed manager of the Erith branch of F. W. Woolworths, hiding her emotions behind a stern exterior. Things would soon change once Betty's own child came into the world.

Freda rubbed her face and immediately knew she had oil from her motorbike's engine smudged across her cheek. That would give the men at the Erith fire station something to joke about. She was often the butt of their friendly banter, but lately she'd grown tired of it all and was the first to agree that this had something to do with Sandy McGregor, who'd recently joined the volunteer fire staff. She felt like a schoolgirl whenever he glanced her way, and wanted to die of embarrassment when her cheeks turned scarlet. It wasn't as if she hadn't had a boyfriend in the past, she thought to herself as she scrubbed at her cheek with a handkerchief. Not that any of her romances had amounted to much.

'You've missed some,' a familiar voice said. 'Here, let me help you.'

Freda turned her face to one side as Sandy took the handkerchief and gently wiped her cheek. 'Thank you,' she stammered, as he handed back the now grubby cotton square. 'I've seen you about. Are you a new fireman?' she asked, pretending she hadn't noticed him around the fire station and overheard the older staff talking about the injury he'd sustained to his leg whilst on the beaches of Dunkirk, although nothing seemed to stop him mucking in with tasks around the station.

He gave her a gentle smile before holding out his hand and speaking in a soft Scottish accent. 'I'm Sandy McGregor, a new volunteer.'

She took his hand and shook it, surprised at how firm it felt. 'How do you do? I'm Freda Smith. I work at Woolworths and the rest of the time I'm a dispatch rider based at this fire station.' She didn't like to say that she already knew his name from hearing idle talk around the station – and that he had returned from the war with a leg injury.

'And you find time to help out at the Brownies and Girls Guides, too,' he added.

Freda was puzzled. 'How do you know that?'

Sandy laughed. 'Don't look so worried. I've been a life-long member of the Boys' Brigade and decided to offer my support to the troupe at Queen Street Baptist Church while I'm down this end of the country. They mentioned you are a great help to Mrs Missons. Perhaps I'll see you at the church parade on Sunday?'

Freda gave him a smile. 'Yes, I'll be there. I take it you don't come from these parts?'

'Is my accent that obvious?' he laughed. 'My home is in Edinburgh.'

'I've heard it is a beautiful part of the country,' Freda said, noticing how laughter lines appeared around his eyes when he smiled. 'You must miss your hometown?'

'I've not been back for a while now,' he added wistfully, looking lost in thought for a few seconds before remembering his manners. 'Your accent isn't local either.'

'I'm from Birmingham, but Erith is my home now. There's nothing left for me in the Midlands anymore,' Freda answered, reminded of the fact that she no longer had any family back where she was born.

'No young man, then?'

Freda felt herself start to blush. Was he checking to see if she had a boyfriend? 'I'm footloose and fancy free, as the saying goes,' she grinned as she turned back to her motorcycle to collect her jacket, which lay across the seat. 'How about you?'

Sandy was quiet for a second or two. 'I'm the same, so why don't we take a walk after church and perhaps find somewhere to have a bite to eat?'

'I'd like that,' Freda said, giving Sandy a shy smile. 'That's if you don't mind taking a walk with someone who is wearing a Tawny Owl uniform?'

'I'd deem it an honour. However, as it is February and the sun is bound not to shine we will have our overcoats to cover any embarrassment,' he added with a grin.

Freda was already thinking ahead and thanking God that Maisie had passed a decent forest green woollen coat to her, stating that it would no longer fit around her waist since she gave birth to the twins. She had a passable black felt hat and knitted gloves, so wouldn't look too badly turned out. 'Then a walk it shall be. But I'm not sure we'll find anywhere open to eat, so why not come back to my landlady's house for dinner? She is always telling me I should invite my friends home. That's if you don't mind a noisy house full of people?' she asked, wondering if she had overstepped the boundaries of their new friendship.

'A house full of people sounds just great,' Sandy said. 'That's if it's all right with your landlady. I don't wish to impose.'

'Don't be daft . . .' she started to say.

'Oi, McGregor, Smith, stop your bloody billing and cooing and get your backsides in here. There's work to be done,' came a man's voice from an open window of the upper floor of the fire station.

Freda felt embarrassed to think that the men on duty had been watching her talking to Sandy and thought they'd been . . .

'I'm sorry if you've been offended,' Sandy said, noticing Freda's look of consternation. 'I'd hate to think you were embarrassed.'

Freda forced herself to laugh. 'It's fine, honestly. I've grown a thick skin working here. You'd be amazed at the things they say at times.'

He squeezed her arm to reassure her. 'As long as you are all right? I'll have a word with the boss if they overstep the mark. It's not always nice for a young lady to be the butt of their jokes.'

'Honestly, Sandy, I'm fine. It's nice of you to stick up

for me, though,' she said, turning away from him in case he could see her broad grin. She could tell he really liked her, and if they had been billing and cooing she'd not have minded one little bit.

Sandy gave her a wink and headed back to the building, while Freda picked up the tools and cleaning clothes from where she'd been working on her motorbike and wheeled the machine into the shed at the side of the building.

'Freda!'

Freda almost jumped out of her skin as she heard a familiar voice call from the front of the yard. 'Gwyneth, whatever is wrong?' she asked as the pretty Welsh woman hurried up to her.

'Betty told me I should come over and let you know that Sarah is having the baby,' Gwyneth puffed before leaning against the wall and taking a deep breath.

Freda was concerned by the worried look on Gwyneth's face. 'Is there a problem? Sarah was in labour this morning before I left for my shift. I thought she'd have had the baby by now.'

'They've taken her up to the Hainault. We don't know any more than that. Betty wondered if you would go and find out?' Gwyneth added, looking at the motorbike now parked in the wooden shed.

'It won't take me long to run up there,' Freda said, knowing she'd be in deep trouble if she took the motorbike without permission.

'But it's been an age and no one seems to know what is happening,' Gwyneth said with a beseeching look.

'Stay there and watch the bike. I don't want any of the local kids messing with it. I'll run up and get permission,'

Freda said, knowing she would also have to face the men's jokes about her friendship with Sandy. Well, this time she'd stand up to them. Many of them knew Sarah's family and what they been through in recent months, so they could shut up and be polite for once. If her best friend was in trouble, she wanted to be there by her side as soon as possible.

2

Bob Jackson scratched his head. 'I'll be blowed if I can tell them apart,' he said, looking to where David Carlisle held a twin in the crook of each arm. 'I've got to hand it to you, David. You're a dab hand at caring for those two babies as well as having young Ruby hanging onto your legs. I'd offer to give you a hand, but I'd not know where to start.'

David roared with laughter, then quickly fell silent as one of the babies stirred. 'There are subtle differences, but even I took time to notice them. Maisie swears she can tell who is crying from another room in the house, but I'm not that confident to even guess. I just thank God we have a boy and a girl, or goodness knows what I'd be like.'

Bob peered closely at the contented babies. 'This one has blonder hair,' he said, pointing to one who had a few wisps of fair hair sticking out from beneath a pink crocheted bonnet. 'Is it the girl?'

David's mouth twitched as he tried hard not to laugh. 'Let's just say that little girls wear pink, shall we?'

Bob slapped his hand onto his forehead. 'I was thinking too hard about it. I suppose we will have to rely on the colour of their clothes until they can speak and tell us who they are. Now, what can I do to help you? Ruby's last words to me before she dashed off to the Hainault to see Sarah were to make myself useful.'

David smiled at the older man. 'I'm going to get these two settled down for their nap, and hopefully young Ruby junior here will join them. Perhaps you could walk up to the school and collect Bessie and Claudette? Myfi will be due out soon as well. I told Gwyneth that we'd collect her along with the younger kids and have them here until we know Sarah is on the mend and our womenfolk can collect their offspring.'

Bob was relieved that he didn't have to take on the care of the babies and nodded his head in agreement. 'That's not a problem, I can do that for you. I'll take them over to the allotment and collect some spuds and parsnips Ruby wants for our supper. Do you know if anyone has spoken to George yet? God knows how he will be feeling, knowing his only child has been carted off to the hospital with his wife not long dead.'

'I spoke to him just now. With Alan away on duty, George reckons they might let him go up there, so he's dropped Georgina back at Maureen's. Mind you, my Maisie's already there with Ruby, and God help them if they turn those two away,' he chuckled. 'I know it's a bit of a cheek, but do you think you could look in on Maureen before you go up to the school? She must be worried sick about Sarah, and not being able to move about much yet on that bad leg of hers, she can't get out of the house as much as she'd like. At least she's got Georgina with her to take her mind off things. But all the same . . .'

'I know what you mean. I'd best head off now, then I can have a bit of a chat before collecting the girls.' Bob chuckled to himself. 'Let's just hope Sarah's next one's a boy. We seem to be overrun with young ladies.'

David's face took on a serious look. 'There is a chance that Bessie and Claudette will soon be leaving us. I've finally managed to find out where Maisie's brother, Fred, is based. There's a letter winging its way to his commanding officer, notifying them of the circumstances that have led to the two girls living with us.'

'It will break Maisie's heart if they are taken away from her after all this time. Why, it must be all of two years since the pair of you took them in?'

'It is, and I'll miss them like hell. Lord knows what Fred will decide,' David replied, staring hard at a point beyond Bob's shoulder.

Bob could see that he was finding it hard to control his emotions. 'I'm here to help you all I can,' he said, slapping him on the shoulder. 'I'll be off now to see Maureen and relieve her of our Georgina for a little while. That kid is so full of beans,' he added proudly.

'She's lucky to have you as a great-granddad, Bob, you always have time for the children,' David said quietly as he tried to compose himself.

'I'm not quite a relative yet. Me and Ruby have still to set a date for our wedding.'

David laughed. Friends and family had been waiting with bated breath for Ruby to finally walk down the aisle with Bob Jackson, and they all knew it wouldn't be too long now. 'Good luck with that, Bob. You're a braver man than I,' he said as Bob headed out of the door to look in on Maureen Gilbert.

'They must have some news soon, we've been here hours,' Maisie said as she walked up and down the waiting room, nodding to a young man who sat nervously in the corner of the room. He'd chewed his nails down to the quick and was now fiddling with a pack of Woodbines. 'Look, love, why don't you pop outside and stretch yer legs? You could have a quick fag at the same time. If there is any news, I promise ter come straight out and call you.'

The man looked grateful. 'If you don't mind, I'll do that. I had no idea it would take this long.'

'Babies come when they're ready and not a minute before. There's no knowing how long they can be,' she grinned as the man made a quick exit.

Ruby looked up at a large clock on the cream-coloured wall. 'It's been an hour since they rushed our Sarah through those doors, although I admit it feels longer. Lord knows what's going on. I just pray her and the little one are going to be all right.'

Maisie threw herself down onto one of the hard wooden seats. 'It don't seem five minutes since I was in here 'aving the twins. As nice as the nurses were, I was glad ter get out of the place and 'ome wiv me family.'

Ruby nodded her head in agreement. 'Just as Sarah will be two weeks from now. She should make the most of it and put her feet up for a while to get over the birth. Her Georgina is a lively one, and what with Alan away doing his bit and Maureen with her bad leg, it'll be down to her to do most of the work round the house. Yes, she should make the most of her stay in here and treat it like a bit of a holiday.'

Maisie grinned as she tried to make herself more comfortable on the hard seat. 'I can think of better places ter go fer a bit of an 'oliday. At me lowest point I just wanted ter die. I know that's not a nice thing ter say but it's the honest ter goodness truth,' she added, seeing Ruby glare at her.

'Childbirth isn't the greatest thing to go through, but it's soon forgotten, and look what you have at the end of it all: a beautiful baby, in your case, two beautiful babies.'

Maisie picked up her cigarettes with shaking hands before throwing them down, as the packet was empty. 'I can't get over how that strange thing 'appened just before the twins arrived, when Irene turned up and told me ter keep going and how she'd be there ter 'elp me and I was ter look out for Sarah's baby.'

'I don't doubt it happened,' Ruby said thoughtfully. 'I've heard of such things.'

'Well, I told Sarah, but I've no idea how she took it as she was almost out fer the count at the time. I hope, if she remembers, she ain't angry wiv me. I'm not sure if she's one fer believing such things.'

Ruby delved into her bag and pulled out a white cotton handkerchief. 'If it's of any help, I do believe you. Irene could be a funny so-and-so at times, but she was a decent sort. I could imagine her wanting to help you girls. I shall miss her,' she added, dabbing at her eyes.

Both women looked up as the door to the waiting room

opened and a nursing sister in her smart navy blue dress and white starched apron and cap walked into the room.

'If you want the young man, he's popped out to stretch his legs,' Ruby said, hoping against hope that the sister had not come to give them bad news.

'No, it is you I've come to speak to. Mrs Gilbert has just delivered a healthy baby boy. We don't usually allow this, but I feel that a family member should sit with her for a while. She is very distressed. I understand Mrs Gilbert has not long lost her mother, and that her husband is serving in the RAF?'

Ruby got to her feet and picked up her bag. 'That's right. Her dad George, my son, should be here before too long. We sent a message to his work. Could I go and see her?'

Maisie jumped to her feet and stood next to Ruby. 'I'd like ter go and see her too. We are like sisters and I'm really worried about her.'

Ruby took Maisie's hand and squeezed it. 'We will both go and see Sarah,' she told the nurse, daring her to disagree.

The nurse gave an understanding smile. 'Follow me.'

The two women followed her along a short passage, aware that their shoes were making a noise on the black tiled flooring which seemed to echo off the walls.

Stopping at a pair of double doors, the nurse turned to Ruby. 'Mrs Gilbert is very tired, so no more than ten minutes. And please don't excite her,' she added, giving Maisie a stern look.

'As if we would,' Maisie muttered as she followed Ruby into the room.

Ruby hurried over to where Sarah was propped up in bed, her face as white as the crisp pillowcases she lay against. 'Look at you, laying there like lady muck,' Ruby said as she gave her a hug. 'Maisie's with me but she's been told not to get you excited.'

Sarah gave a weak smile. 'So no hokey-cokeys around the room, eh?'

Maisie snorted with laughter as she leant over to give her friend a kiss. 'We can save that fer tomorrow. I must say you look bloody awful. Was it that bad?' she asked as she perched herself on the end of the bed.

'It seemed to take forever. Not a patch on when I had Georgina. He's a lot bigger than she was. The nurse told me that was the problem and I'll be as right as rain in no time. You'll never guess who I saw?'

Maisie gasped. 'Not you too! What did yer mum say?'

Sarah frowned. 'Whatever do you mean?'

'Your mum, Irene, I mentioned it earlier but you was almost out fer count. She spoke ter me when I was in labour wiv the twins . . . I know I must have imagined it, as it was the day of the . . . but . . .'

Sarah blinked at Maisie. 'I was about to say I saw the nurse who helped us when Vera's granddaughter was in here. What do you mean, you saw my mum?'

Maisie waited, hoping that a large hole would open up and swallow her. 'It was nothing. Just me mouth running about wiv me – forget I said anything. Now, are we going ter see yer son?' she added, doing her utmost to be cheerful.

'I want to know what you meant,' Sarah said in a shrill voice.

'You'd best tell her, or she'll never rest,' Ruby advised, adding, 'You are not to get upset, Sarah. It won't do you any good.' She reached out for her granddaughter's hand and patted it reassuringly.

Maisie took a deep breath and started to explain what had happened, rushing her words as she could see the look of alarm spreading across Sarah's face. 'I didn't know about yer mum having died until later, and wouldn't have mentioned it fer all the world, but . . .' She had no idea what to say next.

The room fell silent as Ruby and Maisie watched for Sarah's reaction. Ruby felt Sarah's fingernails dig into her hand before a small sob escaped.

'How can you think that my mum would have come to see you after she had died? Don't you think that if the dead returned, they'd go to see their loved ones? Surely Mum would have been here with me today if she could. Why would she have said you've got to look after me?'

Ruby tried to comfort Sarah as her granddaughter became more distressed. 'I'm sure she is looking over you. She loved you dearly, Sarah.'

Sarah snatched her hand away from Ruby and raised herself from the pillows. 'She did love me, and she would have been here if it were possible,' she spat at Maisie. 'Whatever made you think she would want to see you on the day that she died? Just because you never saw your mum until it was too late, you have no right to take mine. Just go away, Maisie. I don't ever want to see you again,' Sarah cried before sinking back into the bed, pulling the sheets to her face as she sobbed.

'But it wasn't like that. I never meant . . .' Maisie looked to Ruby for help as tears started to run down her face.

'Perhaps it's best if we go,' Ruby suggested, even though she didn't like to leave Sarah in such a state.

'Whatever is all this noise?' the sister said as she burst through the door. She took one look at her patient and held the door open. 'I suggest you leave right now.'

'Come on, love, we'd best do as we are told,' Ruby said, taking Maisie by the elbow and steering her away from the room.

'I'm sorry, Sarah,' Maisie whispered as she allowed herself to be led from her friend's hospital room.

The two women walked from the maternity home and headed slowly down Lesney Park Road towards the town. 'I didn't mean that ter 'appen,' Maisie said quietly. 'Not in a million years. When I thought about Irene coming ter see me and tried ter make sense of what 'appened weeks after the twins were born, I got great comfort from thinking about it. She could be a frightful snob, but deep down Irene was all right. She only wanted what was best fer 'er 'usband and child.'

Ruby stopped walking and turned to face Maisie. 'Don't you ever apologize for what happened. You thought that Irene came to see you on the day she died, and I truly believe you. I'm a great believer that our loved ones look out for us after they pass over. She no doubt knows that Sarah has many people who love her and are here for her. She knew you hadn't been close to your family for a long time, even though you'd taken in your brother's kiddies. You know she told me not long before she died that she thought you were a good person, and she wished she could be more like you.'

Maisie was incredulous. 'Irene said that?'

'She did, and I believe that is why she gravitated to you at a time when she needed help and so did you. In time Sarah will come to realize that, so don't you go worrying your head off over it.'

'I truly hope so,' Maisie said, as Ruby took her arm and they headed home.

'From the look on your face, I reckon all is well and we have another grandchild?' Maureen said as she opened the front door to George Caselton and led him into the house.

George kissed Maureen on the cheek. 'A bruiser of a boy, and mother and child both doing well, from all accounts,' he grinned. 'I was on my way up there when I saw Mum and Maisie heading home. They'd seen Sarah and she was well. The pair of them looked all in.'

'Thank goodness for that. I don't mind telling you, I've been that worried since they carted her off in that ambulance. No wonder she was exhausted if he was a big baby.' Maureen sat down, pulling a handkerchief from the cuff of her cardigan. 'Now I'm coming over all weepy. Whatever must you think of me?'

George sat beside Maureen and patted her hand, chuckling gently. 'You're not the only one. I had a few tears myself when I received the news. Not very manly of me, was it?'

'Blimey, George, you more than anyone are allowed to

have a cry. Even men have to let go sometimes. When I think of what happened to your Irene, and now Sarah and the baby. Why, it doesn't bear thinking about, does it?'

George gave Maureen a sad smile. He'd always thought she was a plucky woman ever since he'd first known her, way back when they were young. She'd coped when she lost her husband, and whatever the war had thrown at her she'd remained strong. 'The pair of us have faced a lot in the past three months. You are still getting over your injury, and with Alan not at home it doesn't help.'

Maureen jutted out her chin in defiance. 'I'd pay anything to have him back home here with us, especially now he has a son as well as a daughter, but the RAF's need is greater than ours. As long as he returns home without being injured again, I'll be a happy mum.'

'That's all we can hope for. Many haven't been so lucky. Now, how about I put the kettle on, then I'll pop up and see our Georgina and let her know she has a baby brother?'

'Leave her while she's sleeping. The poor little cock was crying for her mum earlier, and whatever I said, it didn't seem to help. I coaxed her to help me make a few fairy cakes and used up all our margarine allowance for the week. It calmed her a bit and then I put her down for a nap. I wouldn't mind that cup of tea, though. Here on my own I couldn't be bothered to struggle to my feet just for a cuppa.'

George gave her a hard look. She was rather pale, and he'd put it down to worrying about Sarah and being on the go looking after young Georgina on her own. 'Is your injury playing you up? I know you have to keep exercising the leg, but perhaps we are expecting too much, leaving you to cope with the little one. I'm booking a few days off work to give you a hand. No, I insist,' he added as Maureen started to protest. 'Now I'll get the cup of tea, and perhaps I'll try one of those cakes; then we can listen to the news together. What do you say?'

'I'd say that's a good idea. Thank you, George.' Maureen gave a small smile as she thought about having a grandson. Perhaps she could knit something in blue as a present before Sarah came home from the Hainault? Leaning heavily on the arm of the settee, she pulled herself to her feet and used her walking stick to go to the sideboard for her knitting patterns. Looking at the clock, she could see it was a little early for the news broadcast, but she switched on the wireless to give it time to warm up. Tucking the knitting patterns under her arm, she turned to go back to her seat and then stopped as she heard the faint melody of a memorable tune coming from the wireless.

All at once she was a young girl back in 1916, visiting nearby Crayford for a dance. She closed her eyes and could see George, on leave from the army, coming over to say hello with a couple of comrades by his side. My, but he did look smart, and she felt her heart flutter. Although George had never said as much, Maureen just knew that before too long they would be courting, and she looked forward to their future with great anticipation. They'd grown up together, attending the same school and living only a street apart.

Unconsciously she started to sway to the melody as the wireless sound grew in strength. George had asked her to dance and his mate had done the same with her friend and workmate, Irene. As George steered her through the crowd of dancers, she felt he wasn't paying attention. His eyes seemed to be on Irene as she laughed in delight as she was twirled around the room. When George asked Maureen who her friend was, she knew he was lost to her. She'd never seen him glance at her in such an adoring way.

'What's all this, then? Are you dancing without me?' George asked, as he put the tea tray down and removed the knitting patterns from Maureen. Taking her in his arms, he stepped gently round the room, taking care not to cause her pain in her bad leg. Maureen was too stunned and taken up with her memories to complain, even if her leg had hurt. 'I recognize this tune,' he said, cocking his head to one side to listen. 'Isn't it . . . ?'

'*If you were the only girl in the world,*' Maureen murmured, trying hard not to break the spell her memories had cast.

George gave a delighted chuckle. 'That's right. *And I was the only boy.* It was playing the night I first met Irene at the church social evening.'

'It was the Rodney Hut at the Vickers factory,' Maureen said. And it was the night I lost you, she thought wistfully.

Betty sat down at her desk, kicking off her stout brown leather shoes with a sigh. No one had told her that her feet would suffer so much when she first became pregnant. She recalled the words 'glowing' and 'eating for two', but nothing about swollen ankles and tiredness. For God's sake, woman, pull yourself together, she muttered to herself. You can run a busy Woolworths store, so carrying a baby should be a piece of cake. She really couldn't see why there was such a fuss. Taking a sip of lukewarm tea that had been sitting on the desk since she first walked into her small office, she grimaced and placed the cup back in the saucer. She'd call for fresh tea when Mr Porter arrived for his appointment. Goodness knows why head office had sent him in to see her. No doubt it was something to do with the light bulb order she'd complained about. There was ten minutes before then – just time to tackle a pile of correspondence that had been sitting in an untidy heap on the desk for the past few days.

Using a brass letter opener that had been a gift from her husband, Douglas, she made a pile of letters that required answering and a pile of invoices she would need to check before sending on to head office for payment. Coming across a stiff cream manila envelope imprinted with the Woolworths logo, Betty frowned. Since the war started, head office had taken to using brown envelopes. This must be important to use such impressive stationery.

Betty was still staring into space when there was a quiet knock on the door and it opened. Gwyneth popped her head round the door and gave Betty a concerned look. 'Mrs Billington, your three o'clock appointment, Mr Porter, is here.' She'd hardly finished before the door was pushed open wide and a short, thin-faced man pushed past Gwyneth and marched to Betty's desk.

'Mrs Billington, I am Cecil Porter, the new store manager.'

Gwyneth would long remember Betty's pale face and the way her hand trembled as she nodded her head to the man and glanced briefly at a letter in her hand before throwing it into a wastepaper bin. Perhaps she wouldn't ask if there was any news about Sarah. It didn't seem to be the right time.

'My God, you look awful,' David said, rushing to help Maisie to a chair as she walked into the house, her face as white as a ghost. 'What's happened, is it bad news? How is Sarah? Please don't say she's lost the baby,' he added as he turned to a glass cabinet that housed a precious half bottle of gin along with a bottle of whisky.

Maisie threw herself down onto the settee. 'Thank you, that would go down a treat. Sarah and the baby are fine, she 'ad a little boy,' she said, as David passed her a glass of gin and she looked about the room. It looked tidier than usual, and there was even a smell of furniture polish and something nice cooking in the kitchen. 'Cheers, someone's been busy. Where are the kids?'

David sat down beside her and slung his arm across the back of the chair. 'If you hadn't noticed, it is half past seven. Ruby went out like a light while she was eating her tea. Bob had been playing with the kids for ages and she spent hours toddling after them, screaming her head off most of the time. I fed the twins, so we have a few hours before they stir, and I've told Bessie and Claudette they can read in bed until you go and say goodnight to them.'

Maisie looked amazed. 'And you found time ter tidy up as well? Blimey, p'raps we should change places. You'd make a wonderful 'ousewife. I love all the kiddies, but I'd kill ter go back ter work.'

David laughed before noticing the look on his wife's face. 'You're serious, aren't you?'

'I'm too tired ter crack jokes,' she said.

David knocked back the remains of the whisky and wiped his mouth with the back of his hand. His wife was not one for a quiet life and by now he was used to her hare-brained schemes, but was she serious? 'Darling, no one expects you to do war work. You've more than provided for the future of the country with our three adorable children.'

'Five,' Maisie corrected him. 'We 'ave five children.'

'Fair enough. You have your hands full caring for five children, but two of them are not ours, and before too long they will be returned to their parents. Even so, there is no way you are expected to return to work. Why, it is a preposterous idea,' he said, starting to lose his temper.

Maisie stood up and glared at her husband. 'You sit there saying I'm not supposed ter do another day's work, and in the next breath I 'ave ter give Bessie and Claudette back ter me good-fer-nothing brother, who hasn't given a damn about 'em these past couple of years? Blimey, David, I thought you knew me better than that,' she spat at him before turning to leave the room. 'I'm going ter see the kids, then I'm off ter me bed.'

David held out his hand to his wife. 'But dinner – you've not yet eaten.'

'I'm not 'ungry. I think it best if you sleep down 'ere tonight,' she said, storming from the room.

3

'Who the hell is banging on the door at this time?' Ruby said as she put down her knife and fork.

'I'll go and look, you get on and finish your dinner. I hope it's all right,' Bob said nervously, looking at the plate of food he'd just put in front of her. 'It's been in the oven for a while.'

'It's warm and filling, and most welcome after the day I've had,' she said, giving him a gentle smile.

Bob pulled back the heavy curtain from the front door that helped keep the cold draughts from getting into the house. 'Hang on a minute,' he muttered as there was another knock.

'Sorry, Bob. I left my key at work and try as I might, I couldn't pull the string through the letterbox to get at the spare,' Freda said as she stood there in her Fire Service uniform. 'It's perishing cold out here.'

Bob checked the spare key, which was always kept on a string on the inside of the door. Usually one tug and it came through the letterbox, so friends and family could let themselves in. Only for a short time, at the beginning of the war, had Ruby removed the key when she thought

Adolf Hitler was about to invade Erith. 'It's caught up in the curtain,' he said as he tugged it free. 'Get yourself inside and warm up in front of the fire. I'll get the kettle on while you have your dinner. It's warming in the oven.'

'Cheers, Bob,' the young woman said as she hurried into the room where Ruby was eating. 'Is there any news of Sarah?' she asked her landlady as she started to peel off the official Fire Service uniform she wore over her siren suit before rubbing her hands together in front of the fire. 'I was about to ride up to the Hainault when we had a call to go to an incident. I've not heard a word since.'

'It's a boy. Mother and baby are doing well,' Ruby beamed.

'Thank goodness for that,' Freda replied, heading into the small kitchen to wash her hands at the sink. 'That smells good, Bob. I'm starving. I missed tea at the station.'

'It's only fish pie, and more potato than fish at that,' he apologized as he used a tea towel to carry the hot plate to the table. 'Where were you?'

'We were over Belvedere way. A rocket came down and wiped out half a street. Our watch was two men short so I stayed to give a hand, as I wasn't needed as a dispatch rider.'

'Was it bad, love?' Ruby asked, wiping her mouth and nodding to Bob as he removed her empty plate.

'Half a dozen dead, and quite a few injuries,' Freda said, reaching for a slice of bread. 'I'll never get used to how one minute people are going about their lives and the next minute hell drops from the sky.'

They all looked up towards the ceiling, and Ruby shuddered. 'Bloody Hitler. I've said it before and I'll say it again: I'd love to get my hands on the murdering so-and-so for just five minutes.'

'Wouldn't we all, love? You'd have to stand in a very long line to have your chance to black his eyes,' Bob said as he took away the dirty plates. 'No, you stay there and rest your bones. I'll put the kettle on and make a fresh pot of tea.'

'There's nothing like being spoilt. Thank you, Bob. You'll make someone a lovely wife,' Freda grinned.

Ruby snorted with laughter. 'Keep your hands off him – he's all mine.'

'Then you'd best name the day and be quick, or I may just take up a better offer,' Bob called from the kitchen.

Freda held her breath and waited. Ruby had been keeping Bob waiting for a couple of years, and even though at the end of last year she'd made her mind up that he was the man for her, she'd still not named the day. They were devoted to each other, but unusually for someone who was normally the first to make a decision, Ruby had kept everyone on tenterhooks.

'How about the eighth of May?' Ruby called out.

A broad grin spread over Freda's face as she waited to hear Bob's answer.

Bob walked into the room with a tea towel in his hand. 'Are you sure?'

'I've always thought it would be nice to marry on my birthday. At least you'd never forget our wedding anniversary,' Ruby added in a matter-of-fact voice.

Bob swept Ruby up in his arms and gave her a big kiss. 'You've made me the happiest man in the world,' he said, trying to dismiss the fact that he'd forgotten Ruby's birthday last year and Sarah had had to remind him halfway through the day. 'Let's walk up to Saint Paulinus church and see the vicar in the morning, shall we?'

'We'll do just that,' Ruby said, patting his hand. 'Now, where's that tea?'

'Maisie? Can I come in?' David Carlisle spoke quietly for fear of waking the children as he tapped on the closed bedroom door. He waited for a reply but there was silence. David opened the door and walked slowly into the room.

Maisie was lying on her back on top of the pink satin bedspread staring up to the ceiling. 'What do you want?' she asked without looking at him.

He walked closer and sat on the edge of the bed. In the half-light from the partly closed curtains he could see her tear-stained face. 'It wasn't my intention to hurt you or make you cry, Maisie,' he said, reaching out to take her hand.

She pulled away and huddled up on the pillows, tucking her feet underneath her body. 'I don't understand why you can't see that I want ter be in the outside world holding down a job as much as you do. As much as I love our kids, all five of 'em,' she said shooting a look that defied him to argue, 'I don't see me place in this family as being chained ter the sink and cooking yer dinner.'

'Why have you never explained this to me before?' David asked, staring at the wall above her head. It broke his heart to see her so distressed and he knew he would break down if his eyes met hers.

'Why have you never asked?' she whispered back.

There was silence in the room as they both thought on the few words that had been exchanged.

'Do you hate me fer wanting more than what we have?' Maisie asked.

David shook his head violently. 'God no, I could never hate you, not in a million years. I'd die without you by my side. Please don't ever think of leaving me,' he begged, and as an afterthought added, 'I thought you were happy being a mother?'

Maisie gave David a hard stare. 'I love being a mum. I'm surprised you even have ter ask me that. I've always dreamed of 'aving a big family and now we 'ave five kiddies. I just don't see meself as being a stay-at-'ome mum. Betty manages all right,' she said, jutting out her chin in defiance.

David sighed. 'Betty is a marvel. However, she is not going to be working much longer now she is expecting a baby, is she?'

Maisie gave a frown as she thought about what David had said. 'I've never thought about Woolies without Betty in charge. She gave me my job and that's when I met Sarah and Freda. We were all new girls together,' she added. 'Blimey, I wonder if she has thought 'bout her future? It will be a big shock ter her. I'd better go and 'ave a word wiv her tomorrow,' she said.

Whatever frame of mind his wife was in, she always considered her friends and their feelings. It was one of the things that had attracted him to her long before they were courting. 'Why don't you tell her you'd like to return to work for a few days each week to start?' he suggested with a smile. 'I know I can't win when you set your mind on something.'

'What? Do you mean it?' she shrieked, launching herself across the bed into his arms. 'But what about the kids . . . and yer dinner?'

He laughed, happy to have his smiling wife back with him. 'Don't you worry about it. I have an idea that may just work. Leave it with me.'

Maisie snuggled into his arms. 'It doesn't mean I don't love all the kids – and you. I just feel I want ter do more wiv me life. Does that make me sound ungrateful? You've given us a lovely 'ome, and I simply adore being Mrs David Carlisle, but . . . '

'But you were put on this earth to do more?' he suggested, kissing her forehead and brushing her hair from her face where it had fallen from the carefully placed pins.

She snorted with laughter. 'Don't be an idiot. You make it sound like I want ter be a vicar or something. I know I'm not clever enough ter do a proper job, but I just think I can do more than be a mum and housewife.'

'You are a very able woman, Maisie Carlisle, I'll not have you say you aren't clever. Headstrong maybe, and pretty irritating at times, but you are one clever woman. Look at how you can turn your hand to transforming an old piece of material into a new dress for the children. Your friends are the best-turned-out women in town thanks to you and your sewing machine. I do wish you'd consider setting up a sewing business of some kind. I know I've mentioned it in the past, but it could be a good venture.'

Maisie wrinkled her nose. 'I do enjoy making things out of nothing and copying the fashions from magazines, but I ain't trained or anything. People would laugh at me.'

'Irene never laughed at you when you made her a gown. And look at Sarah's wedding dress. I know I only ever saw the photographs George took, but she was a beauty, as were the bridesmaids. One in particular was spectacular – but then I'm biased,' he added, kissing the tip of her nose.

'I . . . I . . .'

'Darling, whatever is wrong?' David said as he watched a look of distress cross her face. 'We're all upset that Irene died, but I thought you were coping with it?'

'It's not that. I fell out wiv Sarah. Earlier today I told her something I haven't told you before, either . . . that I believe Irene came ter see me, and told me ter take care of Sarah, while I was giving birth ter the twins. I didn't know Irene had died earlier that day. I feel bad not telling you before now. When I found out Irene had died, I kept it ter meself in case people thought I was mad.'

'I don't think you're mad. Stranger things have happened. I've seen it in my job. I take it Sarah was none too pleased?'

'She acted as though her mum thought more of me than she did of her own daughter. You see, Irene never went ter see Sarah when she had a bad time giving birth. I don't know why either, but now it's as if I've lied, and I swear I didn't,' Maisie cried.

'Sarah must have been exhausted and not thinking right. Perhaps when she's had a good night's sleep she will see things differently? Why don't you take a walk up to the maternity home tomorrow and see if you can make things up with her? The pair of you are best friends – she is bound to remember that, given time.'

'I hope so. P'raps I'll do that after I go into Woolworths and see Betty. Yer never know, she might come wiv me. They can be a bit sniffy about who visits, but no one'll argue wiv Betty.'

David gave her a gentle kiss. 'I'm glad that's all sorted. Now, shall we have something to eat?'

Maisie wrapped her arms round David and pulled him close. 'In a little while, eh?'

'Hello, ducks. Is Betty up in her office?' Maisie greeted Freda with a peck on the cheek as she met her on the staircase leading up to the staff quarters of the Woolworths store.

'She is, but she's not alone. Her replacement is in there with her,' Freda replied, screwing up her face in distaste.

'The woman's not yer cup of tea, then? That'll cause a few problems while Betty's on leave if you don't like her,' Maisie grinned. 'I 'ope she's OK wiv me coming back,' she added.

Freda squealed with delight. 'You're coming back to work? That'll be grand. I've so missed you and Sarah. It'll almost be like the old gang is back together – apart from the fact that Betty will be leaving, and Sarah'll be busy with her baby. Come to that, what's going to happen with your lot if you are here?'

Maisie shrugged her shoulders. 'David said he'd sort it all out, so let's not worry. I'll catch up wiv you later. I'm hoping ter go up and see Sarah this afternoon and thought Betty might be able ter slip off and come wiv me.'

'Good luck with that. The new manager seems to have Betty on her toes already – and it's a man. I'd best dash. I have a couple of new assistants on the counters and they need watching until they've settled in a bit more. I'll catch you later for all the news. Give Sarah a big hug for me,' she added before hurrying down the staircase.

Maisie continued up the stairs to the long passage with its numerous doors leading off to storerooms, the staff canteen and the manager's office. The office door was ajar and as she approached she heard low voices. Without giving it much thought she knocked on the door and walked straight in, as she always had.

'Excuse me, would you wait outside until you are called,' a thin-faced man told her in an annoyed voice as he looked up from where he was seated behind Betty's desk.

'I'm sorry, I was expecting ter see the manager in here,' Maisie said, taking an instant dislike to the man.

'I'm here,' Betty said from behind the door. 'Is that you, Maisie?'

Maisie pulled the door closed and saw Betty standing on a small ladder, reaching up to where she kept old paperwork on a shelf. 'What the 'ell are you doing up there?' she asked as she grabbed Betty's arm and helped her down. 'You shouldn't be climbing up ladders in yer condition. Any gentleman wouldn't allow such a thing.' She glared at the man.

'And you might be?' he asked, giving her a cold stare.

'This is Mrs Maisie Carlisle. Maisie was one of my best

supervisors before she left to have her twins. How are they doing, Maisie, and what news of Sarah since yesterday?' Betty said, straightening her jacket and giving her friend a strained smile.

'The kids are all well. In fact, I came ter see you about . . .'

'Can you please stop all this social chit-chat and let me get on with my work, ladies?' the man sneered. 'Mrs Billington, we have work to do.'

Betty gave a look at the clock on the wall and reached for her handbag. 'It is time for my lunch, Mr Porter. I shall be back promptly at two o'clock. Good afternoon.' She took Maisie's arm and they left the room at a brisk pace.

Halfway down the staircase, they waited while Betty caught her breath.

'Are you all right, Betty? What was all that about?'

'I'm fine,' Betty laughed, holding her side as she did so. 'Ouch – I have a stitch. Such strange things seem to be happening to my body at present. I had no idea.'

'There will be more delights, believe me,' Maisie said, stepping aside as a young shop assistant rushed up the stairs.

'Oh, Mrs Billington. Someone's been sick and I can't find the cleaner,' she gasped.

'Jenny, I'm off to lunch. Mr Porter will assist you. He's in my office.'

The girl almost curtsied to Betty before dashing off.

'Come on, let's get out of here before that intolerable man catches us and asks me to wield a mop and bucket.'

Maisie took Betty's arm and they bustled down the stairs, through the shop and out into the cold afternoon.

'Now will you tell me what the 'ell is going on?' she asked, as they crossed the road to Hedley Mitchell's department store and stood in line for a table in the tea room.

'That, my dear Maisie, is my replacement. It seems that my services will no longer be required by F. W. Woolworths once I am a mother.'

Maisie froze on the spot. 'Why, they can't do that ter you, can they? They'd have been lost without you these past six years,' she said indignantly before adding, 'and ter think I came ter ask if you could do with a part-time worker.'

'You would like to come back to work?' Betty asked as they were shown to a table. 'What does David have to say about this?'

'He supports me decision,' Maisie answered as Betty raised a quizzical eyebrow. 'Betty, is it so wrong of me ter want ter do something outside of the home? I love the children dearly but I feel so unfulfilled. Just ter be able ter do something for meself rather than fer the home and family is all I ask.'

'But the twins are only three months old. You really want to leave them?'

'Would you?' Maisie asked, before giving her order to a waitress who hovered with a pad and pencil in hand.

'I envisaged having my baby and returning to work at the Erith store at some point. I didn't expect to be told by head office that my position would end, and if I wished to work for the company a position would be found for me in one of the stores as a staff supervisor, just as I was before the war started.'

'It seems so unfair, after all you've done fer the company,' Maisie sighed.

'They've not got rid of me yet. I don't plan to leave for a few months, so if you would like to come back to work I'd welcome you with open arms. I'm still the manager until I walk out of the front door of the store for the last time, whatever that jumped-up little weasel thinks,' Betty grinned, trying hard not to let her friend see her chin wobble as she fought off the desire to burst into floods of tears.

'P'raps you should see how you feel. After all, you're no . . .' Maisie froze, as what she wanted to say could offend Betty.

'You mean I'm no spring chicken? Believe me, I know that, so please don't feel you've said anything out of place,' she replied, seeing that Maisie's face had turned red. 'I plan to work for as long as I can before taking leave. Now, tell me why you are so keen to come back to Woolworths when you have those delightful children to care for. I hope there are no problems at home?'

'Gawd, no,' Maisie said quickly. 'It's me. I'm feeling restless, as if I should be doing something wiv me life rather than being a housewife. David sees me, all right, but I want . . . ter be honest, I don't really know what I want. He suggested I go back ter work fer a few hours a week and see how I feel then. Between you and me, I reckon he hopes I'll find it too much ter cope wiv,' she grinned.

'I can see why he would think such a thing, as my own thoughts are for the children. Who would have them – Ruby?'

'My goodness, I wouldn't expect Ruby ter take on me kids. We sat up chatting part of the night and David says he has an idea and ter leave it wiv 'im. I trust 'im,' Maisie added. 'Now, the other reason I wanted ter see you was ter ask if you could spare half an hour ter go up and see Sarah. I know we aren't supposed to visit, but I thought what wiv Alan being away and her 'avin' a bit of a bad time, they might let us pop our heads in fer a while. What do you think?'

'That is a very good idea. I don't know about you, but this sandwich does not look very appealing to me. I can't eat another morsel. Why don't we go right now?'

'What about the chap in yer office?'

'That man has made it perfectly clear he is superior to me, so he can take charge for a while. I'll leave a message,' Betty giggled.

'I can't believe you're rebelling, but it's great fun. Come on, there's a bus due in five minutes. If we hurry we'll just about catch it.'

Betty picked up her handbag from the floor and followed Maisie from the busy tea room. When she thought of the woman she had employed back in 1938, wondering at the time whether this brash, worldly-wise person would fit in with her staff, it seemed suprising that they now got on so well together. Perhaps they weren't so different after all, with their hopes and dreams?

David put the brake on the large Silver Cross pram and checked the babies, who were sound asleep inside, before walking up the short path to Vera's house and knocking on the front door. He knew Ruby's friend was home, as he'd seen the curtains twitch as he checked on his children. The door opened within seconds. 'I'm sorry to bother you, Mrs Munro. I wondered if your Sadie was at home?' David Carlisle said politely, as Vera peered from behind the half-opened front door.

'She is. Come on in, David. To what do we owe the honour of this visit?'

David followed her into the living room, where Sadie was sitting spooning strained vegetables into the mouth of a chubby-faced toddler. From the amount smeared around Arthur's face, it looked like she had a fight on her hands. 'Hello, Sadie, I wondered if you'd consider doing us a favour?'

'Take a seat, David,' Vera said, moving her knitting from an armchair. 'Now, what's all this about? Had enough of your Maisie and come courting our Sadie, have you?' she chuckled while raising her eyebrows at her granddaughter.

David joined in with her laughter, although he felt rather uncomfortable. 'Nothing like that, Mrs Munro. Maisie and I are very happy. I – that is, we – wondered if Sadie could do with a few hours' work each week? We're looking for someone to care for the children while Maisie goes back to work.'

Vera screwed up her face and stared hard at the handsome RAF officer. 'And why would your wife be wanting to go back to work only weeks after giving birth to two babies, and with three others under your roof? Something's not right . . . not right at all.'

David felt confused. 'I'm sorry; I simply came here to

offer your granddaughter a few hours' work, as I felt she would be perfect for the job. I can assure you, Mrs Munro, there is nothing wrong at all.'

Vera crossed her arms over her chest and scowled at David. 'Don't come into my house asking me for my help and then arguing with me. I can tell there's something wrong with your marriage, and you are here to get my Sadie involved. What's your game, David Carlisle?'

David felt confused. Why did Vera always see the bad side of something, even when there wasn't one? As for using his full name, it made him feel like a schoolboy in trouble with his mother, who was prone to still making him feel ten years of age when she wanted to make a point. Even Maisie never resorted to such tactics, being inclined to more flowery language. 'Perhaps I'd better go,' he said, standing up and giving Sadie an apologetic smile. Try as he might, he'd not been able to have more than a few words with the young woman.

'I'll see you to the door,' Vera said, 'and I'll thank you not to bring your problems to my house again.'

David found himself speechless as the door was closed behind him. Checking the children were still sleeping soundly, he kicked off the brake and headed down the road to Ruby's house, where he found Bob cleaning the windows.

'Hello there, David – I see you're in charge of the kids today,' he said, climbing down from his ladder and throwing a cloth into a bucket of water. 'Fancy a brew?'

'I could do with something stronger if truth be known. I've just had a run-in with Vera.'

Bob chuckled as he helped David manoeuvre the pram

into the narrow hallway of number thirteen Alexandra Road. 'That is one woman I neither understand nor wish to clash swords with. What did you do to upset her?'

'I wish I knew. I only went in to ask Sadie if she'd like to earn some money taking care of the children, and the next thing I know I was being accused of deserting them and failing in my marriage.'

'Have you finished those windows?' Ruby called out from the kitchen.

'As near as damn it. We have a visitor who needs resuscitating with a strong drink,' Bob shouted back as he helped David release baby Ruby from one end of the large pram where she'd been top and tailing with the twins. 'This one won't fit in there much longer,' he said as he took the still sleepy child and gave her big kiss on her cheek. 'Come on, let's go and see if your namesake has a biscuit in the tin for you, shall we?'

David checked the twins before following Bob through to the living room, where his daughter was already sitting on a rag rug in front of a coal fire with Bob on the floor before her. 'I'll watch her if you need to chat to Ruby,' he said with a wink.

'Then take her coat off, or she'll not feel the benefit when she goes out in the cold,' Ruby said as she came in with a tray. 'Here, make a bit of room on the table, David, love. Bob's been sorting out his seed packets and made an almighty mess. They'll be in the dustbin if he doesn't put them back in his shed soon.'

David pushed the piles of packets to one side along with a shabby-looking notebook and the stub end of a pencil. 'Planning the garden, Bob?' he asked as Bob looked up from where he was playing peekaboo with Ruby Junior.

'It's for the allotment. I thought if I was careful like, I could put a few rows of flowers between the vegetables. For our wedding,' he added, in case David hadn't understood. 'I've got some more notes in the shed if you want to come and take a look. I could do with a hand if you've got the time. I'd ask our Mike, but he's rather busy these days now he has a wife and child.'

'Don't you think David's got his hands full too, you old fool?' Ruby joshed as she placed a plate of biscuits down next to the teapot. 'There's five kiddies in his house, and he has an important job doing whatever it is in London for the RAF.'

'I don't mind giving you a hand. Your Mike is a newly-wed, after all. Maisie and me have been together a while now, and I do get let off the leash from time to time; that's when I'm not doing my important job in London,' David said with a smile. 'It won't be long before I'll have more time on my hands.'

Ruby passed Bob his tea and looked thoughtful. 'Does this mean you'll be leaving the RAF?'

'I've been discussing it with the powers that be. The way things are going, the war won't last forever, and I've decided not to stay on afterwards.'

'But you have an important job,' Ruby said, looking concerned.

'Once the war's over I want to move on, have a job where I'll be home at regular times and be with Maisie and the family.'

'You know best, lad. What are you thinking of doing?

Our Mike said they're always on the lookout for decent coppers. It kept me in employment most of my working life.'

'If I was younger I'd jump at something like that, Bob. But I'd like to have my own business. Something like Douglas Billington's.'

Ruby looked surprised. 'What, you mean you'd be an undertaker?'

'No. One undertaker's enough in any circle of friends; whatever I do, it would be more management.'

'What does Maisie say about all this?' Bob asked as he picked up the pieces of biscuit young Ruby had dropped on the rug. 'Shall we take this out to give to Nelson?' he asked the toddler as he helped her to her feet and carried her to the kitchen door.

'I've not discussed it yet, so I'd be grateful if you didn't say anything,' David called after him.

'You don't need to worry about me mentioning what's been said. I'm not nosy like Vera Munro. As for Bob, I'll remind him not to say anything,' Ruby smiled, as they watched Nelson gently take the pieces of biscuit from the child's hand. 'She's a good kid. That's the first food I've seen the old boy eat in a few days,' she added, with a worried edge to her voice.

'Now what's this you said about having a run-in with Vera?' Bob called from the door, as he coaxed young Ruby away from hanging onto the dog.

David explained to the pair how he'd approached Vera's granddaughter to consider taking on a paid part-time job to care for his children so that Maisie could return to work at Woolworths. 'I seemed to leave with a flea in my ear and

Vera assuming I had a problem with my marriage. I have no idea why,' he sighed.

'She's a rum one and no mistake,' Bob muttered.

'She gets herself het up over nothing. Don't you go worrying yourself. I'll have a quiet word with her and put her straight. Would you like me to help out? I don't want paying, mind. Maisie's like one of my own and I don't take money from my family.'

'I don't want to take up too much of your time, Ruby, but you'd be doing us a big favour. What if you did some of the time, and if I can get Sadie to help, she can take the rest of the load?'

'Leave it with me and I'll see how the land lies when I chat with Vera. I know the girl could do with the money. She never did get her job back in London and she's not that happy working at the Co-op. Now, shall I get the bottles ready for the twins? They'll be stirring before too long. There's no time like the present to start work. Why don't you take young Ruby out the back garden? Bob can show you the plans he has for the flowers he wants to grow at the allotment.'

Bob had just opened the door to the shed when the two men felt the ground shake under their feet. Young Ruby shrieked with fear and burst into tears in her father's arms.

'What the hell . . .' Bob said as he tried to calm Nelson, who started to howl.

'Sounds like a rocket's come down up past Avenue Road,' David said as he sheltered his eyes against the winter sun. 'Yes, look, there's a cloud of smoke the other side of town.'

The wooden frame of a sash window scraped and Ruby shouted from an upstairs window, still holding the nappies she had gone to collect from the airing cupboard. 'It's over near the Hainault, where our Sarah is.'

David felt the blood pound through his head as he remembered that Maisie had gone to visit her friend, and could also be in danger.

4

Maisie waited for Betty to catch her breath as they walked up the tree-lined lane towards the maternity home. 'Do you think they'll let us see Sarah? They only allowed David in ter see me when I had the twins.'

'I do hope so. I intend to do my utmost to ensure we get in. Perhaps I can fall on their mercy as someone who will be having her child there in a few months' time. Look, there's a low wall. Can we sit down and rest for a few minutes? Who'd have thought carrying a baby could be so tiring?'

Maisie led Betty to the wall that edged a large Victorian house and they both sat down, letting out a sigh. Although it was only February, the day was a mild one and the women both wore heavy woollen coats. 'Take yer coat off fer a bit; it'll help you cool down,' she said. 'I'll carry it fer you.'

Betty shrugged out of the coat and thanked Maisie as she neatly folded the garment and handed it over. 'This is a delightful road. Did you not live round here some-where?'

'Back down the Avenue a bit, but we only rented rooms.

You'd need ter be filthy rich ter own a house like this one,' Maisie said, indicating the property they sat in front of.

'I don't know. There are some terraced houses over the road. I shall make it my business to search out prices. It would be so handy for work.'

'But you ain't going ter be working at Woolworths in a few months, and . . .'

Maisie's words were cut short by a loud whooshing sound, and then an explosion that had the two women reaching out to each other in fear as they were almost knocked from the wall.

'Stay there,' Maisie shouted at Betty as the noise still rang in her ears. 'I'm going ter see if I can 'elp.' She rushed across the road and round the corner towards Erith Cottage Hospital and the maternity home that stood nearby.

'Stay back, love,' a man shouted as he ran from his house. 'You don't know what's happened over there.'

'I know I 'ave a mate in the maternity 'ome, and I want ter make sure she's all right,' Maisie shouted back without slowing down. '*Please let no one be hurt*,' she prayed aloud as she reached the side of the hospital and rushed to the back of the building as a short cut to where she remembered the wards and nursery of the Hainault were situated.

The garden area was a complete mess, covered in glass, fragments of burning wood and masonry from a rear wall. With a quick glance she could see right into the nursery, where the wall was now completely missing. In amongst the debris she heard a small noise like the mewling of a kitten coming from beneath the metal bars of a broken crib. Flames licked the edge of the bedding. Without thinking, Maisie threw herself forward, pulling the debris from where she heard the noise. A louder cry had her lifting the broken crib back and underneath, protected by a sheet and blanket, she found a baby boy covered in dust and bellowing at the top of his lungs. 'Why hello, young fella, what 'ave you been up ter?' she asked as she picked him up and hugged him close, uttering soothing words until his tears subsided. She pulled back the cuff of a blue knitted matinee coat to read the tag around his small wrist. 'This is a strange way ter meet you, Master Gilbert, but I'm yer auntie Maisie. Welcome ter the world,' she said, giving Sarah's newborn child a gentle kiss on the cheek while other babies in the nursery started to cry in protest at the disturbance. 'Yer a lucky little fella and no mistake.'

Betty and Maisie sat beside Sarah's bed in a side ward as staff cleared up the mess. Relieved nurses had supplied tea for the trio and, after making sure that Sarah was tucked up snugly, had left them to chat and get over their fright. The baby had been given a thorough check, and was none the worse for his adventure. Word had soon arrived that no one had been injured in the rocket attack, so spirits were high, with nursing staff and mothers coming to visit the little miracle.

'He was in the nursery at the back of the building and close to the window, so that's how he ended up being blown into the garden. I dare not even think of what could have happened,' Sarah said in a shaky voice. 'Thank goodness you found him so quickly,' she added, giving Maisie a grateful look.

'He's all right, a proper little bruiser. I reckon he'll be down the boxing club as soon as he can walk and knocking nine bells out of the big kids and busting their noses flat ter their faces. I don't know if you've named him yet, but I'm going ter call him Buster.'

Betty flinched. Yet again Maisie had surprised her with her language, but she had to smile at the choice of name. 'Does he have a name – a proper name, I mean?' she asked as Sarah passed the baby to her for a cuddle.

'We'd decided on Alan if it were a boy, as it was my Alan's granddad's name and runs in the family, and Irene if it had been a girl . . . after Mum.'

The women fell silent, thinking of how Sarah had fallen out with Maisie.

'Look, Sarah. I was on me way 'ere ter say ter you as how I didn't want us ter argue. I'm sorry fer what I said about yer mum appearing like that when I was in labour wiv the kids. The last thing I wanted ter do was ter upset you. I could kick meself fer saying anything. I should 'ave kept me gob shut. No doubt I imagined it all.'

Betty held her breath as she watched the two girls. Their friendship balanced on a knife's edge.

Sarah looked Maisie straight in the eye. 'I wasn't myself when I had a go at you like that,' she said.

'You had every right ter speak as you did,' Maisie interrupted.

'No. You see, I do believe that Mum came to you after she died. She could be a right snob at times and drove me up the wall with what she said about people, but she meant well, and we all loved her . . . and we miss her,' Sarah added with a tremor in her voice, 'but I do believe she meant for you to look out for me, and you did. If you hadn't been there to rescue . . .'

'Buster?' Maisie prompted her.

Sarah smiled. 'If you hadn't been there to rescue Buster he could have died, so we have Mum to thank for that.'

Maisie raised her cup of tea. 'Ter Irene and Buster!'

Betty joined in, although she had a worried look on her face. 'You will christen him Alan, won't you?'

'Excuse me, ladies,' a nurse said, after politely knocking on the door. 'There's a gentleman outside wishing to speak to his wife.' Sarah's eyes lit up until the nurse continued, 'It's a Mr Carlisle.'

Maisie leapt to her feet. 'It's David – he must be worried about the explosion. I suppose we'd best go and let you have some peace and quiet,' she said, giving Sarah a quick kiss on the cheek. 'Thank you,' she whispered to her friend before hurrying out of the room.

Betty followed more slowly, but still stopped to kiss Sarah and to bend and stroke the baby's cheek. 'Buster . . .' she muttered to herself in a puzzled tone before leaving the room.

'I'm pleased to see you have graced us with your company, Mrs Billington,' Cecil Porter said as he checked his wristwatch. 'It is almost time for staff afternoon breaks, and I've still to go through the stock sheets with you.'

If Betty had felt tired earlier, now she was ready to drop. However, the man's arrogance had annoyed her. She'd not left the employ of F. W. Woolworth yet, and she was still in charge of this store. 'If you don't mind, Mr

Porter, I would like to sit at my desk. You may have the visitor's seat over there.' She pointed to the corner of the room where he had placed his coat and briefcase. 'As manageress of this store, which I am until the day I leave, I will decide what you have to learn about being a manager. Is that clear?'

Cecil Porter gave her a cold stare, but did not argue. Betty went on, 'I'm in receipt of a letter from head office where they have instructed me that you will be my replacement. However, they have included a copy of your curriculum vitae, which I find sadly lacking. You've had very little experience of working in any branch of Woolworths, which I find somewhat worrying. Therefore I will devise a training schedule so that my store will be handed over to someone capable of keeping up the high standard customers expect when shopping in Erith. Do I make myself clear?'

'I trained at head office in the personnel department,' Cecil said haughtily.

'It is as I thought; you do not yet have the skill to be a manager.'

Cecil frowned. 'My uncle happens to have an important position in the company. He recommended me for this store.'

Betty gave him a charming smile. 'You have just confirmed that you do not yet possess the skills. I'll do all I can to assist before I leave.'

Cecil nodded his head and vacated his seat.

'Now, before you make yourself comfortable I suggest you go to the staff canteen and make tea for us both. I would appreciate something to eat as well, so please see what is available. Hurry along now.'

After Cecil left the room Betty reached for the heavy Bakelite telephone, dialled the number for her husband's business and waited to be put through to him. While she did so she opened a notebook and wrote the heading 'Cecil Porter Training Schedule'. She would enjoy educating this man in the way she liked her store to run. 'Douglas? Hello, my love. I wondered if you would collect me from work. I'll be finished on time for once. I'm feeling fine – you've no need to be concerned. I have much to discuss with you, and it would be nice to sit down to a meal together first.' She listened as her husband spoke, then said goodbye. It would be good to have a cosy night at home with Douglas, she thought as she kicked off her shoes and started to compile the training schedule. She'd only written a few words when Freda entered the office.

'I'm sorry, Mrs Billington. I heard you'd gone to see Sarah, and I wondered how she was? I've been up to the Hainault twice now and they wouldn't let me see her.'

Betty gave her a sympathetic smile. 'I find the visiting rules so archaic,' she said. 'But it will only be another ten days before Sarah comes home, and then we can see her and young Buster as much as we like.'

Freda looked startled. 'Buster?'

Betty smiled at Freda's shocked face. 'Maisie had a hand in that. In fact, our Maisie has been extremely courageous today. Pull up that chair, and I'll tell you all about it. You can put the briefcase and coat on the floor.'

When Cecil Porter entered the room carrying a tea tray, it was to see the manager of the store laughing with one of the younger members of staff. 'I have our tea, Mrs Billington,' he said, looking straight through Freda as if she didn't exist and putting the tray on the desk.

'Thank you, Mr Porter. You may take your break now. I'll have you back here in fifteen minutes. Not a minute late, mind you,' she added. 'Now, Freda, help yourself, and I'll explain about Irene's ghost.'

Cecil glared at the manageress as he left the office. With luck, Mrs Billington would be leaving this store sooner rather than later.

Freda gave Sandy a shy smile as she opened her umbrella. 'It's so good of you to wait for me. So many of the Brownies' mothers wanted to speak with me today.'

'You should be firmer with them. You are entitled to your own time,' he said, reaching out and taking her hand. 'Now, are you ready?'

'I'm raring to go – but where are you taking me?' she asked as they headed away from Queen Street Baptist Church towards the station. Sandy had left a note for her at the fire station to say he was taking her on a surprise trip.

'Just follow me and all will be revealed,' he said.

'Gosh, I hope it's nowhere posh, what with the way I'm dressed. I'll look a right nitwit turning up in a Tawny Owl uniform.' Freda was wearing her uniform of navy serge skirt and blue shirt. In her handbag, under the squashed official felt hat, were her tie and brown leather belt with the brass Girl Guide buckle. She wore her best hand-knitted navy blue cardigan under her smart green coat, and hoped this would be enough for casual onlookers to assume she hadn't just left a Brownie meeting. She might have been foolish to force the hat into her bag, as it would need a good steaming over the kettle to get it back into shape.

'Don't be a fool,' he said, as he took her elbow to steer her over the road to the train station. 'You look fine, very fine,' he added in his soft Scottish accent.

Freda felt a warm rush of happiness flow through her despite the persistent rain and having to hurry to catch the train that was already waiting in the station. 'Phew, I didn't think we'd make it,' she said, collapsing down onto the seat before closing her brolly.

'Here, let me take your coat or you won't feel the benefit when we get to London.'

Freda grinned. She was used to Ruby saying such things, but wiggled out of her coat and folded it neatly before handing it to Sandy to place on the string coat rack above their heads, then sat down opposite. The carriage was empty as it left the station on the up line to Charing Cross.

Sandy noticed her smile. 'I take it your mother said the same? My mother says such things so often, I'm afraid they tend to slip out when I least expect them to.'

If only my mother had been that caring of me and Lenny, Freda thought to herself. 'No, it's my landlady, Ruby, who says such things. My mother passed away last year, but we weren't very close,' she added apologetically.

'I'm sorry for your loss. I find my parents to be a great support in my life even though we live far apart.'

'You must be a great blessing to them,' Freda said, not

knowing how else to answer this polite young man. 'I wondered if there was a reason you didn't return to live with them after . . . after . . .'

'After I was injured at Dunkirk?' he finished for her, knowing that it was common knowledge at the fire station.

'Yes, I'm sorry. I wasn't sure you wanted to be reminded,' she said, wishing she hadn't started the conversation.

Sandy raised his hand to dismiss her concern. 'What's done is done. My wish was to return to my regiment, but what use is a man who couldn't defend his country with a leg that refuses to bend properly? It was suggested that I should continue with the engineering apprenticeship I started before I joined up. Vickers offered me a job, and the Baptist church arranged lodgings, so here I am,' he said, giving her a charming grin. 'We are both outsiders who've been welcomed with open arms by the good people of Erith.'

'I count myself very fortunate. I know I'm not supposed to ask, what with walls having ears and all that, but do you by any chance work with George Caselton?'

Sandy gave a dramatic look left and right in the empty compartment before whispering loudly. 'He is a very important man who heads our division. I doubt he knows I exist. Why do you ask? Are you a spy working for Hitler disguised as a Tawny Owl?'

Freda giggled. She couldn't imagine George being considered a very important man when she'd seen him on the floor in his slippers playing with his granddaughter and beating them all at tiddlywinks at the weekend. 'I'm sure a spy would have a much more glamorous life. George is the son of my landlady and father of my best friend,

Sarah. He's been like a father to me since I came down from Birmingham.'

Sandy was quiet for a moment. 'I understand he lost his wife recently?'

'Yes, Irene died in November when a V2 hit some-where she was visiting. It was extremely sad.' Even though they were alone, Freda did not feel that she should men-tion how the Woolworths branch in New Cross had been decimated and many lives lost. She was also unsure if she should disclose too much about George's life, if he was such an important man in his job. She already felt as though she'd said too much. Why, she'd only known Sandy a little while, and here she was chatting away nine-teen to the dozen.

'You are fortunate to have good people to live with,' he said. 'My landlady is rather too fond of cabbage, and the smell tends to linger in the house for much of the time. But she is a good God-fearing woman, so I can't ask for more.'

Freda thought she was lucky to live where she did, as Sandy's landlady sounded none too appealing. 'It could be worse,' she said.

The train stopped at Woolwich and the door opened as two women laden with shopping climbed into the car-riage. Sandy helped them with their bags and moved to sit next to Freda. They sat in silent thought for a while, with Freda very aware of Sandy being so close.

'You've still not said where we are heading. I'm worried I'm not dressed appropriately,' she said, noticing that Sandy was not wearing the uniform of a leader in the Boys' Brigade but had on a tweed suit that looked smart, if a little worn. It was like something George or Bob would have worn.

He patted her knee, and quickly withdrew his hand when he noticed the women opposite watching his every move. 'You look extremely smart and presentable. I wouldn't worry.'

However, Freda did worry, and as she gazed out of the smoke-smeared window as the train rushed towards London, she feared her attire would let her down. Where could he be taking her on a Sunday afternoon? There were very few theatres open on a Sunday, which was a shame, as she loved the grandness of the theatre and the excitement as the curtains opened and the lights dimmed. Perhaps it would be tea in a hotel? She groaned inwardly at the thought of how eyes would follow her across the room as she walked to their reserved table in her drab serge skirt and navy jumper. Nothing could disguise the fact she was wearing the clothes of a leader of a Brownie pack, even though she'd removed some of the more obvious signs. It was at times like this Freda wished she had joined up and could be admired in a uniform from one of the women's services. Her fire service uniform was more functional than smart.

The train pulled into Charing Cross station and Sandy helped the two women from the train before reaching for Freda's coat and umbrella, making sure she was ready for the next part of their outing. Turning right out of the station, they walked down the Strand, with Freda exclaiming at the bombed-out buildings and boarded-up windows where bomb damage had occurred. Turning up a side street, they walked on for several minutes before stopping in front of an imposing church. It seemed to have escaped the bombing by the Luftwaffe, but its grim front and tall spire gave Freda the shivers as she looked upwards to the large cross at the top of the building. Surely they weren't going to church? She'd attended once today already.

'We go down here,' Sandy said, indicating a passageway at the side of the building. Pulling hard on a stout door, he ushered her inside. They were greeted by the sound of an accordion playing a lively Scottish tune.

'I hope you enjoy Scottish country dancing?' he asked as he handed over a couple of coins to a dour woman sitting at a table just inside.

Freda's spirits plummeted. A wet Sunday afternoon dancing Scottish reels in a teetotal church hall was not quite what she'd expected. She'd liked to have spent some time alone with Sandy to get to know him more.

Ruby stepped back from the sideboard and gave the shining new black Bakelite telephone a sideways glance. Even with a crocheted doily underneath, it still scared the daylights out of her. 'I can't get used to it being there. It looks so sinister, as if it's about to bite me or something.'

Bob chuckled. 'It can't go anywhere else apart from the hall, and you didn't want it there. The Post Office men explained to you that the telephone has to be near the front of the house so that the cables can go out to the pole up the road.'

'People like us don't need a telephone. We're not ones for making out to be something we're not. The neighbours will think we're putting on airs and graces, having such a thing in the house.'

George gave Bob a grin. He was surprised the telephone had even been allowed house-room at number thirteen, as his mother had been adamant she was not having one under her roof. 'Mum, you're doing me a big favour having a telephone here. It means if there is an emergency, we can call for help. Besides, if I decide to move back this way, you can take messages for me. You know how important my work is?'

Ruby huffed and folded her arms in front of her chest. 'If you say so, George, but I still think we will rue the day we had that thing installed. It will attract trouble, mark my words – but what's this about you moving back to Erith? Isn't your place in Crayford closer to your work?'

'It is, but I'm not so happy there anymore. The place holds too many memories for me. I'd rather be in Erith with my family and be of help to Sarah now she has the two kiddies. I have use of a car, so I won't have to worry about using a pushbike or public transport for work.'

Ruby nodded her head. 'I can see where you're coming from, son, but don't make any hasty decisions. Grief can be a funny old thing, and you may come to realize you shouldn't have moved after all.'

'Ruby has a point,' Bob said as he settled down in an armchair by the fireplace. 'Although after my wife passed away I was all for selling up and coming back here to be with Mike. Retirement by the seaside is no fun on your own, and if truth be known, it wasn't really my idea to move down there in the first place. It took the Luftwaffe to make me come to my senses and move back home, and I couldn't be more happy about how things turned out,' he said, reaching for Ruby's hand and giving it a squeeze before she pulled away and cuffed his ear.

'You daft bugger,' she said affectionately. 'I wonder when it will ring?' she added, giving the telephone a stern look. 'I'll not have it interfering with my day.'

A tap at the door had George on his feet.

'It's Vera,' Bob said. 'I could see her walking up the path.'

'Is it working yet?' Vera asked, before anyone could say hello to her. She pulled her coat off and approached the telephone slowly. 'Where do we put the coins in?'

'Yes, it is, and no, we don't,' Bob replied, trying hard not to laugh as Vera delved into her purse to count out some pennies.

'You can be a funny so-and-so sometimes, Bob Jackson. I thought it would be neighbourly of Ruby to allow those of us without a telephone to make use of it.'

'Ignore him, Vera. Now why do you need to use the telephone? Is it urgent?' Ruby asked.

'You could say that,' she replied, giving a look to Bob and George to insinuate they shouldn't be listening.

'Would you like to come and see my onions, George? They're coming along a treat,' Bob said.

'I do believe I would like to see them. Thank you, Bob,' George replied. 'If you would excuse us, ladies.' He made a comical bow and followed Bob from the room.

'They're a bit keen to go out in the garden. It's still drizzling out there,' Vera said with a frown as she sat in the armchair just vacated by Bob.

'It may have something to do with the brown ale I saw him smuggling down to the shed earlier today,' Ruby said.

'Now, tell me – what's had you rushing down here in the rain?'

'It's our Sadie. She's got a bit of a problem, and I thought that with you having a telephone I could sort it out for her.'

'Please don't tell me she's got herself in trouble again?'

'No, it's nothing like that, it's the chap who fathered the baby. They'd come to an arrangement where she wouldn't name him or return to where they worked together, and in return he would send her a monthly postal order,' Vera explained.

Ruby thought the man had got out of his responsibilities very easily, but she knew Vera was still impressed that he was some kind of big nob in London and not the usual run-of-the-mill scoundrel who got young women pregnant without a by-your-leave. 'I take it the postal orders haven't arrived?'

'Not for the past three months they haven't. Our Sadie wrote a very polite letter, but he hasn't replied. I thought if I made a telephone call to his office and asked him politely, he could tell us what the problem was. It's probably the post not getting through,' she added as she saw the look on Ruby's face.

'Yes, it would be a good idea to get in touch with the man. But why isn't your Sadie doing it?'

'She reckons he wouldn't speak to her. I thought if he spoke to me we might get to the bottom of things,' Vera said.

Ruby thought there was more chance of getting blood out of a stone than the father of Sadie's child coughing up to help support him, but she dared not say that to Vera.

She knew the woman wasn't doing so well money-wise, and didn't want to dampen what little hope she had. 'There is something else you've not thought of,' she said, trying hard to be kind.

Vera frowned. 'Please don't try and stop me speaking to him, Ruby. I can always go and use the public phone box.'

'You are welcome to use my phone anytime, and I don't want your money. The problem is, it's a Sunday, and he's highly unlikely to be at his desk. More likely he's home with his wife, and I doubt you have a telephone number for his home, do you?'

Vera looked shocked. 'I hadn't given that a thought, and I'd not like to upset his wife. This is between him and our Sadie.'

'You and Sadie are welcome to come down tomorrow morning and use the telephone.'

Vera mumbled her thanks and got up to go.

'While you've got a minute,' Ruby said, 'I wondered why you turned on David as you did when he offered Sadie a few hours' work? I thought you'd both have been in need of the extra cash at the moment?'

Vera sighed and sat down again. 'It's so difficult, Ruby. I worried that our Sadie might become tempted again.'

Ruby snorted with laughter. 'What do you mean, tempted?'

'It's no laughing matter. Look what happened last time she was in close quarters to a man. She ended up with a baby.'

'Vera, getting pregnant isn't an illness. Do you mean

that she's likely to leap on any man who comes within spitting distance?' Ruby asked, trying hard not to laugh.

'I wouldn't say that exactly, although I do keep an eye on her to be on the safe side.'

Ruby looked at the woman she'd known since God knows when. The years had not been good to Vera, and the added worry of her unmarried granddaughter having a baby out of wedlock seemed to be the final straw. 'Vera, your Sadie is a bright, intelligent girl. She simply fell in love with the wrong man, and he took advantage of her. She's doing a good job caring for that little lad and you should be proud of her.'

'But . . .'

Ruby raised her hand to silence her friend. 'You are doing David Carlisle a disservice by thinking he would step outside his marriage and dally with another woman,' she said, thinking that Maisie would rip the limbs off any woman who approached her husband with the wrong intentions. 'Why don't you tell the Carlisles that you and Sadie would be prepared to help with the children?'

'I don't like to, after what I said to him. I don't think I can even face him, I'm that embarrassed.'

'Then perhaps we should leave it for now. I'll see you tomorrow morning for that telephone call. Why don't you bring Sadie with you? I've not seen that baby of hers in a while. I'll make a bite for us to eat as well.'

Vera's eyes lit up. 'That's really neighbourly of you, but you won't go running up to Maisie's to tell her I'll be down here, will you?'

'Of course I won't be running up to Maisie's house. I've got much more important things to be getting on with.'

Ruby gave a small smile as she showed her friend out of the door. Yes, she'd invite the Carlisles down as well. She liked it when a plan fell nicely into place.

Approaching the new telephone with trepidation, she picked up the heavy receiver and dialled the number she had written on a piece of paper. 'Hello, Maisie, it's only me . . .'

5

'Tea or lemonade?' Sandy asked as he led Freda to a seat at the side of the church hall.

'Lemonade would be lovely, thank you. I never knew Scottish country dancing could be so energetic – not that I've tried it before,' Freda said as she collapsed onto the hard wooden seat. Although she'd removed her navy cardigan, not worrying if anyone spotted her uniform, she was still pink-cheeked and feeling hot.

She gazed around the dusty hall. It wasn't an inspiring place, with grubby windows covered in blast tape and faded cream-painted walls. The wooden floor needed a good scrub and polish, but no one seemed to care as they danced away, following the more expert amongst them. There was much laughter when some forgot their steps, and a round of applause at the end of each set.

'It's been a lovely afternoon. Thank you for inviting me,' Freda said as she accepted the glass of lemonade. 'I was surprised you seemed to know all the dances.'

Sandy shrugged his shoulders as he sat down next to her and took a gulp of his drink. 'I grew up with it. Did I tell you my grandfather is a minister back home? If there was something going on in the hall behind the kirk then we were expected to participate. That's why I'm still with the Boys' Brigade. He made me promise that wherever I went in the world, I'd stayed involved. '

'Kirk?'

'It's what we call our church,' he explained.

'I thought your family were farmers? Sorry if I'm being nosy.'

'Not at all,' he smiled. 'My mother's family have always farmed and when her father passed away and there wasn't a son to take on the farm, my dad stepped in. It did cause a problem, as he was expected to follow Granddad into the clergy. There was some ill feeling for a few years, but all is well now.'

Freda thought for a moment. 'So well that you decided to become an engineer?'

'I knew that the church and farming were not for me. Farming can be a hard life, and my mother told me to follow my heart and learn a trade. I'm pleased with my choice,' he replied, giving her a gentle smile.

Freda felt a small thrill run through her as she handed back the empty glass. Did Sandy mean he was pleased with her, or just his choice of job? 'That was most refreshing. Has the dancing finished?'

'Goodness, no! We have a Virginia Reel and the Dashing White Sergeant,' he said, nodding to a blackboard where the dances were listed. 'Why, did you want to head for home?'

'Not at all, I'm having a wonderful time, thank you for inviting me. Perhaps you would like to join my friends and me next time we go to Erith Dance Studio on a dance night? I can't guarantee a Gay Gordons, but we enjoy a waltz and foxtrot.'

'There's nothing I'd like more than to dance a waltz with you,' he said gently, holding out his hand. 'Now, let's take our place on the floor for the Virginia Reel.'

Freda took his hand and followed him onto the dance floor as she dreamt of being held close in Sandy's arms and gently waltzed around the floor, something they couldn't do in Scottish country dancing.

All thoughts of romance slipped from her mind as she was spun round the room to the lively music. An hour passed too soon as Freda enjoyed dance after dance.

'Will you come again?'

'Is that an invitation?' Freda asked as they left the brightly lit hall and stepped into the chill of the late afternoon. What remained of the wintry March sun was beginning to set. 'If it is, I'd love to go dancing with you again, but don't forget my invitation still stands to join my friends and me at the dance studio. We've had some lovely times there. In fact, there's a dance coming up in a couple of weeks to raise funds for something or other. I guarantee you'll have a jolly time.'

Sandy took Freda's arm and tucked it through his own, keeping hold of her hand. 'I'd like that very much. Now, would you like to see what I do next whenever I come to London?'

'I'm intrigued,' Freda said, more than a little thrilled that Sandy was holding onto her. 'Is there anywhere open at this time on a Sunday?'

'Wait and see,' he replied as he guided her down the darkened streets, taking care as they crossed roads.

'Oh my,' Freda said, taking a deep breath. 'The River Thames. I never grow weary of watching it flow past our little town of Erith, and here it is in London. It looks much more majestic here,' she said, leaning against the wall of the embankment and watching as the water flowed calmly downstream. Even with barrage balloons overhead and naval ships docked nearby, there was still something romantic about the river as night fell and the moonlight glinted on the water.

Deep in thought, they leant against each other, contemplating their calm surroundings, until a familiar sound could be heard in the distance heading up the Thames.

'Oh no,' Freda called out in some distress. 'A doodlebug – can you see it?'

Sandy put his hand to his eyes to shield them from the moonlight and stared hard. 'Yes, it's coming this way. Get down.' He pushed her down hard against the wall of the embankment, and before Freda had time to think he'd pulled her into his arms and held her close. She could feel their hearts beating fast as they listened to the *phut-phut* sound, before it cut out.

Douglas handed his wife a small glass of port and lemon before joining her on the sofa. Betty had her feet up, and he rested them on his lap and gently massaged her ankles. The heavy green velvet curtains were drawn against the night sky, with a single standard lamp lighting the cosy room.

'That's bliss. Please, don't ever stop,' she sighed. 'If only you could come to work with me tomorrow and be on hand to rub my feet when they start to ache.'

'Couldn't you have your replacement do that for you?' Douglas said with a hint of laughter in his voice. 'You could add it to his list of duties.'

'Douglas, it is no laughing matter. The man is useless at his job. How can I leave to have our baby, knowing he is so incompetent? Why, the store could be ruined within days. I was thinking perhaps I shouldn't leave my job when I'm six months gone, and try to remain a little longer. What do you think?'

Douglas ceased rubbing his wife's feet and looked at her tired face. Even in the dull light from the lamp he could see her face lacked its usual rosy glow, and small lines were forming around her eyes where once there had been none. He knew how distressed she'd been when he collected her from Woolworths only a few days before and she'd shown him the letter from head office. 'Darling, I've been pondering their suggestion that you let Cecil Porter take over command of your ship from the end of this month. Perhaps you should consider leaving earlier. Isn't it time to hand the reigns over to someone else and plan for your future as a wife and mother? I know the girls would adore having you home when they return from school each day. Why, you might even have time to finish those baby garments you started knitting before Christmas.' Betty's attempts to knit had become a joke amongst her family.

She slid her feet from her husband's lap and placed them on the floor before finishing her drink. Taking a deep breath, she faced Douglas. 'I was thinking I would write to head office and inform them I planned to work as long as possible, and that after my confinement I could return to my position.' She held her breath and watched as Douglas let her words soak in.

Slowly he shook his head before letting out a sigh. 'I just knew you were thinking of doing something utterly preposterous,' he exclaimed. 'There is no need for you to work. Aren't we comfortable enough? Am I a bad provider? Why, I've never heard anything so ridiculous in all my life. What would people think if they knew I allowed my wife, and the mother of our baby, to abandon us all to go to work?'

'But Maisie is returning to her job, and her twins are only a few months of age. I've said she can work three mornings each week, and David has agreed she may.'

Douglas stood up and paced the floor. 'I'm not David Carlisle. I've told him he is mad to allow his wife to leave his family for this fancy of hers.'

'Fancy? You think my wishing to continue my job is fanciful? David, this is the twentieth century. I am not your chattel. If it weren't for women in this war and the last, this country would be on its knees. Next you will be dragging me by my hair like a caveman.'

Douglas returned to sit beside her. 'I've made a total mess of explaining how I feel,' he said, attempting to reach for her hand, which she snatched away. 'The girls spent years without their mother after she passed away, and although I did my best, it meant I had to rely on a housekeeper while I worked. I just thought that this time I would have a wife who would be here for us all, and it would make us a proper family.'

'I can't believe what I am hearing,' Betty raised her voice. 'Douglas, I was in an important position when we first met. Whatever made you think I'd ever stop being a working woman with a responsible job? Woolworths kept jobs open when their male staff went off to fight for their country. It stands to reason women should also be allowed to return to their management positions.'

Douglas took a deep breath. As much as he loved his wife, he was alarmed that she hadn't thought through her situation. 'Read the letter again, my love. Woolworths are effectively giving you notice. As a woman expecting a child, this is what happens. You have also not considered that when this ghastly war ends, men will return home and take back their jobs.'

Betty jutted out her chin in defiance of Douglas's words. 'Mr Benfield has passed away. We have no male manager returning to the store.'

'Your superiors seem to think otherwise. Why else would they have sent this Porter chap as your replacement?'

Betty went over to the tiled fireplace and pulled the offending letter from behind an ornate clock that had been a wedding gift from Douglas's aunt. She scanned the typed lines several times before lowering it and looking at her husband with tears in her eyes. 'You're right, Douglas. They have no need of me anymore.'

Douglas soothed Betty as she all but collapsed in tears at his feet. Leading her to sit down he held her in his arms and thought hard about the situation as he soothed her. There was no doubt that his wife would be unhappy if she didn't work after giving safe delivery of her child. It went against everything he held dear to agree to what she wanted. It seemed that the people at Woolworths head office were of a similar opinion.

'Sshh,' he soothed Betty. 'If you keep on like this you won't be fit for work tomorrow morning, let alone for a few months more.'

Betty raised her tear-stained face. 'You mean you agree that I should work on for a few more months?'

'Against my better judgement, I do agree, if only to see a smile back on my pretty wife's face. However, I do feel you shouldn't return to work after the birth, but perhaps we can come to some arrangement?'

'Arrangement? Whatever do you mean?'

'Perhaps you could come and work for me for a few hours each week, just as Maisie will do at Woolworths.'

Betty wrinkled her nose as she considered his sugges-tion. 'But if Maisie is able to return to Woolworths, why shouldn't I?' she asked.

'Because Maisie is a shop girl and you, my dear, are a manager – and I fear that most managers at F. W. Wool-worths have never had a baby before. You are charting new territory.'

'Well, that was one reason I thought I might write a letter to inform them of my plans.'

Douglas knew that Betty would never give in to his request to be a wife and mother and stay at home. 'With Mr Porter already in place I fear you wouldn't be able to remain afterwards, but I can see no reason not to inform them you are fit and well and can work on a while longer. However, I have a better suggestion. You should speak to head office in person rather than by letter, and take with you a letter from our doctor stating you are fit for work.'

Betty was delighted. 'What a super idea. Perhaps I could even speak to them about returning to my job after the birth?'

'I feel it best if we wait and see how you feel, and broach the idea at a later date.' He saw Betty's smile drop a little, and added, 'My concerns are for you, my love. I've buried one wife and don't wish to bury a second. At least not for another forty years,' he added with a gentle smile.

Betty put her hand to her mouth as he said his words. 'My goodness, I never gave that a thought. What an utter prig you must think I am, acting like a spoilt child when you are thinking only of me.'

Douglas was relieved to see his wife happy again. As he pulled her to him to seal the deal with a kiss he thought of Alan Gilbert, who had been the trainee manager at the Erith branch before joining the RAF. He too would be after a managerial role when the war ended. He doubted a decorated Spitfire pilot would be turned down in favour of a woman, no matter how intelligent or hard-working she was.

Freda snuggled into Sandy's chest as the doodlebug came closer. She knew it would be a matter of seconds before it came down and exploded, causing death and destruction close to where they sheltered against the embankment wall. She thought back to when she'd been on duty and seen the aftermath of one of these deadly bombs. She'd also experienced the full force of a blast when one landed in the street behind Betty's home and she was flung across the garden, landing with just a few scratches and bruises. Others had not been so fortunate. 'Sandy, may I ask a favour of you?' she whispered.

'Of course,' he replied in a surprised voice.

'Would you kiss me? I'm not usually this forward but I'd hate for us to die and not have kissed. But if you don't wish to . . . ?'

Sandy needed no second bidding as, with a small groan, he put a hand at the back of her head and pulled her even closer than they already were, covering her face with tender kisses before their lips met. They were oblivious to an explosion from just across the river, and for several minutes delighted in their closeness.

A polite cough had them stopping to look up to where a slightly embarrassed policeman stood. 'Excuse me, sir, madam. I do believe it's time for you to take this young lady home, if I may be so bold. The danger seems to have passed for now.'

Sandy helped Freda to her feet and brushed down her coat as she straightened her hat. Neither was able to look at the other. 'Thank you, officer,' he said politely as the policeman continued his beat. Taking Freda's hand, he gave it a tender squeeze. 'We'd best catch our train. There's a long wait if we don't.'

Freda didn't care if they had to wait for all of eternity. 'Yes, I suppose we should. I must apologize for being so forward,' she murmured. 'I thought we might have died and I'd have missed . . .'

Before she could say another word, Sandy leant towards her and brushed her lips with his own. Freda wrapped her arms round his neck, pulling herself as close as possible before closing her eyes and responding. She didn't care that they could have died, or that she was in her dowdy Tawny Owl uniform. As far as she was concerned, she was in heaven, and she intended to stay there for as long as possible.

'Something smells rather nice. Have you been cooking?'

'When do I ever stop cooking in this house?' Ruby said as she led Vera and Sadie through to the living room. 'Sit yourselves down, and Sadie, why don't you lay the boy down on the armchair and put those cushions round him? He looks dead to the world.'

'I've not long fed him, Mrs Caselton,' Sadie replied in a quiet voice.

'Call me Ruby, I've told you before, love. Now, I'll just check the sausage and tomato pie. We don't want it burning before we're all ready to eat, do we?'

'You're so inventive with your meals, Ruby. I don't know where you get your ideas from,' Vera said as she licked her lips.

'It's nothing special. I used a recipe from one of those booklets they handed out. They've got some good ideas in 'em. Surely you had them as well?' Ruby said as she used a tea towel to pull an enamel baking tin from the oven and check the food.

'I flung them all onto the fire when I was short of coal,' Vera said.

Ruby tutted to herself. She knew that Vera had hit hard times last year, but had thought she was over the worst until her news yesterday. 'You can borrow mine if you want, and copy out the recipes.'

'I'd like to do that, Mrs . . . Ruby,' Sadie said. 'I like to do a bit of cooking when I can. The smell coming from your kitchen is wonderful,' she added shyly.

Ruby returned to the room, rubbing her hands together. 'Now, that won't be too long. Would you like to use my telephone while I make us a cup of tea? I've got some Camp coffee if you prefer. The telephone's in the front room, so you can be private while you talk to your boss, Sadie.'

Sadie gave Vera a frightened look. 'Can you do it, Nan? I wouldn't know what to say if he was horrid to me again.'

Ruby sat down and leant towards the young woman. 'Why would he be horrid to you, Sadie, love? You had his child, even if you weren't wed. Any man should be proud of his own child and want to see him fed and cared for.'

Sadie's chin wobbled as she stared back at Ruby. She had the look of her nan, but so far the harsh lines of bitterness that Vera wore with pride had not been etched on her young face. 'He didn't want me to have it, Ruby. He said he'd pay for me to get rid of it. He's got children with his wife and didn't want her to find out about my Arthur. I walked out of his flat and my job with only a few clothes and a couple of quid in my purse.'

So that was what was behind all that business from last summer when Sadie had turned up on her nan's doorstep asking for money, Ruby thought to herself. The poor kid. 'You say he now sends you a monthly postal order?' Ruby asked, trying not to judge the girl. She knew that no one was perfect, and both Sadie and her nan were on their uppers.

'Yes, I sent him a letter after Arthur was born and told him we needed his help and support. That's when he told me he would send some money each month, as long as I kept my mouth shut and didn't name him on the birth certificate.'

'He doesn't sound like a very nice person, does he?'

'I thought I loved him. He took me to nice places and bought me beautiful clothes. Then when I found I was expecting his child, he changed.'

Ruby recalled how the girl would come home from her job in London dressed up to the nines, and how proud Vera had been with her only grandchild working in an office in London. 'It sounds as though he just wanted his bit of fun,' she said sympathetically.

'And don't we know it,' Vera huffed. 'She gave into him far too easily, just because he said he would leave his wife.'

'It's the age-old story, but we mustn't worry about that now. Let me show you where the telephone is and perhaps you can speak to him, Vera?'

'Oh no, not me. I'm not good on the telephone, and if he says anything awful I'll not be able to keep my temper. Would you do it for us, Ruby?'

Ruby took a deep breath. She'd had a feeling it would come to this. 'All right, I will. But can we write down what you want said, Sadie? I can be as sharp-tongued as your nan at times, and just as likely to put my foot in it and make things worse.'

Sadie thought for a few minutes before carefully writing on the piece of paper Ruby had supplied.

Vera peered over her shoulder. 'Ask if he would like to see his child. We could always take Arthur to London to meet him.'

Sadie wasn't keen, but added it anyway. 'I think that's it, Ruby,' she said, handing over the list.

'You have beautiful handwriting,' Ruby said as she read through the few sentences. 'Come on – let's get this done before I change my mind.'

Vera picked up her sleeping grandson and followed the two women into the front room, where the telephone sat on a white crotchet mat on the sideboard.

'Does it cost much to have one of these?' Vera asked as she peered at the instrument from a safe distance.

'I have no idea. George arranged it all. He said it would be useful after us all rushing around trying to find news when Irene and Maureen were involved in the explosion at New Cross. It hasn't rung yet, and when it does I'll be that worried about answering the thing,' Ruby said as she nervously picked up the receiver and slowly dialled the number that Sadie had added to the list of her questions. After a short while she spoke into the handset. 'Good morning, I wish to speak to Mr Gordon Davenport,' she said in a voice she reserved for speaking to the vicar and her doctor. 'My name? I am Mrs Ruby Caselton and I'm speaking on behalf of Miss Sadie Munro.' There was a short pause before Ruby answered. 'I see. Thank you very much.'

'Well?' Vera asked.

Ruby replaced the receiver and polished it with the

edge of her pinny. 'You could hear that I didn't get to speak with him. He's in a meeting. I think we should give it an hour and then try again, don't you? Now, let's go and have that cup of tea.'

They'd hardly sat down before they heard the key being pulled through the letterbox and the door opening. 'Coo-ee, it's only us,' Maisie called out before entering the room with a twin in each arm. David followed with young Ruby, who was crying loudly to be put on the floor, and set her down gently.

'She'll get covered in dog hairs,' Ruby complained. 'I've not had time yet to put a broom over the floor or give the rugs a beating. Nelson's moulting all over the place.'

'You should get rid of that dog with children in the house. It's not nice to have the mangy old thing around kiddies,' Vera moaned.

'A bit of dog hair won't hurt anyone,' Maisie said. 'Besides, the kids all love Nelson. I'm rather fond of the old dog meself. I've been thinking we should 'ave a dog ourselves fer the kids.'

'Good morning, ladies,' David said, ignoring his wife's comments. 'How are you today?'

Ruby gave him a crafty smile. 'I'm very well. I was just saying how it's nice to be able to earn a few extra bob from time to time. I understand you are looking for someone to keep an eye on the children, David?'

David walked through to the kitchen as the kettle started to boil and made a pot of tea before Ruby could get to her feet. 'I am, but it would have to be someone responsible. We'd not trust just anyone to look after our brood, would we, Maisie?'

'Too true we wouldn't. Someone like Sadie here would be ideal. Could you come ter our house and do a bit fer us? David would pay you well, wouldn't you?' Maisie asked as he walked into the room with a laden tea tray. 'Mind you, I reckon he should stay home and be a house-wife.' She laughed at her own joke.

'That'd be quite a day when men did such things,' Vera scoffed.

'I would be interested in working a few hours, if I could bring Arthur with me?' Sadie replied to David, ignoring what her nan had just said. 'It would mean not having to bother his dad for money.'

'Not bother him?' Ruby exploded with rage. 'He got you into this position, so he ought to be paying. Don't let him off the hook that lightly, my love.'

'Are you 'avin problems?' Maisie asked.

The women explained what had happened while David handed out tea and gave a biscuit to Arthur and young Ruby.

'Watch they don't choke,' Ruby commanded.

'So he's in a meeting, is he?' Maisie asked thoughtfully. 'Would you like me ter see if I can get 'old of 'im?'

Sadie gave her a shy smile. 'Would you?'

'I'd love ter. Here – take one of these each,' she said, handing a twin to Ruby and one to Vera. 'Come on, luv, let's go and give 'im what fer,' she said, picking up Sadie's list and heading to the front room.

'God help the man. I'd not want to be on the receiving end when Maisie lets rip. Now, what one have I got here?' Ruby said, peering at the twin she was holding.

David stopped patting Arthur on the back to dislodge

a soggy biscuit and turned to look. 'The blue one is Oliver and the pink is Carol.'

'Adorable,' Vera said as she cuddled Oliver. 'You can never have enough babies around the place,' she added with a smile.

'Why, Vera, I think you're softening in your old age,' Ruby grinned as she hugged Carol.

'Hey up, what's all this?' Bob asked, coming in from the back garden. 'Have you opened a children's home?'

'It feels like it sometimes,' David said, getting to his feet and shaking Bob's hand. 'How's the garden?'

'I've not done much today. I've been in the shed with the dog. He's not so good. I think we should bring him indoors where it's warmer. There's a bit of a nip in the air, and he ain't as young as he used to be. Have you got a blanket we could use, Ruby?'

'There's a couple of old army blankets under the stairs that we used in the air-raid shelter. Can you get one for me please, David?' Ruby said, looking worried. 'Bring him in now, Bob, and he can sleep by the hearth next to my armchair,' she instructed, passing Carol to Vera to hold.

They'd just settled Nelson when Maisie and Sadie appeared. The latter had a broad smile on her face.

'There's a postal order in the post, and he should toe the line fer a while,' Maisie said. 'I laid it on a bit. Told him how as Sadie and the kid were almost on skid row, chances are that she'd have to send the kid to live wiv him if he didn't cough up.'

'It was marvellous to watch Maisie as she told him off, Mrs Caselton. I could never have done that, even on the telephone. Would you like me to finish off the dinner so you can sit with Nelson? He doesn't look so good, does he?' Sadie said, leaning down to give him a gentle stroke. 'It's been a few weeks since I've seen him going up the alley to visit Mrs Hawkins' dog. They always used to play together.'

Ruby gave the dog a gentle pat. 'That would be a big help, Sadie, thank you. The spuds just need mashing and the sausage and tomato pie is keeping warm in the oven. Why don't you bring the twins' pram through, David, then they can have a kip while we eat. Vera looks weighed down holding both of 'em. God knows how she will eat holding those two little bundles otherwise.'

'They're no problem,' the old woman said with a gentle smile. 'But I'd be grateful to have at least one hand free to eat my dinner.'

Maisie started to clear the table so they could eat. 'It's good of you ter take on working for us, Sadie. I really appreciate it, you know,' she called through the open door.

'I'm looking forward to it,' the girl replied as she started to mash the potatoes. 'If you want, I could do a bit of housework and put some dinner in the oven for you as well? I could borrow Ruby's recipe leaflets like she said.'

Maisie hurried into the kitchen and hugged the surprised girl. 'That would be bloody marvellous. I could get some sewing done when I get in, and not 'ave ter worry about burning something fer David,' she grinned. 'You might as well make enough ter take 'ome wiv yer. I reckon yer nan would appreciate it, wouldn't you, Vera?'

'That's generous of you, Maisie,' Vera said. 'I'll look after our Arthur when you're working for Mr and Mrs Carlisle. He's teething at the moment,' she mouthed to

Ruby before nodding to the young child, who had dozed off on the rug, as if he had something seriously wrong with him.

'Blimey, I've just had a thought.' Maisie burst out laughing, making Arthur jump awake with a wail. 'This means we've got staff, just like yer mother, David. Ain't that posh!'

6

'Mrs Billington, I need a word with you,' a large buxom woman called to Betty as she walked through the Woolworths store doing her morning inspection.

'Yes, Doris, what can I help you with?' she asked, stopping by the vegetable counter where the red-faced assistant worked.

'It's that Mr Porter. He's been interfering with my vegetables again. I arrived this morning to find he'd re-arranged the spuds and Brussels. Now he's saying as how I've got to wash the spuds before they go on sale as customers don't like dirty produce. Then he says as how I've got to make the carrots all point the same way. I've gave him a piece of my mind, and now he's told me he'll have me sacked for answering back.'

Betty felt her face twitch as she tried not to laugh. This was the third complaint of the morning about Cecil Porter, and although inside she was fuming, she couldn't help but smile at the thought of Doris washing the piles of potatoes that were delivered from a nearby farm. 'Don't worry, Doris, I'll make sure Mr Porter is aware of how vegetables are sold.'

'Thank you, Mrs Billington. I knew you'd see sense. I told him that you were the boss here and the day you left I'd be following you out the door. I'll not have no jumped-up schoolboy tell me how to do my job.'

'Don't worry, Doris. There won't be any changes here for a while yet. Just leave it with me.'

'I will, thank you,' she replied, turning away to serve a customer. 'He should work a day on this counter, then he'd know what's what,' she muttered.

Betty continued on her way with Doris's words echoing in her ears. How could she tell her staff that the man interfering in their jobs had no skills, and hadn't even been a trainee manager like Alan Gilbert had been before he joined the RAF? If only Alan was back working in the store, she knew he would be the perfect person to take on her job when she left to have her baby. Woolworths needed more people like Alan and Sarah. Instead she had the nephew of someone from head office taking over, who knew nothing about the store. He couldn't even use a broom. It was then an idea came to her. Stopping by the haberdashery counter where Gwyneth Jackson was tidying a display of darning wool, she called over to her. 'Gwyneth, if anyone needs me I'll be in my office for the next hour and I don't want to be disturbed. Can you ask Freda to come and see me when she returns?'

'Certainly, Mrs Billington,' Gwyneth replied in her gentle Welsh voice. 'Freda will be back from her tea break soon. I'll tell her then. Is there anything I can help you with?'

'Thank you, Gwyneth, that's very kind of you to offer. I'll have a word with you later. You could say I've just seen the light,' Betty said as she headed off to the door marked 'staff only' with a determined look on her face.

Reaching her office, Betty took a notepad from the desk drawer and carefully drew a series of boxes entering each department of the store, followed by dates and times. When Freda knocked on the door ten minutes later she found Betty deep in thought.

'You wanted to see me, Betty?' she asked, carrying in a tray of tea and sandwiches. 'I thought you could do with a mid-morning break. There's no cake, so I brought a Spam sandwich to keep you going now you're eating for two.'

'Oh, you wonderful girl,' Betty said, clearing room on her desk for the tray. 'Take a seat and tell me what you think of our Mr Porter?'

'Crikey, I tend to keep out of his way. I can't say he likes me, although I can't think why. He always speaks to me as though he has a bad smell in front of him. I know staff despise him as he is so bossy. He's only been here a week and he's putting everyone's back up. Where is he, by the way?'

'I sent him to the storeroom to fill out a stock sheet. It will keep him out of my hair for a while. Now, you do know that I'll be leaving Woolworths once I've had my baby?' Betty said, trying hard to keep her face expressionless.

Freda, however, was a different kettle of fish, and looked shocked. 'I'd not thought about it. How silly of me. I just imagined you'd be here forever. Woolworths won't be the same without you,' she added sadly.

'It's the way of the world, I'm afraid,' Betty said, passing a cup of tea to the young woman. 'I will be visiting head office to plead my case, but inside I know they will expect me to stay at home with my child, even though I feel I could have the best of both worlds and keep my job. My feeling is that Mr Porter will be my replacement, and this makes me somewhat uneasy. He does not know the way we work, and if I have to leave then I want the store left in capable hands. So my plan is to train our Mr Porter on every counter until he knows the job backwards. He may still be unpleasant, but at least he will know what the words "hard work" mean.'

Freda spluttered as she sipped her tea. 'Oh my goodness. I fear he may resign. Which wouldn't be a bad thing,' she said as she wiped tea from the front of her overall. 'Isn't it a shame that we no longer have our trainee managers to fall back on?'

'I thought the very same, but we shall just have to work with what we have, won't we?' Betty said with a twinkle in her eye. 'Here, have a Spam sandwich.'

'I always enjoy this stroll up to the church,' Ruby said as they reached the end of Perry Street and could see Saint Paulinus Church up ahead. 'Are you sure you don't mind me leaving these flowers on Eddie's grave? I've got a small bunch for Irene as well. I must say, it feels a little strange to be visiting one husband while seeing the vicar to arrange marrying the next.'

'Don't be so daft, woman. I'd be doing the same myself if I didn't know Mike had cycled up a couple of days back and tidied up his mum's grave. I may just pop round to say hello while you tend to your Eddie. That's if you don't mind?' Bob smiled as he took her arm to cross the road.

'Of course I don't mind. We should always make a point of going to visit their graves. The pair of them played a big part in our lives. I shared a big part of my life with Eddie and I have our kids and grandkids to show for it. You're the same, although she missed seeing your Mike marry Gwyneth. She'd have been that proud.'

Bob nodded his head in agreement. 'Did you know, Gwyneth placed her wedding bouquet on the grave afterwards. I thought that was most generous of her.' He slowed down to look over the wall at the graves of the German airmen whose plane had crashed on a nearby golf course several years before.

'It gives me the shivers every time I see those graves,' Ruby said.

'Why? Because they are the enemy?' Bob frowned. He'd not thought of Ruby as being bothered that young men, albeit the enemy, who'd fallen in battle should be buried in their family churchyard.

'No, it upsets me that those lads are buried so far from their homes and families. That could be our Alan, or any one of thousands of English men who die on foreign soil. I just hope that come the end of this war, someone will be able to arrange to have them taken home and laid to rest in their own country.'

Bob patted her hand before they walked on towards the old lychgate. 'I'm sure it will happen. There are always fresh flowers on the graves, and they are tended as well as any others in the churchyard. We could ask the vicar about it come the time?'

Ruby kissed Bob's cheek. 'You're a good man, Bob Jackson. I'm a lucky woman to be marrying you.'

'Well, you took your time deciding to accept my proposal and to name the day,' he replied, running his fingers around his tight collar and going a little red as he spotted the vicar watching them.

'Hello, Vicar, thank you for agreeing to see us,' Ruby said as he ushered them into the church whilst making polite talk about the weather being good. She felt a bit daft holding a bunch of flowers. 'I'm going to leave these on a family member's grave,' she explained, not wanting to say it was her late husband's. She noticed Bob give her a conspiratorial smile, and grinned back.

'Would you like to set them down here until you leave, Mrs Caselton? The church is quite cool at the moment.'

Ruby placed the flowers down on a wooden seat and shivered. After their walk in the February sunshine she felt it was rather chilly inside the church.

'I'm sorry I can't offer you tea in the vicarage. My wife is in the throes of an early spring clean, and she has members of the WI helping her. We can sit in the vestry out of harm's way,' the vicar said, giving Bob a wink.

Ruby was pleased not to be visiting the vicarage, as it was a little too posh for her liking. Sitting in the vestry after the vicar had moved a pile of hymn books suited her well enough. 'I was hoping you could fit us in for May the eighth as it's my birthday. That way all the ki . . . children wouldn't have to make two journeys to visit their old mum,' she explained.

The vicar thumbed through his diary until he reached the date and ran his finger down the lines of writing.

'Hmm; I'm afraid there may be a problem. I must say, May is a popular month. I have three weddings that afternoon already.'

Bob could see the disappointment on Ruby's face. 'How about the morning?' he suggested. 'We could marry around eleven and then back to our place for a bite to eat, then have a booze-up later on.' He looked pleased with his suggestion until he spotted the look of horror on Ruby's face. 'Not that we are much for drinking,' he stuttered.

'No, just a sherry to toast the King,' Ruby said in the poshest voice she could muster.

It was the vicar's turn to try and hide a smile as he watched Ruby glaring at her intended. 'I'd be most disappointed if you didn't celebrate your nuptials, Mr Jackson. In fact, after a busy day I'd quite like to join you, if you agree?'

Ruby nodded enthusiastically. 'It would be an honour to have you visit, Vicar. Please bring your wife along as well.'

'I'm afraid my wife is not one for drinking,' he said. 'I'll come alone on my bicycle. Now, shall we go through the formalities – and then you can visit your loved ones in the graveyard?'

'That didn't go so badly, did it?' Bob said as they stepped out into the daylight from the gloomy interior of the church. 'Shall we have a walk down into Crayford and find somewhere for a cup of tea after you've left your flowers?'

Ruby looked up at the clock on the church tower. 'No, I want to get back to Nelson. I don't like leaving him on his own while he's not so good. He likes me to sit where he can see me now his eyesight's fading, the poor old bugger.'

Bob didn't argue. He knew that when that old dog left this earth he would leave behind one distraught owner. He would also miss Nelson, who liked to accompany him when he was in the garden and take a snooze in the sunniest available spot. 'Then let's get cracking, shall we?' he said in a hoarse voice, trying hard to swallow the lump that was forming in his throat.

'Welcome home, love,' Maureen beamed as Sarah entered the small front room of the house in Crayford Road. 'We have missed you. Here, let me take this young man from you so Georgie can say hello,' she added, holding out her arms for her new grandson. 'Why, he is the most beautiful boy in the world, and quite a size too! Buster is certainly a good nickname.'

Sarah gave her mother-in-law a kiss before picking up her daughter and swinging her round. 'He's over a pound heavier than this young lady. No wonder it was such a struggle to bring him into the world.'

'Be careful, Sarah,' George said, staggering into the room laden down with a suitcase and a large shopping bag, plus a bunch of flowers tucked under his arm. He dumped the bag and case and handed over the flowers. 'These are from all of us for presenting us with a bonny grandson. And this,' he added, reaching into the pocket of his overcoat for a small box, 'this is for Georgina, from her little brother.'

The girl scrambled from her mother's arms and reached for the box. 'From Buster?'

'Oh dear, I was hoping she'd call him by his proper name,' Sarah grinned. 'I supposed I'd better write to Alan and explain.'

'Look, look,' Georgina shouted with excitement as she pulled a silver necklace from the cotton wool in the box before running over to tug on Maureen's skirt until she lowered the baby down to Georgina's level. 'Thank you, Buster,' she said, giving him a gentle kiss.

'Oh my, what beautiful manners, that reminded me of . . . of . . . of her other nanny. She'd have been so proud,' Maureen said as she passed the baby to George and reached for a handkerchief tucked up her sleeve.

'Wouldn't she have loved to have seen her grandson?' Sarah said as her chin started to wobble. 'I'm not sure she'd have approved of us calling him Buster, though. Maisie would have been in trouble for coming up with that name,' she sniffed. 'My goodness, we will all be in tears soon if we don't talk of something happier.'

'I'm sure she is looking down on all of us and smiling,' Maureen reassured her. 'And talking of happy things, look what arrived this morning,' she said, pulling a letter from where she'd placed it behind the clock on the mantelpiece. 'I do believe it could be from a certain young man's daddy. Now I'll go and put the kettle on and Georgina can help me with the special cake we made for mummy's home-coming. George, put the case in Sarah's bedroom while she has a minute or two to herself in peace.' She nodded at Sarah, who was staring at the letter with a sad expression on her face.

'What do I do with this little bundle?' he enquired.

'Oh, give him here and I'll put him in the pram. He looks as though he's out for the count and won't stir for a while. I gave the pram a good scrub ready for his arrival,' she said, in case anyone thought it was still covered in dust from where it had been stored in the garden shed. 'Come along Georgie, let's get the tea made,' she said, holding out her hand to the little girl.

Left alone, Sarah sat down and looked at the looping handwriting on the envelope. It could only be Alan's writing. She always savoured the arrival of his letters, wondering what he had to say and how he was doing. Although they were heavily censored and not allowed to give away his location, she knew he would hint at it in some way if he could. She ripped open the envelope and spread out the two pages inside. The letter was dated the day after she'd given birth to their son. She was aware that David Carlisle, with all his contacts in the RAF, would have got word to Alan about the birth if he could. Quickly scanning the closely written lines, she could see that he knew. Her heart quickened as she read his words of love and deep regret about not being there to meet his son, and how he hoped to be home before too long, and to give the baby a big kiss from his daddy.

Sarah put down the letter to wipe her eyes. It didn't seem fair that a man couldn't be with his loved ones to meet his child. Damn Hitler and this war for all he had done to keep families apart. She closed her eyes and prayed that it would all soon be over and they'd be together again soon. Yes, she was lucky and hadn't lost her husband as so many women had done, but she'd not count her blessings until Mr Churchill announced the end of the war and sent Alan home to be with her for the rest of their lives. Then they'd be able to continue their lives as they'd planned. Alan would continue his job at Woolworths, and would no doubt be a manager before too long. She would be at home to care for their children and greet him each evening. She thought of the money she had managed to save from the hours she'd worked at Woolworths. There might even be enough for a deposit on their own home, although she would have to be careful that he thought she'd saved the money from what he sent home to her. It was important for Alan's pride not to be hurt if he thought his wife had earned the money herself. If rumours were to be believed, then just perhaps this year her nan would be right, and there would be peace by Christmas.

Returning to the letter with hope in her heart, she read his final words:

My love, I'm told that it won't be forever before I'm home and we can once again be a family. As I am now teaching men how to fly and not part of our essential frontline staff there's a chance I'll be demobbed as soon as the end of war is declared. Nothing is definite yet but hold onto the thought that I'll be with you soon. I have such plans, my love. You wouldn't believe how I've lain in my bed at night thinking of our future life. You've always said you'd like a home with roses round the door, and I plan to work hard to make your dreams come true . . .

Sarah clutched the letter to her heart. She just knew that Alan thought the same way that she did. 'Come home soon, my darling,' she whispered.

'Good news?' Maureen asked, looking hopefully to the letter in Sarah's hand as she entered the room with a laden tea tray.

'I do believe so,' she said, giving Maureen a delighted smile. 'Alan's services won't be required when the war ends, so he could be home with us soon afterwards. We've just got to hope that the end of the war is in sight and we will see peace this year.'

Maureen placed the tray of tea onto the sideboard and rushed as fast as her bad leg would allow her to hug her daughter-in-law. 'Oh that's such wonderful news. If I was one for praying, I'd be on my knees right now.'

'What's all this about praying?' George asked as he entered the room. 'Has something happened?'

Sarah explained what Alan had written in his letter, as Georgina ran about excitedly shouting that Daddy was coming home.

'That is certainly good news. It's about time we had something to celebrate,' he grinned.

'Aren't you forgetting our grandson's safe arrival?' Maureen reminded him. 'I'd rate that as just as highly as Alan being home. At least the little lad will grow up without his daddy rushing off to defend our country. Let's hope they lock up Adolf for a good long time.' She gave George a small hug before starting to pour the tea.

Sarah looked between her dad and her mother-in-law. Something wasn't right, but she couldn't quite put her finger on what made her feel uneasy . . .

*

'Let me do that,' Freda said as she bent down to make Nelson more comfortable on the pile of old blankets Ruby had placed by the fireplace. 'You shouldn't be trying to move him. You'll do your back in,' she scolded.

Ruby had to admit that she was feeling quite weary with moving the dog around and keeping him comfortable. He lay there giving her a doleful look before glancing towards the biscuit barrel on the table. Ruby automatically dipped into the container and pulled out a piece of broken biscuit, which she handed to the dog.

'No wonder he's so hard to lift,' Freda sighed, 'he's full of biscuits. They can't be doing him any good.'

'Does it matter now?' Ruby said softly as she stroked the dog's head. 'He's been a good friend to me and I'll not let him go without, for as long as he's still here with me.'

As if he understood, Nelson raised a paw for Ruby to hold.

Freda turned away to wipe her eyes. Nelson was the only dog she'd known, and she was very fond of him. He had crept onto her bed on many occasions when she first moved to number thirteen and had been a comfort to her when her life was in turmoil. 'Do you think it will be long?' she asked.

Ruby shook her head slowly. 'I'd not think so. He's very old and doesn't appear to be in pain. It's as though the light inside him is slowly dimming and he seems to know.'

'Oh Ruby, I can't bear it,' Freda started to sob as she threw herself down to hug the woman and the faithful dog.

'There, there, love, you don't want to go upsetting yourself,'

Ruby soothed her. 'He's been a grand friend to us all, and we have to accept that his time is near.'

'I just can't think of this house without him. He fits in with all we do and has always been here. The kids are going to be so upset,' she sniffed.

Ruby nodded. She knew just how the girl felt, and wasn't far from bawling her eyes out as well. 'We'll never forget him. He's been as much a part of my family as everyone else who has slept under this roof. Do you remember when we were stuck in the Anderson shelter and he created blue murder until someone came along to help?'

Freda laughed and gave a small hiccup as she fought not to sob again. 'You always say that memories are important, and he will feature in many of mine,' she said before giving the dog a gentle kiss on his head. 'I'll stay up with you tonight to keep you company.'

'I'd appreciate it, love, but you do have your work in the morning.'

Freda grimaced. 'Don't remind me. It's my turn to be with Cecil Porter. Betty wants me to show him how we complete the stock sheets and check the storeroom. I'm not looking forward to that one little bit. There's something not nice about the man.'

'Then you need to keep your wits about you, and that means a good night's sleep,' Ruby scolded her.

Freda looked to where the dog lay peacefully with Ruby still holding his paw. 'No, I'm staying with you. Nelson needs his family with him right now. If I feel sleepy I'll kip in the armchair.'

Ruby knew she wouldn't be able to change the girl's

mind, and she'd be grateful of the company. Bob had gone up to his bed hours ago and would be sound to the world all night. 'In that case, let's have a fresh brew and see if there's something in the pantry to eat, shall we?'

They both laughed as Nelson's eyes opened and one ear pricked up at the mention of food.

Ruby stretched her back and yawned as she pulled back the curtains. Dawn was just starting to break and it looked chilly outside, with a frost on the ground. Indoors it was warm and cosy, as she'd fed the fire throughout the night, not wanting Nelson to become cold. He'd slept soundly, although at times his breathing was shallow and she'd thought the time had come. As if he knew she was thinking of him, the dog opened his eyes and gave a very small yap, holding out a paw.

'I'm here, lovey, don't you fret,' she said quietly, not wanting to wake Freda, who was snoozing. As she bent to hold his paw, the dog gave a small shudder and slipped away.

Her tears dripped slowly onto Nelson's head as she cuddled him for one last time, telling the dog how much the family would miss him and how important he had been in their lives. The minutes ticked by as Ruby spoke to her faithful friend, completely unaware of her surroundings, until an arm was placed around her shoulder.

'Come on, girl, you've said your goodbyes, now's the time to put Nelson to rest. I've prepared a nice spot near the shed where he used to sit in the sun and I've got some bulbs we can dig in once he's settled,' Bob said gently, with a catch to his voice.

Ruby allowed Bob to help her to her feet and watched as he covered the dog with a blanket before carefully lifting him. Freda stepped in to help with tears coursing down her face.

'You have somewhere prepared already?' Ruby asked.

'I did it a couple of days ago when he started to slow down. I thought it would be better than waiting until the time came. I can tell you, it nigh on broke my heart knowing he'd be there before too long. Now, can you open the back door while we take him outside? Do you want to come and help?'

Ruby headed to the door, averting her eyes from the large bundle that had once been her faithful companion. 'I'd rather not, if you don't mind. I'll come out when it's all done,' she said, turning away to put on the kettle. 'You'll need something to warm you both up once you've done the deed. I'll put on the porridge as well. It's a bit early still, but I doubt you'll go back to your bed.'

Ruby bustled about starting breakfast and relaying the fire before picking up the blankets to give them a sniff before folding them carefully and placing them in the cupboard under the stairs. 'These'll need an airing later on when it stops drizzling, Nelson,' she said before stopping in her tracks. 'I'm a daft mare,' she muttered. 'There's no one to listen to me anymore.'

The teapot was on the table keeping warm under its knitted cosy and Ruby was dishing up bowls of porridge when Bob and Freda returned to the house. Both took their shoes off at the back door and headed to the kitchen sink to wash their hands.

'I'll leave your porridge on the table and go down the garden to say goodbye to the lad,' she said, reaching for an old cardigan she kept hanging behind the back door. 'I won't be long.'

Bob poured out the tea and handed a cup to Freda. 'It's going to be strange not to have him about. I'll miss the old boy,' he remarked quietly.

'Do you think we should have another dog?' Freda asked. 'It won't be the same, but the kids will be asking.'

'Give it time,' Bob muttered gruffly, reaching for a large white handkerchief from his pocket and loudly blowing his nose.

7
~

Betty hurried into the staff cloakroom and found Freda, who had just hung up her coat and was locking her handbag away in one of a row of metal lockers. 'Freda, I've made a list for you . . . Oh my goodness, whatever is it?' she asked as Freda turned towards her. 'You look washed out. Has something happened?'

Freda nodded, but found it hard to speak. 'We didn't have a very good night. Nelson died, and we are all a little upset,' she said as she blew her nose and tried to compose herself.

'Oh my,' Betty said, raising her hand to her mouth. 'I'm very sorry to hear that. He was such a lovely dog. I know my girls will be very sad to hear this news. They loved Nelson. In fact, they've done nothing else but beg us to have their own puppy, but it must be like Nelson. I foolishly said yes in a moment of weakness and they haven't stopped reminding me. How is Ruby? I know he was very special to her.'

'Bob's with her, he's going to take her out to try and cheer her up. The plan is to buy her a new hat for the wedding, but I fear it will take much more than that. I've never seen her so sad.'

Betty stepped to one side as a group of chattering staff came into the room. 'Would you come to my office, please, Freda?' she said, adopting the clipped tones of a shop manager as opposed to that of Freda's friend. 'I have an urgent job for you.'

'Yes, Mrs Billington,' Freda replied, following her from the room and receiving sympathetic glances from some of the newer staff, who had no idea of Freda's friendship with the Woolworths manager. It was only a couple of yards to Betty's office, where she sat down and looked at the list Betty passed to her. 'Is this to do with Cecil Porter's training?' she asked, a smile flitting across her pale face.

'Yes. If the wretched man is to take on my job when I leave then he's going to know how to run this store. I refuse to allow standards to drop once he is in charge of the ship.'

'So you want him to undertake all the jobs on this list?'

'Yes, and today if at all possible, as I wish to pass him on to another member of staff tomorrow. Cecil needs to experience every aspect of work at Woolworths. One cannot manage a store without being able to step into any staff member's role with confidence,' she said sternly, although Freda detected a twinkle in her eye. 'Are you up to the challenge, dear? This could be a tad stressful, and if you are not feeling quite well . . . ?'

Freda grinned. 'I have a feeling this is just the job I need to cheer me up. Talking of being cheered up, we're going to the Erith Dance Studio tomorrow evening. Will you and Douglas be joining us? It seems an age since we've all been out for a little fun.'

'I'm not sure I'm fit for dancing at the moment,' Betty said, placing her hand on her expanded stomach, 'but I'd like to sit and watch. Douglas can dance with you. That's if you don't mind taking him off my hands for a while?'

Freda's pale cheeks turned a little pink. 'Actually, I'm bringing someone with me – but I'd like to dance with Douglas as well,' she added quickly.

Betty clapped her hands in delight. 'You have a boyfriend? That is splendid news. Do we know him?'

'I don't believe you've met Sandy. I met him at the fire station. He helps out as a volunteer there, and with the Boys' Brigade too. We went Scottish country dancing in London on Sunday,' she explained.

'I look forward to meeting him,' Betty said, more than happy that Freda had met a young man. It did worry her that while all her friends had settled down, the youngest in the group was yet to find the love of her life. She did wonder if a Scottish dancing churchgoer was the right person for Freda, but would hold off judging this unknown person until she met the young man.

'Mrs Billington, I thought that I'd go through the staff rotas today. Some of your female staff aren't putting in the hours,' Cecil Porter said as he barged into the room. He froze as he spotted Freda. 'Shouldn't you be at your counter, Miss Smith?'

'Mr Porter, would you please knock before entering my office. I was in the middle of an important meeting. However, as you are here I'd like to give you your orders for the day,' Betty said, giving him a stern look.

'But . . .'

Betty raised her hand to silence the man. 'No buts, Mr Porter. If, in time, you are the one to take charge of my store, I wish to ensure that you know the business inside out. I have given Miss Smith the task of overseeing your first training session. She has my instructions and understands what is required. Now,' she said, giving him a hard stare, 'are you ready?'

'But . . . but . . .' he blustered. 'She's just a young girl. How can this person tell me what to do?'

Betty stood up. Anger was evident on her face. 'Mr Porter, Freda has more experience of working in a Woolworths store than you have of flying a Spitfire.'

'I say,' he exclaimed. 'There's no need for talk like that. I have a medical certificate and my uncle is . . .'

Betty raised her hand again. 'I know who your uncle is and I know that is why you were moved here. Do you not think I checked your credentials? That is why I have devised this training scheme – so that you come up to the standard of the women who know much more than you, even though they earn less. Do you have any questions?'

An angry flush spread over Cecil Porter's face, but he remained silent.

'Very well, then. Miss Smith, perhaps you could start in the storeroom so that Mr Porter understands our system? If there are any problems please come straight to me. Once Miss Smith is happy that you understand this side of the business, you will spend the next month working in the storeroom and ordering our stock. Is that clear?' Betty asked, holding out a notebook. 'You will need this to take notes.'

Cecil took the book, but looked sullen. 'I'll be speaking to my uncle about this. I'm here as management, not as a storeman.'

'Fear not, Cecil, I do have the support of head office,' Betty said as she crossed her fingers, knowing she had told a little white lie. 'A word of advice I was given when starting the climb from shop assistant to manager was that we cannot undertake to manage staff unless we can do their jobs. Take note of that, Cecil. Now, off you go and find yourself a brown overall. We can't have you in the wrong uniform, can we?'

Freda grinned at Betty as she left the office. This would be an enjoyable task, and it would most certainly keep her mind off the loss of Nelson.

'What about this one?' Bob said as he took a blue felt hat from a display, much to the chagrin of the elderly, po-faced sales assistant. He'd taken Ruby to Hedley Mitchell's department store in Erith, knowing it was the best place in town to purchase such items. The girls had told him enough times for him to remember.

Ruby knew he meant well, but her heart wasn't in choosing finery for their wedding when Nelson wasn't yet cold in his grave. 'I'm sorry, Bob, I don't want to appear ungrateful, but I can't seem to think straight today. I'm liable to pick the wrong colour hat and spoil my outfit, the mood I'm in. Then I'll have Maisie after me as she's making my frock for the occasion. It is good of you to try and cheer me up, though. Why not let me buy you a cup of tea in their tea room? You never know, they may have Victoria sponge, and you know how much you enjoy that.'

Bob didn't need any second bidding. He quickly handed the hat back to the assistant, who checked it over for damage even thought it had not reached Ruby's head. 'It's all right, love, we had a bath last Christmas even though we didn't need one.' He grinned as he followed Ruby through the various departments until they came to the tea room. Thank goodness it wasn't the day they had the Palm Court concert party. He couldn't stand their squawking when he was trying to enjoy a cup of tea.

'Well, blow me down, look who's over there,' Ruby exclaimed, ignoring the waitress who was showing them to a table for two and heading to the back of the room.

'Hang on, Ruby, they may not want us interrupting their afternoon tea,' Bob said, catching her by the arm.

'Don't be daft, it's only our George and Maureen. Why wouldn't they want us to join them? He's my son, for goodness' sake,' Ruby said as she tugged her arm free and continued towards the couple, who had spotted them. 'They're only having a cuppa like we plan to do.'

Bob shrugged his shoulders and followed at a slower pace. If he wasn't much mistaken, this was more than a casual cup of tea. George was wearing his best suit, and wasn't Maureen wearing her best outfit – the one she'd worn to Mike and Gwyneth's wedding last September?

'Hello, you two, caught you at it, have we?' Ruby laughed as George jumped up and pulled out a chair for his mother.

'Not interrupting you, are we?' Bob said apologetically as he sat in the remaining spare chair. 'We've been trying on hats for the wedding, but Ruby wasn't in the mood after . . . you-know-what this morning,' he added, lost for what exactly to say in case Ruby became tearful. She'd used the telephone to let family members know of their loss, fortified by a strong cup of tea with a dash of rum to give her strength.

'Not at all,' George said as he indicated for a waitress to bring more tea to their table. 'We just fancied a bit of fresh air, and I suggested to Maureen that I take her out in her wheelchair – and where better to stop than here for a bit of afternoon tea?'

Maureen nodded in agreement, although Bob could see that she was thin-lipped and didn't have much to say on the matter.

'How are the wedding plans progressing?' George asked as the tea arrived along with fresh cakes. 'I take it the do will be held at the Prince of Wales?'

As Bob nodded yes, Ruby spoke out. 'No, it'll be a nice family get-together at home after the church service. Bob's growing salad stuff down on the allotments, and we can make up the rest with what we've got. There is a war on, after all, and we have to remember the family is in mourning.'

'For Nelson?' Maureen said, looking rather shocked.

Ruby shot Maureen a glance sharper than diamonds cutting glass. 'No, our Irene. It would only have been six months since she was killed.'

Maureen had the good grace to look ashamed, and kept her eyes down towards her lap until George spoke. 'Mum, I don't think for one minute that Irene would have wished you to have a quiet wedding because of her. In fact, I insist that we throw a big party, and it'll be my treat. As the person giving the bride away, I insist on footing the bill.'

Ruby looked shocked as she thought of what her son had said. 'If you put it that way, I'll say thank you very much, but I would still like a family meal at home if it's all the same to you. Perhaps we could have the party in the evening,' she said, explaining that it would be an early service.

'I'd like to help if you'll allow?' Maureen said. 'Perhaps I could help with the lunch?'

Ruby patted her hand and smiled. 'That's very good of you, love, but you need to think of your health,' she said, nodding to where the wheelchair was parked behind their table. 'We'll be blessed simply to have you there as a guest. Things could have been much worse.'

'But I'll be back at work by then, so if it's all the same, I'd like to help as much as possible?'

'Back at work?' Bob and George said at the same time.

'This was what I was going to tell you this afternoon,' she said to George. 'My doctor said that I could go back to doing a few hours a day, but not to tire myself. I only use the wheelchair when someone takes me out for a long walk and it's too far for me to walk home without discomfort. I intend to go in and see Betty once we leave here. If that's all right with you?' She looked at George.

'If you're sure?' George said, looking dubious. 'If this is about money, I can give you something towards Sarah and the kids' board to help out?'

Maureen laughed out loud. 'Goodness, no, but thanks all the same. I just want to get out and do something worthwhile before I go mad. Betty is as short-staffed as ever and I'd like to go back to covering the dinner and tea breaks in the staff canteen. I miss seeing everyone. Sarah's home with the kiddies for now, so I'm not required for looking after the grandchildren, although that might change in the future if she wants to put a few hours in herself.'

'If you are sure, then we'll pop over the road and see her shortly,' George said, giving her hand a gentle pat. 'Now who wants more tea?'

Bob held out his cup to George, but couldn't help notice how Maureen gazed at her hand where the man had just touched it and how her cheeks had turned a pretty shade of pink. Thank goodness Ruby had been busy tucking into a slice of cake and had missed the exchange. Things could get very tricky indeed if she thought another woman was trifling with her son's affections so soon after the death of his wife. Deep in thought, he was startled by the sound of the air-raid siren starting to wail.

'This is where we enter the number of items,' Freda said as she passed her clipboard and pencil to Cecil, pointing out one column amongst many.

He chose to ignore the proffered paperwork. 'I don't think this is the kind of work I'm expected to do,' he said, picking a small thread from his overall. 'I'm management material, and managers don't dirty their hands.'

Freda was livid. 'Mrs Billington takes an interest in all sections of the store. That's what makes her a top-notch manager,' she answered, continuing to hold the clipboard in front of him and tapping her pencil on the paperwork. 'Now, shall we get on? Or we'll be here all day, and I don't wish to miss my dinner even if you do.'

Cecil turned to count the crockery stacked on the shelf behind him. 'Twelve dinner plates and ten cups and saucers, and you know I earn more than your Mrs Billington, so she cannot be senior to male management.'

Freda sighed. She'd been shocked when Sarah told her friend about the differences in pay. In all innocence she'd assumed anyone in Woolies who did the same job would receive the same pay packet. 'Then it's all wrong, and someone should do something about it,' she retorted, getting rather angry, although she held back from mentioning that Cecil wasn't earning a penny of his wage.

'It's because she's a woman, and that is the way of the world,' he said, shrugging his shoulders. 'And by the way, it's time for luncheon.'

Freda squared up to him even though he stood a good foot taller. 'What do you mean?' she snarled.

'I mean, dear shop assistant, that only the working classes have their dinner in the middle of the day.'

'I do believe you are a snob,' she answered back, 'and I have no interest in what you think. Our manager has given us both a job to do and do it we will, whether you like it or not.'

He gave her a cynical smile. 'Let's get this job done, shall we, before I have to report you to head office? Be sure that when I'm manager of this store, you will be back on the shop floor serving customers,' he said.

'And be assured that if that day comes, it will be the day

when hell freezes over and Hitler comes marching up Pier Road,' she retaliated, shoving the clipboard into his hand. She hated stooping down to the man's level, but if he wished to act that way then so could she. 'Here, you do the paperwork. Then, when it is wrong, you can answer to the manager of this store. Once we've counted the stock, I'll show you how to pick the items requested by the counter staff and transport them downstairs. Once the stock has been signed over, this list will require changing. Oh, and hurry up, as there's a delivery due in this afternoon and you will have a lot more counting to do before you add up all those columns. You can add up, can't you?' she said, jutting her chin out at the man and waiting for his reply.

'It seems simple enough,' he replied, turning to a stock of light bulbs on the next shelf. 'I thought there was a shortage of these?'

'There is, and that is why once we've checked stock levels they have to be taken downstairs. Customers are waiting, so hurry up.' Freda didn't give the man time for a breather as she hurried him through the counting of stock before sitting him at a small table in the middle of the room to add up the many columns. 'I'll check them once you've finished,' she said, standing by his shoulder as he started the laborious task.

'There's no need,' he said in a cold voice.

'There's every need,' she snapped back. 'It's company policy to double-check everything, otherwise mistakes can be made. I'm surprised you haven't been taught that since joining Woolworths?'

'I'm management. We don't have to do a job when our

staff are paid to do it,' he replied, although he put his head down and got stuck in with adding the columns of figures.

'I'll leave you to it for half an hour as I have a small job to complete,' Freda said.

Cecil nodded without looking up. Once he heard the door close he turned to look at the stock of light bulbs and gave a knowing smile.

'Betty, can you spare me a minute or two?' Freda said as she tapped on the manager's door.

'Come along in, Freda, I was just about to make a visit to the storeroom to see how the training session is progressing.'

Freda explained how belligerent Cecil had become. 'I was wondering if you could find out exactly what training the man has had? I know I'm speaking out of turn, as it is down to you, what with you being our boss – but I'm confused by what he does know about running a store. It doesn't seem to be much.'

'I was thinking the same thing, and will be making a telephone call to someone I know at head office this very afternoon. What is he up to at the moment?'

'Adding up the stock sheets we checked.'

'Have you not told him we have a mechanical adding-up machine?' Betty said, looking at a large metal contraption with rows of numbered buttons and a lever at the side.

'Ah! I knew there was something I'd forgotten,' Freda said with a grin.

*

'What shall we do?' Ruby asked as the air-raid warning sounded. 'Is there time to dash across the road to Woolworths and use their shelter, do you think? I'd prefer that to using Mitchell's one. If I'm going to sit in a cellar for ages then I'd rather it be amongst people I know.'

Bob looked at George for support. If a raid were imminent they'd be daft to risk it, but so many had been false alarms of late that Ruby's suggestion would be preferable. 'Come on – let's make a dash for Woolworths,' he said, passing Ruby's coat to her and helping Maureen into her wheelchair.

George threw some money onto the table as they headed out of the tea room, ignoring the cries from staff to stay put. Entering Woolworths, they joined the queue going down into the cellar underneath the store. George left the wheelchair where it wouldn't get in the way and helped Maureen down the steps.

'I can do this on my own, George,' she insisted, although she enjoyed him putting his arm round her waist as they went downstairs in the half-light from a bare light bulb.

'Hurry along, please,' Freda called from just below them.

'Hello, love,' Ruby said as she reached Freda's side. 'This is a bit like old times. We've not had a raid in a while.'

'I thought the same,' Freda said as she pointed to some spare benches where they could sit. 'Most likely a false alarm, but better to be safe than sorry, eh?'

'You've lived with Ruby far too long,' Bob laughed. 'You're beginning to use her sayings.'

Ruby gave Bob an indignant nudge. 'Stop with your cheeky comments and hurry up, there's a crowd of people waiting behind us on the stairs. If it is a raid they'll go to their graves blaming you,' she huffed.

'Always the cheerful one, isn't she?' he whispered to Freda as he followed Ruby to a bench.

'How's it going?' Betty asked as she joined Freda. 'I didn't see anyone left on the shop floor, and I've ticked off the list of staff that are on duty.'

'What about Cecil?' Freda asked.

'Oh dear, I never thought to add him to the staff list,' Betty said with a worried look on her face. 'Do you suppose he is still in the storeroom? I'd best go check.'

'You'll do no such thing,' Freda said. 'For goodness' sake, think of your baby. Now, sit down over there and take the weight off your feet. I'll go and look for the wretched man.'

The words 'Be careful' followed Freda as she left the cellar and headed through the empty store. Reaching the door that led to the staff quarters and the upstairs storeroom, she was knocked off balance as the door swung open. Grabbing a nearby shelf to stop herself from falling, she saw Cecil hurry out in his outdoor clothes carrying a shopping bag. 'Mr Porter, you must go down into the cellar at once. Surely you know the rules?' she called after him as he headed to the front of the store and tried to get out, rattling each door in turn as he found them all locked.

'How am I supposed to get out of these bloody doors?' he demanded, a thin sheen of sweat appearing on his upper lip.

Freda felt a little bad for enjoying his discomfort. 'Surely you know the drill for air-raid warnings in store? I know we don't have many these days since the doodle-bugs and rocket attacks, but we still have to follow orders all the same, and as a potential manager of this store you should lead by example,' she scolded him. She shrugged her shoulders. What did she care? Her future with Woolworths would be short if the man became her boss.

'Just open the damned door,' he snapped, his hands shaking as he pushed the brass plate of the door.

Freda reached into her pocket. Betty had insisted that at least three staff members held the keys to doors in case of emergencies during enemy attacks. It had become second nature for the women to collect the keys each morning from her office. 'You are in luck, as it's my turn to be one of the key holders. However, I must insist you take cover, as your life may be in danger.'

Cecil called out something she didn't quite catch as he pushed through the partly opened door and ran off down the road.

As Freda watched him turn the corner, the all-clear sounded. She wondered if he would return, and breathed a sigh of relief when after a couple of minutes he did not appear.

'Most strange,' Betty said, after she'd seen every customer out of the cellar and work had resumed. 'Most strange indeed. Perhaps I'll make that call to personnel before I forget.'

'Mrs Billington, may I have a word?' Maureen called as she caught up with Betty at the staff door.

'Why, Maureen, what a delightful surprise. How are you?'

'I'm well, and ready to return to work,' Maureen said as she held onto a counter to support herself. 'I wondered if you'd like me back to do a few hours each day?'

Betty looked at the woman, who was most certainly not as steady on her feet as she should be, and then at George, who was pushing a wheelchair towards them. 'Why don't we go upstairs to my office and discuss this? Are you all right with stairs, Maureen?'

'I'll wait down here for you,' George said, steering the chair away from customers who were trying to get to the counters to continue with their shopping.

'Freda, would you keep an eye out for Mr Porter and ask him to come to my office at his earliest convenience, please?'

'I'm not holding you up, am I?' Maureen asked as she started to follow Betty up the steep staircase.

'No, not at all,' Betty replied, trying not to think about the mound of work piling up on her desk. She was glad to walk at Maureen's pace, as she found climbing the stairs could be tiring at times. Goodness knows what she'd be like a couple of months from now.

'Nothing changes up here,' Maureen said as she sat down in Betty's office. 'You seem to be just as busy.'

'I like it this way.' Betty smiled at the woman sitting in front of her. She didn't add that in the odd quiet moment when she had time to think, she would imagine her future life and a wave of panic would engulf her. 'Now, tell me how you really are, now that we don't have an audience? You've been through such a lot since . . . since . . .'

'Since Irene was killed?' Maureen said gently, knowing how hard it was for Betty to put what had happened into words.

'Yes, I'm sorry. I wasn't sure how to put it,' Betty replied, suddenly feeling quite tearful. 'Goodness, look at me, I'm an emotional mess.'

'It's the baby that'll be making you act like that,' Maureen said. 'It happens to us all when we go through carrying a kiddie. Next you'll be giving that nice husband of yours what for without any reason.'

Betty smiled. She'd done just that yesterday evening, when Douglas had been five minutes late collecting her from work. 'I never knew such things. I'll keep it in mind for the future. Now, how do you feel about coming in for two hours a day, and we can see how you feel after a couple of weeks? I'd hate to get in your doctor's bad books and have you end up back in hospital.'

'That suits me down to the ground, thank you. Perhaps I could come in and prepare the main meal, and bake a few cakes for the tea breaks? I wouldn't be putting anyone out of work, would I?'

'Goodness, no – it would free up some of my ladies to go back on their counters. We've been praying for the day you walked back in here and asked to return to work. However, you've got to promise me one thing, Maureen.'

'Anything at all,' Maureen beamed.

'That when my baby is born you will make the christening cake. No one can beat your cakes. I'll provide all the ingredients.'

A wave of relief crossed Maureen's face. 'It's a deal. I thought you were going to ask me to teach Maisie to cook,' she laughed, and Betty joined in. 'That would have been an impossible task.'

Maisie held Claudette and Bessie in her arms until they'd finished crying. She'd dreaded telling the two girls that their favourite dog had died. 'Nelson was a very old dog, and now he's gone ter 'eaven he can run and play just like he did when he was a puppy. You should be happy that he can do that, me darlings.'

'Will he come and see us now he's a puppy again?' Claudette asked, as Maisie wiped the young girl's nose for her.

'No, he can't do that, but he wants you ter remember how much you loved 'im and ter look after Nanna Ruby now she doesn't have him by her side. Can you do that?'

'Is Nanna Ruby very sad?' Bessie asked as she scrubbed her eyes with her fist.

Maisie loved that Ruby had told the two girls to call her Nanna Ruby, as it made them all feel like one happy family. 'Yes, she is sad, but she knows that he is no longer old and stiff and can run and bark as much as he wants ter in doggy 'eaven.'

The two girls thought for a little while. 'We could draw some pictures of Nelson for Ruby to keep,' Claudette suggested.

'I think that's a jolly good idea. P'raps tomorrow, as it's getting close ter yer bedtime. Why not go and have a wash and put yer nighties on, and then we can read fer a little bit before David comes home.'

The girls scrambled off Maisie's lap and hurried away.

She started to tidy the room, picking up toys and checking it was presentable before David came in and they could relax. She had hardly finished when she heard a key in the lock and he walked into the room, pulling off his overcoat and taking Maisie in his arms. 'How did the girls take the news?' he asked.

'Not so good, but they'll get over it. Considering how they coped after me mum died, I'm surprised how upset they've been over the death of a dog. I'm thinking it's because they loved that dog and he seemed ter love all the kids, whereas me mum didn't care much fer anyone. At least they are loved here, and I'll make sure nothing 'appens ter 'em.'

David looked as though he had the cares of the world on his shoulders. 'Are they in bed?'

'Not yet, the pair of 'em will be down shortly once they've got their nightclothes on. I said they could have one story before you came home.'

'Then you'd best see this now,' he said wearily as he reached inside his jacket and pulled out an envelope. 'It came via internal channels. To be honest I'd given up thinking we'd ever hear from your brother.'

Maisie snatched the envelope as David held it out to her. 'It's been opened, 'ave you read it?' She saw the raw anguish in his eyes as she pulled out the one sheet of paper and quickly read the scrawled lines. 'No!' she shouted. 'He can't do this. He can't take the girls away from us, not now. No, no, no!'

8

'You looked pleased with yourself,' Sarah said when Maureen came into the house followed by George.

'It's been an eventful day. Did you manage to get yourself down into the cellar all right?' Maureen asked.

'Yes, Georgie helped me, didn't you love?' Sarah said, trying to get the young child's attention. Georgina was too interested in the wheelchair that her granddad was wheeling into the house. It had a parcel wrapped in newspaper placed on the seat. 'That air-raid warning was a fuss over nothing. Buster didn't like being woken up. He's been rather fractious ever since.'

'Better to be safe than sorry,' Maureen said as she took off her coat and hung it on a coatstand in the corner of the room before rubbing her hands together in front of the fire to warm them. 'Here, let me take him for a while. George has treated us all to fish and chips for our tea as it's a little late to start cooking.'

'I wasn't sure whether to start,' Sarah said. 'What took you so long? I thought you'd gone out for a stroll and a cup of tea at Mitchell's.'

'We met Ruby and Bob and started talking about their

wedding. Then after the air-raid warning went off I had a word with Betty, and she's offered me my job back. Well, a couple of hours a day to start with. That's when I decided I ought to walk more, and George has been pushing the empty wheelchair around the town,' Maureen said, giving George a grateful look. 'Then we went to the Odeon to see *Waterloo Road.* I've been very spoilt all afternoon.'

'And so you should, after what you've been through,' George said, patting her shoulder as he went into the kitchen to fetch plates for their tea.

Sarah felt a lurch of sadness course through her. Granted her mother-in-law had been injured when a rocket exploded at the New Cross Woolworths, but her mum had died. It looked to her as though her dad had forgotten he'd lost his wife, the way he was fussing around Maureen.

'Not enjoying your meal?' George asked, noticing Sarah pick at her food.

'I could boil you an egg if you prefer?' a concerned Maureen said. 'You need to keep your strength up.'

Sarah gave them both a weak smile. 'I'm not that hungry, thank you all the same. Perhaps I'll bundle up what's left and take a slow walk round to Nan's tomorrow with the children. Nelson will enjoy the leftovers.'

George looked at Maureen who gave a subtle nod back.

Sarah frowned. 'What's going on?' she asked, looking at their concerned faces.

George cleared his throat, looking uncomfortable. 'It's like this, love. I don't want you getting upset, but . . .'

Sarah started to get annoyed. 'But what? What is it you're trying to tell me?'

George looked distressed and seemed unable to speak,

so Maureen took over. 'Sarah, love, what George wants you to know is that Nelson passed away early this morning. We were going to wait to tell you when . . .' she nodded towards Georgina, who was busy eating her chips. 'When little ears here wasn't about.'

Sarah didn't believe what she was hearing. With a stifled sob, she left the table and rushed upstairs to her bedroom. Why was everything changing in her life? First her mum, and now Nelson – nothing would ever been the same again in her life. She couldn't wait for the day when Alan came home for good and life returned as much to normal as was possible. As she lay on her bed, trying hard to remain calm, she could hear chatter from downstairs before footsteps and the creak of the wooden staircase told her that someone had come to see her.

There was a tap on the door. 'Sarah, can I come in?'

'Yes, Dad, come in,' she said in not much more than a whisper.

'Brrrh, it's a bit nippy in here,' he shivered as he sat on the edge of the bed. 'Here, let's wrap this round you.' He took hold of the edge of a pink floral eiderdown and pulled it around her shoulders. 'Now, what's all this about? I've never known you turn down a nice bit of fish.'

'I'm probably being daft, Dad, but so much is changing. Hearing about Nelson just made things so much worse. Do you think I'm being silly? I feel so frightened at times.'

George put his arms round his daughter and hugged her until she could hardly breathe. She could smell his shaving soap, and the tobacco he liked to smoke in his pipe. Both were strong, reassuring smells. 'There's nothing daft in feeling frightened. Why, I've been frightened and more than a little worried for so many years, I've lost count.'

Sarah leant back and looked her dad in the face. 'You've been frightened? But you're a man and you have an important job. You tell people what to do. Why would you feel frightened?'

'I have a lot of responsibility, I'll have you know, young lady,' he said, tweaking her nose like he had done when she was a child.

'And I'm a grown woman with a husband and two children, so stop doing that,' she laughed, pushing his hand away.

'And we are both allowed to be a little frightened and worried at times. I worried as soon as your mum told me she was expecting you, and a day hasn't passed since without me worrying for your safety and your future. I worry about your Alan and the brave job he does, and I worry for all the lads who use the equipment I help make at Vickers. That's a lot of worry, I'll have you know,' he said, giving her a gentle smile. 'Don't go thinking you have the monopoly on worrying.'

'But being a man, you mustn't show such things?'

'That's about it.'

Sarah thought for a moment. 'I nearly lost my Alan that time he went missing in action.'

'You are no different from many other young wives.'

'No, I mean the way he was acting when he was home on leave. He was so distant and acted so strange, I thought he didn't love me anymore. Then . . . then when we thought he wouldn't be coming home, and I met David . . . I acted

139

like a complete fool and almost lost him for good,' she said, her thoughts many years away.

'It all worked out for the best,' George said, bringing her back to the present.

'I know why he acted like he did – it was because he was worried, and afraid. He couldn't say much, but that last time he was home he knew he was going on a dangerous mission. I took his grumpiness to mean he'd met a different class of people, what with being in the RAF. I thought I wasn't good enough for him anymore, but the truth was, he was frightened. My lovely husband was frightened to death.' She burst into tears as she thought of Alan and their past.

'There, there,' George said, reaching into his pocket for a handkerchief. 'It all came out in the wash, didn't it?'

Sarah nodded her head and gave him a watery smile. 'Yes, but now, when I'm worried or frightened it makes me think I may have gotten things wrong again, and lately, what with Mum . . .'

George took her by the shoulders so she could do nothing but face him. 'We are a right pair, aren't we? Your mum must be up there screaming her head off at the two of us right now. In a way I wish you were more like her, as God knows I need someone to tell me what to do at times.'

'Are you saying you'd like me to nag you sometimes?'

'I just miss your mum being around and organizing . . .'

'Organizing our lives?' Sarah said sadly.

'That's about it. That's why I thought I needed to change my life before I became a miserable old man, and why I've been over here in Erith more often . . .'

Before George finished speaking the bedroom door flew open, and Georgina rushed in and jumped on the bed.

'I'm sorry, Sarah, it's past her bedtime and she's had her wash. I didn't mean to interrupt the pair of you,' Maureen said, going to a small chest of drawers and pulling out Georgina's nightdress. 'I can take her back downstairs, if you've not finished your chat?' she added, looking between the two of them.

'I think we've finished our little chat, don't you?' George said, giving Sarah a quick kiss on her forehead and standing up. 'It's a good job we have you to keep us organized, Maureen, or Georgina would be still running round at midnight. I'd best be off. I've got an early start in the morning,' he said, squeezing past Maureen as she stood in the doorway.

'I'll warm this by the fire for a few minutes while I see your dad off,' Maureen said, taking Georgina by the hand and leaving the room.

Sarah straightened the eiderdown thoughtfully. Dad was over in Erith quite often . . . and he liked being organized by Maureen . . . 'Oh God, he's in love with Maureen,' she said out loud. 'No, it can't be so. It's far too soon, and Maureen is my mother-in-law.'

The door creaked and, looking up, she saw Maureen standing there. 'I forgot Georgina's dressing gown,' she said, without looking Sarah in the face.

Sarah glanced away. Had Maureen heard what she'd said?

*

'Mrs Billington, Mr Grant will be with you shortly if you'd like to take a seat,' the prim secretary said, indicating to where a hard-looking bentwood chair had been placed in the corner of the office.

Betty had thought long and hard about visiting head office to enquire about her future with the company. Although she was interested in Douglas's suggestion of working a few hours a day with his business, she couldn't help but think that Woolworths should at least offer her the chance to return to a job she'd done selflessly throughout the war years. Why, if the war continued to drag on as it was, then the company would still be short of men to run the stores. Surely they would be glad to make use of her skills?

Sitting on the edge of the seat so as not to crease her skirt, she felt confident that this Mr Grant would see before him a professional woman who knew her job and would not be fazed by carrying a child as well as running a busy store. Maisie had lent her a very smart red wool swing coat with a black velvet collar that hung loosely over her tweed suit. Again, Maisie had come to the rescue and let out the seams of the skirt, so hopefully it would last another month or so. Betty wore the smart black felt hat that had been purchased for her wedding. Maisie had impressed upon her that feeling confident starts with wearing the right clothes and make-up. Betty had refused the use of Maisie's favourite red lipstick.

The door opened and a short, thin-faced man stepped out. 'Miss Billington,' he called out, and disappeared before Betty could speak. Placing her handbag over her arm, she followed him into the room. It was stiflingly hot in the small room from a paraffin heater situated close to the man's desk, and there was a faint odour of the fish paste which, no doubt, had formed part of his lunch. Betty removed her coat, and as he did not offer to take it, she folded it carefully and placed it over her knees. Reaching into her handbag, she pulled out a cotton handkerchief that she'd dabbed with lavender water and held it to her nose. It helped mask the fishy smell.

'Miss Billington,' he began with a frown, staring at Betty's stomach.

'It's Mrs Billington,' Betty smiled, holding up her left hand to show the thin gold band on her wedding finger.

Mr Grant looked relieved. 'I did wonder,' he replied stiffly, looking down at a beige folder with her name written in one corner. 'It does state "Miss" here.'

'I married a little over a year ago. My maiden name is the same as my husband's,' she explained, trying hard to keep a pleasant smile on her face.

He nodded approvingly. 'Keep it in the family,' he said, looking over the frame of the spectacles that were positioned on the end of his nose.

'Certainly not,' Betty snapped back. Whatever was he inferring? 'I can assure you my husband was no relation to me before we were married. Our marriage was above board.'

Mr Grant waved his hand to stop her explanation. 'It is of no concern to me. What is important is that you seem to be working at our Erith store whilst . . . whilst in this . . .' He started to wave his hand in the air, again trying to grasp the right word.

'Whilst expecting a much-wanted child?' she replied.

'That's as may be, but it is most unprofessional. We've never had a manager in this situation before.'

Betty stifled a grin. 'I'm sure you haven't, Mr Grant, considering there have been few women in management positions who have been of childbearing age.'

Mr Grant gulped loudly, causing his Adam's apple to move up and down and his eyes to bulge slightly. 'Well, really, Mrs Billington, there's no need for such crudeness.'

'I'm facing facts, Mr Grant. My situation is somewhat unusual, and I wish to put my cards on the table.'

He reached for a packet of Senior Service and lit one without asking Betty if she would like one. She coughed as he blew smoke in her direction. 'I can't see a problem,' he said. 'You will be leaving our employ very soon, and we have an excellent replacement in Cecil Porter.'

'I'm sorry, Mr Grant. I know you are new to the personnel department, but I've already filed a report about Mr Porter being unsuitable for the job. However, that is neither here nor there, as I intend to work for as long as I can – and then I'd like to return, once my child is here. We already have a very good housekeeper who cares for my stepdaughters, and if necessary I will engage a nurse. I want to keep my job, Mr Grant.'

'I don't wish to know about your domestic arrangements, Mrs Billington. You should be at home with your child. Hopefully, this coming year will see our men returning home and they will want their jobs back.'

'Sadly our manager, Mr Benfield, passed away, so we don't have a manager who will return to the Erith store,' Betty interrupted.

He raised his hand to stop her speaking. 'Please let me

finish. We also have trainee managers returning who have been on our payroll since being called up. Would you deny them a job because of your fanciful ideas?'

Betty stopped to think for a moment. It was true that both Alan and young Ginger would at some point return to their jobs. By staying, would she be denying Alan the chance to bring home a wage to Sarah and the children? 'You are right, I can see that. However, as things stand, these men are still serving their country and we are still at war. The person you sent us is not suitable, as he has no idea how to serve a customer, let alone run a store. We had an air raid recently, and the wretched man ran away with no care for the customers or our staff. I need time to train him before I leave. At least give me time to do that, please?'

He lit another cigarette, and again blew the smoke in her direction. With the heat of the room and the abhorrent odours, Betty was already feeling a little light-headed and sick. The stress of the situation did not help one iota. As the smoke wafted across her face, she felt her stomach heave. Looking round desperately, she spotted an aspidistra plant in an ornate china bowl on the window ledge. She only just managed to reach it as she brought up her lunch and the cup of tea she'd enjoyed at Lyon's Corner House when she reached London.

'My goodness, Mrs Billington, whatever are you doing?' Mr Grant demanded, jumping to his feet. 'My dear wife gave me that plant to celebrate my promotion.'

Betty wiped her mouth and turned to collect her coat where it had fallen to the floor. 'I'm sorry. I think it would be best if I left now,' she said, walking towards the door.

She hoped that he would call her back and make some kind of comment about her employment, but there was silence as she left the room and closed the door behind her.

'Would you mind terribly if I asked for a glass of water. I'm not feeling very well,' Betty said to the secretary as she sat down on the seat she'd vacated not ten minutes before.

The woman nodded her head politely before picking up the telephone. 'Mr Grant, I have your nephew on the telephone. Putting you through now, Mr Porter . . .'

Betty knew then that she could not win. Oh to have been born a man, she thought to herself.

Maisie shrieked with laughter before clamping her hand to her mouth. 'Gawd, I'm sorry, Betty, but being sick in his pot plant! Oh my goodness. I'd 'ave paid good money ter see that.'

'I have to say, I laughed myself when I'd left head office and started for home. To think that was the awful Cecil's uncle, and I was sick in his pot plant! I'm not sure how to face Cecil when he gets in to work.'

'It's best if you pretend nothing 'appened. Play the cool, calm, collected boss and stare straight through 'im.'

'Yes, that is a good idea. I have a job for him, so at least he will be out of my way for the day.' Betty looked up at the clock on the office wall. 'He's late, as usual. How the heck he thinks he will be able to run this store when I've left, I just don't know. He's always the last to arrive in the mornings. Some days the store is open before he makes an appearance.'

'Give 'im the sack,' Maisie advised as she finished the last of her tea and got to her feet.

'I have the feeling that if I did, his uncle would override my decision and make a mockery of me. No, it will have to be something more than lateness for me to be rid of him. Until then, I will continue training him in every department until he hates me and the store so much, he trips up and does something wrong.'

'Or leaves?' Maisie suggested, getting to her feet. 'So what poor sod's got 'im today?'

Betty raised her eyebrows and gave Maisie an apologetic look.

'Oh, bugger it,' Maisie swore. 'I just knew he'd land on me counter before too long. It's bad enough helping out Doris on the veg counter without 'im being there. We've got a delivery coming in at ten from the farm and it's been raining all day. I'm going ter be muddy and miserable by the time I get ter see Sarah on me way 'ome.'

'You could delegate,' Betty suggested. 'Freda told me he hated getting a speck of dust on his hands when he was in the stores.'

Maisie's eyes gleamed. 'Hmm, p'raps I can make good use of 'im. I'll get me overalls on and be ready for 'is lordship when he comes in.'

'I'm sorry to land him on you like this, Maisie,' Betty apologized. 'Although it's a little light relief after being at head office yesterday. It's been good to share it with you.'

'Any day,' Maisie grinned. 'By the way, what did Douglas say about it?'

A cloud passed over Betty's face. 'I didn't tell him I went to beg for my job. I've promised him I won't rush to return to work after the baby arrives. If truth be known, he wants me to finish work soon.'

Maisie sat back down. 'Blimey, you'd be lost if you didn't work here.'

'We had words about it the other day. I'm afraid I used you as an example of women who continue working after having children.'

'I'm not sure I'm a good example ter give 'im. You're a manager wiv a responsible job, whereas I just want time ter do something worthwhile. I just don't know what it is . . . oops, sorry, I didn't mean I don't like working here, but . . .'

'I know what you mean, Maisie. We are so alike in so many ways.'

Maisie hooted with laughter. 'Me and you are alike? Blimey, I must be getting posh in me old age.'

Betty smiled. Maisie was like a breath of fresh air. 'I mean that we want more than just being wives and mothers. Unlike our Sarah, who wants nothing more than to make a good home for Alan and have his children.'

'You're right there, she can't wait for 'im ter leave the RAF and play 'appy families fer the rest of her life.'

'I wonder what it is Freda wants? I've never really asked her. She's been through such a lot for a young woman.'

'She wants ter be loved,' Maisie said straight away. 'Sounds simple enough, but Freda's yet ter find the right man ter love her and for her ter love 'im back.'

*

'You look lovely,' Sandy said as Freda opened the door to number thirteen and invited him inside.

'Thank you,' she blushed. 'My friend made it for me out of two old dresses. I wish I could sew as well as Maisie.'

'Don't put yourself down. You can knit better than all of us. I swear she's kitted out most of the Navy with woolly socks. I'm Ruby Caselton, Freda's landlady,' Ruby said, holding out her hand. 'That lump snoozing in the armchair is Bob Jackson. No, we're not married,' she said, as Sandy raised an eyebrow. 'Now come along in the warm while Freda finishes getting herself ready.'

'The wedding's in May,' Bob said as he opened his eyes.

'I beg your pardon, sir?'

'Me and Ruby, we're getting married in May. Until then I'm banished to the back bedroom.'

'Bob, I hope you're not embarrassing Freda's young man?' Ruby demanded as she followed Sandy into the room. 'You'd not think he was a retired copper at times, the way he speaks,' she said, pointing to a chair. 'Sit yourself down.'

Sandy did as he was told, glad of the warmth of the fire. 'It's rather chilly out there. Are you not coming to the dance this evening? Freda mentioned that friends were attending.'

Ruby took a liking to the young man. He had nice manners, and didn't look too shocked by Bob's joshing. 'Not this time, although we do enjoy dancing. I do believe my son George is going along, and so are Maisie and her husband. I'm just off down to their house to look after the children for the evening, so I'll say goodnight and hope the pair of you have a really nice evening. You make sure Freda brings you round for tea some time. I understand your family don't live round here?'

'No, Mrs Caselton, they live in Scotland. I'm in lodgings down here while I finish my apprenticeship.'

Ruby nodded. She knew she shouldn't assume such things, but she could see Freda settling down with this nice young man. 'Well, my door's always open if you fancy popping round any time.'

'Thank you, Mrs Caselton,' he said politely, standing up as she walked from the room.

'And call me Ruby. Everyone else does,' she replied as she pulled her coat from the hallstand and waved good-night.

'You live with nice people,' Sandy said, taking Freda's hand as they left.

'They are like family to me. In fact, they are my family. There's only my brother Lenny and me now. Ruby's looked out for me since I came to Erith in 1938. I don't know what I'd have done without her, and my friends from Woolworths.'

'You have the friendship of our church as well,' he said as they crossed the road towards the town.

'To be honest, I go there more to help Mrs Missons with the Brownies and Girl Guides. Since her daughter, Molly, went into the Land Army she's been short-handed. I miss Molly a lot, as we got on so well. I do attend church parades to help keep order amongst the girls, though.'

Sandy's hold on Freda's hand stiffened. 'Surely your faith is more important to you than helping out at Brownie meetings?'

'I'm not sure I have a proper faith,' Freda said, trying to wriggle her fingers in his grip. 'I've seen enough in my childhood and this war to know that it is nice people who count in this world, and I like to think those who don't attend church can be as decent as those who put on their best hats and coats and turn up every Sunday to kneel and pray. I admire anyone who does have a faith – they are to be commended.'

'How would you feel if one person in a marriage believed in God when the other treated going to church as a social occasion?' he asked stiffly.

Freda held her breath. She had the feeling that her answer was pivotal to her future romance with Sandy. 'I believe a couple who truly love each other would bring their own views and beliefs to a marriage, and each should respect the other person's views,' she said seriously.

'I suppose you are right,' he replied, although Freda could still detect a slight iciness in his voice.

'Here we are,' she said, feeling slight relief. She'd not expected such a conversation to dominate their walk to the Dance Studio. The memory of Sandy's kisses were still fresh in her mind from the last time they'd met, and she'd hoped there would be an opportunity for them to repeat the experience as they walked through the dark streets of Erith. A tingle of anticipation ran up her spine. Perhaps on the way home things would be different, even if it was a gentle kiss goodnight on the doorstep of number thirteen.

'Over here,' Maureen waved as the young couple left the cloakroom.

'Oh good, Maureen and George have saved seats for us,' she said as they started to weave their way across the crowded dance floor. 'I wonder if Betty and Douglas are here yet?'

'Who are these people?' Sandy asked as he held her elbow to slow her down.

'Betty is my boss at Woolworths and her husband, Douglas, runs a funeral business. Maureen also works at Woolies and she is the mother-in-law of my friend Sarah – Ruby's granddaughter. George is her dad. My goodness, that sounds confusing to me, and I know them all,' she said with chuckle. 'Maisie also works at Woolworths and her husband, David, is in the RAF. He does something terribly important in London working with the government. It's no good asking me what, as I have no idea,' she said, noticing his frown.

'So, George is George Caselton?'

'Yes, that's right. Is there a problem?'

'He's my boss at Vickers.'

'Then you know him. He's such a darling. He's almost like a dad to me. Hurry up, we're in the way of the dancers and someone might pinch our seats.'

'I'm not sure I should be socializing with someone so important. It's not really the done thing,' he muttered.

'Don't be daft,' Freda laughed. 'You're not at work now, are you?' she added, as they reached the table Maureen had saved.

She was still making introductions when Maisie and David appeared. 'So this is yer young man we've been 'earing so much about?' Maisie said, shaking his hand.

'I've not said much about you,' Freda whispered to him as they moved up to make room for Maisie to sit down.

She could feel her cheeks burning. 'Anyone would think I'd not had a boyfriend before.'

'Not too many, I hope?' he whispered back before turning to listen to George, who was telling David how they'd started to downsize some of the workforce. 'We must be careful, sir. Walls have ears, you know.'

George frowned as he stared at Sandy. 'Do I know you from somewhere?'

'Yes, sir, I'm lead apprentice in your department,' Sandy replied somewhat pompously.

'Ah yes, you lads all look the same in your work overalls.'

Sandy looked a little put out. 'I was top in my year at college.'

George nodded his head thoughtfully. 'Well done. Keep up the good work and they may be able to offer you a job at the end of your training. Now, who wants a drink before these ladies expect us to take to the dance floor?'

Sandy looked pleased with himself. 'Do you think so, sir? I'd be grateful if you could put in a good word for me.'

George didn't answer, and avoided Sandy's eager gaze as he left the table with David and Douglas and headed to the bar.

Sandy looked excited. 'Did you hear that?' he said in a low voice to Freda. 'Mr Caselton says I'll be taken on by Vickers at the end of my apprenticeship.'

'That's not what I 'eard,' Maisie said, leaning over to speak before Freda had even opened her mouth. 'Now, why don't you be a good chap and go help the men carry the drinks?'

Sandy nodded politely and left the table as Freda kept her head lowered so as not to catch his glance.

'Sorry, ducks, but he was getting a bit up 'imself there. Next thing you know he'll be asking me David fer an introduction ter Hitler, or Douglas fer a cut-rate funeral.'

'Sandy's not like that. I think you were a little harsh with him,' Freda threw back at her friend. 'I like him. I like him a lot.'

'Sorry, Freda, I didn't mean ter offend you. I'm not meself at the moment. You could say I'm a bit on edge.'

Freda was at once contrite. 'Whatever's wrong – you aren't ill, are you?'

Maisie looked over to where the men were still at the bar, then waved at Betty to move closer so she could hear. 'We've finally received a letter from me brother, Fred.'

'Oh, Maisie, I'm so pleased for you,' Betty said, squeezing her hand. 'You've not said anything, so I assume you've just heard?'

'It was a couple of days ago, but David wanted to check out how we stood legally.'

'You mean he's not going to let you keep the girls with you? I thought after all this time they'd be with you for keeps!' Betty was upset for her friend.

'Ter be honest, so did I, and it's been a bit of a shock, especially now we've been told we ain't got a leg ter stand on even though it's been two years since I took 'em both in and . . . and treated 'em like me own,' Maisie said, reaching into a smart crocodile clutch bag and taking out a handkerchief to dab at her eyes. 'I love those kids like they are me own. I can't think of a future without 'em,' she went on quietly, trying hard not to draw attention to herself from people sitting close by.

'It seems strange that Fred want the girls back when he's still in the army and his wife did a bunk with that Yank,' Freda said. She'd been with Maisie the night Maisie took the girls home after their grandmother was killed in Bethnal Green back in 1943. Since then, she had seen how her friend had bonded with the children and just how much they adored their auntie.

'Is he still overseas?' Betty asked.

'David said he's back at Catterick and that's how he finally managed ter track 'im down. Ter be honest, I thought he was dead, it's been that long.'

Freda was fond of Bessie and Claudette, and couldn't imagine them leaving the close family of friends and their children. 'What happens next? How will he care for the girls when he's in the army?'

'Cynthia's back on the scene, that's Claudette's mum. It seems that the Yank left her and went back ter his wife. She's still in America but has begged Fred ter take her back when she gets 'ome.'

Freda looked suspicious. 'From what you've told me about your brother, I feel he just wants someone to care for those girls, and having Cynthia back in the picture would make his life easy. What will you do?' she asked, noting her friend's distress.

'I intend to carry on as normal fer now. David has an uncle who works in the law, and he's going to 'ave a word wiv 'im. We won't give up the girls wivout a fight. From the little things the girls have said, they didn't 'ave a good life wiv Claudette's mum. From all accounts it sounds like she was as good a muvver as me own. I may not be perfect, but I can do a damn sight better than they did.'

Betty placed her hand over her growing tummy. She knew she too would fight tooth and nail for her child, just as she would for her two stepdaughters, even though they could be a nightmare to live with at times. 'Whatever it takes to keep those two girls with you, you have to keep fighting. If there's anything Douglas and I can do to help, we will.'

'That goes for me, too,' Freda said, giving Maisie a hug. 'You're not alone. Just remember that.'

9

'That was a successful evening,' Sandy said, taking Freda's arm as they left the dance.

'I had a lovely time, thank you,' she said quietly. Maisie's dilemma had hung heavy over the evening, although it hadn't been discussed again. The women had danced and made small talk, but their thoughts were on the plight of the Carlisle family. Betty had had a quiet word with Maureen to let her know what had been said, and she was as distressed as the others to hear about the dilemma Maisie and David were facing.

'How long have you known George Caselton?' Sandy asked.

'I thought I'd told you,' Freda snapped back. 'Since I came to Erith at the end of 1938. What is this interest in George? He's a lovely, fatherly man, and has welcomed me into his family with open arms.'

Sandy shrugged his shoulders, seemingly unaware how much his question had irritated Freda. 'I must have heard wrong as I thought his wife had died, but there she was dancing with him.'

Freda snatched her hand from Sandy's and turned to

face him. 'Yes, his wife died tragically in the rocket attack at New Cross. Her name was Irene and we all loved her very much. Maureen is George's daughter's mother-in-law, and she tried to save Irene. She was injured, and has had a rough time. Anyone who says there is something going on is a hurtful person, and no friend of mine. Now, if you don't mind, I'll walk home alone,' she said, storming off towards Alexandra Road.

'Freda, wait . . .' Sandy called as he hurried to catch her up, but he was hampered by his injured leg. 'Freda . . . please . . .'

Freda had reached the corner of her road when she tripped on the uneven pathway and crashed to the pavement. 'Damn,' she shouted, getting to her feet and finding a large hole in the knee of her best pair of stockings. The heel of her shoe was hanging loose. She pulled off the shoe and started to hobble up the road. It gave Sandy time to catch her up.

'Wait, you silly woman,' he said, grabbing her arm and forcing her to stop. 'You've got me all wrong. Please wait and hear me out.'

Freda nodded and sat on the low front wall of number one. She needed to catch her breath after her fall. 'Hurry up and speak. I've not got all night,' she huffed.

'First, did you hurt yourself? You went down with a bit of a crash.'

'I'm fine, thank you. I've had bigger tumbles on my motorbike,' she said, jutting her chin in the air.

'Of course you have, but then you had your uniform to protect you. Tonight you have on your beautiful dress and looked so wonderful.'

Freda felt her heart lurch in her chest, but tried to remain angry with him. 'I've ruined my shoes,' she whispered, holding out the one in her hand. She didn't like to mention her stockings as it seemed too intimate.

Sandy sat next to her and took the shoe from her. 'I think it can be fixed. I'll take it to work and sort it out for you. Here, give me the other one as well.'

Freda slipped the remaining shoe from her foot and handed it to him. He put both into the large pockets of his overcoat. She went to stand and he caught her hand. 'The ground's wet – let me help,' he said, scooping her up into his strong arms and sitting her on his lap.

Freda felt suddenly vulnerable. 'I'm not hurting your leg, am I?' she asked, aware of his injury.

'Not at all,' he replied, gently kissing her throat. 'I could hold you in my arms for an eternity.'

'Oh . . .' was all she could say, until she pulled herself together and scolded him. 'I'm still angry with you.'

'Blame my upbringing,' he replied. 'My mother always wanted to know what was happening in our small community and who was related to whom. All your friends and the way they were connected had me confused, and more than a little nosy.'

Freda laughed. 'We don't need two Veras,' she chuckled.

'Vera?' he asked, resuming the gentle kisses around her throat and towards her ear.

'I'll tell you later,' she replied, turning her face to his and allowing him to pull her close and kiss her. She closed her eyes and melted against him. At this moment she could forgive him anything.

'I've never met anyone like you,' he whispered breathlessly into her hair. 'I could carry on kissing you forever.'

'Don't let me stop you,' she murmured, surrendering herself to him once more.

An insistent tapping on the windowpane of the house they sat in front of brought them both to their senses.

'Perhaps it was time for me to take you home,' he said, kissing her tenderly one more time before standing up and carrying her to the doorstep of number thirteen. He set her down on the doormat. 'Goodnight, my sweet princess,' he smiled.

'Goodnight, my handsome prince,' she whispered into the night as she watched him walk away.

Maisie stood defiantly in front of Betty's desk. 'I'm ready ter show Cecil how ter sell veg, now he's decided ter turn up fer work.' The man had not turned up in days and informed Betty somewhat arrogantly that his services had been required at head office. He was now in the staff canteen drinking tea.

'Are you sure about this, Maisie? I can easily have one of the other women keep an eye on Cecil.' Betty was still concerned about the news Maisie had shared at the dance. 'Why not go home and spend the time with the girls?'

'Before they're taken from me, do you mean?'

'Yes, dear. I know I always harp on about making memories, but it isn't just you who should enjoy the last days of living with the girls. They may need to hold onto memories in the days ahead as well.'

'I'd not thought of it that way. But they're at school. I'll start me memory-making another time.'

'And David? How does he feel about the situation? He dotes on Bessie and Claudette as much as his own children. Why, if I was in your position I'd be distraught.'

Maisie sat down, put her head in her hands and started to cry. She lifted her tearful face to her friend and gave a weak smile. 'I'm sorry, Betty, I was being selfish. I know David is as hurt as I am. We've not even said anything ter Bessie and Claudette, as we didn't wish ter alarm 'em. They've settled in Erith and they love their school. God knows 'ow they'd cope going back ter live wiv Cynthia and our Fred. I doubt they'd be as cherished as they are now. If there was only something we could do.'

Betty, who had left her seat to comfort her friend, shook her head. 'It does seem to be a dilemma. I still feel you should be at home today. I take it Sadie is looking after the younger ones? Then why not take your husband out for a few hours and spend some time alone? God knows you can't have much time together.'

'But what about sorting out Cecil?'

'Don't you worry about him. He will not get away with anything, I promise you that. Now be off with you before I change my mind.'

Maisie gave her friend a kiss on the cheek. 'You're a diamond, Betty. I 'ope I can do the same fer you one day,' she said before rushing off.

Betty gave a wry smile. Why was it that the nicest people in the world had such problems? Maisie was someone she could rely on, and now it was time to repay the debt – but how?

She took off her tweed jacket and headed out of the office, stopping at the stores department to collect two brown twill overalls. Pulling on the smaller one over her skirt and smock top, she entered the staff canteen. She waved to Maureen, who was working behind the counter preparing the staff's midday meal, before heading to where Cecil was lounging back in his seat reading a newspaper. 'Mr Porter, your services are required.'

Cecil Porter dropped his newspaper with a start and glared at Betty. 'I'm in the middle of my tea break,' he said, looking down his nose at her.

'No employee of F. W. Woolworth has a tea break before putting in a few hours' hard graft. Follow me, Mr Porter. We are about to start grafting.'

She strode into the corridor and waited there until a sullen Cecil appeared. 'Here, put this on,' she said, holding out the overall. 'It is clean, so there's no need to pull a face like that.' She watched as he removed his jacket and pulled on the overall. 'You can leave your jacket in my office for now. Please follow me.'

They headed downstairs with Betty leading the way, marching across the store and not stopping to speak to staff or customers until they reached the vegetable section. Betty sought out the staff member in charge of the section. 'Doris, you have two willing staff members here to help you out for the rest of the morning.'

Doris raised her eyebrows at the unlikely pair of workers standing in front of her. 'I'll not have you lifting anything heavy, so stay away from that end of the counter,' she said to Betty, nodding to where a young woman was weighing potatoes on a large set of scales before pouring them into a customer's shopping bag.

'As for you, I need these collected from the downstairs storeroom. The sack barrow's missing a wheel, so you'll have to carry them one at a time across the store on your back,' she continued, handing a list to Cecil, who looked quite put out. 'And remember, the customers always come first, so be polite and don't step in front of them or get in their way – and don't leave a mess on the floor, or you'll be the one scrubbing it clean. Off you go.' She handed him the list. 'Oh, and don't take all day – we 'ave people here waiting for onions,' she called after him.

Betty couldn't help but giggle as she watched Cecil head back through the busy store. 'He is not a happy man,' she said to Doris.

'He's not one of us like you are,' Doris replied. 'The word is he's taking over from you, and none of us are happy about it, Mrs Billington.'

'I'd stay on if I could, Doris. I'm going to miss you all, but I promise to come in to purchase my vegetables, and I'll be visiting to show off my baby.'

'You make sure you do,' Doris sniffed. 'I've got a lot to thank you for, Mrs Billington. You got me back on my feet after I lost my old man, and I'll never forget that as long as I live.'

The two women stood looking at each other. Betty wanted to hug her employee, but it wouldn't have been the right thing to do in the busy store. She didn't feel she'd done anything of importance by giving Doris more working hours when she became the only earner in her family after her husband died whilst serving his country.

'You are a hard worker, Doris, and I know I leave this section in good hands. Thank you. Now, what's this about a problem with the sack barrow? I could have had it fixed if I'd known.'

Looking slightly ashamed, Doris reached into her overall pocket and produced a couple of screws. 'It'll work properly when I slip these back on.'

Betty's faced twitched as she tried to look stern. 'I wonder what happened there?'

'When I heard the young twerp would be paying us a visit, I thought how I'd like him to learn what proper work was like. Humping about sacks of spuds for the day would soon teach him. I hope you aren't angry with me?'

Betty held out her hand, and Doris passed over the screws. 'I'll make sure the sack barrow is repaired . . . tomorrow,' she replied and turned to a customer. 'How can I help you, madam?'

'You're home early,' Sadie said as Maisie crept into the front room. 'The twins are sleeping and I've put young Ruby down for her nap along with my Arthur. Would you like a cup of tea?'

'No, ta. I had a cup wiv Betty before I left work. She sent me 'ome ter be wiv me 'usband.'

Sadie looked concerned. 'There's nothing wrong, is there? Can I help at all?'

Maisie thought how different Sadie was to her grandmother. Vera would have dived in to find any interesting morsel of information without worrying if she was upset. 'I'm very well, thank you for asking. It's the girls – their dad, that's me brother, wants ter take 'em back. From what we've heard, his wife's back wiv him and they want their kids returned – after two years.'

Sadie looked upset. 'That's shocking. To begin with I thought they were your children as they are so happy here. This makes my problem look small compared with yours.'

Maisie sat down on the sofa next to the girl. 'We'll manage. David is getting some legal advice. We won't let Fred take 'em without a fight. I just don't want the kids ter find out.'

'I won't say anything – and I won't tell my nan, either.'

Maisie snorted with laughter. 'You know her very well.'

'She's a good sort in her way, but sometimes it's wise not to tell her everything.'

'So you've not shared yer problem wiv her?' Maisie said, hoping the girl would confide what was worrying her.

Sadie sighed. 'It's Arthur's dad. He's not sent any more money since you kindly made that telephone call to his office.'

'What a sod!' Maisie exclaimed. 'How did you get involved wiv this snake? No, don't tell me. Posh lunches and he sweet-talked you into 'is bed. Told you 'is wife didn't understand 'im?'

Sadie looked sad. 'I fell for it all hook, line and sinker. I'm such an idiot. The one good thing to come out of all this is my little Arthur, but he doesn't even want to see the lad. Can you believe it?'

Maisie could, but wasn't about to say so. She thought for a moment. 'Is me David 'ome ?'

'Yes, he's up the garden sorting out your vegetable patch. Bob's helping him.'

'How long will it take you ter get yer glad rags on?'

Sadie looked puzzled. 'Not long, but Arthur's asleep upstairs. Why do I need to get dressed up?'

'Just go and get yer smart clothes on. You and me are off ter London. David can keep an eye on the kids fer a few hours. Now off wiv you, while I call in me darling 'usband and give 'im 'is duties fer the rest of the day.'

It was as Maisie was dashing upstairs to change that she remembered why she had been sent home from work. It can wait, she thought to herself.

Leaning from the back bedroom window, she called out to David. 'Yer wife needs you indoors immediately, Mr Carlisle!' She could hear Bob chuckling as she closed the window and went to her bedroom to pull out an outfit that suited the plan she had in mind.

'I wasn't expecting you home for another three hours,' David said as he wrapped his arms around his wife.

'There's no time for that,' she scolded him. 'I've got ter go ter London and sort out the chap who got Sadie up the duff. The blighter's not sent 'er any money. I need you ter keep an eye on the kids.'

'Yes, ma'am.' He saluted her and grinned. 'Any other orders?'

'Please remember to collect Bessie and Claudette, won't you? The other week they 'ad ter walk home on their own. If Ruby hadn't spotted 'em going the wrong way they'd 'ave ended up in Crayford.'

A shadow crossed over David's face, and he sat on the edge of the bed.

'What's up? You've 'eard something, 'aven't you?' she said, sitting next to him.

'It's no good, love. It seems that if Fred and his wife want the girls back, we haven't got a leg to stand on. They are their legal parents.'

'Bessie isn't Cynthia's child . . .' Maisie said with hope in her eyes. 'P'raps we could keep Bessie wiv us?'

'Fred is her father, and Cynthia did look after her for a while before she went off with that other man.'

'But . . .'

David took Maisie's hands so she had to face him. 'Would you split the girls up? If they go to live with Fred then they will need each other.'

Maisie knew he was right, but the pain she felt knowing they would lose the girls was unbearable.

'How long have we got before they leave us?' she asked, trying hard not to show David how upset she was. It wouldn't help at all. She wanted to keep calm and think about the situation.

'I'm going to see if I can pull a few strings and find out when he has leave, so we can sort this out man to man. I want him to understand that the girls must be prepared for this – he can't just walk in and take them away. I want to impress on him that it wouldn't help for Cynthia to turn up alone, either. The girls will only have memories of her going away, and them being dumped on your mum.'

'That all makes sense. Once we know what's 'appening we can sit 'em down and talk, make 'em understand this ain't their fault. We need ter tell 'em how we will keep in touch, and they can come and visit as much as they like.'

David smiled and kissed her gently. 'That's my girl.'

'I still feel as though me heart's been ripped out,' she said.

'Me too, my love, me too. Now, get yourself off to London with Sadie and try to make that chap understand how a father is supposed to act. I'll take care of the kids – and I promise to remember to collect our girls.'

'I wonder how much longer they will be our girls?' she said.

'We need another sack of spuds, and can you get us some carrots as well? These will be sold before too long,' Doris instructed Cecil as he stood wiping his sweaty brow.

'Can't a man have a break for a minute? My back's killing me.' He glared at her.

'All right, but not for long, or we'll have customers complaining if we run out of carrots and they have to wait for you to get them. Come to think of it, the cabbages are a little on the low side, so perhaps you should get some of those as well. But have your rest first; we don't want you collapsing on us. Serve that lady while you're standing there.'

Cecil begrudgingly turned to the customer and asked her what she wanted.

'Three pounds of potatoes, a pound of carrots, six onions and a nice big cabbage, please, young man, and try and look happy about it,' she said, giving Doris a wink as Cecil started to throw potatoes onto the brass scales. 'Mind you, don't bruise them, or my old man'll be down here with something to say about shoddy goods.'

'That'll be, er . . . that'll be . . .' Cecil said, scratching his head as he looked at the numbers he'd written down as he served the woman.

'Oh, here you are, the money's correct,' the woman said, passing over a handful of copper. 'This one needs to go back to school,' she called to Betty as she waved good-bye to Doris.

'That was not a very good example of how to serve customers,' Betty snapped at Cecil. 'Where did you train?'

Cecil raised his eyebrows at Betty. 'Train as a shop assistant? Never. My uncle spotted my management potential. It would be a waste of company time and money to have me work on the shop floor. I'm here to run this store, not to work in it.'

'Some would say managers work as well. Take our current manager – she never stops working,' Doris spat at him as she went to serve a customer.

'Some staff will no longer have jobs when I take over this store,' Cecil said, directing his words towards Doris, who glanced at Betty with a worried expression.

'There's no need to worry, Doris, your job is safe here. I think we've seen enough of your skills in this section. It is time to move to another.'

Cecil unbuttoned his overall and left it on the counter. 'My choice would be this department,' he said, looking across the store to where staff were weighing out nails and lengths of cable as well as testing light bulbs before selling them.

'In a while. I have another job for you for the rest of today,' Betty said, taking him to where Freda was working on the haberdashery counter. 'Freda would you show Mr

Porter how this section runs on a daily basis? I suggest you instruct him on how to serve a customer and count change back properly, as well as handling stock.'

'With pleasure, Mrs Billington,' Freda replied, giving Cecil a cool glance.

'If you would return to my office in two hours, Mr Porter, I will show you the next part of your training.'

'Two hours? What about my lunch?'

Betty checked her wristwatch. 'You will take the third lunch shift today.'

'I have plans to meet someone. It is not convenient for me to take a late lunch.'

Betty approached the man until she was nose to nose with him. 'You will do as you are told while you are working in my store. You will be polite to our customers and pleasant to our staff. You will arrive to work on time and you will not slide off early. Step one inch from what I've just said, and you will be collecting your cards at the end of the day.'

Cecil shifted uncomfortably from foot to foot. 'You cannot tell me what to do.'

'Oh yes I can, Mr Porter, and you, my man, are onto a sticky wicket. Play ball, or you will be out on your earhole. Do you understand what I am saying? Now pin a smile on your face and get to work,' Betty all but snarled at him. Turning to Freda, who was watching with interest, she said, 'Miss Smith, would you pop in to see me later this afternoon?'

'With pleasure, Mrs Billington,' she smiled. 'Come this way, Mr Porter, you can start by putting out these knitting patterns. Then I will show you how we lay out the wool, and how to keep the book where we list what is put by for our customers.'

Cecil glared in Betty's direction and followed Freda behind the counter.

Betty made her way upstairs to the staff canteen to see how Maureen was getting on. She'd not long started back to work, and Betty was concerned she was taking on too much too soon.

It was warm in the canteen and empty of staff, although before too long the place would be buzzing with chatter as hungry workers started their lunch breaks.

'Maureen, you shouldn't be doing that,' Betty scolded as she caught the woman wiping down the oilcloth table coverings. 'Where is the girl who's supposed to be helping you? The last thing we want is for you to have a relapse.'

'I sent her off for her break before we get busy. Don't worry about me, Betty, I have a sit down every so often, and my leg is holding up well. Would you like a cup of tea? Or some Camp coffee?'

'I'd love a coffee, but here, let me get it, and you take a rest for a little while.'

'Don't be daft. You need to be resting up as well.' Both women burst out laughing. 'We're a right pair, aren't we?' Maureen said.

Between them they made the drinks and sat down. 'It was good to see you at the dance the other night,' Betty said.

'I must say it was nice to get out and have a bit of fun. As much as I love Sarah and the children living with me, it's nice to get dressed up and escape for the evening.'

'Yes, I agree. I can't remember the last time Douglas

and I went somewhere without our girls. I did have a problem finding something to wear. Maisie has done a fine job of letting out all the seams on my black gown, but I fear it won't be long before it has to go into mothballs for a while.'

'You looked a picture,' Maureen smiled. 'What did you think of Freda's young man?'

'He seemed rather earnest and overly polite to me, but Freda is truly smitten. I was surprised to hear he was an apprentice at Vickers. Surely he should be in the forces?'

Maureen nodded in agreement. 'I thought the same and asked George about it as he walked me home. It seems the lad was injured, he's got a gammy leg like me, and he returned to continue his apprenticeship that he'd started before the war.'

'Poor boy,' Betty said. 'Where was he injured?'

'I can't remember, but from all accounts he was almost caught by the enemy in France somewhere and it took weeks for him to get back to his regiment because of his injury.' A worried look crossed Maureen's face. 'George reckons he can't take to the lad.'

'Why would he say such a thing?'

'I have no idea. He wouldn't be drawn on why he'd said what he said, and you know me well enough to know I tried. Perhaps it was a gut feeling. We all have them from time to time.'

Betty sipped her coffee and thought about what Maureen had said. 'George isn't someone to say things without reason, and I feel he wouldn't speak out of turn just because of a gut feeling. Something must have happened for him to say what he did.'

'True. Perhaps we should keep an eye on our Freda, all the same. We don't want the girl's heart broken. Now, I've made a tasty savoury tripe casserole, or there's a mince pudding, and for afters we have spotted dick with a drop of custard. Can I put something by for you before it all goes?'

Betty's stomach lurched at the thought of tripe. 'I'd love a little of the mince pudding and some spotted dick, if I may?'

'I'll keep it warm for you and add a little more now you're eating for two,' Maureen smiled.

'A small portion will suffice, thank you. Otherwise I'm liable to fall asleep over my desk this afternoon while I'm instructing our Mr Porter on the ways of the payroll system.'

'Now that's another strange one,' Maureen said as she took the empty cups to the sink. 'I hear you're giving him some lessons on how the stores ticks over? If you'd lend him to me for a few hours, I'd like to show him how we work in the kitchen,' she said, waving her dish mop in the air.

'That's the building over there,' Sadie said, pointing to a building across the road from where they sat in a Lyon's Corner House. 'His office is on the first floor.'

Maisie peered through the window to where Sadie was pointing. 'Once we've 'ad our cheese on toast we will put me plan in action. Are you sure he's in work today?'

'Yes, I heard him talking when I rang this morning. He told his secretary he didn't wish to speak to me. In fact, if you look to the left of that window, she can see him sitting at his desk.'

'Are there any other exits apart from the front door?'

'Not to my knowledge,' Sadie replied. 'We all used those doors and walked up the stairs. There's a reception room at the top, and a waiting room for several companies who use the building.'

Maisie had a gleam in her eye. 'Now this is what we do . . .'

Half an hour later the two women crossed the road and entered the building.

At the bottom of the stairs, Maisie delved into a large bag she'd been carrying and pulled out a cushion. 'Shove this up yer top and act like you're eight months gone. After I've gone upstairs, give me ten minutes and follow me. You remember what ter say?'

'Yes, I remember,' Sadie grinned as she arranged her clothes over her new bump.

Maisie did the same with her cushion and headed up the stairs. Entering the reception area, she staggered up to the desk, huffing and puffing. 'Excuse me, love, I need ter see me 'usband urgently,' she gasped.

The prim secretary looked Maisie up and down. 'Your husband is . . . ?'

'Mr Davenport . . . Mr Gordon Davenport. Can you tell 'im it is urgent, please? I need ter see him at once.'

'If you would take a seat, I'll call his office,' the secretary said, reaching for her telephone.

'I can't sit, love, the baby's fast approaching and it's too uncomfortable ter sit down. I'll walk up and down a bit, if you don't mind?'

The woman nodded her head and spoke in hushed tones into the receiver. After finishing her call, she turned her back on Maisie and continued to type a letter, every so often looking towards the glass double doors.

Maisie also kept an eye on the doors, as she knew Davenport's office was in that direction. She thought she spotted the shadow of a man at one point, but he did not enter the reception area. She jumped as the telephone rang and the secretary answered it, looking towards Maisie as she spoke.

'Yes, Mr Davenport, the lady said she was your wife. She seems to be slightly indisposed. What I mean is, she seems to be in distress . . . Yes, sir, I'll let her know.'

Maisie staggered across the reception area towards the windows and opened one to take in great gasps of air. 'Oh, oh, oh,' she groaned, enjoying the attention she was receiving from a couple walking through from the staircase. 'I'll be all right, loves, don't worry about me,' she called to them. 'It's not me first, although me eighth arrived rather quickly. He appeared when I went ter the outside lavvie.'

The couple hurried away as quickly as they could.

Maisie knew Sadie had arrived when the secretary let out an audible gasp.

'I'd like to speak to my husband, Mr Gordon Davenport. Can you tell him to hurry up, please?' she said, leaning on the desk and panting hard. She and Maisie ignored each other.

Again the secretary used her telephone, and again Maisie saw the man-shaped shadow appear through the glass doors. The telephone rang and the secretary answered it.

'Yes, sir, they both gave your name. No, sir, I can assure you I heard correctly,' she hissed down the receiver. 'Yes, I'll tell them both . . . Excuse me, ladies, Mr Davenport says you must have the wrong person. His wife is at their home in Surrey, and she is not . . . not . . .'

'In the club?' Maisie helped her finish her sentence. 'I am Mrs Gordon Davenport, and this,' she said, pointing to her large stomach, 'is not Scotch mist. Tell me 'usband his kid is about ter drop on this posh carpet if he doesn't 'urry.'

On cue, Sadie spun to face Maisie. 'Did I hear you use my husband's name?' she enquired primly.

'I used *me* old man's name, if that's what you mean,' Maisie replied, squaring up to her.

'Perhaps there are two Mr Davenports?' the secretary suggested, trying to calm the situation.

'What, in the same building?' Maisie asked. She turned to Sadie. 'Tell me, how tall is yer 'usband?'

'Six foot.'

'So's mine. What colour hair does he 'ave?'

Sadie raised her chin in defiance at Maisie's question. 'Dark brown hair and blue eyes. He has a small scar on his chin as well.'

'And so does me 'usband.' Maisie gave a manic laugh. 'So do you still think there are two Gordon Davenports?' she glared at the secretary. 'There may be only one of 'im, but it sure looks like he 'as two wives. Now get 'im out here, and fast. I can't hold on much longer,' she screeched, holding her stomach.

'Me neither, 'Sadie groaned, clutching her tummy. 'Oh my God, no!' she screamed, looking down to the carpeted floor, where a puddle of water had formed. 'My waters have broken.'

'Bloody 'ell, so 'ave mine,' Maisie groaned, looking at her feet, where an identical puddle had appeared. 'I think I'll be giving birth right 'ere.'

'Me too!' Sadie cried.

The secretary fled through the double doors with her hands over her ears, trying to shut out Maisie and Sadie's groans.

Sadie started to giggle, but Maisie gave her a sharp look. 'Keep it up. We've got ter be convincing.'

'Whatever is going on here?' a grey-haired man demanded as he barged into the reception area, followed by the secretary.

'Both ladies are asking to speak to their husband – Gordon Davenport,' she explained.

'Davenport? I thought his wife was older . . . ? Get the damned man out here now,' the man growled as the frightened woman fled. 'Now, ladies, I suggest we sit down and have a little chat, shall we? I'm Davenport's boss, Frederick Whitely. I run this company. Please tell me what this is all about?'

Maisie nodded and took the lead, explaining how Sadie used to work for Davenport and he had fathered her child, and now would not keep up payments for young Arthur.

'We didn't know what else ter do, so we thought we'd shame 'im in front of his colleagues.'

Frederick Whitely thought for a moment before a rumble of laughter came from deep inside his large frame. 'Very enterprising, ladies. How old is your son, madam?'

Sadie delved into her handbag and pulled out a photograph that George had taken at Christmas of the children with Father Christmas at Maisie and David's house. 'Just coming up to twenty months, sir,' she said, handing over the photograph and pointing to Arthur. 'He's the apple of my eye, and worth all the trouble Gordon has caused.'

'The other children?'

'Some are mine, and the rest belong ter friends,' Maisie beamed. She liked this man.

'I take it Davenport doesn't have a hand in any of these?'

Maisie burst out laughing. 'Gawd, no, they belong ter me and me 'usband. He's an RAF officer based at the War Office,' she said proudly. 'We just wanted ter 'elp young Sadie here.'

Gordon Davenport burst through the doors and came to an abrupt halt as he spotted his boss. 'Sir – I have no idea who these madwomen are. I can assure you . . .'

Frederick Whitely raised his hand. 'No more, Davenport, this isn't the first time we've had to put up with your shenanigans. I believe this young lady and her friend.' He turned to give Sadie a closer look. 'I do believe I recognize you.'

'I used to be a secretary here. Until he gave me the sack, and my life became hell.'

'We can't have this, can we?' Frederick said. 'From now on, my company will forward your allowance each month. It will be taken from Davenport's salary. I wish you both good day, and congratulate you on your enterprising plan.'

The two women left the building, not caring that they still had Maisie's cushions tucked inside their clothing or that their shoes squelched as they walked.

'I think we should find a pub and celebrate, don't you?' Maisie grinned.

10

April 1945

'What a lovely surprise! I didn't expect you today, not that you aren't welcome here at any time,' Ruby said, ushering Sarah into number thirteen.

'I just had to come and tell you – Alan's coming home and should be able to attend the wedding. Isn't that wonderful?' she said, her eyes shining.

'That is good news. Is he home for long?'

'He doesn't say how long. I have the letter with me – you can have a read of it.'

'I don't want to read your personal letters. Telling me is good enough. You must be over the moon, love?'

'I am, Nan. I'm counting the days until the war is over and Alan comes home for good, and we can get back to being a normal family. One forty-eight-hour leave over a month ago isn't enough when young Buster here is growing so quickly. Even Georgina had a funny few minutes and went shy when her daddy walked through the door on his last trip home.'

'Just imagine what it must be like for kiddies who

haven't seen their dads for years on end,' Ruby sighed. 'What are his plans for when he leaves the RAF? With all this talk about the war soon being over, it makes me wonder how the young men will cope when they're back on civvy street.'

'Our life is mapped out,' Sarah said. 'Alan's job is safe at Woolworths and with Betty leaving to have her baby, I've no doubt he will be offered the manager's job and we can find a home of our own. Who knows; there may even be another great-grandchild or two on the horizon for you,' she sighed happily.

Ruby frowned. It seemed to her that Sarah was looking at the world through rose-tinted glasses. 'Are you sure about that?'

'We've always said we wanted lots of children.'

'I meant about Alan's job. Haven't they put some chap in the store to take over from Betty?'

'Maisie says he is next to useless, and Betty is at the end of her tether with the man, so he won't be there for much longer.'

'Don't you be so sure, my girl.'

'Perhaps I'll pop round to Woolies and have a word with Betty,' Sarah decided.

'Best you leave such things to Alan. You don't want to start interfering, do you?'

'A friendly word isn't interfering, Nan,' she smiled.

'Now, let's get you all out of your coats. Come on through to the living room,' Ruby said, taking Georgina's hand. 'I may just have a biscuit in the tin for my favourite youngest great-granddaughter. Would you like that?'

'Yes please,' the little girl replied politely.

'She's such a joy,' Ruby said. 'It's as if her Nanny Irene is speaking, with her posh ways.'

'Oh, Nan, you are a laugh,' Sarah said. 'Though I'm sure Mum would be proud of our Georgie.'

'Irene would also have loved this little lad, although I'm not sure she'd have liked his nickname. There would have been some raised eyebrows whenever we called him Buster. Oh my goodness, he is getting heavy. What are you feeding him on?' Ruby asked, as she lifted Buster from his pram. Sarah helped Georgina unbutton her coat as her little fingers fumbled with the large buttons.

'I'm having to give him an extra bottle these days, he's that hungry. Maureen said Alan was the same at this age.'

'Are you copying your dad?' Ruby said, tickling the baby under his chin, which produced a gummy smile. 'You are certainly going to be a heartbreaker,' she cooed. 'Here, you take him and I'll make us a cup of tea. Bob will be home soon. He's down the allotment fussing over something or other. He's more worried about feeding people for the wedding than he is about the bride,' she joked.

'Is there anything I can help with?' Sarah asked. 'I feel as though I'm not contributing enough towards your wedding.'

'Don't you be so daft! You've got your hands full with this little lad. I also hear you've been helping Maisie make the outfits.'

'Oh, Nan, I've hemmed Georgie and Myfi's bridesmaid dresses and stitched on a few buttons. That's not exactly hard work.'

'They're going to look as pretty as a picture. I'm so

pleased you talked me into having a couple of little bridesmaids to stand with you, Maisie, Freda and Gwyneth in your pretty dresses.' Ruby had been adamant that she didn't want an entourage in long fancy frocks, and insisted they all wore summer dresses that could be worn again rather than hung in wardrobes without getting as much use. They'd made a trip to Woolwich market and picked up fabric in different shades of blue, so the four women would look similar but not identical.

'I suggest you try on your dress again before the big day in case you decide to have the hem turned up a little, Nan? I know you were unsure before.'

'No, it's fine as it is, I'll not worry about the dress now. What I'd like you to do is to look at that list on the table and see if I've left anyone off the guest list. I'm sure there will be someone.'

Sarah picked up the list and checked through the names. 'Nan, is there a reason you've invited the butcher?'

'He was in the Home Guard with Bob and they play bowls together,' Ruby called from the kitchen. 'Did you think I was after extra meat above the rations?'

Sarah grinned. 'I'd not put it past you,' she whispered to herself.

Ruby came in carrying a tea tray. 'How's it going? Have I left anyone off?'

'Not that I can see,' Sarah said, running a pencil down the rows of names. 'There'll be no one left in Erith that day, going by this list.' She stopped and frowned.

'Have I added someone twice?' Ruby asked as she poured their tea.

'No, but I wondered why you put "George and

Maureen" together, as if they are a couple?' Seeing her dad's name linked with Maureen's brought back the flicker of suspicion Sarah had previously felt about their relationship. No – it can't be true, she thought, pushing the idea away. She must have been mistaken. Surely her dad wasn't becoming romantically involved with her mother-in-law.

'Excuse me, is Betty here?' Sarah asked as she knocked and walked into her friend's office at Woolworths.

Cecil Porter looked up from where he was reading a newspaper. 'Mrs Billington has had to go out for an appointment. Can I help?'

Sarah sighed with annoyance. She had thought and thought about speaking to Betty, and had finally decided to leave the children with Maureen, who had just arrived home from work, and walk round to Woolies to have a chat with her friend about Alan's future. Oh well – in for a penny, she thought. 'I wanted to speak to the manager about my husband, Alan Gilbert.'

He indicated that she should sit down. 'What exactly do you want to say about your husband?' He recalled Gilbert's name being on a list of staff who had left to join the services as war broke out.

Sarah felt it prudent not to mention him taking the manager's position when Betty left her job. 'My husband has indicated that it may not be too long before he is no longer required by the RAF. I simply wished to notify Bet . . . Mrs Billington that Alan would be free to return to his job.'

'And your husband's job was?'

Sarah didn't like this man's arrogant attitude. Maisie had told her how much he was disliked in the store and how he shied away from hard work – unlike her friend's husband, who'd taken on any task, however menial, when he'd worked at the store. 'My husband was a trainee manager, and if the war hadn't intervened he'd have been a manager by now,' she told him, jutting out her chin in an obstinate manner.

Cecil Porter gave her a cool stare. 'We cannot be responsible for every private in the army being handed back their jobs after all this time.'

Sarah felt her blood start to boil. 'For your information, my husband signed up for the RAF and not only flew Spitfires in combat but was shot down, injured, and had to escape from France. He now works teaching younger pilots. He was promised his job would be here waiting for him after the war.'

Cecil sneered and picked up his newspaper. 'Have him come in and enquire about a warehouse job when he returns home. I prefer not to deal with wives begging for work,' he said, dismissing Sarah.

She stared at him for a moment, then turned on her heel and left. What was the point of getting annoyed with this horrid man? However, if he was right, how would they cope when Alan left the RAF? Her dreams for the future looked set to crash around her feet. Would Betty be able to help? Chances were that she would have left her job before Alan came home for good. What would they do then?

She walked slowly down the staff stairs and back to the

shop floor. Freda was busy with a queue of customers, and there was no sign of Gwyneth. Sarah so longed to talk with a friend. Having no need to stay, she left the store and walked several yards down Pier Road before she heard her name being called. Looking across the road, she spotted Betty waving.

'Phew! You were in a daydream. I thought you'd never hear me,' she laughed.

'I'm sorry, Betty, I had something on my mind.'

'Why, Sarah, you look upset. I don't have to be back at work for a little while. Come – let's have tea at Mitchell's. I have something to tell you.'

Sarah nodded and followed Betty into the tea room, where they were shown to a table in a quiet corner. 'You look pleased with yourself. What has happened?'

'I am. I've been to see my doctor, and he says I'm as fit as a fiddle. As long as I don't start lifting heavy boxes or climbing ladders, there is no reason why I can't continue working for a few more weeks.'

'You really ought to be careful, Betty,' Sarah said as they ordered tea from a waitress who hurried to their table with a beaming smile. 'You don't want to harm your child just because you wish to remain at work a little longer, do you?'

'I promise I'll be sensible. You seem to be of the same mind as Douglas. He has done nothing but talk about me staying home and putting my feet up. There's only a little while to go, then I will be at home all the time. Do you know he had the cheek to mention my age the other day? How ungallant of him!' Betty chuckled, even though deep inside she dreaded the thought, until she saw the sadness on Sarah's face. 'My dear, whatever is the matter?' she asked.

'It's Alan. I had such dreams of him being back at Woolworths and either continuing his training to be a manager, or perhaps even being offered a store of his own. For some time I've even wondered if he could be the one to take on the Erith store when you leave to have your baby, but now . . . now it's unlikely he'll even have a job to come home to, and all my dreams will have been for nothing,' Sarah said, as her chin started to wobble and tears threatened to start falling.

'Sshh, my dear,' Betty said as she reached across the small table between them and squeezed Sarah's hand. 'What makes you think Alan won't be allowed to take back his old job?'

'I've just been to Woolworths. I was hoping to have a word with you about Alan's future. I thought it would cheer him up to know he was wanted back in his old job or . . . or . . . perhaps even . . .' she sniffed.

'. . . perhaps even offered a promotion to store manager,' Betty finished her sentence. 'Yes, I must say that if I had any say in who would take over the reigns it would be your Alan, but sadly head office may just decide to send him elsewhere.'

Sarah wiped her eyes with the napkin on her lap. 'I don't understand? Woolworths doesn't want him back.'

It was Betty's turn to look confused. 'Who told you that? We've already had men returning to their old jobs around the country. I was reading about it just the other day.'

'Mr Porter said so when I went to your office. I'd just left the shop when you called out to me,' she said.

'Oh, that wretched man! He will be the death of me,' Betty exclaimed, causing nearby diners to look her way in consternation. 'He had no right to tell you any such thing.' She tapped her forehead. 'I've had it up to here with him. He'd have gone long ago if it weren't for his uncle holding an important position at head office. It's time I did something about it.'

'Be careful, Betty – it won't do the baby any good if you go getting yourself upset.'

'Don't worry about me. I want you to get yourself back home and write to that husband of yours. Tell him from me that the day he comes home for good, there will be a job waiting for him at Woolworths. And whether I'm still there or not, I'll be rooting for him to be made a manager before the year is out. Woolworths stands by its promise that every male employee will have a job to return to.'

Sarah almost danced down the road. For a while she'd felt as though her dream had been snatched away from her, but now she could almost smell the roses round the door and see the years ahead with her making a home for her husband, Alan Gilbert, manager of a Woolworths store. That sounded just right, she thought as she crossed from the Prince of Wales to Crayford Road and approached Maureen's house. Perhaps they'd be able to move before too long? As lovely as her mother-in-law was, she longed to be the mistress of her own household.

Taking a key from her handbag, she quietly opened the front door on the off chance Buster was sleeping. She stopped in her tracks as she heard crying. It wasn't Georgina – it was a woman, and she sounded quite upset. Hurrying into the front room, she found her dad comforting Maureen with his arms round her.

'Don't get yourself upset, Maureen. Telegrams don't always bring bad news,' he said, eyeing an envelope lying on the table.

'I've just got a feeling it's something bad,' she sniffed as he continued to hold her.

'What's happened?' Sarah snapped, not liking that her dad was being so familiar with Maureen.

'A telegram came for you just now. If it wasn't for Maureen getting herself upset I'd have walked round to Woolworths with it. But you're here now,' he said, noticing his daughter's strained expression.

Sarah picked up the buff-coloured envelope and walked to the kitchen, closing the door. If it was bad news about Alan she wanted to be alone with her thoughts. Maureen seemed to have George to care for her. She just had a long-distance husband – or not, depending on the contents of the envelope. She ripped it open and read the few words, trying hard to focus as she read the line over and over again.

I'll be home tomorrow and I'll never leave home again. I have such plans my love!

Sarah screamed as she realized what this meant, causing George and Maureen to rush into the room, and from upstairs came the wail of young Buster. This time it was Sarah's turn to fall into the arms of George as she sobbed, 'Alan's coming home. He's coming home for good.'

Maureen, who had snatched the telegram from Sarah's fingers, started to sob again. 'I thought I'd lost him. This close to the end of the war, I thought I'd lost my boy.'

George held out his arm, and Maureen joined the pair as they hugged each other.

A little voice could be heard from the doorway. 'Mummy, why is Nanny crying?'

Sarah scooped Georgina up in her arms. 'Daddy's coming home, and he's never leaving us again,' she explained as she showered her daughter with kisses. 'Isn't that wonderful? From now on, everything we do will be done as a family. That's you, me, Buster and Daddy.'

The little girl was overwhelmed with the news, and seemed confused. 'Can he be a bridesmaid for Nanny Ruby with me and Myfi?'

George roared with laughter and picked up his granddaughter, swinging her round the room. 'I'd like to see that!'

'I'd better get his best suit out of mothballs for the wedding,' Maureen said, 'and perhaps we should throw a party to welcome him home.'

'No,' Sarah all but shouted. 'No party. The war's not over and we shouldn't be counting our blessings just yet. Besides, not all of our family will be here to celebrate,' she said, her eyes going to the framed photograph of her mum in pride of place on the mantelpiece.

*

'I've been wanting to see this film for ages,' Freda said, taking Sandy's hand in the cinema as the lights started to dim.

'What is it with you and this actor chap, Johnny Johnson?' he chuckled. 'If I was one to get jealous I'd be blacking his eyes right now. Who else goes to the cinema to see the B film rather than the main attraction?'

'Me and my friend Molly do for a start. We particularly like the spy films where he plays Clive Danvers. He's so handsome.' Freda shivered with delight.

'I'll have to have a word with this Molly. She seems to be leading my girl astray.'

Freda squirmed in the plush velvet seat with delight. Sandy had called her his girl. She'd never been someone's girl before. Yes, she'd had her romances, but with Sandy it was something special. 'Don't you dare, I'm as much to blame as Molly. Although I do believe she has a couple of photos cut from magazines in her bedroom. I do miss her,' she added. 'In her last letter she said that it won't be too long before she is home to visit.'

'She may be home for good before too long. If your friend Alan is being demobbed from the RAF, then chances are Molly will be from the Land Army.'

'I hadn't thought of that. But I suppose there's no call for pilots to be taught how to fly planes anymore when we are hearing that the war in Europe will be over before too long, whereas we will still need cabbages?'

Sandy laughed out loud, and was rewarded by people sitting nearby hushing him to be quiet. 'Freda, you are a tonic,' he said, leaning over to kiss her cheek.

I'm also your girl, she thought to herself as she

snuggled down against his shoulder as the Pathé News came up on the large screen.

If Freda had expected a quiet evening with her boyfriend at the Odeon, she was to be disappointed. News of the Russians reaching Germany brought cheers from the crowd and despite the usherettes walking up and down the aisles flashing torches at the noisiest customers, the festivities continued into the B movies, with people booing and cheering as the ace secret agent searched out the baddies and got his girl.

Things are really changing, Freda thought as she joined in the cheering along with Sandy. The days and years ahead would not be spent wondering if they would be alive come morning, or if loved ones would be lost. Even her brother Lenny had mentioned he would be visiting before too long, although his life would still be at sea, as he loved the life. And she had a feeling he would have some news to do with the lovely nurse, Sally, who they'd both met when their mother was gravely ill in a Birmingham hospital.

'Did I tell you I'd heard from my brother?' she whispered in Sandy's ear.

'Only a dozen times,' he whispered back, making the hairs on the back of her neck tickle. 'He means a lot to you, doesn't he?'

'He's the only proper family I have,' she said.

'Not for much longer,' he replied, squeezing her hand in the darkness.

Freda was still on cloud nine as they left the cinema. Never had she heard the national anthem sung with such gusto as it was that night as the curtains closed on the evening's entertainment. 'Do you fancy some chips? My treat,' she said, digging into her handbag for her purse.

'I wouldn't say no. My landlady isn't the best cook in the world, but it's filling. I didn't have a chance to eat in the works canteen today. But you can put your purse away. I'll not take money from a woman,' he added sternly.

They hurried across the road to join a long queue outside the chip shop. 'Why did you miss your meal at work?' Freda asked. She didn't like to see a man not eat properly, especially when he had a hard day's work to get through.

Sandy shrugged as he tightened the belt on his overcoat and pulled up the collar against a light chill in the late evening air. 'We were called in to be interviewed by people from the ministry. It took ages because we had to wait in a queue in the passage outside the offices.'

'What? The whole factory?' Freda gasped. She knew that Vickers was a very big factory in Crayford.

'Mainly my department, and some of the office staff. George was sitting in the room when we were interviewed.'

'Did he recognize you?' Freda asked. 'You have met on a few occasions now.'

'I don't think so. He seemed to be writing in a notebook most of the time I was in the room. The thing is, Freda . . . I wondered if you'd have a quiet word with him and put in a good word for me?'

Freda stepped back from the door to let someone out of the chip shop before stepping into the warm interior. She breathed in the aroma of vinegar and licked her lips. 'I didn't realize how hungry I was.'

'So will you speak to George?'

'I don't understand why I need to speak to George. This has nothing to do with me.'

'You wouldn't want to be linked to someone who has done something wrong, would you? If you speak to George, it may help him to see me in a good light.'

Freda felt confused. 'Why would he think of you in a bad light? I don't understand what you're saying,' she exclaimed as they reached the counter and put in their order. 'Lots of vinegar for me please, Vi,' she called.

'It's just important for me not to have a blemish on my employment record. Will you speak to George?'

Freda sighed. 'Oh all right then, anything for a quiet life. Although I have no idea what to say to George.'

'You could point out what a good chap I am and ask him what was said about me after I left the interview.'

'Oh, I don't know about that. He will think I'm poking my nose into something that doesn't concern me,' Freda said, passing him his chips wrapped in newspaper. 'Watch out, they're hot.'

Sandy nuzzled her ear and kissed her neck. 'I'd be so grateful,' he murmured for only Freda to hear.

She felt her knees turn to jelly and a shiver ran through her body. 'All right, I'll do it.'

'Oi! That's enough of that,' Vi called from behind the high counter. 'You'll be curdling the vinegar doing things like that. Be off with you.'

Freda ran giggling from the shop, followed by Sandy.

They walked slowly back to Alexandra Road, nibbling on the hot chips until they'd had their fill. 'Give me your paper. I'll get rid of it indoors,' she said, holding out her hand to him. Sandy grabbed it and pulled her close.

'You promise you'll speak to George?'

'For goodness' sake, I told you I would, didn't I? Now be off with you before your landlady locks you out.'

Sandy kissed her long and hard. 'Don't forget,' he said as he walked away into the darkness.

Freda opened the gate and walked up to the door, deep in thought. Why on earth did he want her to speak to George? Sandy was a good bloke – why did he need to prove this to anyone?

At the door, her foot hit something on the doorstep. She kicked it again, and a small yap sounded from inside. Reaching into her pocket for a torch, she shone it onto the box as the top flap opened and a small furry face peered out. 'Oh my goodness, aren't you a cute little puppy,' she said, kneeling down to pick up the young dog just as a second popped its head out of the box.

Freda banged on the door in excitement as she tried to stop the two puppies escaping. 'Hurry up,' she called out.

'What in heaven's name . . . ?' Ruby exclaimed as she opened the door, to be met with the sight of Freda sitting on the cold path with a puppy licking her face.

'You shouldn't sit on the cold ground or you'll get piles,' Bob said, peering over Ruby's shoulder.

'Wherever did you get these from?' Ruby asked, leaning down to take the puppy so that Freda could get up.

'I didn't. They were here when I came home just now.'

'They?' Ruby and Bob said at the same time.

'There's another in the box,' she answered, pulling back the flaps. 'Correction: there's another three.'

Bob helped Freda carry the box indoors while Ruby closed the front door after looking up and down the street. 'I can't see hide nor hair of anyone. What a strange thing to have happened! The poor little buggers must be frozen. I've got Nelson's old blanket in the cupboard under the stairs.' She bustled about, moving items, and eventually emerged holding an army blanket that had seen better days. 'Bob, you'll have to fetch Nelson's basket from the shed. They'll be cosy in there for the time being.'

'They're lively little blighters,' Bob said as he held two of the black-and-white puppies in his arms while Freda dived under the table to retrieve the others.

'I wonder where they came from?' Ruby said.

'What you mean is, who dumped them on our doorstep? They obviously know you're a sucker for every waif and stray in the neighbourhood.'

'I took you in and gave you a bed, didn't I,' Ruby huffed as she picked up the box from the table where Bob had left it. 'What's this?' she said, taking a sheet of paper from inside between two fingers. The page had been ripped and chewed by the pups, and was damp with a yellow stain. 'Well, I'll be blowed. Look at this, Bob.'

Bob placed the puppies onto the floor, where they started to fight playfully together on Ruby's best rag rug, and took the note. He read the few words and burst out laughing. 'It looks as though Nelson had a lady friend in his final days, and these are his kids.'

'No!' Freda laughed. 'The old scoundrel!'

'It says here that the owner of his lady friend isn't prepared to keep them and her husband would have drowned them in a bucket of water if he'd had his way. She had no choice but to leave them with us,' Bob said.

'There's no name or address, I suppose?' Ruby asked, as

she shooed off one of the four who was now hanging from the hem of her pinny.

'Of course not,' Bob scoffed. 'Would you dump them on someone and leave an address?' He watched the lively pups for a while. 'I suppose you'll be wanting me to get a bucket of water out and be rid of them . . . ?' he asked with a slight grin.

'Don't you dare,' Ruby scolded as she bent down and flipped each one on its back. 'Four girls – I should have guessed as much. Our Nelson was always one for the ladies.' She picked up the one who had taken a liking to hanging from her clothes, and gave it a close look. 'This one's the spit of her dad. Look, she's even got one black and one white ear, like my old boy did. This is the one I'll be keeping, and I shall call her Nellie.'

'That's all well and good, Ruby,' Bob said, scratching his head, 'but what's going to happen to the other three?'

11

George banged on the top of Maureen's kitchen table with a glass pint pot. 'If I may have your attention, please,' he called above the hubbub of neighbours, family and friends chatting nineteen to the dozen. 'I'd like you all to raise your glasses and toast Alan as he returns to the bosom of his family. Without lads like my son-in-law, Adolf Hitler would be marching through London right now and our grandchildren would be speaking German. The war's not over yet, but God knows the tide well and truly turned. Let's look to the future and raise our glasses to peace and happy times.'

'To Alan, and peace,' they all cheered.

'Thank you,' Alan said, raising his glass. 'I never expected such a homecoming. I thought I'd come home and simply get on with life with my wife and children, work towards having our own home and face whatever the future threw at us. All the same, I thank you all. Cheers,' he added.

'I can't believe you are home for good. I swear I'm going to pinch myself and wake up and it will all have been a dream and you will be off somewhere putting yourself in danger,' Sarah said as they strolled hand in hand into the small back garden of Maureen's house.

Alan pulled his wife into the small shed where his beloved motorbike was stored and closed the door behind them. 'I thought we'd never be alone,' he whispered before they clung together in a heated embrace.

'Alan, Alan,' Maureen called from the garden. 'Where are the pair of you? We have a surprise.'

Alan pushed open the door of the shed as Sarah straightened her hair and her clothes. 'Hello, Mum, I was checking out Bessie. It won't be long before I can take her out for a spin now I'm home.'

Maureen raised her eyebrows. 'That's as may be, but there are people here wanting to speak to you and wish you well. You can look at motorbikes another time,' she said pointedly. 'But before you go inside, George has got something for you both.'

'Dad?' Sarah said as she spotted her father nearby trying to light his pipe. 'What's going on?'

George reached into his pocket and pulled out an envelope, passing it to Sarah. 'We both thought you'd like to have a few days away before you go back to work and get on with your life together. It's not much, but . . .'

'Dad, this is wonderful. Look, Alan, it's Whitstable, where we spent our honeymoon. This is so generous of you, thank you,' she said, flinging her arms round her dad.

'It's only a couple of days, what with your nan's wedding coming up fast. Maureen chipped in as well. She's going to look after the children so you can have a bit of time alone.'

'This is very good of you, sir,' Alan said, shaking

George's hand and kissing Maureen. 'I don't suppose . . .' He started looking towards the shed where his motorbike stood covered by a tarpaulin.

'No, Alan,' Sarah shot him a stern look. 'I refuse to get onto the bike and travel all the way to Whitstable with you. You know I hate the wretched thing. If I had my way it would have been handed over for scrap to help the war effort years ago.'

'But, love . . .'

'It's all right, Alan, you can use my car for the week-end.' George grinned, knowing how much his daughter hated riding pillion on Alan's pride and joy.

Maureen tucked her arm through George's, causing Sarah to frown. 'Come along, you two, let's get back to the party. There's still some beer left, and I managed to make some sausage rolls, although I've had to pad out the fill-ings with breadcrumbs and herbs. They should be about ready to take from the oven. Help me hand them round, Sarah, then we can have a sing-song.'

Sarah nodded and followed her mother-in-law into the house, waving to Freda as she passed. Was she the only one who thought Maureen and her dad seemed far too friendly?

'Your friends like to enjoy themselves,' Sandy said as he accepted the glass of beer Freda had collected from David Carlisle, who'd been put in charge of the beer barrel.

'We are happy Alan is home and safe.' She looked round the room at the smiling faces, counting in her head the number of people who had lost loved ones during the past six years, and shuddered. It was far too many.

'Why did you shudder? Are you cold – would you like my coat?' Sandy asked.

'I was thinking about how many people here have lost family due to this bloody war. I just hope it was worth the sacrifice.'

He shrugged his shoulders. 'Unless something unexpected happens, you will have won this war. How do you think the Germans feel, to have lost so many and to have lost the war as well?'

Freda was surprised at his words. 'You seem almost bitter about this war. How can you have feelings for the Germans when they have taken over so many countries and done such despicable things? You were injured too. Do you feel no hatred for what they have done? I know I do for them killing Irene, and Maisie's first husband, Joe. I still live in fear of my brother being killed at sea, and thank the lord that he too will be home on leave soon, and that our Alan will never fly another Spitfire again.'

'War makes us bitter, and not all of us hate the Germans,' was his only comment after her outburst, as he drained the last of the beer from his glass. 'Did you put in a good word for me with your friend George?'

Freda sighed. She'd hoped Sandy had forgotten his request. 'There's not been an opportunity as of yet.'

'Why not now?' Sandy was beginning to slur his words. 'He's over there talking to the brave Spitfire pilot. Go and talk to him while I get another beer.'

'Don't you think you've had enough? Shall I get you something to eat?'

'Do it,' he said, getting unsteadily to his feet and heading over to the beer barrel.

Freda knew she'd have no peace until she'd done Sandy's bidding, although what to say to George was another matter.

'Hello, kid,' Alan said, draping an arm round her shoulder as she approached where he and George stood. 'What's this I see? I go off to fight the enemy, and you find yourself another boyfriend?'

'Don't be daft, Alan. How can I be faithful to you when you're married to my best friend? It's best we are brother and sister,' she kidded him. Freda had loved Alan like a big brother ever since he'd started courting Sarah. In return Alan had treated her like the sister he'd never had, teaching her how to ride a motorbike and wiping away her tears when she had boyfriend problems.

'Sarah might have something to say about it,' he laughed good-naturedly. 'But seriously, how's the romance going? Do we have another wedding on the horizon?'

'Don't you think this family has had enough of weddings for the moment? We've yet to see Ruby and Bob walk down the aisle. She could still change her mind and put the date off once again.'

George groaned. 'Don't say that. My mother has dallied over this wedding long enough. She knows Bob is a grand chap, but she still has her doubts.'

'It's because she loved your dad so much. It must be a hard choice to make.'

'Dad's been gone nigh on eight years now. She should have come to terms with it by now,' George said. 'Look at Bob – his wife passed away in the same year, and he's raring to marry Mum.'

'It's different for men,' Freda said, showing knowledge

beyond her years. 'They cope differently. When women find the right person they never stop loving them,' she said, glancing to where Sandy was walking none too steadily back to his seat. She hoped he didn't spill beer on her best coat, which was draped over the back of her chair.

'You have got it bad,' Alan said, noticing where she was looking.

'Sandy's all right. I've had fun going out with him. He's a decent sort. Wouldn't you say so, George?' she asked, crossing her fingers behind her back in hope that George would say something she could take back to Sandy.

George had a serious look on his face as he too watched Sandy. 'He's a hard worker and wants to know everything about the job,' he said seriously.

Freda breathed a sigh of relief. That was more than enough to keep Sandy happy. She made a little more small talk and headed back to share the news.

George frowned as he saw Sandy questioning Freda, and glanced away before the man spotted him watching.

'What's going on?' Alan asked. 'Don't you like the chap? And why was Freda asking you about him?'

George looked about him and then took Alan's elbow to guide him from the room. 'Let's have a word out-side ... I'm just going outside to smoke my pipe,' he called to Maureen, who hated the smell of tobacco inside her little house.

Alan followed his father-in-law to the end of the small garden, where they leant against the wall so they could see anyone approaching. 'Spill the beans,' he said, reaching into his jacket pocket for his cigarettes.

'I'm telling you this in the strictest of confidence, in the hope you can keep your eyes and ears open.'

'That sounds mysterious,' Alan grinned.

'It is, and you'll stop grinning like an idiot when I tell you that it affects young Freda.'

Alan frowned. 'I'm listening, so tell me everything. I'd hate the kid to be in trouble.'

'We've had a breach in security.'

'What, at Vickers? You're joking, aren't you? I'd have thought security was pretty tight at the factory.'

'It is, but we've been aware for a little while that designs are moved about, and chances are they are copied. When the ministry arrived to say they had evidence of the enemy coming up with information that could only have come from my department, we had to not only become even more vigilant, but also question the loyalties of our staff. Sandy is one of my staff, and I know very little about him apart from that he was injured at Dunkirk. He came out of the army to continue the training he started before the war.'

'Blimey, this all sounds like comic magazine stuff. Or one of those spy movies Freda likes to watch.'

'Let's hope not. At the moment we've been asked to keep an eye on the men in our department and report anything that seems suspect. I know the majority of men on the list of suspects, and I was able to report on them. It is Sandy who is the problem. He was moved to my department in the past year, and his manager before me has since died. The lad keeps himself to himself.'

'So how can I help?'

George smiled. 'I'm glad you've asked. Can you get to

know him a little and see what he gets up to outside of work? If you have any suspicions at all, we'll call for help. No heroics, mind you. The last thing we want is for you to be injured.'

Alan grinned. 'And there was me thinking I'd miss the action now I'm out of the RAF. Will you tell Freda?'

George tapped his pipe on the garden wall and started to fill it with tobacco. 'No, it's best we keep this between ourselves. The bosses will be none too pleased if they know I've spoken to you. It's having Freda involved with the man that makes me feel we should be doing something more than keeping an eye on him at work.'

Alan agreed. 'True. If anything happened to the kid and we'd known and not done anything, I'd never forgive myself. I'll not mention it to Sarah either.'

'That's the ticket,' George said. 'I knew I could rely on you, son.'

'There's something I want to talk to you about, George. It's been on my mind for a while now. I've been thinking about my future and wondered if you could give me some advice?'

'I will if I can,' George said as they leant against the wall, and Alan started to talk.

'We can't have all these puppies in the house what with the wedding in less than a week,' Bob said grumpily. 'I've almost worn out the mop swabbing the decks after this lot have been fed and watered.'

'Don't go on so,' Ruby scolded. 'I've got it all in hand. Two of them are going to their new homes later today. In fact, that sounds like them right now,' she said as the front door opened and she heard Gwyneth call out. 'Come through, love, I'm in the kitchen.'

Bob's daughter-in-law came into the room, pushing her daughter in front of her. She had her hands clamped firmly over the child's eyes, and they were both giggling.

'Mummy, what is the surprise?' Myfi asked, wriggling behind her mother's hands. 'It's not even my birthday.'

'Stand still for a moment and you'll find out,' Gwyneth said in her sing-song Welsh voice. 'But I don't want you making a noise, do you understand?'

Myfi nodded her head. 'I understand,' she said quietly.

'Now put your hands out.'

Ruby stepped forward and placed one of the puppies into the young girl's arms, and Myfi shrieked with delight as she opened her eyes. 'Oh, you dear little thing,' she said, burying her face in the puppy's warm fur as it tried to lick and nibble her face. 'Is this your new dog?' she asked Ruby as her eyes shone with delight. 'I do miss Nelson. He was a very special dog.'

'He was, my love, but no, he's not mine. Mine is out here,' Ruby said, opening the door to the kitchen and scooping Nellie up as the other puppies came gamboling in. 'These are Nelson's children. You have the one with the black paw,' she said as she watched the little girl's eyes shine.

'She's mine to keep?' Myfi asked, looking between her mother and Ruby.

'All yours, and I trust you to be the one to look after her and feed her.'

'Oh, I will, I will.' Myfi was almost crying in delight. 'I

shall call him Sunny, and then we will both have a part of Nelson's name in his puppies,' she exclaimed before thinking for a moment. 'Ruby, did Nelson . . .'

Gwyneth raised her eyes to Ruby in consternation. Was the child going to ask how Nelson had fathered the puppies?

'Ruby, did Nelson send the puppies to us because he knew how much we all missed him?'

Ruby brushed a tear from her eye. She'd been thinking the same thing. 'Myfi, I do believe you are right. Nelson has sent us a gift from heaven,' she smiled.

'But what about the other two puppies – who will they go to live with?'

'Just you wait and see. Now, how would you like to take Nellie and Sunny into the garden to play for a little while? Bob will help you,' Ruby said, handing Nellie to him and ushering them into the kitchen and out the back door just as there was a knock at the front door.

'I'll get that for you,' Gwyneth said as Ruby reached for the mop to wipe up a small puddle.

'I swear these puppies produce more liquid than they consume,' she muttered as Gwyneth led David Carlisle and Douglas Billington into the room. 'Hello there. You can take your pick of the two girls that are left. They're as alike as two peas in a pod, so there's not much of a choice.'

David bent down and picked up the plumper of the two puppies. 'The kids will love this one. She has the look of Winston Churchill, don't you think? I'll tell Bessie and Claudette her name is Winnie,' he laughed. 'What about yours?'

'I'll let Clemmie and Dorothy decide. They're going to be over the moon. We've never had a dog before, and Betty is just as excited.'

Bob and Myfi came back into the house with the other pups. Myfi was overexcited, so after making their goodbyes Gwyneth took the child back home.

'Not long to the wedding now,' Douglas said. 'And who'd have thought we'd be celebrating the death of Adolf Hitler in the same week?' he added, waving his newspaper for all to see.

'There were times when I thought it wouldn't happen, I don't mind telling you,' Bob said as he took the paper and scanned the page quickly for news. 'There's not much more here than we heard on the radio,' he said, passing it back to Douglas. 'Don't forget it's Ruby's birthday as well. That's why we chose the day,' Bob added.

'I'm too old to be thinking about birthdays. I just want everyone to have a nice day, and then we can have the party round the Prince of Wales in the evening. I'm not one to celebrate people's deaths either, but that Hitler is one death I'll raise my glass to,' Ruby said, glancing to where the newspaper lay on Douglas's lap.

'Hear, hear!' the men agreed.

'Talking of raising glasses, can I offer you a glass of something?' Bob said.

'I'll not have guests in my home going back to their wives half sloshed, Bob Jackson. They won't thank me for that. I'll put the kettle on. Let's save the drinking for the wedding, eh?'

The men nodded in agreement and watched Ruby head

to the kitchen. 'Will you be having a stag night?' David asked.

'I will,' Bob said, giving a sideways glance to the kitchen. 'In this house it's called popping round to the pub to check everything's in order, if you get my drift,' he winked, tapping the side of his nose at the same time. 'Mike will be having a word with you. I've left it all to him to sort out.'

'Don't think I can't hear what you're talking about,' Ruby called out. 'Just promise me you'll be bringing Bob home in a fit state to be married the next morning. And I don't mean with any black eyes or the likes – I know what you men get up to at things like that.'

Betty stretched slowly and winced as the pain in her back increased. She had another hour to work, then she could head for home. Thank goodness Douglas had taken to picking her up from work, and these days she didn't care if she travelled in one of the company's hearses.

One month to go and their child would be here, and she couldn't wait to hold the little one in her arms. As much as she loved Clemmie and Dorothy, they were not her children, whereas this baby would be solely hers and Douglas's. It would make their family complete. However, at the moment, Betty's thoughts were on her other child, the Erith branch of Woolworths. In the past few days she'd come to terms with the fact she would be passing the store over to someone else to care for. Chatting to Sarah had given her hope that Alan would soon be back working in the store, and with his splendid war record she was in no doubt he would be the ideal candidate to take over as manager. Perhaps she would even leave work sooner rather than later. She felt her cheeks burn a little with embarrassment at how she'd deceived her employers by saying the child wasn't due until late July. Being men, they'd not thought about the size of her bump or asked about dates. Serves them right, she said to herself. They'd been less than helpful lumbering her with Cecil. Speaking of which, where was the wretched man? She'd sent him to the storeroom to search for the bunting they had packed away. She wanted the windows of the store prepared for decoration, as any day now they'd be required to celebrate the end of war in Europe now that despicable Adolph Hitler was dead. Talk was it could be the seventh or eighth of May, so not long to wait.

She left her office intent on heading to the storeroom when she bumped into Freda. 'Oh dear, whatever is the matter? You look as though you've lost a pound and found a penny,' she said, rather proud that she had remembered one of Maisie's sayings.

'You could say I have in a way,' the young woman said. 'I've been laid off down the fire station. It seems I'm surplus to requirements now the war is all but over. I know I've not done much recently apart from take telephone messages and help wash the fire tenders, but it was a shock all the same. I'm going to miss working there.'

Betty patted her shoulder. 'I'm sure you must feel very down at the moment, but their loss is our gain. Will you be able to go back to full working hours?'

'I'd like to, if I may? There was a suggestion that I join the Fire Service but I'd never be allowed to undertake the same job as the men. It's a shame, as I'd love the excitement of attending fires and rescuing people. Then again the job would be tedious at other times.'

Betty's heart skipped a beat. If Freda left Woolworths she would lose yet another trained employee. It was such a shame Freda was considered too young to take up management training, even if the company would consider a woman as suitable for the job. She would have to tempt Freda to stay and enjoy her work.

'I do have an idea that may interest you. Why not walk with me to the storeroom while we discuss it? I'm looking for Cecil. He went to sort out the bunting two hours ago. No doubt he is skulking somewhere enjoying his newspaper and a cigarette.'

Freda was interested in what Betty had to say. 'I'm all ears, even though I have no idea what you are going to offer me,' she said, falling into step beside her boss.

They reached the storeroom as Betty explained that she'd like Freda to take on supervisor duties, with the aim to make it a permanent post by Christmas. 'By then we will know which staff are returning to Woolworths when they leave the forces, and also which women are giving up work now their menfolk are home for good.'

Freda beamed at the suggestion. 'Thank you, I'm honoured that you think I'm up to the job. There is one thing, though . . . You would have left Woolworths by then, so will whoever takes over honour my promotion?'

Betty felt a small lurch in the pit of her stomach, and it wasn't her child moving. It was the reminder that she would no longer be part of the Woolworths family. 'Never you fear,' she said, trying hard to put on a brave face. 'I'll draw up a proper contract so no one can change my offer.

Besides, I'm hoping the new manager will be Alan Gilbert. Won't that be good?'

'Alan?' Freda tried not to shriek out loud. 'That would be wonderful. It would be just like the old days before the war,' she grinned.

Betty nodded her head in agreement. It would, but with one exception. She would no longer be sitting in her office overseeing the running of the store.

'Oh Alan, I can't believe we are back here after nearly six years. Wasn't it wonderful of Dad to treat us to these few days away? I feel like a bride all over again.'

Alan looked at his wife's flushed cheeks and sparkling eyes as she lay in bed beside him. 'You're not quite the shy bride I brought here last time, are you?' he grinned as he ducked the pillow she raised ready to throw in his direction.

'And you are no longer the fumbling young lad either,' she reminded him as she moved closer to snuggle into his arms. 'What shall we do today?'

'I'd be happy to stay in bed all day, but no doubt you have plans?'

'Alan! We may be married but that's a shocking thing to say. Whatever would the hotel staff think?'

'They'd think I'm one lucky man to be here with such a wonderful woman.'

'There's nothing wonderful about me. I'm just a housewife and mother.'

'You are much more than that. You've kept this family afloat while I went off to war. You've even managed to fit in being an air-raid warden and work at Woolworths. In my book that's certainly wonderful. That's why I've been able to make plans for our future, knowing you will support me in whatever I do,' he said, kissing her before she could ask what he meant. 'Come on, let's go and find our breakfast, I'm famished. Then we can head out for the day. I wonder if that cafe where we dined on our honeymoon is still open? We could pop in there for lunch?'

'You never think of anything but your stomach,' Sarah laughed as she pulled away to get out of bed. She could already see her dream coming true, and just perhaps they would one day have that little house with roses round the door.

They decided to skip breakfast in the hotel and headed out into the sunshine, walking down the busy high street until they came across the cafe they'd visited on their honeymoon. 'Oh good, it's still there,' Sarah said, pleased at the opportunity to revisit a happy memory.

A face they recognized looked up as they entered the low-beamed cafe. 'Come along in, the kettle's always on the hob. Why not sit near the fire? The sun may be out but there's still a bit of a chill in the air,' the woman said, bustling about straightening the tablecloth and placing a menu in front of Alan and Sarah as they took off their coats and sat down. She stepped back and looked at them both with a thoughtful expression on her face. 'I've seen you before . . . No, don't tell me.' She put up her hand to stop Alan speaking. 'It'll come to me in a minute. Hmm . . . yes, I know. You were honeymooners and work at Woolworths.'

'My goodness,' Sarah gasped. 'You have a very good

memory. We got married the day the war started. A lot of water's gone under the bridge since then.'

'I'm very pleased to see that you've both survived, and honoured you've come back to see us. Now, let me get you some breakfast and then perhaps we can have a catch up over a cup of tea?'

They tucked into eggs on hot buttered toast, each having two thick rashers of bacon and sliced fried tomatoes. The cafe owner gave a crafty wink when Sarah asked how she could supply such a feast. 'Only for my favourite customers,' was her reply.

After they finished and a fresh pot was brought to the table, she sat and listened as Sarah told of their two children and life back in Erith. 'How are your family?' she asked tentatively. From experience she knew it wasn't always good to ask such a question. The war had taken the lives of so many loved ones.

'I have another grandchild,' she beamed, 'but my old man went in 1941.'

'Oh, I'm so sorry,' Sarah said, remembering what a jolly couple they'd been. 'Was it quick?'

'You could say that. I found out he was carrying on with the barmaid at the Neptune and I booted him out there and then. I don't hold with any of that kind of thing.'

Both Alan and Sarah were lost for words and sat quietly wondering what to say next.

'I've got a new husband now. He's out collecting the eggs from down the farm. Perhaps if you pop in again you'll meet him. He's ten years younger than me,' she guffawed, nudging Alan so hard he almost fell off his chair. 'It was the best thing I ever did. Everyone should have a second husband.'

Sarah giggled. 'My nan's getting married again in a few days' time. She's taken her time making up her mind. My granddad died ages ago,' she added, not wanting the woman to think that Granddad Eddie had run off with a barmaid.

'Give her my best wishes and tell her to pop in when she's down this way. It's a glorious week to be married, what with them saying we'll be celebrating the end of the war in Europe any day soon. Let's hope those blokes in charge hurry up and sign their bits of paper, then we can have a bloody good party to celebrate.'

They both nodded in agreement as Alan took out his wallet to pay the bill.

'No, I'm not wanting your money. You've been good company and reminded me of my days when I worked in Woolworths. Now the war's as good as over, you come back and bring those kiddies of yours,' she said, glancing again at the small photograph Sarah had taken from her handbag to show her. 'I take it you'll be back working there before too long?'

Sarah beamed as she thought of her dreams of a happy-ever-after life.

'No, I have plans that don't include Woolworths,' Alan smiled as he helped Sarah on with her coat. 'Thank you again for our meal.'

With the invitation to call again soon ringing in their ears, they stepped outside and headed towards the harbour front. When they were out of view of the cafe, Sarah spun on her heel and glared at Alan. 'What the hell do you mean, your plans don't include Woolworths? I've even been to see Betty to make sure your job is still there waiting for when you return.'

Alan shrugged his shoulders and looked sheepish. 'I've changed, love. I don't feel Woolworths is right for me anymore,' he said apologetically.

'Not right for you anymore? What's happened to you, Alan? Have you become too posh, mixing with your RAF chums? Oh, it's been all right for me to have to go to work at Woolworths to put by some money, hoping we can build a future for the family. I didn't have any choice but to stay at home and play my part while you swanned off flying your bloody planes,' she shrieked, storming off along the seafront.

Alan tried not to laugh as he hurried after her. 'Darling, I wasn't exactly playing at flying planes . . .'

Sarah stopped suddenly, and he almost cannoned into her. 'I'm sorry. That comment wasn't called for – but I'm so annoyed with you. I had this dream, you see . . .'

He took her arm and led her to a wooden bench and they sat down side by side, looking out to sea. 'It looks as though we both have our dreams,' he said gently. 'It's a shame we never thought to share them with each other. Tell me more about yours.'

Sarah looked out over the estuary. Even with the sun shining it looked rather bleak, with grey ships moored offshore and gun emplacements dotted each side of the shore. 'I thought that once you returned home you'd go back to your old job and perhaps we might have another child, even two. And we could find a little house so we weren't reliant on your mum for a roof over our heads.

Not that I'm complaining, as she's been great caring for us while you've been away. I just thought the end of the war would mean a fresh start for us all. I'm sorry, I should have said something.'

Alan reached out and took her hand. 'I have dreams too. I wanted more for my family. I could see you in our own home with a growing family where you'd be waiting for me to come home every evening after a hard day at work. Don't laugh, but I even imagined roses round our door.'

'Me too,' Sarah exclaimed. 'What colour were yours?'

'Yellow,' he smiled.

'Mine were red, but we could have both. But if you don't want to go back to Woolworths, what are we to do? Betty thought you'd be her ideal replacement when she leaves to have the baby. She was going to speak to head office and she reckoned they would jump at promoting you from the trainee manager position you had back in '39.'

Alan groaned. 'Now I feel even worse,' he said, running his hand through his hair in despair.

'Then tell me a little more about your dream,' she said gently.

'I want to start my own business repairing motorbikes, perhaps even selling new ones. You know I'm good with my hands and I think I could make a go of it. I had a word with your dad the other day and he said he'd help find me a workshop and pass any work my way that he heard of. What do you think? Then again, if you are dead set against it I'll go back to Woolworths and we'll never mention it again.'

Sarah stayed silent for a while as she digested what Alan had told her. She knew he'd be unhappy if he didn't at least have a go at running his own business, and she would hate to see him unhappy. 'Money would be tight for a little while until business picked up, though . . . Did I tell you we had some money put by for a rainy day?'

'We do? How did we manage that?' he asked, looking puzzled.

'I took a part-time job at Woolworths up until Buster was born,' she grinned. 'Perhaps I'll see if Betty will take me back – it would help out while you run the family business . . . ?'

Alan hugged her tight. 'You mean it? You don't mind me not taking on the Woolworths job?'

'Woolworths will always be there,' she smiled.

12

~

'Why ever did you ask Freda to bring us along to this awful dance?' Sarah hissed at Alan. 'Scottish dancing reminds me of my school days, and I was next to useless even then. By rights I should be at home helping Nan get ready for the wedding. There's so much still needs doing, and it's only a couple of days away now.'

Alan tried to ignore the pain in his feet where a hefty lady had jumped on his toes during the Gay Gordons. 'Just smile and pretend you're enjoying yourself. We are here to support Freda with her boyfriend. It's not much to ask, is it?'

'Then stop limping and smile yourself. I could kill a port and lemon – is there a bar?'

'No, just tea and lemonade,' he muttered. 'Don't you think I've looked?'

Sarah giggled. 'Just think, it's not a week since you've been home, and look at what we are doing? I never thought we'd be hopping and skipping about in a dusty church hall in London. Why did we have to come to this place? Surely there's dancing closer to home?'

Alan felt awful not being able to confide that he was

here following George's request to keep an eye on Sandy. 'From what Freda said this is somewhere that Sandy visits quite often. Perhaps it's some kind of Scottish club.'

'That makes sense,' she said, looking around her. 'There aren't many young people here, though. It's a bit strange if you ask me. But if Freda is happy, who are we to question things?'

'She does seem happy with Sandy,' Alan agreed, looking across the room to where their friend was dancing with Sandy.

'Why are you looking so glum all of a sudden?' she asked, seeing a shadow cross her husband's face.

'Was I? Perhaps I was thinking of that beer I'd like to sup right now.' How could he tell Sarah he was worried about how Freda would react if Sandy was caught up in wrongdoings at Vickers? 'Come on, let's have another go. I'm determined to get round the room once without tripping over my feet,' he laughed, grabbing Sarah by the hand and pulling her onto the dance floor.

'Oh no,' she giggled as the music stopped. They'd danced no more than a dozen steps when an announcer declared it was time for an interval.

'I'll get you that drink,' Alan said as he spotted Sandy leaving Freda alone and walking over to an older man. The pair of them went out a side door of the hall, deep in conversation. Alan followed, trying hard not to be seen. He was unsure of the layout of the church hall and had no idea of where the men were heading. Pushing the door open slowly, he could hear hushed voices up ahead. He was in a short passageway that ran alongside the stage; a heavy curtain at the far end hid Sandy and the man as they spoke. He crept as close as he could and leant forward to listen. It sounded as though Sandy was annoyed, by the tone of his voice.

'I tell you, I've had enough. I've done as you instructed. I want no more to do with this. The Fatherland will not win this war – it is obvious to anyone. The Führer is dead. Why continue this madness?'

Alan couldn't believe his ears and moved closer to hear more, although he could only make out angry mutterings from Sandy's companion.

'I tell you, no. I handed over what you asked a year ago, and now I want to be free to live my life. I'm looking to settle down with my lady friend and my father wishes me to go back to Scotland to take over the farm. I've done what was asked of me. Please . . . I want no more.'

There were more threatening murmurs from the other man, but try as he might, Alan couldn't catch more than a word. It suddenly fell silent. Alan took a few steps back and opened the door behind him, making sure to create a noise. The curtain flew back to expose Sandy and the older man. 'Hello there,' said Alan. 'I'm looking for the gents?'

Sandy just stared back, his face paler than usual. 'It is at the other side of the stage,' the older man growled in his thick Scottish accent, giving Alan a surly look.

'Cheers, mate,' Alan said, trying hard to look cheerful as he walked away. He could hear footsteps behind him so he headed for the gents before rejoining Sarah, who was now sitting with Freda.

'What happened to our drinks?' Sarah asked. 'Don't bother, I'll go myself. You sit and have a chat with Freda.

We don't see nearly as much of her as we'd like now she has a serious boyfriend,' she grinned, leaving them alone to talk.

'So, kid, what's all this with you courting. Is it serious?' Alan asked, leaning back in his seat so he could keep a discreet eye on Sandy.

'I like him,' Freda said, jutting out her chin as if daring Alan to make fun of her.

'He seems a decent sort from what I've seen. How did you meet him?'

Freda relaxed and explained that Sandy helped out with the Fire Service and the church Boys' Brigade. Her eyes sparkled as she chatted away.

Alan felt like a heel for having spied on the man who was making his favourite girl, apart from Sarah, so happy. 'Do I hear wedding bells?' he asked.

Freda shrugged her shoulders. 'He hasn't asked me, if that's what you mean?'

'Would you say yes if he did ask you?' he asked tentatively, dreading her reply.

'Now you ask, I might just do that,' she grinned. 'Why do you ask – do you want to give me away?'

'You only have to say the word.' He smiled, while inwardly dreading the day his friend would face the end of her romance.

'Betty, whatever are you doing up that ladder?' Sarah shrieked as she entered the Woolworths store. 'Here, help me get her down!' she called to Cecil Porter, who was standing nearby gazing out of one of the large glass windows that looked out over Pier Road as people rushed up and down hugging friends and acquaintances with beaming smiles on their faces. 'There are plenty of other staff who can put up bunting. It may be the end of war in Europe but we don't want our celebrations being spoilt by you being carted off to hospital.'

'I'm fine, Sarah, I just wanted to join in with the celebrations and do my bit like the rest of the staff.'

Sarah waved a finger at her friend. 'Then go upstairs and bake a cake with Maureen. Honestly, Betty, I'm so angry with you. Not only could you have hurt the baby if you'd slipped, but you could have done yourself harm. And as for you,' she added to Cecil, 'call yourself a trainee manager? You're supposed to have eyes in the back of your head at all times in case there is a problem in the store, and here it is happening right in front of you. You don't deserve your job title, you lazy so-and-so,' she said, facing him nose to nose.

Cecil simply looked at her and sneered. 'If she wishes to climb a ladder, who am I to stop her? Besides, I'm the manager of this store now, so please don't assume I'm a trainee and not worthy of the title. I'm assuming your husband did not get offered his job back?'

Sarah wanted nothing more than to stamp her foot in frustration and punch him on the nose. Betty was no help, as she simply laughed. 'Come upstairs to my office, Sarah. I have some news you might like to hear. Cecil – clear this mess up and arrange for tea to be sent to my office, and make it snappy. After that, you can help out on the electrical counter. They seem to be short of light bulbs yet again. I swear the people of Erith must be eating them, we are getting through them at such an alarming rate. And don't look at me like that,' she glared. 'No one is a replacement manager here until the day I leave.'

Sarah followed Betty as she slowly climbed the familiar steep staircase up to the first floor. She could see that Betty was having trouble now her due date wasn't so far off, and by rights she should have given up her job long ago.

'Sit yourself down,' Betty said as she collapsed into her own seat. 'Now, you are probably wondering what I have to tell you?'

Sarah made the right noises, but prayed that Betty would say she was leaving her job.

'You won't have to worry about Alan's future anymore. Head office have told me they want him to return to Woolworths as soon as possible, as an assistant manager. My gut feeling is that he will soon have his own store, and the way Cecil is performing, it may even be the Erith store.' Betty beamed as she finished giving the good news, then spotted Sarah's sad face. 'Oh my dear, is there something wrong?'

Sarah nodded her head. 'I've lost count of the times I've sat here and cried or had to share bad news,' she said as Betty looked on with concern. 'I'm afraid Alan will not be returning to Woolworths. He has decided to be his own boss and run a workshop repairing motorbikes. In fact, he is with my dad looking at premises this very afternoon. A day before my nan's wedding and he is looking at grubby workshops,' she added, looking sad.

Betty clapped her hands together in delight. 'Why, I call that splendid news; every man should have his own business at some point in his life. He can always return to Woolworths if he decides he isn't cut out for the motor-bike trade. The skills he learnt here will never leave him,' she smiled.

'I suppose not,' Sarah said, although she couldn't get quite as enthusiastic as Betty. 'This just brings more problems, though.'

'Then tell me your problems. You know what they say: a trouble shared is a trouble halved.'

There was a knock on the door, and a young assistant carried in a tray of tea. Sarah jumped up to clear a space on the desk and take the tea tray. 'I don't think this is something that can be halved,' she said, pouring milk into the cups. 'Alan becoming his own boss is sure to bring money problems. We can't expect Maureen to support us, and I know my dad will give us what we need but I don't want to ask him; if you know what I mean?'

Betty took the cup and saucer and stirred the tea thoughtfully. 'I know exactly what you mean. You'd like to stand on your own two feet, and I do know how you can do it. Sarah, with Cecil still here and me no doubt leaving very soon, I feel you would be an asset in this office.'

Sarah was dumbfounded. 'What do you mean?'

'I mean you should come back to Woolworths and help bring in some money for your family until Alan's business can support you. I could do with someone to run the office. What do you say?'

'I would love to, and in fact I'd thought of asking you for a part-time job. But Buster is still too young to be left, and Georgina has to be dropped off at school. Did I tell you how well she is doing?'

'Well, if you can find someone to help with the children, please consider it,' Betty pleaded. 'I need to know the store is in good hands, and with Freda back full-time and you and Maisie doing a few hours every day, I could rest easy.'

Sarah had never seen Betty so anxious. 'All right – I may be able to ask Sadie to help. She does a good job caring for Maisie's little ones,' she said, thinking aloud. 'The money would come in handy while Alan builds up the business. I'll see what he has to say. Thank you for thinking of me, Betty. This isn't how I expected my life to be when Alan came home – but I suppose roses round the door are rather overrated,' she added sadly as she sipped her tea.

'Life never is as we expect it, my dear; we just have to make the most of things. Now, what's all this about the men having drinks at the Prince of Wales this evening with Bob? They will be fit for the wedding tomorrow, I hope?'

'They'd better be, or Nan will have Bob's guts for garters. I've warned Alan to be on his best behaviour, and I heard Maureen having a word with Dad.'

'They seem to be close, don't they? It must be a comfort since they lost your mum?'

Sarah nodded her head, but was unable to reply as a lump formed in her throat. Now others had noticed it was going too far. She'd have to say something before too long. Her mum hadn't been cold in her grave more than six months, and people were thinking of her dad and Maureen as a couple. It just wouldn't do.

*

'Over here,' Bob shouted to David and Douglas above the noise of the busy public house.

'Is this turnout all for you?' David said loudly as the men shook hands.

Bob laughed. 'If only it was, I'd be awash with rum by the time the night was out. There's a ship in at the docks and the men are drinking to the end of the war. It's going to be one big celebration tomorrow, now they've announced that the eighth of May is to officially be known as "Victory in Europe Day".'

'Who'd have thought we'd be celebrating a wedding and Victory in Europe all on the same day?' Douglas said as he shook hands with Mike Jackson, who was still in his police uniform. 'I'll get a round and bring it through. I take it we are in the hall at the back?'

'Yes, Alan and George are just setting up the last of the tables. It's a good job we booked the hall, as no one's going to be able to move in the pub tomorrow evening. It looks like the whole country's going to be out having a party. Ruby certainly picked a good day for our wedding,' Bob grinned as he took one of the trays of drinks and led the way into the hall.

'Hello, hello, what's going on here then?' Mike joked as he greeted his mates. He waved to Bob's friends from the allotment society and the police male voice choir, who'd been coerced into hanging up some of the bunting that Maisie had run up on her faithful Singer sewing machine.

'Are you here on official business?' George asked with a nod to Mike's police helmet, which he'd placed on a nearby table.

'I've been called in for a late shift because of the celebrations that seem to have started since the news was announced for VE Day. I couldn't really say no when I've booked tomorrow off for the wedding. That's why I'm the only one drinking lemonade,' he grinned, raising his glass. 'However, it won't stop me making a toast. Gentlemen, please raise your glasses to my father, Bob, and his bride-to-be, Ruby, as we wish them health, wealth and happiness on the occasion of their nuptials tomorrow. It is a special day for the country – or should I say the world? Who'd have thought when Ruby chose her birthday to marry this old scoundrel here, that it would also be VE Day?'

'Oh, bugger!' Bob said, looking alarmed by what his son had just said.

'It's too late now,' George said. 'Mum will hound you to the ends of the earth if you don't marry her now she's finally agreed to set a date.'

'No, it's not that,' Bob replied, turning rather pale. 'I forgot it was her birthday. I've not bought her a present.'

Once the roar of laughter had died down, Mike reached into his pocket and pulled out a small box. 'Gwyneth thought you might have had too much to do to remember to buy a birthday gift, so she picked this up yesterday.'

Bob carefully opened the box. Nestling in a layer of cotton wool, he found a silver brooch consisting of small glass stars cascading from a larger silver star. 'It's perfect,' he sighed. 'I'm sure Ruby will like it.'

'Gwyneth spotted Ruby looking at it in Selfe's the Jewellers window the other week, so it's a safe bet it will be acceptable.'

'That girl's a diamond. You picked a good one there,' Bob said, wiping his perspiring brow with a handkerchief.

'We both did, Dad. I reckon Mum is looking down on us both right now and wishing us well, don't you?'

The two men tapped their glasses together in a silent toast to Mike's mum and Bob's first wife.

'I'm sure she is, son, I'm sure she is. And wouldn't she be proud of you, with a wife and child?'

Mike agreed. 'I wish she was here to meet Gwyneth and Myfi, but then, if she was here you'd not have met Ruby.' He stopped and frowned. 'Now that is a confusing thought.'

David interrupted the father-and-son discussion. 'I'm going out to the bar. Can I get you anything?'

'Not for me, thanks, but put another lemonade in Mike's glass before he heads off to work,' Bob said.

'I'll come and help you,' Mike said, draining his glass and following David out to the main bar of the pub.

They'd just reached the bar through the crush of happy drinkers when the landlord called out, 'David, there's a couple asking about your Maisie. They're standing over by the piano.'

David left Mike to deal with the drink order and went over to where a squaddie was standing talking with a woman in a tatty fox-fur stole that must have walked the earth when Queen Victoria was on the throne. Her hair was a brittle blonde, and the red lipstick smeared around her lips highlighted her yellow teeth.

'I understand you are asking after my wife?' he said politely. 'I'm David Carlisle, Maisie's husband.'

The man looked him up and down. Like Mike, David

was still in his RAF officer's uniform; an impressive sight compared to the man in front of him in his ill-fitting khaki. 'So my sister's married an officer? It looks as though she did all right for herself,' he slurred.

'You must be Fred?' David said, holding out his hand to shake Fred's. It was ignored.

'You've got our kids,' the brassy woman said. 'You've had them years, by all accounts.'

David nodded slowly. This couple required careful handling. 'I believe your mother also had them for some time before her untimely death. We've been writing to your division trying to get hold of you since March 1943.'

'Well, I've been busy,' Fred shrugged. 'We don't all have cushy office jobs,' he sneered.

'Don't yer know there's been a war on?' the woman cackled.

'I do, madam,' David replied, gritting his teeth. 'So to what do we now owe this social visit?'

'I want me babies back.' The woman started to snivel, and let out a wail.

'Sshh, Cynthia,' Fred said as people nearby started to look. 'All in good time; let's see what this gent is going to offer us first.'

Davis frowned. 'I'm not sure what you mean?'

Fred winked. 'You've chased me enough these past few years, so you must be keen to take 'em off my hands. That means you're willing to pay, as far as I'm concerned.'

Cynthia stopped her wailing and gave David a sly look. 'You look the sort who's got a few bob put by. Name your offer and we can start the negotiations, otherwise I'll scream and stamp until the whole of this town knows you pinched our kids at a time when I'd lost me dear old mother-in-law.' She began to sniff dramatically.

David wanted nothing more than to drag the pair of them out of the pub and have it out with them. Was this why the man hadn't bothered answering any of the numerous letters he'd sent since Bessie and Claudette came to live with his family? In his heart he knew he'd pay a king's ransom to have the two girls, who he loved as much as his own offspring, stay with him and Maisie; but he'd be damned if he would weaken that easily.

'I thought you'd run off with an American serviceman?' he said, shooting Cynthia a dismissive look. This stopped her snivelling in an instant.

'Who told you that?' she asked warily, looking to her husband as he glared at David.

'Mrs Dawson informed Maisie the evening she passed away.'

'Then she was telling lies,' Cynthia spat back.

'Maisie was not alone. There was a witness. If it weren't for my wife, your children would have been alone in the world and most likely ended up in an orphanage . . . or worse. Not that you seem worried, as it has taken this long for you to track them down.'

Cynthia whimpered and looked at Fred for support. He simply sneered and nodded to where a group of rowdy squaddies stood drinking and watching them. 'Don't think you can get one over on me,' he threatened. 'Perhaps I need to go visit that sister of mine and remind her who is head of this family now.'

David took a step closer to his belligerent brother-in-law. 'You'll not threaten my wife,' he glared, although he knew that in most situations his wife was more than capable of handling herself. There again, Fred hadn't met his sister in many years, so would not know how strong she'd become since running away from home.

Fred seemed not to be swayed by David's warning and he too took a step closer, so that the men were almost nose to nose. 'I'll be back here tomorrow night. Make sure you either have the money with you, or I'll take the kids.'

Cynthia leant forward and, almost in a whisper, said, 'Or some of the money, and I'll just take my Claudette.'

Fred shoved her out of the way. 'The money – or we take both my kids,' he growled at his wife. 'You might only have birthed one of 'em, but they are both as valuable to me.'

'Is there a problem here, gents?' Mike said, joining the group. Cynthia backed away at the sight of the policeman.

'Nothing to worry about, officer,' David said politely. 'This man and his wife were just leaving.'

Fred and Cynthia left the bar. David noticed that the other squaddies followed quickly behind while giving the policeman a wary look.

'Is there a problem?' Mike asked, seeing the tense look in his friend's face.

'There could be, Mike. Can you spare me five minutes before you go on duty?'

The pavement outside Saint Paulinus church in Crayford was packed with friends and family, there to see Ruby Caselton marry Bob Jackson and to wish them well in their future life together. The gentle May sunshine warmed the well-wishers, who chatted in excitement, not only because a wedding between two senior citizens was something to behold, but also because the day brought to an end six years of hostilities in Europe and was a time of celebration.

'Well, the sun shines on the righteous,' Vera said as she stood by the lychgate of Saint Paulinus church. 'I don't think I've ever attended a Caselton wedding where the Lord didn't make the weather glorious.'

'While she made a pact wiv the devil ter turn everything sour,' Maisie whispered to her husband with a grin as she pushed the pram through the narrow gates, trying hard not to wake the twins. 'Now, try and put a smile on yer face fer a while, eh?'

'I was wondering if the girls were all right,' David said, glancing about for any sign of uninvited guests. He'd decided not to say anything to his wife until after the wedding.

'They'll be fine. Freda's in charge of 'em at Ruby's house, and Sarah's 'elping her. They take more notice of her than they do me,' she grinned. 'Just be thankful we're free of three kiddies fer a little while. It's luxury, ain't it?'

'We can always trust Vera to come up with the right words,' Bob Jackson laughed as he arrived along with Mike and Gwyneth. Shaking hands with the guests, he made his way slowly towards the church.

'Not having any last-minute nerves, Dad?' Mike asked, looking at his dad's jovial expression.

'There's not one nerve in my body. I've waited for this day for a while now, and unless something happens in the next fifteen minutes to stop Ruby arriving on time, then my plans to invade and capture Ruby Caselton will have succeeded.'

'You've done better than Hitler ever did,' Alan said as they reached the church where he was handing out hymn books. 'Who'd have thought the coward would top himself rather than face trial for all his sins?'

'He will face his trial, never you fear,' the vicar said as he shook hands with Bob and welcomed him inside the church.

'I'm a friend of the bride,' Vera said, hurrying up behind. She was followed by Sadie, who was trying valiantly to hold on to a lively Arthur.

'Ah, Mrs Munro, it's been a while since you graced our doors,' the vicar said, stepping aside to allow her through.

'If you wrote livelier sermons, you might see more of me. For now I'll stick to funerals and weddings,' she told him, heading for the front pews and overtaking other guests as she did so.

A young chorister hurried up to the vicar and whispered in his ear. 'It seems our blushing bride has arrived. I'll leave you in the capable hands of your best man; or should that be best son?' He chuckled at his own joke as he hurried away.

'No turning back now, Dad,' Mike said as they knelt to pray.

'I've not changed my mind, although this kneeling lark is playing the devil with my knees,' Bob said. 'I must say, David is looking a bit on the glum side. Have him and Maisie had a falling out?'

Mike looked over his shoulder to check who was sitting behind them. One never knew when Vera Munro would appear to pick up a juicy morsel of gossip. 'It can wait. I don't want to worry you on your wedding day.'

'Well, now you have. So spit it out before Ruby gets down the aisle and I have other things on my mind,' Bob said.

'He's had a run-in with Maisie's brother, Fred. He turned up in the Prince of Wales last night and is threatening to return there this evening.'

'Why is he threatening to turn up? All are welcome at our party.'

'He's not wanting to come and join in the celebrations. He wants money off David – otherwise he's taking his girls away. The pair of them aren't fit parents.'

'I thought the wife had sodded off with an American?'

'She's back. I got a look at them last night and they are quite a pair, I can tell you. You'd not want them to look after a dog.'

Bob thought for a moment. 'Make sure you tell Douglas and Alan, and between us we can keep an eye on David. Best not tell Maisie, or she'll kill her brother with her bare hands. We can have Sarah and Gwyneth keep an eye on the two children so they're safe.'

'I'll see to that. I did tip them off at the station that there could be trouble brewing this evening; but with the world and his neighbour celebrating today, they're going to be hard pressed to help with our little problem. One thing did cross my mind, so I'm having it checked out –

I'm thinking our mate Fred and his merry band of friends may have gone AWOL from the army.'

'Good thinking, son. We'd best get off our knees now, or people will wonder what we've got to pray about,' Bob said. 'I don't want trouble on my wedding day, so I trust you and our friends to look out for Maisie and David as well as the nippers.'

'You look a picture,' Freda sighed as she handed Ruby her bouquet, 'and these flowers are the finishing touch. Bob was crafty growing them without you knowing,' she added, taking a final sniff before bending down to talk to Georgina, who was hopping about on one foot and taking no notice of what was going on around her. 'Now, be a good girl and copy me when we walk down the aisle. Do you understand?' Georgina nodded her head and carried on hopping whilst poking a finger up her nose.

'The child's a lost cause,' Sarah sighed. 'I knew it would be a mistake having her as one of your bridesmaids, Nan. If you want, I can take her inside the church to sit with Alan?'

'You'll do no such thing. I don't care if she hops or dances down the aisle. Those children play a big part in my life and I want them with me when I get married. Our Pat is already miffed that I didn't ask her girls to be bridesmaids. I'm beginning to wonder if I made a mistake. You know how she can moan for weeks on end. She grumbled that I invited Maisie's three girls over some of my grandkids, but when those girls live in my street and Maisie made the frocks it's the least I can do. Can you do a head count, Sarah? I'm sure we have some missing. I just want to peep inside the church to check that everyone is there.'

'You can't do that, Nan. Bob might see you, and that would be unlucky. Enough things have held up the pair of you marrying, let alone you starting off married life with a curse hanging over you both.'

'Who are you looking for? I may be able to take a quick look for you?' Freda asked.

'It doesn't matter,' Ruby said. 'Here comes the vicar to give me a pep talk. Don't let him go on too long, Sarah. We've still got a pile of things to do when we get home if we're to feed all this lot.'

'I told you, it's all taken care of, Nan. Maureen's been busy, and she said she'd get stuck in as soon as we're home if there was anything left to do. I think it's wonderful of you to share your wedding reception with the whole street.'

'I couldn't really have a party in my own home knowing the rest of Alexandra Road were celebrating the end of war in Europe without us, could I? Besides, we'd lose some of the guests once the singing and dancing started and they opened the barrel of beer I see being set up in front of number fourteen.'

'Excuse me, are we too late for this wedding?' a man with a Brummie accent asked as he tapped Freda on the shoulder.

Freda turned with a surprised look on her face, and shrieked with delight. 'Lenny, what are you doing here? How did you know . . . ?' She was lost for words as her brother hugged her tight and lifted her off her feet.

'Someone wrote me a letter and invited us to the

wedding. I made it to shore by the hair of my teeth, and then the train was held up with everyone trying to get to London for the celebrations . . .'

'We?' Freda asked, looking past her brother to where a pretty blonde woman stood looking shy. 'Sally? It's nurse Sally who we met when Mum was ill,' she explained to Sarah, who had met the woman on several occasions and liked her very much.

'Sis, I'd like you to meet Mrs Leonard Smith. We married on my last leave home two months ago, but wanted to tell you in person. You don't mind missing our wedding, do you? It was just the two of us and a couple of witnesses, as I only had a twenty-four-hour leave.'

'Of course I don't mind. There is a war on . . .' She stopped as her friends laughed at her. 'I suppose we can't use that excuse anymore,' she grinned.

Freda struggled out of his arms to greet her new sister-in-law, and Sally whispered into her ear as they hugged. 'I'm going to be an auntie? Already . . . ?'

Ruby wiped her eyes on the back of her white glove. She loved a happy ending. 'Now, you two get yourself into the church. There's a man in there most likely wondering what the hell is going on out here. He may even think I've changed my mind again.'

The girls laughed as they lined the children up behind Ruby, and George stepped from the back of the church to take his mother's arm. They started to walk slowly up the aisle as the organ struck a note. Sarah gave her daughter a warning look as the child reached up to poke her finger back up her nose.

'This must be the happiest day I've ever known,' Freda whispered to her friend. 'It's a perfect day. From now on, we won't have to live in fear or be worried for the future.'

13

'I take my hat off to Ruby, she certainly knows how to organize a do,' Alan said as he joined George, who was sitting on a bench set up in front of number thirteen.

The families who lived in the two long terraces of houses that faced each other across Alexandra Road had pulled out all the stops to mark the end of war in Europe. A hotchpotch of chairs and tables, including some made from doors taken off their hinges and propped up with bricks, ran down the middle of the road. Women had brought out their best tablecloths and cutlery along with all the chairs they owned, so that every child and older resident had a seat. The tables groaned under the weight of food; families who had more shared with neighbours who had struggled through the past six years. Cans of food that had been hidden away – no questions asked – were produced and passed to the team of women buttering bread. It might still have been grey National Bread, but it was eaten with relish by those looking towards a future free from war. With only days to prepare, children had made festive headwear, even if it was boat-shaped and folded from newspapers, while men and women took their best clothes out of mothballs in honour of the nationwide party to beat all parties.

Above the large bay windows, bunting was hung from each bedroom window across to the facing house on the other side of the road. Maisie had shown neighbours how to cut and sew scraps of rag, old fabric or in fact anything that would flutter in the breeze, to make the peacetime celebrations extra special.

'It was generous of Ruby to donate all the food from her wedding reception to the street celebrations. It's made a big difference to the day. She seems to have a bottomless bucket of energy today,' Alan added.

'She certainly does,' George smiled, as he watched his mum ushering the children of Alexandra Road into a row for the judging of a fancy dress competition. 'Where did the parents find all these costumes? They seem to be quite inventive,' he grinned. 'Look at Maisie's eldest three dressed as the ARP, the Navy and the Air Force. What a sight, even if the costumes are hanging off them.'

Alan chuckled. 'I had a hand in that. Maisie borrowed my RAF jacket and cap, as it was smaller than David's. The ARP items were donated by Bob; the Navy by Freda's brother. The poor chap had to borrow some clothes off me as he was wearing his uniform to the wedding.'

George laughed. 'No one argues with Maisie.'

Alan looked more serious. 'Let's hope not.' He went on to explain to his father-in-law what had happened at the pub the night before with Maisie's brother, and how Mike had asked them to step in and keep an eye out for David at the party that evening.

'Count me in,' George said, looking more than a little

angry. 'As you know, I think of Maisie and Freda like my own daughters, and I wouldn't see one hair on their heads harmed. She's never said much about Fred, but for a bloke to not get in touch for over two years means he's not the best of fathers. I'll do all I can to help out. But best we don't let on to Mum, or she'll want to sort the chap out with her own bare hands.'

Alan nodded his head solemnly. 'She certainly would. They broke the mould after Ruby was born. It would be awful if she was carted off to the clink for causing an affray,' he grinned.

George guffawed, causing people nearby to smile in his direction. It was certainly a day for happiness. 'No doubt it would be her new stepson who would do the arresting.'

'I think Mike would rather break the law than arrest Ruby.' Alan joined in with the laughter. 'But where's Pat and the kids? They're usually running amok by now, with Pat trying to keep them under control.'

'She hurried off home. It seems the farm has a bit of a do on to celebrate the end of the war and she's doing the catering. She's also got to help with the milking.'

'Blimey, who'd be a farmer's wife?'

'Not me and that's for sure.' George started to laugh, and Alan joined in.

Once the men had calmed down and taken gulps from their glasses of beer, George looked about to check no one could overhear them. 'Have you come to any conclusions about Sandy? I heard you went Scottish country dancing with the pair of them, which in my book means you deserve a medal. I take it nothing happened to cause you alarm?'

Alan also glanced around, mindful that Vera from up the road had an annoying habit of turning up just as the juiciest piece of gossip was being discussed. 'Yes, my toes suffered the day after, I can tell you. There was something I wanted to tell you about. What with the women having us jump through hoops for the past couple of days, I've not had chance to speak with you alone.' He went on to explain about seeing Sandy talking to the stern-looking man, and the few words that he'd heard. 'It could be nothing at all, I suppose. After all, Sandy does travel up to London to socialize with his church friends. On the face of it, I know it might seem unlikely he's involved in any skulduggery whilst doing the Gay Gordons.'

George thanked Alan for the information and looked thoughtful.

'You do think there's something in it all, don't you?' Alan asked, looking hopeful. 'I say, sir, do you think he's a spy? Is our Freda in danger? Are there even spies, now we're no longer at war?'

'There will always be spies, and as for Sandy being one . . . I just don't know. What you heard certainly doesn't sound good. Perhaps he's been caught up in something and now has doubts. As for Freda being in danger, I'm wondering more whether the girl's heart will be broken? She's clearly smitten with the man, that's for sure. She's not left his side all day. I'll take what you've said back to the people who know best, and all we can do is keep our eyes peeled.'

'While we wait to pick up the pieces when the kid's

romance fails,' Alan muttered angrily. 'I think that angers me even more than Sandy possibly stealing secrets from Vickers. I'll go have a word with them, and keep up the pretense that I like the chap.'

'Be careful, Alan. We don't need any heroes. If the lad is guilty of anything, he will be caught given time. I'm going to make a quick telephone call. I knew that Mum having a telephone would come in handy one day. Then I'll give Bob a hand with that beer barrel.' He nodded to where Bob was rolling a fresh barrel up the road to the makeshift bar.

Alan wandered across the road and sat down next to Freda. 'Hello, kid, are you having a good time?' he asked, draping his arm across her shoulder in a brotherly way.

'It's been marvellous,' she sighed, 'and we still have the wedding reception in the pub to look forward to this evening. I'll probably sleep all day tomorrow.'

'Lucky you. It's the first day of my new business, and I have work to be getting on with.'

'Sandy, did I tell you that Alan is setting up his own motorbike repair business?' she said, turning to her boyfriend, who was staring ahead without taking in what was happening around him. 'Wake up, sleepyhead,' she joshed, nudging his arm when he didn't respond.

'Sorry,' Sandy said. 'I was miles away.'

'No need for apologies – it's been a bittersweet day for many of us. I've been thinking back to my comrades who never made it through the war. You must feel the same, as well as having your family living so far away. Will you be going to see them some day soon?' Alan asked, hoping he wasn't being too inquisitive. He had a boyish hankering to solve this spy problem for his father-in-law.

'That would be lovely, Sandy, perhaps I could take a few days off and visit your family with you? I've never been to Scotland,' Freda said, looking thrilled with her idea.

'No!' Sandy said, getting to his feet. 'I don't remember my colleagues, and I won't be heading to Scotland any-time soon.'

'Steady on, old boy, I was only being friendly. I believe it's not uncommon to forget what happens when we have a nasty accident. I was the same when I came down over France. I had a right headache for a while and could easily have ended up in the hands of the Nazis,' Alan said with feeling.

'Alan, I'm so sorry. You've never really said what happened. Well, not to your friends anyway. Was it really that awful?' Freda slipped her arm through Alan's. 'I'd hate to think of those brutish Nazis giving you a bad time.'

'It's all in the past now, kid. The war's over in Europe and we can start afresh. What are your plans, Sandy?' he asked the man who was still standing in front of them.

Sandy sat down again and seemed to relax. 'I plan to finish my training at Vickers and then go travelling. There are places I'd like to see before I settle down.' Again his eyes seemed to be staring into space.

Alan could see that Freda was upset, and tried to lighten the situation. 'Hey, kid, when I'm set up and running properly you can come and work for me selling second-hand motorbikes and charming my customers. What do you say?'

Freda gave him a watery grin. 'I'll hold you to that, but I want my name over the shop. No one's going to take advantage of me and get away with it,' she said, defiantly shooting a glance towards Sandy, who seemed oblivious to the conversation.

'Then it's a deal. Gilbert and Smith it is,' he said, holding out his hand.

'Make it Smith and Gilbert and I'll agree,' she said, extending her own small hand.

'You strike a hard bargain, Miss Smith,' Alan grinned, giving her a tight hug. 'It may take a few years, but I promise you there's a place for you in my business. We've got to keep the business in the family, and you are part of my family.' Alan knew that at that moment he'd have promised Freda the crown jewels just to see her happy. He swore to himself that no man would ever upset the girl again.

'What's all this, then?' Sarah said, joining the pair of them. 'Shunt up so I can sit down,' she added, as they all moved along the bench to make room for her.

'Alan's just given me a share in his new business,' Freda said cheekily.

'Considering he has just the one bike in for repair and I'm having to go back to working at Woolies to support the family, you may find he's being over-generous,' Sarah grinned. 'However, if the day comes when he can hire staff I'll remind him of his promise. That's if I can have my cottage with roses round the door as well,' she laughed.

'Your wish is my command, my love,' Alan said. 'Do you have any other wishes?'

Sarah cocked her head on one side and thought for a

moment. 'I'd like two, if I may? First, enough new fabric for Maisie to deck us out for the summer months, without us having to worry about make do and mend or those wretched coupons. And the second is that I'd like to be a bridesmaid again.'

Alan looked shocked. 'You've only just been a bridesmaid for your nan, and not many women can say that,' he laughed. 'Who is the lucky bride next time?'

'I was an attendant for Nan, as she didn't want grown-up bridesmaids. I was there more to check that the girls all behaved – not that I could stop our Georgie picking her nose in front of everyone. I could cheerfully have swapped her for one of the other bridesmaids.'

'If it's any help, Mum said I was the same at that age,' Alan grinned. 'I thought she was most endearing.'

'Oh, you would,' Sarah scoffed.

'So who is the chosen bride?' he asked, getting back to his wife's request.

Sarah grinned in delight. 'Freda. I want to walk down the aisle behind my friend here when she marries Sandy.'

Freda and Alan fell silent as Sandy took one look at his girlfriend and walked away.

'Oops, have I said the wrong thing?' Sarah asked, looking worried. 'Me and my big mouth – it must have been that port and lemon Bob made for me, it was rather strong. I can't keep my mouth shut when I've had a couple.'

Freda watched Sandy walk away from them up the street to where it joined Manor Road and disappear from view. 'Don't worry about him. To be honest, he's been a bit of a bore of late. If he's not quizzing me about George he's wanting to go Scottish country dancing at that dreary church hall in London. Would you want to go there every week?' she asked Alan.

'It's not my cup of tea, kid, but when you love someone you go along with their hobbies, even if you aren't keen yourself. Take my Sarah here. She hates my motorbike and when we were courting she refused to ride pillion after the first time I took her out, but did I give up and find a replacement? No. I stuck in there even though she broke my heart,' he said, putting his hand to his chest and feigning sadness.

Freda bent her head in shame. 'But he hates my hobbies. He's even started to ridicule me being a Tawny Owl and organizing outings for the Brownies. The only time we ever have a sensible conversation is when he asks about George and his work at Vickers. We've got to the point that when we go to the country dancing evenings, he often wanders off to talk to friends and leaves me to make conversation with all the old biddies.'

Sarah reached out and stroked her young friend's arm. 'I had such hopes for this one,' she said, looking sad. 'Sandy seemed quite normal when we went dancing with you.'

Freda shrugged her shoulders. 'It was rather strange, as he was more attentive that evening – almost as if he was putting on a front for your benefit. I thought nothing much of it because I was enjoying the attention. He is rather a good kisser,' she added with a smile.

'Oh, you ladies!' Alan joked, pretending to look shocked and fanning his face.

'Oh, Alan, stop it,' Sarah said. 'We should be thinking

of Freda at a time like this! Do you think you should go after him?'

'I honestly don't think I do,' Freda said. 'Let him go off in a huff. If he comes back with his tail between his legs, I'll give him the old heave-ho. Life's too short to be bored.' She got to her feet, putting on a brave grin. 'Who wants another drink? After that I'm going to join in the dancing with my brother and his wife. This is a party I want to enjoy. It's not often we have a chance to celebrate the end of a war and a wedding all at the same time.'

Alan caught Freda's arm as she started to walk away. 'Before you go off to be merry, can you tell me if you know where Sandy lives?'

Freda looked puzzled. 'I do, not that I've been there. I'm not that kind of girl. He recently moved lodgings as his landlady was moving away. He's got a room down West Street, near the Ship.'

'Would you do me a favour?' Alan said, with no trace of his earlier light-hearted humour.

'What's this about, Alan?' Sarah asked, seeing her husband's serious face.

Alan ignored Sarah's question and kept looking at Freda. 'It may be nothing, but would you go and have a word with George? Tell him all that Sandy has asked you about him and Vickers?'

Freda nodded her head. 'If you think I should, then I'll do it right now. Do you know where he is?'

'In Ruby's front room, making a telephone call. Let's just say that what you tell him could solve a very big problem for George, and for Vickers.'

'Now will you tell me what's going on?' Sarah asked, as they watched Freda disappear into number thirteen.

'Later, my love; let's go dance and enjoy ourselves for a while, shall we? I'm hoping there's been enough excitement for one day,' Alan added, looking to where David Carlisle was twirling his wife around the makeshift dance floor to Maureen singing, *When the lights go on again all over the world* . . .

'Sshh, listen: Winston's about to speak,' Ruby said to the people crammed into the front room of number thirteen.

'I've not missed it have I, Nan?' Sarah said as she perched on the arm of Ruby's chair, wiping her hands on a tea towel.

'No, love, he's about to speak . . .'

'My dear friends, this is your hour. This is not victory of a party or of any class. It's a victory of the great British nation as a whole . . .'

'Do you remember when we sat in this very spot listening to the broadcast from the coast as the lads came home from Dunkirk?' Sarah whispered to Ruby.

Ruby slipped her arm round her granddaughter's waist. 'I do, my love. It seems such a long time ago now.'

'There we stood, alone. Did anyone want to give in? Were we down-hearted? The lights went out and the bombs came down. But every man, woman and child in the country had no thought of quitting the struggle . . .'

Sarah leant her cheek against the elderly woman's. 'Mum would have loved all of this. Your wedding, the parties.'

'She would have taken over and run the whole show and given Winston a run for his money.'

'I say that in the long years to come not only will the people of this island but of the world, wherever the bird of freedom chirps in human hearts, look back to what we've done and they will say 'do not despair, do not yield to violence and tyranny, march straightforward and die if need be – unconquered.'

'For all her faults I miss her so much. I can see her in our Georgina,' Sarah said, fighting hard not to cry.

'I hope it's not when the child has her finger poked up her nose,' Ruby whispered back, causing Sarah to choke on her unshed tears.

'Now we have emerged from one deadly struggle – a terrible foe has been cast on the ground and awaits our judgement and our mercy. But there is another foe who occupies large portions of the British Empire, a foe stained with cruelty and greed – the Japanese.'

The room was filled with boos and a few slurred swear words from the men, whilst their womenfolk scolded and others hushed them up.

'I rejoice we can all take a night off today and another day tomorrow.'

'But I have to open my store tomorrow,' Betty wailed from across the room.

'Stay home and put yer feet up,' Maisie called back to a round of cheers.

Tomorrow our great Russian allies will also be celebrating victory and after that we must begin the task of rebuilding our health and homes, doing our utmost to make this country a land in which all have a chance, in which all have a duty, and we must turn ourselves to fulfil our duty to our own countrymen, and to our gallant allies of the United States who were so foully and treacherously attacked by Japan.

'We will go hand in hand with them. Even if it is a hard struggle we will not be the ones who will fail.'

Family and friends fell silent until the national anthem started to play and then every man and woman in the room stood to their feet and joined in singing as loudly as their voices would allow. As the last notes reverberated around the front room of number thirteen, they raised their glasses.

'To peace!'

'George, hold up a minute!' Alan called out as he spotted his father-in-law coming out of his mum's house in Crayford Road and crossing over towards the Prince of Wales public house, where the family's private party was to be held.

George held back to wait for Alan while Maureen

continued on, calling out, 'I'll see you in there. I have a few things to do before the bride and groom arrive.' He lit his pipe as he watched Alan cross the road. 'Hello, son, are you ready for the next session?'

'It's been a bit of a long day, hasn't it? I've left Sarah round at her nan's putting the kids to bed. Vera's Sadie is going to watch all the children in one house. She'll have an easy job, as they are all shattered after the church service and the street party this afternoon. I'm fair jiggered myself.'

George nodded as he puffed on his pipe. 'I'm looking forward to my slippers and cocoa as well, but hopefully we'll get a second wind for this evening's festivities. Did you want me for something?'

'Yes, I was wondering if Freda spoke to you about Sandy?'

'She did, although she became quite upset. The poor kid blamed herself for bringing the man into the family group.'

Alan was indignant. 'She has nothing to blame herself for and I'll tell her as much. Sandy saw an opportunity to ingratiate himself with the family, and our Freda simply fell in love.'

George relit his pipe thoughtfully. 'It does cloud the situation somewhat. I couldn't tell her much, apart from that we're having problems at the works and I believe Sandy is involved. Of course I had to remind her not to tell a soul apart from you. I hope I didn't speak out of turn?'

'No sir, I'll help all I can. Who'd have thought we had a spy in our midst?' Alan grinned.

George laughed. He enjoyed the company of his daughter's husband and trusted him implicitly. 'I'd not go as far as calling Sandy a spy. My thoughts are he's been sucked in by these people, and from what you overheard, he could well have two minds about continuing. Young men can be idealistic and more than a little hot-headed at times. I like to think he's more than fond of our Freda, and that has helped him see sense.'

'I do believe you're right – but if he has passed on information to the enemy, and even if the war is over, I'm assuming he will be in hot water?'

'Boiling hot water,' George said.

'So what happens next?'

'I've ask Freda to act as if nothing has happened and to try and bring him along to the party this evening as they'd planned. A couple of my . . .' George coughed. '. . . Let's say, my colleagues will be at the party this evening and will take him in for questioning. It will be done quietly and discreetly. No one apart from us will be aware.'

'Freda will be aware,' Alan replied, feeling like a complete rotter for playing a part in the demise of his young friend's romance.

'If it comes to nothing Sandy will then be able to continue with his job and life, rather than have friends and colleagues thinking he has done wrong.'

'He has done wrong though, hasn't he?'

'Yes, enough to be serving time, I would think.'

Alan ran his hand through his hair. 'What a mess, and what a bloody waste of such a talented young man. Do you think I should go with Freda to meet him?'

George shook his head. 'Whatever we do, we mustn't

create suspicion. Freda used Mum's telephone to place a call through to his landlady. She spoke at length to Sandy and convinced him to meet her at the party. He said he was a little jealous of her friends and her not spending more time with him alone. Freda bit her tongue and went along with what he had to say.'

'I'll keep an eye out, just the same. I'd not want the kid to come to harm.'

George slapped him on the back. 'Good lad, but don't forget we are also looking out for Maisie's brother. We're going to need eyes in the backs of our heads at this rate.' He grinned wryly as they walked inside to join the guests who'd already assembled in the private hall at the back of the public bar.

'Bandits at nine o'clock,' Alan hissed at his father-in-law, who looked around blankly.

'Oh, that's an RAF term, isn't it?' he chuckled before turning round to see a group of squaddies sitting round a table which was covered in empty pint pots. 'Hmm, they've already knocked back a fair few. That doesn't bode well.'

'You look worried, sir,' Lenny said as he joined them at the entrance to the hall. 'I've been watching those fellas myself. They've been a bit mouthy to others in the services. I hope they don't spoil the wedding. Mrs Caselton . . . I mean Mrs Jackson has been good to me in the past. I'd not want to see anyone spoil her day. I'm here if you need my help,' he said quietly before leading his wife in to join Freda, who was sitting alone with Sandy and looking quite miserable.

'I said I'm sorry for walking off and leaving you,' Sandy said, trying to take Freda's hand.

She snatched it back and folded both hands in her lap. She was aware that even as they sat there, things were going on that might take Sandy away from her. The bravado she'd felt when telling Alan she was fed up with her boyfriend, and the bravery she'd shown when speaking to George, had now left her, and she felt bereft. Closing her eyes, she tried hard to remember how she'd done her bit for her country and the sights she'd seen working for the Fire Service. She imagined what it must have been like for Irene to die as she did, when the V2 landed on New Cross Woolworths; and try as she might, she could never forget what had happened at Bethnal Green and how she had almost become one of those poor people trampled underfoot in the panic to get down to the underground station and safety. No, she could not forgive anyone for helping the enemy who had brought such tragedy to the country she loved so much. Even if Sandy's kisses made her tingle and she felt safe and happy in his arms, she could never forgive him if he was a traitor, and she'd do her utmost to see him locked up. Just get through this evening and it will all be over, she told herself. Then I will be alone . . .

'There you are,' Sally said, sitting down next to her new sister-in-law and putting her arm through Freda's. 'We've had no time at all to speak and I have so much to tell you. I hope you aren't unhappy that we married without inviting you?'

Freda snapped back from her sad thoughts and smiled at the pretty woman who had kept her sane during the long months she'd spent in Birmingham watching her mum's life fade away. The one good thing to come out of that time had been seeing romance blossom between her brother and Sally. 'I could never be unhappy that you've married my brother,' she said, perking up at once as she realized she would never be alone after all, because for all intents and purposes she now had a sister. 'Now, tell me what your plans are and where you are going to live?'

Sally could hardly contain her excitement. 'As you know, our Lenny is going to remain in the navy, and that means I'm going to be alone for long periods of time,' she began.

'Gosh, I'd not thought of that,' Freda said. 'I promise I'll come and visit you in Birmingham as much as I can . . .'

'You don't have to,' Sally butted in. 'Lenny wants us to live here in Erith. We are going to look for rooms while we are staying at the Wheatley hotel. Perhaps you could help us?'

'Oh, I'd love nothing more,' Freda said as her eyes shone with happiness. 'There's so much to look forward to,' she added, trying hard not to think of Sandy sitting at her other side.

They looked up from their conversation as George stepped onto the small raised stage at one end of the hall. 'Ladies and gents, if I could have your attention please,' he said, raising his voice so those at the back of the hall could hear. 'I've been told that the bride and groom have arrived and we have a special treat for them.' He turned to the side of the room and nodded to a group of elderly men who were standing patiently and watching George for their cue. They filed into three rows in front of the stage. 'With no expense spared, and all the way from the public bar, I wish to welcome the members of Erith's own police force male voice choir, who will greet the happy couple with a song or two.'

An excited murmur rippled through the room as the double doors to the bar opened and Mike ushered in his dad and stepmother. Ruby stood entranced as the men broke into song, hardly noticing as Mike led her and Bob to two seats positioned so they could watch the choir. Bob reached out and took her hand as the refrain from Cole Porter's 'Night and Day' filled the hall. As the guests burst into spontaneous applause the choir went straight into their second song, 'If You Were the Only Girl in the World', and everyone joined in.

'Did you know about this?' Ruby asked Bob as she wiped her eyes. 'I've never heard anything so wonderful in my life.'

'Wait until your hear this,' he said, getting to his feet and joining the choir. 'If I may say a few words? I promise it won't take long, Ruby,' he said, as some of the choir ribbed him for being under his wife's thumb. 'A few years ago, a young woman came into the lives of those of us who live in Alexandra Road. She didn't speak a lot in those days, as I recall,' he added as he searched the room, seeking out his daughter-in-law and son. 'We couldn't have been more delighted when her mum married our Mike and I had a ready-made granddaughter. This song is for our little Welsh granddaughter, Myfanwy, as it was the first words I sang to her when we first met.' Bob stepped back into the ranks of his fellow choristers and the lilting tune of the well-known Welsh song 'Myfanwy' filled the pub. If guests had been moved before, they were now openly wiping their eyes as the rich tones of the choir soared into the heavens. As the song came to an end young Myfanwy ran into her granddad's arms to say thank you.

David, Douglas and Alan carried trays of beer to the choir, who gratefully toasted their fellow member on his nuptials.

'Well, I hope we don't have any more surprises this evening, or I'm going to be a complete wreck,' Ruby said as she joined Sarah and Maisie, and gratefully accepted a port and lemon her granddaughter passed to her.

'I've been bawling me eyes out,' Maisie said, checking her face in a small gold compact and reaching into her handbag for her lipstick. 'Who'd 'ave thought a group of old codgers could sing so beautifully?'

'Watch your mouth,' Ruby said, trying to look stern but failing. 'One of those old codgers is my old codger. It's all legal now,' she grinned, holding out her hand to show off the gold band.

'I hope that's not from Woolworths,' Betty said as she joined them.

'Here, budge up and make room for Betty. You look ready to burst,' Ruby said, fussing around the heavily pregnant woman. 'Perhaps it would have been best if you'd stayed home and put your feet up?'

'I'm fine,' Betty smiled. 'I wouldn't have missed this party for the world. What a wonderful start to the evening!'

'It's about to get even better,' Sarah said as she spotted

her dad helping Maureen onto the stage. 'I do love it when Maureen sings. She has such a lovely voice.'

'Yours ain't so bad,' Maisie said. 'Why, we should 'ave set ourselves up as a singing group. We'd 'ave made a bomb entertaining the troops. England's answer ter the Andrews Sisters,' she laughed.

'Count me out,' Freda said as she and Sally joined the group, having left Sandy behind at their table. 'Has everyone met my sister-in-law, Sally? She married our Lenny a little while ago and they are going to come and live in Erith. Isn't that just wonderful?'

''Ello, love,' Maisie said, getting up to give Sally a kiss. 'We met when we all came up ter see Freda when she was in Birmingham. I'm that pleased ter know young Lenny 'as settled down. He was a bit of a scallywag in 'is younger days.'

Freda raised her eyebrows in mock horror. 'Watch it, Maisie, you might frighten the poor girl off – and her in the family way as well.'

'Lenny's told me all about his younger years, and it will take more than that to frighten me off,' Sally smiled, placing her hand on her stomach. 'I couldn't be happier.'

The women all congratulated her, and the conversation turned to offers of baby clothes and help with finding a new home.

'You wouldn't like a job working in Woolworths, would you?' Betty asked tentatively.

Sarah, Maisie and Freda burst out laughing. 'You never miss an opportunity,' Sarah said, before explaining to Sally that Betty was the manager of the local store where the three girls had first met.

'I will need something to do once Lenny goes back to sea, and I'm not sure the local hospital will take me on as a nurse, what with me expecting a child.'

'Oh, of course – you are the young nurse,' Betty said. 'You must forgive me. My memory is appalling at the moment. But if you do find yourself needing a job, even a part-time one, then come along and see me.'

'But make it quick, as she's about ter leave and 'ave a baby,' Maisie pointed out. 'That's if she ever lets go of Woolworths.'

Up on the stage, Maureen had a word with the three-piece band before starting a medley of Glen Miller songs.

'Oh, it's "Moonlight Serenade", my favourite song. Where's Alan? It's time we had a dance.'

'They were all over the other side of the room talking to Lenny the last time I saw them,' Sally said.

'They're like a bunch of little boys when they get together,' Betty said, making the others laugh. 'There's your dad, if you'd rather dance with him,' she added, pointing to a side door where George was chatting with a couple of men in smart suits.

'He'll have to do,' Sarah grinned, getting to her feet and weaving through the dancers to where George was talking seriously to the men before nodding as they moved away. 'Come on, Dad. Have a dance with your daughter,' she said, linking her arm into his.

'In a moment, love – I've got some business to take care of first. Would you do me a favour and keep an eye on Freda for me? She may become a little upset.'

Sarah was puzzled. 'What do you mean, Dad? Why would she . . .' It was then she spotted the two men speaking to Sandy, who rose to his feet and picked up his hat. He looked over to where Freda was watching. It was as if there was no one else in the room as he gave her a smile and raised his hand in a salute. Sarah watched as Freda got to her feet and ran through the dancing couples, reaching Sandy just as the men led him through the door.

'Sandy, wait . . .'

George nodded to the two men, who let go of Sandy's arms so he could turn and speak to Freda.

'Where are they taking you?' she asked, looking frantically between George and the men, who remained silent.

'It doesn't matter,' Sandy said. 'It's best you forget me,' he added gently. 'You were too good for me – but believe me, I had dreams of changing my life and spending the rest of my years with you.'

Freda flung herself into his arms and sobbed as he pushed her away and turned to go with the men.

Sarah hadn't noticed Alan joining them until he put his arms around Freda and held her as Sandy was helped into a car outside the door and driven away.

'Can someone tell me what's going on?' Sarah demanded.

'Sshh; everything will be all right,' he soothed Freda as she sobbed. 'George will do all he can for him. Do you want to sit out here for a little while until you compose yourself?'

Freda shook her head. 'I'll be fine. I want to go inside and be with my friends, and I owe Sarah an explanation.' She wiped her eyes on the cuff of her cardigan and gave a tentative smile. 'Come on, let's go and celebrate this wedding, shall we?'

They'd not taken two steps inside the hall when there was a bloodcurdling scream from the public bar, followed by shouts and furniture breaking.

'Stay there,' Alan shouted at the women as he pushed his way through the wedding guests and disappeared into the pub area where the scream had come from.

14

Sarah looked on in horror as the men she held dear rushed out into the bar of the Prince of Wales, led by David Carlisle. One look towards where Maisie sat and she could see her friends were following their menfolk, apart from Ruby, who held onto Betty's arm to stop her. If there was a fight, it was no place for a woman who was due to give birth in the next month.

'Whatever could be happening?' Freda asked. 'Shall we . . . ?'

Sarah didn't need any second bidding, and the two girls hurried out to the bar to see the regular drinkers cowering back against the walls while a group of squaddies fought hand and fist with a dozen or so sailors.

'Blooming hell, it looks as though it's all kicked off in here,' Maisie said as she joined her friends. 'I s'pose high spirits are bound ter kick off after a day of celebrating, but look at all this damage. I'm not sure what good the landlord's going ter do with that truncheon,' she added, as the man headed out from behind the bar waving a police truncheon. Behind him, his wife was shouting into the telephone over the screams of the watching crowd.

'David, no!' Maisie cried out as she spotted her husband, alongside Douglas, Alan, Lenny and Mike, wading into the fracas. It was Freda and Sarah's turn to hold Maisie back as they tried to stop her going in to fight for her husband. 'David, come back!' she called out.

David could hear his wife, but he carried on. The landlord of the pub was a decent chap and didn't deserve to have his business destroyed by a bunch of drunks. He'd not given a thought to Maisie's brother until he'd pulled back a sailor from where he was pummelling a soldier who'd been forced to the floor and come face to face with his brother-in-law, his face covered in blood. David's heart plummeted to his boots as he saw the raw aggression in Fred's face, although his first thought was not of his own problems but of stopping the fight. Nearby he could see Alan wading in alongside Lenny – who fortunately was not in uniform, or things could have been much worse for the young man. He grabbed Fred by the lapels and pulled him to his feet.

Fred cuffed the blood running from his nose and gave a sardonic grin. 'Well, well, we meet again. I hope you've given thought to my request?' he said as they were both shoved by men fighting close by.

'Now is not the time or the place,' David said 'But I'll tell you this much. You'll not take those girls from Maisie and me, as they deserve better than you and that tart can give them. And you'll have no money from me. After this evening, you have more than proved your worth as a responsible human being.'

Fred growled like an angry animal and reached into his pocket, pulling out a flick knife.

David felt as though the world had turned to slow motion as Fred lunged at him. Nearby he could hear a sailor shout out 'He's got a knife!' and women began to scream. A few sailors piled onto Fred, who yelled out in pain before going silent. There was silence as the sailors got off Fred, who lay motionless on the floor, the knife now protruding from his chest.

'David, are you all right?' Douglas asked pulling him away from where Fred lay on the ground. 'Oh my God,' he said, looking at the blood spreading from David's arm and chest. 'Can someone help here, please?' he called out as David fell against him.

At once men started to run from the pub, one or two of them even climbing through a broken window to escape as the sound of police whistles could be heard approaching.

As the squaddies and sailors dispersed, Maisie scanned the scene, looking for David before spotting him being laid onto the tiled floor by Douglas and Alan. Lenny knelt over him, checking for injuries, before looking up and seeing his sister. 'Get Sally, and hurry,' he snapped before leaning back over the unconscious man.

Close by, George and Bob knelt at Fred's side checking for a pulse as the landlord held a tablecloth his wife had passed over the bar. By this time Maisie had reached her husband and thrown herself down beside his body. 'No, oh please God no,' she sobbed, shaking David to try and wake him. 'Don't leave me, David. I couldn't bear it if you left me and the kids. Do something . . . please, someone, do something,' she beseeched the men, who stood watching with tears in their eyes.

'He's not dead, Maisie,' Lenny said as he pulled her

away. 'Give my Sally room to take a look. The police and an ambulance are on their way. Everyone will do all they can. Come and sit here where you can see what's going on.' He indicated a wooden seat which seemed to be about the only one not broken. Sarah stepped in to help lead her distraught friend to sit down.

'Is that the bastard who injured me husband?' Maisie asked, as George went to cover Fred's body. 'Let me take a good look at him, so I can see the face I hope will be rotting in hell.' She left her seat and pushed the tablecloth from George's hand. For a moment she froze before shaking her head and moaning, 'No, no, no,' over and over again.

Sarah put her arms round her friend. 'Come and sit down. This won't do you any good, my love.'

Maisie pulled away and got closer to the body, giving it a hefty kick. 'You don't understand. None of you understand. This is me bastard brother, Fred, and I want ter know what the hell he's doing here – and why he stabbed me husband? One of you must know about this,' she glared, as the men present averted their eyes.

Sally pushed past the friends as they stood around David. 'Move back and give him some air, please,' she said as she pulled back his jacket and ripped open his shirt, which was now stained deep red. She looked puzzled as she examined the slash in his chest. 'This is a superficial wound – there must be another . . .'

Douglas squatted down beside her and handed her the knife that had been left lying beside Fred. 'Here, use this to cut his sleeve back. I saw the knife go towards the arm.'

Sally fumbled with the thick fabric, so he took the knife and deftly slit the material back to the area of David's elbow. Loosening the sleeve caused a fresh gush of blood to spurt out, spraying all in the vicinity. Sally leant on the puncture wound, which stopped the bleeding. 'I need to make a pad out of something so that we can keep the pressure on this wound,' she called out with authority.

Alan whipped the clean tablecloth off Fred's body and ripped a wide piece off the linen square, then folded it into a wad. 'Here, this should do, but let me do it. I'm stronger than you and can exert more pressure,' he said, without waiting for an answer. 'Maisie, come here and start talking to your husband. It would help if he was conscious and with us.' Douglas moved away a little and helped Maisie to her knees.

'David, it's me. What the hell are you doing down there, and look at the state of yer shirt! I'll 'ave an 'ell of a job getting that stain out,' she said, trying to keep her voice light and jokey. David mumbled a few words. She leant closer to listen. 'Come on, spit it out. You know I'm a bit Mutt and Jeff,' she said, squeezing his hand. She listened again to David's murmured reply and looked at Alan, who had sweat running from his brow as he kept up the pressure on David's arm. 'He says we 'ave ter stop Fred from taking the kids . . . Is that what this is all about?' she asked, taking in the wrecked pub and her brother's dead body nearby.

No one answered.

Freda sat with Ruby after telling Sally she was needed in the public bar. She was fearful of going back into the pub because of what she might see.

'You say someone's dead?' Ruby asked. Her face had turned pale and her hands shook. 'To think this would happen at my wedding, and on the day we were celebrating the end of the war in Europe. Please God not let it be someone we know,' she muttered, before realizing what she had said. 'Oh, Freda, I'm a selfish, selfish, woman; no one should die, not today of all days.'

Freda clung to the older woman and started to cry. 'It's all so awful,' she sobbed.

Maureen came over from the stage, where the three-piece band was playing a quiet waltz to calm the guests, although no one was dancing. 'Ruby, love, do you think we should tell everyone to go home under the circumstances? They can use the side door.'

Ruby nodded, too shocked to speak properly. 'Would you do that, please, and give our apologies for their evening being spoilt?'

'Darling, none of this is your doing,' Maureen said with sincerity. 'Some drunks in the bar have had a fight and smashed the place up.'

'But there's a man laying dead out there, and David has been injured. It looks bad. That's why I came for Sally's help, as she's a nurse,' Freda looked up with a tear-stained face.

'The dead man is Maisie's brother, Fred,' Sarah said as she joined her family and sat down on the other side of Ruby, who put her arm round her and held her close. 'I was told he was the one who stabbed David. There's blood everywhere.'

A low moan came from close by, and they turned as one to see a blonde woman slump down on a seat nearby and bury her head in her arms. 'I told him no good would come of all this,' she wailed.

'Do you think she was with Fred?' Sarah whispered.

'There's one way to find out,' Freda said, getting up from her seat and going to join the woman. 'Hello, are you by any chance related to Fred Dawson?' she asked the woman. 'I'm a friend of his sister, Maisie.'

The woman nodded, scrubbing her wet eyes with her hands, smearing mascara over her cheeks. 'I'm his wife, Cynthia. Did you know he's laying in there dead?'

Freda nodded. 'I hope you don't mind me asking, but I thought you left him and the girls and went away with an American?'

'Not that it's got anything to do with you, but it didn't work out, and then I bumped into Fred at a dance and we got talking and . . . well, you know what it's like.'

Freda didn't know what it was like at all, but she wasn't about to say so. 'You know your daughters are living with Maisie since Mrs Dawson passed away?'

'So Fred told me. I'll not mourn the old bag – she meant nothing to me.'

'But she'd been caring for your children. Weren't you worried at all as to their welfare?'

'Only the one of 'em is mine. I'm not the motherly type,' she glared at Freda. 'I wasn't cut out to be looking after kids.'

'So why were the pair of you here in Erith?'

Cynthia chewed her fingernail distractedly. 'Fred said there'd be some money coming our way if we let his sister 'ave the kids. We was due to collect it this evening, but he got tied up with some other soldiers, and then there was the fight. I told him I didn't want the kids back and they should be left where they were 'appy, but he was after the money from her rich husband.'

Freda had seen the squalid conditions Bessie and Claudette lived in when they were with Queenie Dawson in Bethnal Green. She doubted their life would be much better with Cynthia caring for them.

'So now it'll be just you and the two girls?' she said, as an idea took shape in her mind.

Cynthia looked appalled. 'How can I look after two kids? I only hung about because he said he'd see me all right when he got the dosh,' she said, reaching for her handbag.

'But what about the girls?'

'Maisie can have them. They won't remember me anyhow,' Cynthia said, getting to her feet to leave.

'Hang on a minute.' Freda reached out to stop her. 'Would you write something down to say you want Maisie and her husband, if he survives, to adopt your children?'

Cynthia's eye glinted. 'Would there be money involved?'

'I daresay, but you'd need to put something in writing to get the ball rolling. Do you have a piece of paper?'

Cynthia dug deep into her bag and pulled out a scrap of paper. 'This'll do. What shall I write?'

'Here – let me do it. As long as you sign your name that'll be all right,' Freda said as she started to write. 'Do you have an address where the money can be sent?'

'I've got a cousin over Woolwich way. She'll be my best contact,' Cynthia said as she watched Freda write, all thoughts of her dead husband having vanished from her mind.

Maureen and Sarah started to sort out the buffet table, making up parcels of food for the guests to take home with them, while Ruby stood at the side door thanking them for coming to celebrate the wedding and apologizing for a spoilt evening.

When there were just a few guests left, the women went back to their table to finish their drinks and wait for news from the bar.

'Hello, what's been happening here? I know I'm a bit late. Have I missed much?' Vera said as she appeared through the door where the guests hadn't long left.

'Not so you'd notice,' Ruby said without raising a smile.

'But Nan, you and Bob should be going off on your honeymoon today!' Sarah said with dismay as Ruby told her they had put off their trip in light of what had happened the day before.

'I'll not go off enjoying myself when this family is in turmoil. It's best I stay here and do all I can to help Maisie by looking after her kiddies while she's at the hospital sitting with David. It looks as though she'll be responsible for her brother's funeral as well.'

Sarah's face took on a determined look. 'Then I'll not go to work so I can give you a hand. Five kiddies is a lot to care for on your own.' She didn't add 'at your age', knowing Ruby would kill her. 'I'll stay and help you until I take Alan's sandwiches up to him. If you want, I can take Bessie and Claudette with me?'

'That would be a great help, love, thank you. Sadie will be back tomorrow and the girls will back at school, so things won't be so bad. It was good of your dad to pay for our trip to Whitstable. He said he can put it off for a week, and hopefully by then David will be on the mend.' She looked to where the black Bakelite telephone sat silently on the sideboard. 'I suppose no news is good news. I didn't want that thing here but it's been a godsend in recent days, although I still jump in the air when it rings.'

'I'm sure I would too, Nan. Now, whatever happens, you and Bob must go off on your trip next week. I've loved staying at the hotel, and you must visit the cafe and say you know us. The lady who owns it used to work at Woolies years ago.'

'I'll do that. My, but it's a small world, isn't it?' Ruby said thoughtfully.

'Now, what can I do to help?'

Ruby looked to where boxes and bags were stacked against one wall of the room. 'Would you be a dear and make a start on that lot? I thought we could bundle up some of the leftover food I put in the larder and give it to the neighbours. It seems such a shame to waste it all after no one got to eat last night.'

'Let me sort this pile out first, then I'll check the larder,' Sarah said as she looked at the boxes and parcels. 'Some of these have your name on the label. Do you think they're presents?'

Ruby frowned. 'Why would anyone give me a present?'

Sarah giggled. 'Because you and Bob were married yesterday, and your friends and guests would have liked to give a small token to commemorate your special day.'

Ruby looked ashamed. 'I never gave that a thought. How very nice of them.' She joined in with Sarah's mirth.

'It has been a long time since I got wed. This is all new to me.'

'Why don't I put the kettle on, and you sit at the table and open your presents? I can sort the girls out while you have a few minutes to yourself. By the way, where are they?'

'Up the garden with Bob – they're teaching the puppies to sit and beg. I don't think they'll have much luck; our Nellie doesn't take any notice of me, and her sisters are just as bad. The kids are enjoying themselves, though, and that's what counts.'

'I'll pop up and say hello, and take Georgie with me. Shall I ask Bob if he'd like to help open the presents?'

Ruby, who was about to unpick the string on the first parcel, thought for a moment. 'I suppose he should be involved,' she grinned, 'but tell him to hurry up.' She placed the rest of the parcels onto the large scrubbed table and marvelled at how generous people had been, when all she'd wanted to do was to share her happy day with everyone she knew. Instead the day had ended in disaster. Who'd have thought such a thing could happen? There they were, through the worst of the war, and this had to happen. Maisie had never said much about her brother. In fact, before the two girls had come to live with their auntie two years earlier, Fred had never been mentioned. What the hell was going to happen now? Ruby wondered. Deep in thought, she jumped when the front door opened. Putting her hand to her fluttering heart, she called out, 'Who is there?'

'It's me,' Freda called back.

'My goodness, you did give me a start,' Ruby said as

Freda came in, flinging off her coat and hat. 'I didn't hear you go out.'

'Sorry. I went round to the Baptist church to have a few words.'

Ruby nodded seriously. 'I sometimes have a few words with him upstairs. I don't know if it helps, but as I see things it can't hurt, can it?'

As miserable as Freda felt, her face twitched as she tried not to laugh. 'I went to speak to the Boys' Brigade leaders. They usually meet today, so I thought I'd see if I could catch one of them and have a few words about Sandy.'

'Sandy? It's funny you should mention him. With all the hoo-ha last night I didn't see him go home. Why would you want to have a word about him? Don't say you two have had words? With everything that's going on, I don't have time for lovestruck youngsters.'

Freda sat opposite Ruby and picked at a piece of string on one of the parcels. 'He's been arrested, Ruby. But because of what he'd done, I couldn't in all honesty have stayed friends with him,' she said with a weak smile.

'Sandy arrested? And him a God-fearing young man?' Ruby almost shouted.

'Goodness, whatever is all this noise?' Sarah asked as she came in the back door. 'Bob said to go ahead and open the presents yourself, and he'll watch the kids. So what's happened now?'

'Freda's young man has been arrested,' Ruby fumed. 'As if we haven't got enough on our plates right now.'

'I know all about it,' Sarah said. 'Alan explained it all to me last night when we eventually got to bed. It probably hurts right now, Freda, but you've done the best thing,' she said, giving her mate's hand a gentle squeeze.

'Is someone going to tell me what happened, or have I got to go down the police station and ask for myself?' Ruby said.

'They won't know much down there, unless Mike has said something,' Freda said. 'George's contacts from the ministry took him away during the wedding, just before that fight kicked off.'

'So George and Mike know . . . so that means they've told Maureen and Gwyneth. That just leaves me and Bob who are in the dark, then?'

Sarah gave Freda a look and tried hard not to smile. 'Dad told Bob, because he was worried about something happening at the party once he passed on the information to the ministry.'

Ruby had the good grace to smile, and soon the three were chuckling. 'That just leaves me and Vera,' she grinned. 'That's a turn up for the books, her not knowing something before everyone else.'

'I think we could all do with a cup of tea – then you can help me sort out the food parcels for the neighbours,' Sarah said to Freda. She stopped as she headed into the kitchen. 'Don't you start worrying about not having a boyfriend. Love will come along when you least expect it. As Nan is always saying, there are plenty of fish in the sea.'

'And look at me; I managed to hook myself a tiddler at my age,' Ruby grinned. 'Mind you, if I'd known it would mean receiving three identical cruet sets in the shape of chickens and eggs, I might just have put the wedding off a little longer,' she added, looking at the row of china cruets lined up on the table.

'Take a seat, Mrs Carlisle,' the consultant said as Maisie entered his office, followed by Douglas. She'd begged him to stay with her, so afraid was she of what the consultant would tell her.

'This is Mr Billington, a family friend. I 'ope you don't mind 'im staying ter listen ter what you 'ave ter say?' she asked. Maisie was still wearing her wedding outfit from the day before. Even though Douglas and Betty had collected fresh clothes for her, she'd not liked to leave her husband's bedside at the cottage hospital.

'Yes, I know Douglas well,' the consultant said, before coughing and running a finger round his collar as if it was starting to choke him.

Maisie looked between the two men and realized why they both looked uncomfortable. Douglas would no doubt collect the deceased from the hospital from time to time, and would be known to the staff. If she wasn't so tired she would have laughed out loud. She knew David would see the funny side. She must remember to tell him . . . 'Can you give me any news about me husband?' she asked, closing her eyes and praying that it wouldn't be bad news.

'You husband is a very sick man, Mrs Carlisle. The knife wound to his chest area was superficial, although there will always be a scar.'

Maisie breathed out. If the man was saying David would always bear a scar, that meant he wasn't about to die. She smiled. 'So he's going ter be all right?'

'It depends what you mean by all right. It was a very deep stab wound to his arm, and some damage has been done. The operation, when he first arrived last night, was successful to some extent, but I fear he will lose the use of most of his right arm. There will be more operations, and we are worried about infection setting in. This is going to take time and patience. I hope your husband is a patient man, Mrs Carlisle?'

Maisie couldn't take in all of what the consultant was telling her. The words *he will lose the use of most of his right arm* kept going round and round in her head.

'Do you have any questions?' he asked.

Maisie shook her head and got up to go. It was as if she was walking in a blur, not quite in touch with what was going on around her. She stopped and turned sharply. 'Can I stay wiv 'im?' she asked.

'We'd prefer you observe normal visiting hours. If there is any change, we'll contact you by telephone,' he said.

Douglas led her from the office and they headed out to his car in silence. 'I'll take you home so you can sleep. You look all in.'

'No, I don't want ter go 'ome. The 'ouse will feel empty wivout David there. I don't want ter be alone wiv me thoughts. Can you take me ter Ruby's house, please?'

'As you wish,' Douglas said as he started the engine. 'Maisie, I hope you don't mind me mentioning this, but in the absence of his wife you are the next of kin for your brother. There's the delicate issue of his remains to be considered.'

'As far as I'm concerned, he can rot in hell,' Maisie spat back.

Douglas was as concerned for his friend as Maisie. 'Hopefully he is already there, but we still have the problem of his body once the police release it. Would you like me to do something quietly? There's no need for anyone to attend.'

'That's bloody good of you, Douglas. Can we leave it fer a while until I can think straight? Whatever 'appens, I don't want you out of pocket wiv this.'

'Let's leave it there, then, shall we?' he said as the car passed the Prince of Wales pub.

'Oh no!' Maisie sighed as she spotted men removing all the damaged furniture whilst several more were puttying fresh panes of glass into frames. 'We've got ter do something about this. Some of this is our fault, and the landlord shouldn't be responsible fer the cost.'

'I'm sure we can all put our heads together and come up with something to help out,' he said, thinking that Maisie might benefit from focusing on a project rather than her seriously ill husband and her dead brother.

'I'll do that,' she smiled.

George walked around the workshop, checking workbenches and tapping on the wooden window frames with a pen. The steady pounding of rain on the corrugated metal roof was the only sound as Alan watched his father-in-law with bated breath.

'I was thinking it would do to begin with,' he suggested, when he couldn't wait any longer for George to speak.

George nodded thoughtfully before shaking the wooden double doors and tugging at a rusty padlock.

'These doors will need changing, and you need a new padlock. Two separate locks would be better. You don't want someone getting in and stealing your tools, and worse still, pinching your customers' motorbikes.'

Alan's face dropped. He'd been excited to show off his new business premises to George, and had expected praise rather than a list of things to change and to beware of. 'Are you saying I've made a bad move renting this place?'

'Goodness, no,' George said, perching on one of two wooden stools set by a workbench. 'With a bit of patching up you'll have a decent set-up to get you started. What made you pick this place?'

'To be honest, sir, it's close to home. I feel bad about Sarah having to go back to working at Woolworths while I get things up and running. With this place being in Crayford Road, I'm only a few steps from home. I can be there in a jiffy to collect the kids, or home for meals.'

'Good thinking. I'd have done the same in your situation. Don't feel too bad about our Sarah. I know she expected different once you left the RAF, but she's always been a bit of a dreamer.'

Alan smiled. 'You've heard about her wish for a cottage with roses round the door, have you?'

George laughed. 'So that's what she's hankering after, is it? I'm sure she'll get her wish in time, but until then she will have to wait. I did think of giving you the bungalow in Crayford. The landlord is after selling it, and since I sold our home down in Devon I've got the readies to buy it outright.'

Alan felt his heart leap. 'You'd do that for us, sir?'

'I would, Alan – you and Sarah are my only family, and I want to invest in your future while I'm still here to see you get the benefit. However, seeing your little set-up here has given me another idea.'

Alan fought hard not to look disappointed. The bungalow in Crayford close to Saint Paulinus Church was the kind of home he wished to provide for his own family one day. There was even a rose garden, which his late mother-in-law had tended every day. 'I suppose it's hard to leave a home when you have happy memories of Irene living there?' he said.

George pulled out his pipe from a pocket in his tweed jacket and tapped it on his head. 'My memories are up here. I don't need places to think of Irene and the life we had together. I can see her in Sarah and the children, although goodness knows what she'd have said to calling the baby Buster. She'd have had a fit,' he smiled.

'It's only a nickname,' Alan grinned. 'To Irene he would have been Alan junior. So what will you do?'

'I'm going to move back to Erith, where I grew up and where my family lives. A little two up, two down will suit me. I don't need bungalows and big gardens. I'm a man of simple means. Instead I'm going to invest in your business.'

Alan was confused. 'But, sir, I don't expect . . .'

'I know you don't, Alan, and that is why I want to help you out. You're like a son to me, and any father would help his son out as much as was humanly possible. I'll come and help you on weekends so we have this workshop in tip-top condition, and I'll pay your rent for the first six months as well as purchase tools and materials. I can also ask around for work. I have contacts, and with so many businesses using motorbikes in their vehicle fleets, you could do very nicely.'

Alan was shocked and didn't know what to say. 'I'm almost lost for words,' he gulped. 'Thank you, sir – thank you from the bottom of my heart.'

Douglas helped Maisie up the path to number thirteen and rapped on the wooden door. 'I'll not come in, Maisie, as I want to get home to Betty and see how she is. I'm concerned that the shock from yesterday will have affected her. She says she's all right, but you know Betty.'

Maisie placed her hand on Douglas's and gave it a squeeze. 'Give her me love. I'm going ter pop into Woolworths tomorrow and rearrange me shifts while David's . . .' Her voice broke with emotion. 'I'm a daft bugger,' she said, trying to smile. 'He's alive, and that's what counts, eh?'

'He's not going anywhere,' Douglas assured her, 'and we are all here to muck in and do what we can, for as long as it takes.'

'I'm bloody lucky to 'ave such good friends,' she said, kissing his cheek. 'They say you can choose yer friends but not yer family, and I've been blessed wiv the people who choose ter be me friends. As fer family . . .' She shrugged her shoulders. 'I won't waste me breath on mine . . . dead or alive.'

Maisie felt the tension in her shoulders melt away as she sat sipping the scalding hot tea Ruby had out in front of her within minutes of her sitting down. 'There's nothing like a good cup of tea,' she sighed. 'The nurses were very good, but their tea was like dishwater.'

'My Pat dropped off some eggs the other day, so I'll do you a couple on some toast. That'll perk you up,' Ruby said, giving her a sympathetic look. 'You need to keep your strength up with all that hospital visiting ahead of you. Now, tell us what the doctors have said.'

Maisie's shoulders slumped as she explained to her friends about her visit to the consultant's office. 'I'd cry, but I don't think I've got another tear left ter shed,' she said sadly.

Sarah felt she could have cried for Maisie too, but thought it best to keep as cheerful as possible. 'He'll pull through this, don't you worry,' she said, 'and we are all here to help while David's in hospital. The twins have been fed and are sleeping it off, and Bob's got the girls out in the garden training the dogs. Why don't you have a bite to eat and then go and have a lie down upstairs for a couple of hours?'

'Ta, I think I'll do that. You've all been so kind considering the wedding was spoilt by me brother. I'll never be able ter make that up ter you,' she added sadly.

'You've nothing to apologize for,' Ruby scolded her, 'nothing at all.'

'Douglas explained how Fred threatened ter come back fer money from David, otherwise he'd take the girls away from us. He stood up ter Fred, and look how he paid fer it. His arm's never going ter be the same again, and no doubt we'll still lose the girls, as that wife of his will 'ave 'em.' Despite Maisie having said only minutes before that she didn't have a tear left, her shoulders shook with heavy sobs. 'It's such a bloody mess,' she hiccupped.

Sarah and Ruby left their seats to cuddle Maisie as Freda, who had been listening quietly, slipped from the room to reappear soon after with her handbag. She pulled out a piece of folded paper and held it out to Maisie. 'I hope this may help a little. With everything that was going on, I didn't have chance to give it to you before now.'

Maisie wiped away her tears with the handkerchief Sarah pressed into her hand. 'What's this?' she asked, looking to Freda for an answer.

'It's something I had Cynthia, Fred's wife, write last night after she said she didn't want to take on the kids. She was ready to run off as she didn't want to be involved with the police, but I hung onto her long enough to make her see sense about the girls needing to stay in their loving home. Did I do right?' She asked, worried that Maisie wouldn't agree.

'Right? You done bloody marvellous,' she cried out, reaching for Freda and hugging her tight. 'If the coppers want her you've even got an address for 'em to find her. What wiv their dad dead and this proof Cynthia's not interested in 'em, I reckon no one'll stop us keeping Bessie and Claudette now. This'll cheer David up no end.'

15

Betty stopped to speak to yet another customer who asked after her health. She wasn't surprised when most of these short conversations turned to the events of Ruby's wedding party at the Prince of Wales public house. Again and again she made the right noises and excused herself, saying she had work to attend to. She knew that most people were genuinely concerned, but couldn't help think that a few of the women were simply being nosy and revelling in the misfortune of others.

Deciding to keep her head down and hurrying as fast as her expanded girth would allow, she headed back towards her office, ignoring someone calling out her name until she was tapped on the arm.

'Are you going deaf?' a familiar voice asked.

'Oh my goodness, Maisie, you are the last person I expected to see today. I'm sorry, what I meant was . . .'

Maisie laughed. 'There's no need fer you ter apologize ter me – I've come in ter apologize ter you.'

They'd reached the door that led up to the staff area of the store. Maisie opened the door for Betty to go first. 'Why would you need to apologize to me, Maisie?'

'Because it's highly unlikely that I'm going ter be able ter come into work fer a while, wiv David needing me while he's in 'ospital and the children ter consider.'

'Let's go upstairs and chat about this in my office, away from prying eyes,' Betty said as she spotted several shoppers looking in their direction. 'Sarah is in there working on the books, and I'm sure she'd like to stop for a chat.'

Maisie had hoped Betty would say just that. 'I'm not taking you from yer work, am I?'

'I'm more than ready to have a break,' Betty said, stopping midway to take a breath.

Maisie thought her friend looked rather flushed in the face. 'You need ter take things easy, Betty; you 'ave under a month ter go now and should really be putting yer feet up. I'm surprised head office are even allowing you ter remain here.'

Betty stopped again and took a shuddering breath. 'Phew, I am rather tired,' she gasped. 'I've been marching around the shop floor for an hour inspecting the counters. Cecil was supposed to have done it, but I was told he went downstairs and disappeared out the front doors. There – I'm at the top of the staircase. I promise not to go down again until it's time to go home,' she grinned.

'Thank goodness it's half day shopping,' Maisie muttered as she followed Betty to her office. 'Now you go and sit down, and I'll pop into the staff canteen ter see Maureen and cadge us all a cuppa, as well as a bite ter eat. I'll be back shortly.'

'It should be me looking after you, not the other way round,' Betty admonished Maisie, 'but I'll not say no.'

'Was that Maisie's voice I heard?' Sarah asked as she

moved from the one comfortable seat in Betty's office over to a hard bentwood chair reserved for visitors. 'Here, you have that seat and rest your feet.'

'Thank you. I'll be glad when I've had this baby and people stop telling me to rest,' Betty said with a sigh as she sat down.

'Believe me, people will ignore you after the birth. They will only have eyes for your child.'

'It won't bother me in the least,' Betty grinned. 'Now, how have you been getting on? I hope the books aren't in too much of a state after I allowed Cecil to take them on? The paperwork is overdue for head office, and there will be an almighty complaint if we miss the deadline. It's never happened in all the time I've taken charge, and I'd hate it to happen just as I'm leaving.'

Sarah had found it to be a nightmare balancing the ledgers but didn't want to worry Betty unduly, although there was something she couldn't let slide. 'We can meet the deadline for head office, but I've uncovered something rather worrying. It is most likely something I've not entered from the stock lists, and you will spot it and tell me where I've gone wrong, I'm sure.'

'Let's have our cup of tea with Maisie, then I'll take a look. You've made such a difference since you came back to Woolworths, Sarah. Why, my office has never been so tidy.'

'You don't have time to do everything, Betty. You've been chasing up Cecil for some time now – in fact, I'd go as far as to say you've been carrying him. Is there nothing head office can do about that man?'

'Believe me when I say I've tried. With his uncle

protecting him, I've not been able to get a complaint through to anyone higher in the company. I live in hope he will move on to another job, and then we can all breathe a sigh of relief.'

'Not all the time he's picking up a very nice pay packet every week,' Sarah said. She didn't like to mention that the man earned more than Betty did, which wasn't fair at all.

'Open the door,' Maisie called from the corridor outside, and Sarah jumped to her feet and helped her friend bring in the tray of tea and sandwiches. 'Corned beef sandwiches wiv some of Maureen's home-made pickle. Me mouth is watering already.'

The friends sat chatting with Maisie as she updated them on how David was progressing. It was now two days since he'd been stabbed by Fred Dawson, and with another operation that morning, Maisie was keen to see him come visiting time.

'Would you like to use my telephone to ring the hospital?' Betty asked as she brushed crumbs from her pretty cotton maternity dress, which had been borrowed from Maisie.

'That's very kind of you. It may be a little early fer news, but you never know,' Maisie said, reaching into her bag for the telephone number of Erith Cottage Hospital.

'Let's have a look at the problem you noticed in the ledgers,' Betty said to Sarah, turning away to give Maisie some privacy while she spoke to the ward sister.

Sarah pulled her notes forward on the desk and pointed to a discrepancy between the stock sheets and the sales taken on the electrical counter. 'I can't understand how we've ordered so much more stock for that department, but sales are the same as they've ever been. All I could think was that we'd over-ordered and the goods are still in the storeroom, but lasts week's stock take shows otherwise.'

Betty was silent as she ran her finger down the columns, then picked up the stock sheets. 'Well spotted, Sarah. I can only think that when the stock count was undertaken, something was missed out.'

'Could we do a recount of those items?' Sarah asked. 'We have the past week's sales figures, so I'll be able to tell if we've missed something off.'

'Yes, that would make a lot of sense.' Betty looked up at the clock on the wall. 'We only have half an hour before the store closes. Would you be able to stay behind, and we could do it then?'

'That's not a problem for me. Nan has Buster, and Georgina is at school. She knows not to expect me, as I said I'd do a bit of shopping on the way home. Freda is downstairs in the shop. Shall we ask her if she can stay a while and help?'

'That's a good idea. Can you ask her now, and also get hold of Cecil and tell him to lock up? Perhaps not mention that we're checking the stock?' she added as an afterthought.

Sarah nodded in agreement. They both understood that the less Cecil knew, the better. 'I'll pop these ledgers back on the shelf for now,' she said.

'I'll lock your notes in my desk drawer,' Betty added as Sarah left the room, taking the empty cups and plates on her way out. She quickly rinsed the bits and pieces in the canteen kitchen, as Maureen had gone home for the day, and then headed downstairs onto the shop floor. She stood taking stock of the counters as customers made their final purchases. Already one supervisor was by the four large doors, holding a bunch of keys. She nodded to Sarah and smiled as she shifted from foot to foot, indicating how tiring her job could be and that she'd be grateful to head for home. 'It looks like it will rain before too long,' she said as they both peered out at the sky. 'I hope I can get home and take my washing in before the heavens open.'

Sarah smiled. It was a common problem with the women who had families to care for, and one of the reasons she hadn't wished to work after Alan came out of the RAF. She prided herself in caring for her family, even though they lived with Maureen and could share the housekeeping duties. She was still in a dream about having her own home one day soon when she spotted Cecil hanging around by the electrical counter. He seemed to be attracted to that section like a magnet, but at least this time he was serving someone, she thought to herself, hurrying to catch him before he did one of his disappearing acts. He wasn't one to hang about come closing time. How he could take his wage packet each week without having it on his conscience, she didn't know. 'Ah, Mr Porter,' she said as she reached where he stood, adding 'Excuse me' to the man who was with him. 'Mr Porter, Mrs Billington asked me to inform you that you are to lock up this afternoon, please. She will be leaving herself once she has finished her meeting.'

Cecil nodded and turned his back on her. Sarah

shrugged her shoulders. She had passed on the message, and now intended to get back upstairs and look into the discrepancy she'd spotted. Hopefully there would be a simple answer to the problem, as she didn't want to think what else could be the cause.

'Here she is,' Betty said, as Sarah reached the top of the staff staircase. 'Maisie's going to help us for a while. Three heads will be better than two.'

'How about four heads?' Freda asked, coming up the stairs behind Sarah and following them into the store-room. 'Didn't you hear me calling out to you?' she asked, nudging Sarah's arm.

'I'm sorry, I was miles away. Are you sure you want to help us check stock?'

'If it means I get to spend some time with my friends without us being surrounded by children, then I adore stocktaking. As much as I love them all, I miss the days when it was just us,' Freda said with a smile. 'Do you know it's over six years since we all met here? I was thinking about it the other day, when I was going back over old times and thinking of the fun we've had – and the sad times when we've supported each other. It's made me think more about the future now that Sandy's gone and my brother and Sally have moved to Erith. I'll be an auntie soon as well.'

'You are already an auntie to our children,' Sarah said gently.

'I know, and I love them all as if they were my own flesh and blood, but you know what I mean,' Freda said. 'Then we all lost our mums within a year or so of each other.'

Maisie sniffed. 'I'm so glad I met all of you. Gawd

knows what would have become of me if I'd not decided to come fer that interview fer a job.'

Sarah gave a small laugh. 'My goodness, look at the four of us. I suggest we get this job done, and then go to the staffroom and have a chat. Maisie will have to go off soon to see David. Was there any news?' she asked.

'He went down for his operation late, so they said not ter go up there until around three. So I've time ter help you.'

'Would you like me to come with you?' Freda asked. 'It would be company if you have to sit about for a while.'

Maisie gave Freda a quick hug. 'I'd like that a lot. Now, what is it you want us all ter check? I take it Cecil's at the bottom of all this?'

Betty groaned. 'Who else? Right – if you two can count the light bulbs, Freda can help me count the boxes over here. I'll note down what we have, and we can take these back to my office and check them there.'

The women worked as quickly as they could, checking electrical stock and calling out figures to Betty. As they worked they could hear staff coming upstairs to collect their coats and calling goodbye to each other.

'I think we have everything. Let's get back to my office and check these against the numbers in the ledgers,' Betty said as she picked up her notes and headed out of the storeroom.

'Why don't I put the kettle on?' Maisie suggested. 'I don't know about all of you, but I'm spitting feathers after working in that dusty room.'

Sarah went with Betty to collect the ledgers and the notes locked in Betty's desk, and they settled down in the staff canteen to work while Maisie raided Maureen's small stock of food. The store fell quiet as closing time came and went as the town started to drift into half-day closing.

'I've found it,' Sarah shouted in glee, causing them to jump in their seats. 'Look here.' She pointed to the figures from when Cecil had undertaken a stock count. 'Now look here. Can you see how he's changed the numbers?'

Maisie squinted at the rows of numbers. 'I ain't that good with figures. Are you saying he's nicked our stock and tried ter cover it up?'

'I'd say you've hit the nail on the head, but we need more proof,' Betty said with a smile. 'I shouldn't be wishing ill on a person, but as far as Cecil Porter is concerned, I'm rather pleased he's been found out. Shall we agree to keep this to ourselves until we can catch him red-handed?'

'The more proof, the better,' Freda said. 'You don't want him to wriggle out of this and continue working here. It would be hell, and he'd make us suffer. I'd be interested to know what he's been pinching?' she said, looking over Sarah's shoulder at the scribbled notes.

'Mainly light bulbs; but there are smaller numbers of other items that all come from the one department,' Sarah said, pointing to her findings in the stock lists.

'The horrid chap is flogging it all on the black market. Don't you just 'ate people like 'im? Mind you, he's got an eye fer the market, what with light bulbs being in short supply.'

Despite the seriousness of what they'd uncovered, Betty couldn't help but smile. Throughout the war, Maisie had been the one person in her group of acquaintances who could lay her hands on things that were in short supply. She always *knew a man* who could find just what she wanted, be it a lipstick or a pair of nylons. Where did she think these things came from? They were stolen from somewhere.

'Do you think we should tell the police?' Sarah asked. 'It would be wrong not to try to do something.'

'But if Betty informs the police they'll speak to Woolworths head office, and then Cecil's uncle might warn him. Perhaps we should have a word with Mike Jackson, but make it a friendly chat rather than an official report?' Freda suggested.

'I agree. Perhaps we could also think of a way to catch him out?' Betty said as she stretched and rubbed her back. 'Ouch – I think I sat still for too long.' She started to stand up before doubling over in pain, gripping the back of her chair for support. 'Oh my goodness,' she exclaimed. 'It can't be the baby, surely?' She gasped as a spasm shot through her.

Maisie and Sarah hurried to Betty's side to support her. 'Have you had any pain before this?' Sarah asked.

'Since this morning I've had a nagging pain in my back, but I put it down to scrubbing out the kitchen cupboards last night when I couldn't sleep, and then walking around the shop floor for a few hours earlier this morning.'

Maisie raised her eyebrows at Sarah. 'This could well be it. Freda, would you be a love and use Betty's telephone ter ring Douglas? Tell him Betty needs ter get up ter the Hainault fairly quickly.'

'The telephone numbers are in my diary on the desk,' Betty said as she winced and held her breath. 'This is too early. I shouldn't be having this child for at least a few more weeks. There must be something wrong. Please hurry, Freda.'

'I'll just be a few seconds,' Freda said as she hurried to the door that led from the canteen and pushed hard. 'That's strange – the door won't budge.' She gave it a hard shove, but it refused to open. Taking the handle, she pushed and pulled, then rattled it as hard as she could. There was a slight clunking noise, but the door still did not open. 'Someone's bolted the door from the outside,' she reported back to the other three women.

'That would have been Cecil,' Sarah said. 'Why the silly man couldn't check inside rooms before he locked up, I don't know.'

'No doubt hell bent on escaping the store at closing time. This will definitely be going down on his staff record,' Betty said in between gasps. 'That's if we ever get out of here.'

'We will,' Sarah said as she made soothing sounds and rubbed Betty's back, although she looked very worried.

'If we can't, then it'll be the first baby born in this store; although, Maisie, I recall young Ruby was almost the first? Thank goodness I have two experienced friends to support me,' Betty said.

'Three,' Freda said, although she looked more than a little worried. 'I was present when Sarah gave birth to Georgina, and the Fire Service gave us a leaflet on what to do if we were ever faced with this sort of situation again.'

'Was it very helpful?' Betty asked, looking a little more hopeful than she had a few seconds earlier.

'To be honest, I never got round to reading it properly.

I had to change a wheel on my motorbike and got oil all over it.'

Maisie laughed out loud. 'We've got ourselves into a few situations in the past, but this one takes the biscuit. Let's think about who knows we're 'ere. Betty, will Douglas be collecting you, by any chance?'

Betty tried to think as she walked around the room, using the edges of tables for support. 'No, he is attending an important funeral down in Belvedere. He told me not to get the bus but to telephone for a taxi-cab. I'd meant to do it earlier but forgot.'

Maisie turned to Sarah. 'How about you?'

'Nan has Buster, and Georgina doesn't have to be picked up from school for a while. Gwyneth had offered to get all the kids. I told Nan I had a bit of shopping to do, and then I was going to walk up to see Alan in his workshop.'

Maisie's eyes lit up. 'So Alan would be expecting you?'

Sarah shook her head in disappointment. 'No, I was going to surprise him.'

Before Maisie could ask, Freda spoke up. 'Sorry, no one is expecting me either.'

'So we're up the creek wivout a paddle,' Maisie declared, looking worried, before trying hard to smile in order to keep Betty in good spirits.

'What about you?' Freda asked.

'Well, I'm not expected at the hospital till late afternoon and I doubt anyone would be worried if I didn't turn up. David will be too groggy ter notice I'm not there. I'd like ter know how he's doing, though,' she added, looking sad.

'I could do with another cup of tea,' Betty said. 'Let's

be thankful that Maureen keeps a tight ship and the room is clean. There could be worse places to give birth.'

'Does this count as overtime?' Freda asked, making them all laugh out loud.

'I'll get the kettle on and see if there's anything we can make use of,' Sarah said.

'I could make use of something ter eat,' Maisie called as she rattled the doors of some metal lockers that lined one wall. 'Look – one of these is open.' She whooped with delight, but soon looked glum again as she pulled out Maureen's comfortable work shoes, a cardigan and two crossover pinnies she wore when working in the kitchen. 'Oh, well, it was worth looking,' she said, pushing the metal door closed.

'We may need the pinnies and cardigan if Betty needs to lie down on the floor,' Freda suggested. 'You can have my overall as well if it's needed. It's a clean one, and I'm wearing a petticoat underneath,' she added in response to Maisie's wide-eyed look.

'You can have mine as well,' Sarah called as she poured boiling water into a large teapot. She wasn't sure giving birth on a hard linoleum floor would be very comfortable, although at least it was clean, as Maureen was particular about her work area. 'I found some bread pudding in a tin. I'm sure Maureen won't mind us having a slice or two under the circumstances.'

'It wasn't supposed to be like this,' Betty said as Freda wiped her glistening brow with a tea towel dipped in cold water.

'Sshh. Save yer energy,' Maisie said as she checked the time on her wristwatch before making sure the makeshift bed hadn't come adrift as Betty writhed on the floor. 'I've never been so 'appy ter see so many clean tea towels and tablecloths under Maureen's counter.'

'They've been there since the last Christmas party,' Sarah said. 'No one knew what to do with them with Maureen still off sick from work.'

Betty gave out a low, gutteral moan. 'It's not supposed to be like this,' she repeated, rolling her head from side to side. 'I'm supposed to be in the maternity home with Douglas waiting outside. He's not even finished painting the baby's room.'

'Your kid's coming whether Douglas has finished decorating or not,' Maisie said, trying to sound cheerful. She checked her watch again. 'Here, Freda, sit down wiv Betty while I get a drink. Watching someone give birth is thirsty work,' she laughed, beckoning to Sarah to follow her to the kitchen area.

'She's not looking good, is she?' Sarah said, looking over to where Freda was again wiping Betty's face.

'It's a first baby, and she's getting on a bit. She should 'ave a doctor or at the very least a midwife who can 'elp her,' Maisie said, her face showing her worry now that Betty couldn't see her.

Sarah tried to wipe the memory of the bad time she'd had with Buster. She wouldn't wish that on her deadliest enemy, let alone Betty, who was the sweetest, kindest woman in the whole wide world. 'We need help, don't we? This isn't something we can do alone.'

'I'm just going to get some fresh water. I'll only be a few

minutes,' they heard Freda reassure Betty, who waved a limp hand to acknowledge the young woman's words.

Freda hurried over to the two women. 'I have an idea,' Freda said. 'I reckon if I go out on the roof like we used to when on fire duty, I could call out to someone for help.'

Sarah's stomach lurched. She'd never liked doing fire duty at the best of times, but she knew the roofing hadn't been repaired properly. Some of the balustrade was missing, and there were loose tiles. Betty had been pushing head office to get it repaired this past year, but to no avail. It was either an excuse about budgets or simply a lack of staff in the maintenance department, due to the building department being needed to rebuild stores damaged in the bombing. Erith Woolworths was a long way down the list of stores requiring repair work. 'I don't know, Freda. It could be dangerous. We don't want you injuring yourself.'

'Or it would be a case of one born and one gone,' Maisie said grimly.

'Look at her,' Freda hissed. 'If we don't do something, Betty could die. We can't wait here until staff arrive for work tomorrow morning.'

Sarah shook her head. 'No, we won't have to wait that long. Nan and Alan will be out looking for me in a few hours.'

'Freda's right. Besides, they will see the store locked up and won't 'ave any idea we are in 'ere. As grim as it is, Freda's idea is the best one we have.'

'Then I'll have my cuppa and head up on the roof.'

'I have a question,' Sarah said. 'How will these people, whose attention you are trying to attract, get into the store?'

'That's buggered up that idea,' Maisie said.

'You need to throw the keys down to them,' Betty said from where she'd crept up behind them.

'Blimey, you made me jump. Shouldn't you be lying down and resting?'

'I'm sick of resting, Maisie. Strangely, I feel better when I'm upright and moving about,' Betty said, before doubling over and using a word none of the girls had ever heard her say before. After a minute or two she breathed out slowly and gave them a grin. 'See, it's much better standing up.'

'I'm glad you think so, as I went through all of that with you,' Maisie said, reaching for her tea. 'It's a shame we don't have a drop of the hard stuff to put in our cups.'

'Freda, take the store keys from my handbag and hang onto them. You seem to be our only chance of getting out of here before the morning. Whatever you do, please go slowly and take care,' Betty said, giving her a smile. 'If you can't face going up on the roof, then I'll understand.'

Freda could see that Betty really needed help, even though she was putting on a brave face. There was a glimmer of fear in her eyes, and her face through the shimmer of sweat was ghostly white. Freda picked up her tea and drained the cup as quickly as she could. 'Right, I'm ready to do this now.'

'You'd best put yer overall back on or you'll scare the natives, going out there in yer petticoat,' Maisie pointed out, and the girls all started to giggle at the thought of Freda climbing over the roof of Woolworths while improperly dressed. Even Betty laughed out loud before gripping her tummy as another contraction ripped through her body. Freda gave her one look and hurried to the tall sash-cord window that looked out over the rooftops of Pier Road. Still buttoning up her maroon Woolies uniform, she swung her legs out onto the crumbling slate roof before turning to wave to her friends.

'Here,' Sarah shouted, hurrying over, 'you need the keys.' She grinned, passing them through to the young woman.

Freda hadn't progressed more than half a dozen steps when she encountered a problem. The earlier rainfall was causing her feet to slip and slide on the slates. She backed up to the windowsill and perched on the edge as she removed her shoes and stockings, throwing them through to Maisie. 'That's better,' she declared before working her way up a slope to the narrow pathway that bordered the front of the building. Holding onto a nearby chimney-stack, she looked around her. It was now drizzling, causing anyone who would have been in Erith when the shops had closed to hurry home to keep dry. How long would she have to stay up here until someone passed by?

Creeping closer to the edge, she gripped the low wall and gulped as large lumps of brickwork came away in her hands. To think she'd spent long hours up here firewatching while enemy planes soared overhead. She shuddered as the memories washed over her. Closing her eyes, she went back in her mind to those fearful nights spent on the roof with her mates as they put out fires and looked out over the roofs of Erith. Thank goodness this damn war was now over and they could sleep safe in their beds. If it meant that people like Sandy were locked up to keep her country free, then so be it. She'd rather die a spinster than marry someone who worked for the enemy. She was so engrossed in her memories that she almost missed the sound of jolly whistling down in the street. Praying the edge of the roof wouldn't give way, she leant forward to see where the sound came from and grinned as she spotted who it was.

'Norman!' she shouted as she saw Norman Missons, the owner of the ironmonger's across the road, bringing in a display of galvanized buckets that had been in front of the shop. Norman's wife, Charlotte, was Brown Owl of the brownie pack where Freda helped out, and their daughter Molly, who was away working in the Land Army was her good friend. 'Norman, up here!' she called out again, more urgently this time.

Norman looked around him. He recognized that voice. Looking up, he spotted Freda. 'Whatever are you doing up there? You know the roofs need repairing in this road. You could fall and kill yourself!'

'We need your help,' she called out. 'We're locked in, and Mrs Billington is having her baby.'

Norman couldn't quite believe what he was hearing. Still holding the metal buckets, he crossed the road and shouted back, 'What was that you said?'

'We've been accidentally locked in the canteen upstairs, and Betty Billington is having her baby. Here,' she called, throwing down the keys to the store. 'Can you let yourself in and come up the staff staircase to the first floor and unbolt the door to the canteen, please? We are in there. Please hurry,' she shouted, knowing that Betty couldn't last much longer and needed medical help.

'I'll be with you in two ticks,' Norman shouted back as he rushed into his shop to call his wife to help.

Freda climbed back across the roof and down to the window of the staff canteen, where she tapped on the glass pane for someone to let her back in.

'Did you see anyone?' Sarah asked as she helped Freda back into the room and passed her shoes to her.

'Thankfully Norman Missons was still in his shop and heard me. I've thrown the store keys down to him and he should be opening up very shortly. Thank goodness we can get help before the baby arrives!'

She'd hardly stopped talking when a feeble wail was heard that grew louder and louder.

'Baby Billington was in a rush ter get into the world,' Maisie beamed from where she was on her knees helping Betty. She held up the wailing child, who was wrapped in a couple of Maureen's best tea towels. 'Meet the latest member of staff. Our youngest Woolworths Girl ever.'

16

~

July 1945

'Good morning, Alan, can I interrupt you?' David Carlisle said as he poked his head round the door of the motorbike workshop where Alan Gilbert was sweeping the floor.

'Come along in. It's good to see you,' Alan said, throwing down the broom and holding his hand out to shake David's after wiping it quickly on his overalls.

David looked at the proffered hand and gave a wry smile before shaking Alan's hand with his left one. 'This bloody thing's not even any good for shaking someone by the hand,' he grinned.

Alan dragged over a wooden chair and nodded for David to sit after flicking a cloth over it to clear the dust. 'Here, have a seat,' he said, perching on the edge of his workbench. 'How are things?' It was two months since David had been stabbed by his brother-in-law, and after numerous operations he was facing a future with a right arm that barely worked.

'I'm free of the RAF at last,' he shrugged, as if he didn't care. 'Maisie's packed me off out of the house, as she says

I get under her feet when she's trying to do her sewing. The noise of that machine whirring away drives me to distraction, so I was off like a shot as soon as she suggested it. I'd got outside the door and halfway down Alexandra Road before I had to think where I was heading. It was you or the pub,' he added without smiling.

'I'm pleased you chose me, mate; it's a long, slippery slope if you start drinking this early in the day. Lunch-times are for sandwiches, not beer.'

David shrugged. 'It's something I can do with one hand. I'm not even much help with the twins unless Maisie puts one in my arm. Look at this,' he said, reaching over with his good hand to show where his wife had stitched a piece of elastic to the inside of the cuff of his sleeve. 'I can't even do up a bloody button on my own,' he said, spitting out the words.

Alan peered closer. 'That's a pretty nifty idea. I might ask her to do it with both sleeves of my shirts. Sarah's always telling me to stop rolling up my sleeves and to wear my shirts properly. I can't be doing with the fiddly buttons. Come to that, I'm not a fan of cufflinks either.'

'Hmm, I've yet to try cufflinks,' David said thoughtfully.

Alan looked down to David's feet to see neatly tied laces on his brown brogues. 'How do you manage . . .' he nodded.

'Bessie and Claudette have made an arrangement where I pay a farthing for them to tie up my laces,' he said. 'It's come to bloody something when I have to ask two kids to do up my shoes. Thank goodness Maisie hasn't stitched elastic on them.'

'I'm sorry, mate. I can't begin to understand how it must be not to be able to use both arms.'

'Neither did I, until this happened,' David said morosely. 'It's not likely I'll find myself a job now.'

'I'd invite you to join me here, but there's not enough work to keep me, let alone someone else.'

'I'd be of no use to you. I've not even mastered how to make a pot of tea yet without spilling it. Thanks for thinking of me, though. I didn't realize things were so bad.'

'If it weren't for my Sarah putting in the hours at Woolworths, we'd sink without a trace. George has been a godsend paying the rent on the workshop and buying some extra tools. He's keeping his eyes open for work, but nothing much has come in yet. The advertisements in the *Erith Observer* and a few cards in shop windows have brought in repairs, but it's not what I'd envisaged when I thought about setting up on my own. Perhaps I should have gone back to Woolworths and finished my training to be a manager.'

'You'd never stick it out, not now you've seen the world. Had you not thought about making the RAF your career?'

'No, the war was enough for me. I'd be one of thousands after a job. I'm not so sure Sarah would forgive me if I'd stayed in the air force. It was hard enough convincing her that I wanted to set up this workshop. At the rate I'm failing, I'll be cap in hand at the staff door of Woolworths by Christmas.'

'You and me both, mate. Not that I can do much with only one working arm. I suppose I can push a broom round the floor,' David said, looking miserable, before slapping his leg and standing up. 'Sitting here feeling sorry for ourselves is getting us nowhere. Let's go and drown our sorrows with a swift half down the pub after all.'

'All right; you've convinced me. Let me just get this lump of old engine out in the yard for the scrap man to collect, and I'm done for the day.'

David grabbed one side of the rusty engine.

'Hey, there's no need for you to carry that – I can manage.'

'It's fine, I can lend a hand. But not two,' David grinned.

'As long you can laugh about it,' Alan said, his voice tinged with respect as they staggered out to the yard at the side of the workshop.

David looked around after they'd dropped the engine next to a pile of scrap pieces. 'It looks as though we should move into the scrap metal trade,' he said. 'You could make a motorbike out of all this old scrap.'

Alan laughed. 'That shows just how much you know about motorbikes. Now, give me a pile of scrap from one model of bike, and I may be able to do just that,' he said, peeling off his overall. 'Come on, let's get that drink before the pub closes.'

David was quiet as they strolled down Crayford Road to the pub. He took a seat on the other side of the bar from where he'd lain almost bleeding to death, trying hard not to focus on the memory.

'Are you all right coming in here?' Alan said. 'It doesn't shake you up at all?'

'I'm fine,' David said as he took his glass of beer and quickly gulped a couple of mouthfuls. 'I've been thinking about your business. There must be a lot of broken-down bikes in the possession of the services that would need a quick fix to get them working again.'

Alan sipped his beer as ideas whirred in his brain. 'You could have something there. I wonder how to find out who to speak to?'

'Leave it with me. If there's a single useful thing I can do with one arm, it's making telephone calls.'

'Cheers for that,' Alan grinned. 'Another pint?'

'Why not – and while we're here, we really ought to have a word with Sid about raising some money to replace the broken furniture in the pub.'

The pair were as good as their word, and two pints later they left the Prince of Wales public house very pleased with themselves for arranging a darts tournament as well as making plans for the future of Alan's business.

Sarah ran her hands through her hair in despair. She'd have screamed and stamped her feet if it wouldn't have startled the customers. Life working at Woolworths had become a nightmare since Betty left work and Cecil Porter took over as manager. Although she'd returned to work to take over the paperwork in the office, she found herself once more on the shop floor most days, working as a senior supervisor.

'Mrs Gilbert?' A young salesgirl approached her. 'We've run out of brown paper bags again,' she said apologetically.

'Do me a favour and check in both storerooms, would you, Jenny? If you can't find any, then go around the other counters and take some from each. I'll go up to the office and find out if Mr Porter placed the order. Was there something else?' Sarah asked, as the young woman stood looking uncomfortable.

'It's the staff rota, Mrs Gilbert. There's something wrong with it this week, as I don't usually work on Fridays and it shows me as working the full day.'

Sarah sighed. This was the third query about the week's rota. She'd have to find an hour to check it through and see what had gone wrong. Heading for the stairs that took her up to the office, she thought about the first query she'd entered in into the notebook she now carried with her due to continuous staff questions; the shortage of light bulbs for the electrical counter. Since the day Betty went into labour two months ago, she hadn't found time to do anything about the errors in the stock books. With staff shortages and so much on her plate since Betty left, she'd reluctantly fallen behind with that particular task. The store always seemed short on the wretched things, and she had a gut feeling Cecil Porter was at the bottom of the situation. Reaching the manager's office, she knocked and stepped into the room without waiting to be invited in. She found Cecil on the telephone chatting away to a friend. He'd taken off his tie and had his feet up on the desk. An open newspaper on the desk showed he'd not been working.

'Mr Porter, I need to speak to you urgently. We have a problem with the staff rota,' she said, ignoring the fact he was chatting on the telephone.

Cecil put his hand over the mouthpiece and shouted at her, 'For goodness' sake, woman, can't you sort out the problem? It's your job to do the paperwork. I can't do everything for you.' He returned to his conversation, laughing about his hopeless staff to whoever was on the other end of the line.

Sarah stood for a moment, seeing red. She was determined that all the good work Betty Billington had put into keeping the store running shipshape would not be spoilt by this awful man. She reached up to a shelf above his head and pulled down the box files that contained staff work rotas, making sure she knocked him on the head as she turned to leave the room, before stopping as she remembered the paper bags. 'By the way, we've run out of bags downstairs. When did they say the order would get here?'

Cecil put his hand over the receiver again and hissed at her, 'What are you talking about, woman? I know nothing about paper bags.'

'You were given the order last week to place with Supplies.'

He shook his head in mock despair. 'Do I have to do everything around here? Sort it out, woman.'

'I will, when you aren't hogging the telephone for your personal conversations,' she snapped back. She stormed out of the room and took her work through to the staff canteen, where Maureen helped her clear a table and settled her down with a cup of tea while she set to work on the rota for that week.

Maureen walked over to take the empty cup and looked at the pages laid out on the table where Sarah had crossed out errors and scribbled notes. She was now writing out a new chart. 'Has he messed up again?' she asked.

Sarah let out a big sigh. 'Oh, Maureen, it's such a mess. I'm running from one problem to another. They've run out of paper bags downstairs and I don't think he's placed any orders. I'd best make a call to Supplies and see if they can send us some urgently until I sort out the stationery and other paper orders.'

Maureen frowned. 'I was in the smaller storeroom earlier trying to look for the veg that should be here for today's lunches, and I spotted a crate in the corner. Do you think that could be the bags?'

'Oh, I do hope so. It would save a lot of problems – although I'd then have to apologize to the man for being so annoyed with him.'

'Don't you worry about him. I've snapped more than a few times lately. It's a shame head office don't have one of their inspections. We could do with them swooping in and catching him out. I'll come with you to check out the crate. I need a sack of spuds, and the new warehouse lad has no idea where to put things.'

'Thank you – perhaps between us we can find those bags.'

'And my spuds,' Maureen said as she followed Sarah down the corridor to the smaller of the two storerooms, where they found a lad in a brown warehouse coat sitting on a wooden crate smoking a cigarette. He jumped and stubbed out the cigarette on the floor, giving them an insolent stare.

'I'm looking for a box of brown paper bags. Have you seen any?' Sarah asked.

The lad shrugged and shook his head. 'No, missus.'

'Do you think you could go to the other storeroom and take a look for me, please?'

The lad nodded, and slowly started to slouch from the room.

'And take this sack of spuds to the kitchen on your way; look lively, or the lunches will be late,' Maureen chivvied him on.

'Before you go, can you tell me what's in this case?' Sarah asked, looking round the wooden crate the lad had been perched on.

'I dunno, but the boss man told me to keep an eye on it as someone was coming to collect it after the shop closes this evening.'

Sarah looked at Maureen as the lad left. 'That doesn't seem right at all. I've not seen any paperwork to show that stock is being returned to the supply depot.'

'What do you think can be in the crate?'

'I don't know, but I'll soon find out,' Sarah said, taking a crowbar from a shelf and prising open the top. Clearing away a layer of packing straw, she gasped in surprise. 'Light bulbs; hundreds of light bulbs! But why would these be sent back, when we are always so short of them on the counter? It doesn't make sense.'

'It does if the toerag is pinching them,' Maureen said, looking grim. 'I always thought he was a bit shifty. What are you going to do?'

Sarah tried to think as she put the lid back on the crate, making sure none of the straw was left on the floor. She knew this could be the key to getting Cecil sacked from his job, but she'd need to think of the best way to do it. 'Leave it with me, Maureen,' she smiled at her mother-in-law. 'Let's get back to the staff canteen. I could kill another cuppa.'

Returning to the canteen, she spotted Maisie and Gwyneth heading to a spare table carrying their mid-morning cup of tea. Perhaps they could help her?

'Come and join us,' Gwyneth called out as Sarah paused to collect her paperwork from a table near theirs. 'It's not often we have the same tea breaks these days, since his lordship took over the preparing of staff rotas.'

Sarah collected the tea Maureen had just poured for her and sat down with her friends. 'I've spent a while sorting out the mess with this week's rota. I'll pin it on the wall shortly. Perhaps you could let the staff know I've rejigged the list, and I intend to do them myself in future?' she said, looking to Maisie, who seemed miles away.

Maisie came to with a jolt. 'Sorry, love, what was that you were saying?'

The two women looked at the usually bouncing Maisie with concern. She had dark shadows round her eyes, and her make-up and hair were not as perfect as they normally were. 'Something up, love?' Gwyneth asked, looking concerned.

Maisie shrugged her shoulders. 'I'm worried about me David. He needs something ter do rather than hang about the 'ouse moping. He ain't said so, but I know the damage ter his arm is getting 'im down. He nigh on bit me 'ead off the other day after I'd sewn some elastic ter the cuffs of his shirts so he could pull 'em on and off wivout asking fer help wiv the buttons. It's hard ter understand how we need two hands ter do things until we lose the use of one. I'm blowed if I know how ter get 'im through this. I told 'im ter go and see Alan at his workshop; I 'ope he doesn't 'old his work up,' she said apologetically, looking at Sarah.

Sarah gave a big sigh. 'David's used to being the provider and the head of your family. This must have hit his pride – especially watching you go off to work while he's stuck at home. If visiting Alan cheers him up, that can only be a good thing. It might cheer Alan up as well.'

Maisie looked sympathetic as she reached for her cigarettes. 'Blimey, what's wrong with yer old man?'

'I don't think he has much work coming in. He's not said anything, and I've not asked; but when I've popped in to his workshop with a sandwich or to say hello, there never seem to be many motorbikes to repair. And he's always got a broom in his hand, sweeping up.'

Gwyneth, who'd been watching her two friends' sad faces, reached out and squeezed their hands in sympathy. 'What a pickle,' she said. 'Alan does have Woolworths to fall back on. At least they both have wives who will stand by them and help as much as they possibly can.'

Maisie gave a cynical laugh. 'We can only 'ope, but ter be honest I'm sick of going out ter work. I love Woolworths, but I don't feel as though it's what I want ter do fer the rest of me life. Keep that ter yourselves, girls; I don't want David finding out, as it might add ter his worries. At least yer Mike has a good job he loves. The town will always need coppers, and we seem ter 'ave enough bad people on the streets for 'im ter keep busy,' she laughed.

'I thought, what with the war at an end apart from those poor souls still fighting the Japs, that our lives would be happy and carefree – not tinged with as much sadness as before, or worries about our futures. I don't think Alan will ever return to Woolworths. He has his own dreams, and they include being his own boss. I dare not imagine his disappointment if the workshop fails.'

Gwyneth nodded. 'I'm just so grateful Mike loves his work; not like our new manager,' she grinned.

Sarah was thoughtful as the women sipped their tea. 'Is your Mike at work today?'

'Only until lunchtime. He's meeting me, as it's my half day, and we are going out for a walk and afternoon tea. Why do you ask?'

'I wondered if he would advise me on something, but I don't want him to be seen in uniform,' Sarah said thoughtfully.

'That sounds intriguing,' Gwyneth laughed. 'I hope he is out of uniform, as sometimes I receive such strange looks when out walking with a policeman.'

'You'll 'ave ter tell us what it's all about, or I'll never concentrate when I go back ter my counter,' Maisie said.

Sarah looked about her to check no one was eavesdropping before explaining what she and Maureen had discovered in the storeroom.

'How will you prove the crate was in our storeroom if it gets shifted somewhere else?' Maisie asked.

'Gosh, I'd not thought of that. Perhaps Mike will advise me on that?'

'The crate could be gone by the time Mike arrives. It only needs him to be held up at the police station, and that crate could be anywhere,' Gwyneth said.

'You need to mark it in some way,' Maisie said as she picked up her handbag and started to rummage inside. 'Ah, I thought it was 'ere.' She pulled out a lipstick and took off the cap. 'Come on, let's go and take a look at this crate of yers before the bell fer the end of our tea break starts ter ring.'

Sarah and Gwyneth followed Maisie out of the canteen.

Sarah stopped at the manager's office door. 'I'll just get rid of these files and check his lordship is busy at his desk so he doesn't catch us out,' she whispered. However, she needn't have worried: Cecil was slumped in his seat fast asleep as she crept in and left the paperwork on the edge of the desk. She was sorely tempted to cough loudly to wake him, but thought it was not in their best interests to do so. Perhaps later, she grinned to herself as she tiptoed from the room.

In the storeroom, Maisie checked out the crate before reaching for the crowbar and reopening the lid. She raked around inside, pulled out a delivery note and scribbled on the back of the sheet of paper before burying it back inside the crate and carefully putting the lid back in place. Taking the notepad that was tied to the belt of her overall, she wrote a few words before pulling the lipstick from her pocket. Using her pencil, she dug out the last of the bright red lipstick and marked the four sides of the crate with a small cross. 'That'll do,' she smiled to herself as her two friends looked on in confusion. 'Come on, it's time ter get back downstairs.'

With no time to chat, Sarah returned to the office, slamming the door closed so that Cecil woke with a start, wiping drool from the corner of his mouth. 'Oh, there you are, Gilbert. There was a call from head office. Some woman is visiting the store . . .' he checked his watch, 'anytime soon. I can't be bothered to speak with her, as I'm off out for a while. You deal with it.'

Sarah nodded without saying a word. What was the point, when he ridiculed her work and treated her like a slave? Going to the files she'd left earlier, she pulled out the revised staff rota and placed it in front of him before leaving the office and heading down to the store. If someone was visiting from head office she'd make sure the staff knew and were on their toes, even if Cecil wasn't bothered. As she walked around the store stopping to talk to staff and pointing out where the counters could be tidied and uniforms straightened, she felt proud to be part of such a well-known chain. They even have shops in America, she thought as she checked the floor in case it needed sweeping. Perhaps one day she'd be able to travel to America and see where Woolworths first started . . .

'Thank goodness I've found you,' Freda said as she rushed up to Sarah, stopping to catch her breath.

'Whatever's the matter? Has Cecil been causing problems again?'

'No, he went out a little while ago. There's a lady here from head office. I've put her in the office with a cup of tea and come to find you.'

'What's she like?' Sarah asked as they hurried towards the staff door.

'Very nice, considering she's someone important,' Freda said. 'Would you like me to stay with you?'

Sarah stopped and thought for a moment. 'No thanks, it's not as if it can be that important, or Cecil wouldn't have gone out, would he? You could go and see if Jenny had any luck looking for paper bags. I'll ask this woman if she can send us some from Supplies.'

'There are plenty under the haberdashery counter. I'll share them about. Anything else?'

'Find Maisie and have her update you on the crate in the storeroom.'

'What?' Freda asked, as Sarah hurried away.

'Hello, I'm Sarah Gilbert, senior supervisor,' Sarah said, holding out her hand to the dark-haired woman sitting in the visitor's chair. 'I'm sorry you've missed Mr Porter.'

The woman shook her hand and gave her a warm smile. 'Gina Jones. I've come to take a look at the records you keep here, and if there's time perhaps you could show me around? I must say your cook has a very light hand with her pastry, and she makes a nice cup of tea, too,' she added, looking to where an empty cup and plate lay on the desk.

Sarah smiled. She seemed very nice. 'It's my mother-in-law, Maureen Gilbert, who runs the staff canteen. We'd be lost without her. She manages to come up with a square meal every day for the staff even when food's been hard to find.'

Gina Jones pulled out a notebook and scribbled a few words. 'How has it been since Mrs Billington left the company?'

'We miss Betty . . . I mean Mrs Billington. Even the customers ask when she's coming back.'

Gina gave an understanding smile. 'She must be a hard act to follow?'

'I'm not in charge, Mrs Jones, Mr Porter is the manager.'

'But I get the impression you are the anchor in this store at the moment?'

'But how . . . ?'

'I've been chatting to a few of your staff, and Mrs Billington did file a comprehensive report once she was over the sudden birth of her daughter. I hear it was an exciting time – and you, Mrs Carlisle and Miss Smith were at hand to help?'

Sarah nodded. 'Betty has become a good friend since I started work here. All four of us have become very close.'

Gina Jones smiled. 'Many friendships are formed at Woolworths. I still have friends from my first days. Now, why don't you show me the paperwork, and then we can take a look around the store and I can meet the staff.'

Sarah felt puzzled as she pulled out the ledgers and sat with Gina Jones while she checked figures and asked questions. When it was time to go over the staff rotas, she was embarrassed to see she'd forgotten to remove Cecil's badly written pages. However, Gina simply smiled as she compared them to Sarah's neatly written charts before writing more notes in the book she kept beside her at the desk.

'I think I've seen all I need to see,' she said after closing the last ledger. 'Let's take a visit downstairs, shall we?'

Sarah nodded and showed the way. Inside she was boiling with fury. Why wasn't Cecil here to show the inspector around, and why didn't Gina Jones seem upset that he wasn't present when he was, after all, the manager of the Erith branch? Cecil wriggled out of everything, and seemed to have a charmed life. Why, if she'd done one job wrong when she'd joined Woolworths, Betty would have had her guts for garters. Even as they started to become friends Betty Billington had always drawn the line between work and friendship. She knew the boundaries and so did the friends who worked alongside her. Glancing at the clock as they reached the bottom of the stairs, Sarah could see it was time for Gwyneth to finish her shift. Was Mike here yet, and would the packing case containing the light bulbs be whisked away as they expected whilst the inspector was still in the store?

'You seem to be doing admirably well considering Mrs Billington left us rather suddenly. The counters are full, and your staff are well turned out and bubbling with enthusiasm. I'd say without a shadow of doubt, this must be one of our star stores. You should be proud of yourself,' Gina Jones said as she finished checking the fresh produce counter, after talking to the counter staff.

Sarah blinked, not quite sure she had heard right. 'But I'm not the manager – I'm not even an assistant manager. Betty . . . I mean Mrs Billington made me a senior supervisor because she wanted me to do the paperwork upstairs, to take the pressure off her in her final weeks. I'd hoped to continue, but Mr Porter thought otherwise, so I've been fitting in where I can and helping to keep the store ticking over.'

Gina nodded her head as if she understood. 'As I mentioned earlier, Mrs Billington sent us an extremely detailed report. I've been given the job of checking everything through, and to be honest, some things don't add up – hence my secret visit here today.'

'But it wasn't a secret; Cecil Porter told me you were coming just before he went out,' Sarah replied, feeling confused.

'Hmm. Someone must have tipped him off,' Gina said thoughtfully.

'That would have been Cecil's uncle. Betty went to see him to ask if she could return to work and he made it quite clear her services weren't required. From the little Betty told me, he was quite rude about mothers who work at Woolworths.'

'That does make some sense,' Gina said thoughtfully. 'One would think that senior staff were above reproach.'

Sarah felt that this nice woman might be a little naive, but decided to keep her thoughts to herself. Perhaps it was time to show her the crate and the old stock sheets she'd tucked away after Betty left the company? 'Would you mind sparing me a few minutes? I have something you may be interested in.'

Gina Jones checked her watch. 'I have half an hour before my train goes. Perhaps we could have a cup of tea at the same time?'

Sarah led the inspector back to the staff canteen and settled her with a cup of tea and a slice of Maureen's gypsy tart before going to a metal locker and unlocking the door. 'These are the stock sheets and list we were working on the day Betty Billington had her daughter, in this very room. It was Cecil Porter who locked us in – which could have had serious repercussions for Betty and her child if Freda Smith had not climbed onto the roof to call for help.'

Gina Jones licked a few crumbs from her lips and

nodded to Sarah to continue talking as she stabbed another piece of the tart with her fork.

'The thing is, we found that there were discrepancies between what should be in our storeroom and what had gone down to be sold in the electrical department. Mainly it was light bulb stock that seemed to be amiss, but there were other items to a lesser extent.' She slipped the folder across the table and Gina flicked through the papers while she sipped her tea. 'I've tried to keep a note since, but now that Cecil Porter has taken over the manager's office it has been hard. He doesn't like me working in there, not even when I have wage packets to fill. I've done my best under extremely difficult conditions.'

Gina closed the folder. 'I'll take this away with me and see what can be done to alleviate the problem.'

Sarah wasn't sure what that meant, so she decided that – in for a penny, in for a pound – she would mention the crate in the storeroom they'd discovered earlier. As she told Gina what they'd done, even mentioning Maisie marking the box with her lipstick and them asking Mike to come in to advise them, the woman listened carefully and then smiled. 'I would like to see this crate, if I may?'

'Follow me,' Sarah said and stood to leave the canteen just as Gwyneth rushed into the room, her cheeks flushed and her eyes wild with excitement.

'You've got to do something,' she called to Sarah. 'There's a problem in the storeroom.'

Sarah and Gina hurried behind Gwyneth to where they could hear muffled shouts and cursing. Entering the storeroom, they saw Mike Jackson handcuffing one loud-mouthed youth while a second young man sat on the floor already cuffed to the structure of the metal shelves, look-ing none too happy.

'It all seems to have kicked off in here,' Gina Jones said. 'I assume this has something to do with the stolen stock?'

'For heaven's sake, let me get up,' an irate Cecil called from where he was sprawled on the hard floor with Freda and Maisie sitting on him. 'Heads will roll for this.'

'Sorry, darling, you're staying down there until the police take you away,' Maisie snarled. 'No one pinches from Woolworths on our watch.'

Freda looked a little worried, but hung on to Cecil's feet to stop him kicking her friend.

'Whatever is happening here?' Gina Jones asked.

Mike finished securing the man and turned to Gina. 'I'm Sergeant Jackson, madam, and my wife is one of your staff. We found these men removing stock from this store – stock that wasn't paid for. I was tipped off that some-thing was amiss, and along with a fellow officer I came down at once. My colleague is detaining the driver of a van outside the building. They had already loaded a crate of goods when we arrived.'

Sarah frowned. What had happened to change their plans? Gwyneth had only said she would ask Mike to have a word when he came to pick her up from work.

Maisie could see that Sarah was looking confused and called out to her, 'You was busy with yer visitor, and we spotted Cecil 'ere instructing these men out the front of the store. Freda used the phone in the office ter ring the police station, and Mike was 'ere in a flash once she'd explained. We didn't 'ave any time ter let you know, and we didn't want ter alarm the customers. It wouldn't have looked good fer Woolworths.'

'There's been a big mistake here,' Cecil said as Mike helped him to his feet, assisted by the rough-handed Maisie. 'I was in the process of having this stock unloaded. It was the light bulbs we'd been waiting for. I managed to source a supply,' he added, puffing out his chest. 'I have some for the Bexleyheath store as well.'

'A likely tale,' Maisie said, prodding him in the chest with a finger. 'You was pinching it, just like you've pinched other stuff from this store.'

'How dare you say such things? You can collect your cards first thing in the morning. Mrs Gilbert, have this person removed from the premises. You can go, too,' Cecil added, jerking his chin towards Freda.

'Hold on one moment,' Gina Jones said. 'Mr Porter, can you explain to me why you are moving stock from one store to another without having completed the necessary paperwork?'

Sarah didn't understand; she'd thought Gina was on their side. 'But . . . ?'

Gina shot her a warning look. 'Answer me, Mr Porter. Where are the documents to support your story?'

He raised a hand and pointed to Sarah. 'She does all the paperwork for this store. Ask her. She was trained by that Billington woman; no wonder everything is a mess. Women shouldn't be in management, that's blatantly obvious.'

Sarah was rooted to the spot in fear. Was he blaming her for the missing stock and everything that had gone wrong?

'Don't start all that malarkey,' Maisie scoffed. 'That wooden crate on yer vehicle has already been in here. You took it out before the coppers arrived.'

'Liar,' Cecil scoffed. 'You're all bloody liars and up to something. You're blaming me to cover yourselves.'

'I can prove that the crate was in this store. And that he pinched it,' Maisie said with a smirk.

'Please do,' Gina smiled, as Mike nodded in agreement.

Maisie put her hand into the pocket of her overall and pulled out a lipstick, passing it to Gina Jones. 'Would you recognize this colour if you saw it again?'

Gina took the lipstick and examined the casing before opening and checking inside. 'Yes, Max Factor. You have good taste – and excellent contacts, as it's been hard to come by. I use this colour myself.'

'Then follow me,' Maisie said, and led Gina and the girls out to the street where several other policemen had joined Mike's colleague. They'd lifted the crate from the vehicle and placed it on the pavement. 'Before you get too close I'd best explain that I marked the crate on all sides wiv a cross using me lipstick. I also wrote a few words on the bill of lading inside the crate.' She whispered a few words into Gina's ear, causing the woman to laugh out loud before she pulled a notebook out of her pocket and jotted down the words.

'Sergeant, perhaps you'd like to check the packing case for us?'

Mike made a thorough check of the outside of the crate. 'There seem to be some red crosses on each of the four sides.'

'This colour?' Gina asked, holding out the lipstick.

'It's exactly the same colour. I take it you now want me to open the crate?'

'If you would, please,' Gina Jones said, 'and take out the bill of lading you will find inside and read the handwritten words you find on it.'

Mike forced the wooden lid off the crate and rummaged in the straw packing for the piece of paper. 'Cecil Porter is a dirty rotten thief,' he read, prompting a ripple of surprised laughter.

'I think we have the proof we require. Please take him away, Sergeant,' Gina said with a smile as she waved her own notebook for all to see the words she'd written down.

As Mike marched Cecil away, Gina Jones turned to the four friends. 'I don't know how to thank you, ladies.'

'You could make Sarah our new manager,' Maisie said as Sarah blushed in embarrassment.

Gina nodded her head. 'That's an excellent idea. You'll be hearing from head office very soon. Can I rely on you to carry on in charge until it is made formal, along with the pay rise?'

Sarah felt her stomach lurch. 'I suppose so,' she whispered.

17

'My oh my, whatever next?' Ruby said to Gwyneth, who'd popped over with a cake she'd baked, as she wiped her eyes. 'The things you girls get up to, and now our Sarah is a manager; I'm lost for words. Here, George, have you heard what happened down at Woolworths when Sarah was made manager?' she called out the back door to where George was enjoying a chat with Bob and Alan.

'Yes, Mum, people have spoken of nothing else. I wish I'd seen Mike taking that chap away,' he called back before returning to his own conversation. 'So how's it going down the workshop?'

Alan shook his head. 'It's up and down. I thought the other week I'd cracked it when a delivery of smashed-up motorbikes came in, but after going through it all I made up one bike out of the load and so far there's not been a taker. The scrap man has done better out of the deal.'

'It's early days, though,' Bob said. 'You've got a good head on your shoulders, and word will get out soon enough; then you'll be rushed off your feet. At least your Sarah's doing all right, from what I've heard? I suppose there's an increased wage that goes along with being a manager?'

Alan was finding it hard to keep a pleasant smile on his face. At a time when he was struggling to bring in even a few shillings, his wife had gone and landed a job that could have been his by rights if he hadn't been so headstrong. Now, if he gave up on his dream of running his own business and went to Woolworths cap in hand for a job, his own wife could be his boss. 'She's doing nicely, thanks Bob. I'm proud of her,' he said – and in truth he was, even if he was uncomfortable feeling beholden to a woman to keep him fed and a roof over his head. It wasn't natural for a woman to be the breadwinner.

'I've got some brown ale keeping cool in the pantry. Do you fancy one?' Bob asked the two men.

'That sounds good,' George said. 'I brought a bottle of sherry for the ladies. We will be celebrating our Sarah's success in style. By the way, where is my clever daughter?'

'She went to meet Betty in town and walk back with her. Douglas was looking at premises as he's intent on expanding his business now the war is all but over, bar us getting those lads back from the clutches of the Japs.'

'It's good to know one business is doing well,' Alan said, trying hard not to look glum. 'I suppose there'll always be a need for an undertaker, even if people don't need a motorbike repaired.'

George watched his son-in-law struggle with his composure and could see a young man faced with a bleak future while his wife's star was on the ascent. Something needed to be done, and fast.

*

'You look very smart, my dear,' Betty said, stepping back to look Sarah up and down after kissing her cheek. 'Being a manager of F. W. Woolworth really suits you.'

'Maisie told me I had to dress the part now I wasn't wearing a maroon overall all day long. Dad treated me to this from Hedley Mitchell, and Maisie ran up a couple of skirts for me. I must admit it felt rather strange walking into work and knowing the responsibility for the whole store was on me.'

'But Sarah, your duties are no different to the ones you were already carrying out. The only difference is that you don't have Cecil Porter getting under your feet or me deciding how you should organize your time. You are in charge now, and you have a bright future,' Betty said, pushing the pram containing her daughter alongside Sarah's pram, where young Buster was sleeping peacefully. Betty held her breath for a moment to stop the wobble in her voice. She didn't want Sarah to see that she wanted her old world back, and could see it slipping further and further from her grasp.

'I suppose you are right,' Sarah said, staring ahead, knowing that her dream of staying at home to care for her family was floating away from her. Perhaps her dreams weren't meant to be? 'What did you think of the premises Douglas wanted to look at?' she asked, moving on to a safer area of conversation.

'They're very good, but so spacious. It's three shops. Two have been knocked into one large premises, and there's a smaller one on the side that someone has been subletting until recently. It needs painting and tidying up, then Douglas can think about letting it out.'

'So he'll sign the lease?'

'I do believe he will. He's so full of plans. He even wants me to run the front of house.' She laughed.

'It will be rather different to running a branch of Woolworths. Will you be able to take young Charlotte to work with you?' Sarah asked, kicking herself for mentioning the store again.

Betty screwed up her face. 'I'd rather not. She has her routine and I'd not like to disturb her. We have a very good housekeeper, and Douglas is all for hiring a nanny, so I've no excuse not to help him.'

'Lucky you,' Sarah said, thinking of her own worries about leaving Buster with someone and arranging for Georgina to be picked up from school. Maisie had been the first to suggest that Buster could join her children, and they could pay Sadie a little more for caring for an extra child. Sadie had been overjoyed at the suggestion; so there was no reason for Sarah to add her children to the list of reasons why she shouldn't accept the job of store manager.

'Yes, I know I'm very fortunate . . . but in some ways I wish my life hadn't changed so much,' Betty said, realizing she needed to unburden her thoughts after all; and to whom better than her friend, Sarah?

Sarah stopped pushing her pram and turned to Betty. 'We're a right pair, aren't we? Here we are with the most adorable babies as well as lovely families back home, and we still aren't happy?'

Betty laughed. 'We should be grateful for what we have. So many women are not as fortunate as we are. We survived the war and have so much to look forward to. We must try to be more positive and pin a smile on our faces.'

'I'll do my best,' Sarah said, knowing that she would have to dig deep to keep her promise to Betty. 'Isn't that Freda sitting on the step of Woolworths?' she added as they crossed the road from Cross Street.

'I do believe it is, and she looks so sad. Come on – let's get these prams over the road and see what the problem is,' Betty said, bumping her pram off the curb so suddenly that young Charlotte awoke and started to cry. 'Blast! I'll never get the hang of caring for a baby,' Betty muttered, as Sarah leant into the pram and soothed the child.

'It takes time to learn,' Sarah said as they hurried towards Woolies.

'You all made it seem so easy,' Betty sighed. 'I'm much better with grown-ups; and it looks as though my skills will be needed with our Freda. The poor girl seems to be sobbing her heart out.'

Both women parked their prams in front of the store. Betty hurried to sit by the younger woman's side, while Sarah checked Betty had set the brake properly in case the baby started to roll down the slight slope of the pavement.

'My goodness, Freda, you look distraught. Whatever has happened? Is it news about Sandy?'

Freda cuffed her eyes and blew her nose on the clean handkerchief Betty passed to her. 'We can always rely on you to have a handkerchief,' she said with a hiccup, referring to when Betty had kept a stock of them in her Woolworths desk drawer when her staff became distraught over something or other. 'You'll have to remember that, Sarah,' she added, trying to raise a smile but failing.

Sarah sat on the other side of Freda and put her arm round her shoulder. 'What has upset you so that you can't come home and share your problem?' she asked.

'I didn't want to spoil Ruby's tea party with bad news. I thought if I sat here for a while I could compose myself, and then I could walk back to Alexandra Road and join in the celebrations for your promotion. Then I passed their shop, and the memories came flooding back of the happy times I've spent with Molly and her family,' Freda said, as the tears returned.

Both women looked across the road to the Misson family's ironmongery business and noticed a few people standing in front of the shop with their heads bowed.

'Oh no, don't tell me something has happened to your friend Molly?' Sarah said. Freda had got her love of helping with the Brownies and Girls Guides from her friend Molly Missons and her mother, while Norman Missons was well known in the town for the busy shop they'd come to rely on over the years.

'No, Molly is fine – it's her parents. They were both killed in a car accident in Canterbury earlier today. I bumped into one of the Brownie mothers and she told me. I popped over to the shop and the staff confirmed the awful news. Molly is on her way home from the farm she works on as a Land Girl. Mr and Mrs Missons have been so good to me and Molly is my only friend apart from you two and Maisie,' she sobbed. 'I can't begin to understand how she must be feeling. She's going to be alone in that big house up the avenue and I don't think she has any family to speak of.'

'The poor girl,' Betty said, trying hard to fight back her own tears. Norman Missons and his wife had been the people who came to her rescue when Cecil Porter had locked them in the store the day she gave birth to Charlotte. In fact, Douglas had suggested they name their daughter Charlotte after Mrs Missons, who was so helpful that day, and also Charlie, who had been Betty's first love and Douglas's best friend in the trenches of the Great War. 'None of us know what is round the next corner, do we?' she said, looking to Sarah, who nodded and gave a weak smile.

'I don't know what to do,' Freda said.

Sarah gave Freda's shoulders a squeeze. 'You are going to be the friend you already are to Molly, and you will keep the Brownie and Guide packs running just as Charlotte Missons would have wished.'

Freda nodded her head vigorously. 'You're right. I was being selfish and panicking.'

'Anyone would under the circumstances. You are also grieving for the friends you've lost. When will Molly be home?' Sarah asked.

'Later this evening. Would it be all right for me to go up there, do you think? I really don't have much idea of what to do under these circumstances.'

'Gosh, yes, and take a bag with a few things so you can stay with the poor girl. Nan can give you some food to take as well, I'm sure,' she suggested. 'Just be there for when she wants to talk and be a shoulder to cry on. You're a good friend, Freda; you'll know what to do, and don't even think about coming in to work tomorrow. Molly is your priority for now.'

Freda gave them both a hug and wiped her eyes. 'Thank you. I think I can do this, knowing I have you all to fall back on. The months to come are going to be rather strange, and so different to what we are used to.'

Sarah and Betty both agreed as their thoughts once again slipped to their own worries and wishes.

'Come on, David, we were due down at number thirteen over an hour ago. If you don't pull yer finger out the kids will 'ave got grubby again and be unfit ter be seen in public, plus the twins will need feeding and changing again,' Maisie said as she looked out of the kitchen window to where Bessie and Claudette were throwing a ball for an excited young Ruby, who was screaming with excitement as it fell from her hands.

David sat at the kitchen table with his shirt undone and two days' stubble on his chin. 'You go, I'll stay here and watch the twins. I can't face all the back-slapping and cheering that will be going on because Sarah's got herself promoted.'

Maisie took a deep breath. 'I don't know what's come over you, David Carlisle, but you ain't the same bloody man I married. Get yourself off yer arse and at least 'ave a shave, even if you don't intend ter go and congratulate our friend. Besides, if I leave the twins wiv you they'll be screaming fer food and stinking ter high heaven by the time I get back. You're about as useful as a chocolate teapot these days.'

David stood up so quickly his chair scraped backwards over the linoleum and crashed to the floor. 'For God's sake, woman, can't you see I don't want to go out? It's not just listening to all their happy talk, but I can't stand the sympathy when they see my arm.'

'But David, they all mean well. No one's mocking you. These are our friends and as good as our family any day – better, in my case,' she said, trying hard to smile. David's mood swings had become progressively worse over the past few days, and she was finding it hard to predict how he would be when she came home from work. Even her excitement over the arrest of Cecil Porter had been met with a blank stare. It was as if he was giving up on life because of his injury. 'I bet you've not tried any of those exercises the doctor told you ter do?'

'What good will they do?'

'You was told it would keep the arm flexible, and it might even bring back a little use while they look at other channels of treatment.'

David ignored her as he watched the girls in the garden. 'I can't even play ball with the children or change a nappy properly, let alone find myself a job and be a proper husband to you.'

Maisie looked away. She'd forgotten the last time they'd shared a bed, as these days David would often fall asleep drunk on the front room sofa. 'You need ter pull yerself together and stop feeling so bloody sorry fer yerself,' she snapped.

'Or what?' he said bleakly, turning to stare at her.

'Or you might wake up one of these days and I'll 'ave sodded off, and taken the kids wiv me. I didn't sign up fer any of this. You've started ter treat me as if it was my fault Fred stabbed you.'

'Well, he did, and there's no denying that,' David shouted back.

'But he paid for it wiv his bloody life, and now he's lying as dead as a doornail in an unmarked grave up Brook Street cemetery. Whereas you might as well be dead, for all the use you are ter yerself and ter this family!' Maisie screamed back.

'Our dad's dead?' A small voice came from the back door, where Bessie stood with her arm round her half sister, Claudette.

'Oh, David, whatever 'ave we done?' Maisie whispered, as both she and David rushed to the girls and pulled them into an embrace.

'We didn't mean fer you both ter find out like this,' she said as she smothered their white faces with kisses, dashing away the hot scalding tears falling onto her cheeks. 'Yes, your daddy has died and gone ter heaven.'

'Does it mean we can stay living with you both forever?' Bessie asked, looking between David and Maisie.

'Both of us?' Claudette added.

'Yes, we want you to stay with us forever. We want to be your new mummy and daddy,' David said in a choked voice.

'Then I'm pleased he's dead,' Bessie said, jutting out her chin.

'Blimey, you're a proper Dawson,' Maisie smiled, 'but you must never be pleased someone has died.'

'Not even Hitler?' Claudette asked, giving Maisie a sly look.

'Well, p'raps we can make an exception fer Hitler,' she replied, not daring to look at David in case she laughed. 'David is going ter see a man who can make it legal so you can be our own daughters. What do you think of that?'

'Are you, David?' Bessie asked, getting excited.

David looked a little shamefaced. 'It may take a little while, but yes, one day we will be your mummy and daddy.'

'Even if one day you might sod off and take us with you?' Bessie asked Maisie.

Oh God, how long were they standing there listening? Maisie thought to herself.

'Now, you aren't ter listen ter us. We was just 'avin' a bit of a barney. It wasn't fer little girls' ears.'

'And no one's going anywhere,' David said, slipping an arm round Maisie's shoulders and giving her a gentle squeeze. 'I love you all too much to let you leave me. I've been a bit poorly lately and it's made me miserable. I promise I'll try harder in future.'

'Is it because of that bloody arm?' Claudette asked innocently.

David's face twitched as he tried not to smile. 'Yes, you could say that, but it should feel a little better if I do my exercises. In fact, you can both help me by playing catch with your ball in the garden. What do you say to that?'

'I'd say that's pretty damned good,' Bessie exclaimed, imitating Maisie's voice. 'Can we start right now?'

'I don't see why not. What do you say, Mummy?'

'Well, we should be going down ter Ruby's fer our tea; but I think p'raps on this occasion we can make our apologies, don't you? We could even have fish and chips later instead.'

The girls cheered and rushed out into the garden as David pulled Maisie close with his good arm and kissed her gently. 'Friends?'

'Friends,' she said, snuggling into his chest. 'But you do need ter 'ave that shave.'

'That's a part of my life over and done with,' George said as he sat down at the dinner table. 'I've been looking forward to this all day.' He picked up his knife and fork as Ruby brought a plate of steak and kidney pudding to the table along with a steaming pile of boiled potatoes, carrots and peas.

'Get stuck into that. There's more vegetables than meat in the pudding, but you'll get the flavour of the meat at least,' his mother said with satisfaction.

'Aren't you eating with me?' George asked, reaching for the salt cellar.

'We had ours earlier. Now, tell me how it went down in Devon. Was there much to shift?' Ruby asked as she sat down opposite her son and watched him eat.

'I met the people who'd purchased our Devon house and they seemed very nice. I managed to move all the furniture out, and bagged up clothes we'd left there when we came up to Crayford.'

'What did you do with Irene's bits and pieces?' Ruby asked, wondering if George had found it hard to go through his late wife's personal effects.

Knowing what his mum was hinting at, he gave her a

wry smile. 'You know, it wasn't too bad at all. If Irene had liked those clothes and bits of paste jewellery she'd have brought them with her when we rented the Crayford house, so it didn't upset me too much to off load as much as possible with the WVS so others can make use of the garments. The jewellery can go to Sarah, and she can decide what she wants to keep or share with her friends. I did keep back some of her posher outfits, as I thought Maisie might find a use for the fabric. I know how she likes to unpick things and make bits and pieces for the kids.'

'That's good of you, George, and I'm pleased it wasn't too painful.'

'I won't say I didn't get down a few times when I was looking at photographs and some letters I came across from when we were courting; but in time I'll be able to smile, and Irene wasn't one to want us to be upset. Sarah can have it all when she's got her own place.'

'That's as it should be; she can pass on what she wants to Georgina and Buster when they are older.' Ruby smiled to herself. 'For all her ways, I do miss her. I just hope the war and our losses will make a difference, or I'll be asking him up above what it was all for.'

'I'm with you there, Mum – then for Winston Churchill to lose the election. What is the world coming to? I've given some thought to going into politics – in a local way,' he said, seeing Ruby's eyes glint. 'There's no need to start thinking of me as the next prime minister.'

'Perhaps once you're settled in your new home you can give it more thought. We need some decent people on the council to speak up for the people of Erith, or they'll be bulldozing it to the ground or other such nonsense. Now, Irene would be behind your plan to be a councillor.'

George chuckled as he put his knife and fork down. 'She'd have been in her element. It would have cost me a fortune in new hats.'

'So, what's next?' Ruby asked as she took his empty plate to the kitchen.

George followed her and leant on the door frame as she placed the plate in a bowl and poured hot water from the kettle on top. 'I'm going to start looking about for a place to buy. I can't keep renting the Crayford house indefinitely. It was supposed to be short-term, while I was going between the Devon plant and Vickers. Now I'm up this end full time, I want a place of my own.'

'In Crayford?'

'I'd like to move back to Erith. It's my hometown, after all, and I'd be near my old mum.'

'Not so much of the old,' Ruby said, flapping a tea towel at George, although she was over the moon at the prospect of having her son so close by.

'I'll need to go through Irene's things at the Crayford house. I've not done a thing since . . . since that day. I've been sleeping in the spare room rather than face it.'

'You can't keep doing that. Are you ready to sort out her things now? I'll come over with you and help.'

George put his arm round Ruby's shoulders. 'Not now, Mum. I'm all in after driving back from Devon. I was thinking of taking my time to look for a new house, as it will be my permanent home.'

'In that case, let me and Bob come over while you're at work and move all of Irene's things into the spare room so you can at least have a decent-sized bedroom to yourself. That room you're using at the moment is no more than a box room. You can close the door on it all until you're ready to tackle it once and for all. Eh?'

George nodded and reached into his pocket for a key. 'Take this one, I have another. But please don't go knocking yourself out doing too much. I know what you're like. You'll be fussing around me, then home to cook for Freda and Bob.'

'Freda's moved in with her friend Molly for a couple of weeks while Molly gets to grips with losing her parents. Bob can have fish and chips with me on the way home from your place, so don't you go worrying about me.'

'The poor kid,' George said, shaking his head. 'More reason for you to go steady and not tire yourself out; we don't want to be standing over your grave any time soon.'

'I'll take care,' Ruby said, turning away from him to put the kettle on for a cuppa while starting to make a list in her head of everything that needed doing.

18

October 1945

'Everything seems spick and span. Do you have any problems or questions?' Gina Jones asked as she closed her notebook and looked at Sarah across the desk.

Sarah smiled politely and resisted the urge to check her hair was still neatly pinned up. It didn't feel right, any more than the constant checking of her lipstick in the small mirror hung on the wall of the office. She'd started changing her appearance on the advice of Maisie, who'd suggested it would make her look a little older and more in command of the Erith store. She longed for the days when a wash with soap and water and wearing a clean overall was all it took for her to do her job. 'I'm comfortable with my job, but would like to implement a few changes,' she said, pulling a sheet of paper from her desk. 'I've found from time to time, with staff off work, we don't have anyone experienced on certain counters. First, I would like all supervisors to have had some hands-on experience in all sections. Secondly, counter staff can cover for other sections of the store if we are short-staffed,

342

and that includes the canteen.' She watched tentatively as the store inspector looked through her notes and scribbled in her own notebook.

'Yes, I can see that this would work. Would you start by implementing a training scheme for your supervisors to develop knowledge of each department in the store? They will then be able to assist you in training your counter staff. I'll watch this with interest as it's something we could copy for our other stores. Now, I must be on my way. I have to visit the Bexleyheath store before returning to head office and filing my report. Perhaps next time we could have lunch together. You do have the best cook amongst all the stores I cover,' Gina smiled.

'I'll tell Maureen you said so. She will be delighted. I have to agree with you – as you know, she is my mother-in-law, and at the moment we live with her while my husband is building up his business,' Sarah said politely as she followed Gina downstairs.

'Ah yes, Alan, isn't it? The motorbike trade's gain is Woolworths' loss. Please give him my best wishes.'

'I will, thank you,' Sarah said as she shook hands with Gina and watched as she got into her car and drove away. If only I could give Alan the message without him going all moody on me, she thought to herself. She'd found it best to get home from work and remove her office clothes, wash off the make-up and turn back into a wife and mother before he came home from the workshop. She tried to make no mention of her job in the hope he didn't feel she was doing better and earning more money than he was. It was a problem getting worse by the day. Not wishing to return to her office to brood, she decided to walk around the store, stopping to talk to customers and passing on her congratulations to staff who'd been worried about the inspector's visit.

'Mrs Gilbert, could yer spare me a minute?' Maisie asked. 'We 'ave a visitor you may want ter be aware of.' She indicated with a nod of her head to where Freda was talking earnestly, in a quiet corner of the store, to a young man.

'My God, isn't that Sandy? I thought he was under arrest somewhere?' Sarah said, trying in vain to remember what the situation was since he'd been taken away on the evening of Ruby and Bob's wedding.

Maisie stood behind one of the central pillars so she could peer round it at the young couple. 'The last I 'eard, he was still in custody and not likely to be released fer a very long time. Perhaps he's been released, but why would he come 'ere ter see Freda? The kid's not long got over being let down by her love life. This will just bring it all back.'

'Freda was more than a little in love with Sandy, but at least she'd started going out with men again. She went to the pictures last week with a new trainee manager over at Mitchell's. I haven't heard that they are going out again, but it's early days; and she's spending a lot of time with Molly at the moment. Oh, this is such a pickle,' Sarah sighed.

'Something seems strange ter me,' Maisie said, standing on tiptoe so she could look over the heads of passing shoppers. 'He seems ter be in some kind of uniform – even if it is dungarees and a pullover.'

'You're right. Oh dear, do you think he's escaped from where he was being held?'

'If he has he could be desperate ter get away, and that's why he's sought out Freda.'

Sarah couldn't help feeling their thoughts were bordering on the ridiculous, but even so . . . 'I think we should speak to someone. Dad would know what's happened with Sandy.'

'We could get hold of Mike Jackson if he's on duty. I've always thought it was handy to know a copper.'

Despite her worries, Sarah raised a smile. 'Gwyneth's not at work for a few days; she did say something about taking a trip to visit her parents in the Welsh valleys. Mike could well have gone with them. I'm going to pop upstairs and make a phone call to Dad. He should be in work today. Would you keep an eye on things for me? But please be discreet, and don't put yourself in danger. If Sandy has escaped detention he could be desperate.'

'What if he leaves the store?'

'Follow him. At least then we can tell someone in authority which way he is heading.'

Sarah hurried to her office and put through a call to her dad. As she waited there was a tap at the door. She placed her hand over the mouthpiece to call out, 'Come in,' and was astounded when Sandy walked into the office, followed by Freda and then Maisie. Lost for words, she nodded to Sandy to take the one seat opposite her desk while Maisie stood guard by the door. Placing the telephone receiver on her desk, she took a deep breath. 'Well, I must say this is a surprise.'

*

David Carlisle gazed out of the window of his office and chewed on his pencil thoughtfully. It was a miserable, damp day, and the river looked grim with its grey ships and muddy banks. This just about summed up his job, he thought, as it was just as grey and miserable. Maisie had been surprised when he took the job after scanning the vacancy columns of the *Erith Observer*. It was local to home, he could add up and he could use a pencil in his good hand, albeit with some difficulty. He could still see her frowning as he picked up their telephone and enquired about the position. Two weeks later he was here, wishing he'd listened to his wife when she said the job would bore him to tears. It had taken him all of an hour to realize he'd made a terrible mistake.

'Mr Carlisle, I wondered if you'd finished those bills of lading I gave you earlier?' a voice said from behind his left shoulder.

David jumped, and caught a smirk of satisfaction from the elderly secretary as he dropped his pencil. She was the senior person in the office and seemed to be their self-appointed boss. He'd bent over to pick up the pencil before he realized he'd reached out with the arm that still failed him. The woman didn't seem the kind to look sympathetically on a person's failing, and he'd be damned if he was going to have her look down her beaky nose at him. Concentrating with all his might, he thought of the times his girls had helped him with his exercises by throwing their balls for him to catch and making him reach out to take something from their hands. If he could do it for them, he could do it to show this woman he wasn't useless. Aware that she was waiting, he leant as far forward as possible until he could feel the pencil at the tips of his fingers. Concentrating until he thought his head would burst, he eased it between two fingers and closed them. Would the pencil stay there as he leant backwards, slowly raising his arm? Within seconds, which felt like hours, he had it in sight and grabbed it with his good hand before it could escape. Trying not to let out a huge sigh of relief, he casually placed it on the table before sliding the documents the woman had asked about towards her. 'If there isn't anything else, Miss Harrison, I'll go for my lunch,' he said, not waiting for a reply as he collected his hat and coat and left the office. He did catch a piece of a conversation in which she used the word 'cripple', but it didn't bother him, as he had no intention of ever going back into the building.

Feeling much cheered, he headed towards the high street, whistling a slightly off-key tune. The sun had come out, and the greyness seemed to have lifted from the river as well as from his heart. It was a good day after all.

'Someone looks happy with himself!' a voice called out from across the road.

David gave a grin. 'Hello there, Douglas, how are you on this lovely morning?' he enquired as he crossed the road to where his friend was standing with a box of decorating materials. 'Will you join me for a pint of best bitter? I'm celebrating!'

'I wish I could, but I have a job of work to do this afternoon. I take it you are enjoying your new position?'

David slapped Douglas on the back. 'I'm enjoying it that much, I have just left the premises and will never return. My decision, not theirs,' he added, in case Douglas thought he'd been fired.

'Then you are the perfect person to help me out this afternoon. Come along inside, and I'll show you around and explain my problem.'

David followed Douglas into his new premises, pointing out how two of the shops had been knocked into one, making it large and airy. 'You know the layout of my other premises in Bexleyheath, don't you?'

'Intimately,' David grinned, thinking back to the occasion when he had helped to deter thieves from the funeral director's premises and rescued Douglas from inside a coffin.

'My problem here is the front office is far too big. I don't have the kind of business where I can display stock in the windows or need a waiting room on view, as most of my clients make private appointments to see me. '

David walked up and down the shop area and had to agree it was rather on the large side. 'What's it like out the back?' he asked, heading to a door.

'Take a look. I've started moving some stock down here from the other premises. It was the large stockroom and parking for our vehicles that attracted me to the building to begin with.'

David wandered around, looking outside and going back into the shop part of the building. 'Do you have some paper and a pen?' he asked, before sitting down at an old desk that had seen better days and starting to sketch. 'Look, I thought that if you partitioned off this part of the shop front it could be used for some kind of complementary service, like a florist. There's a side door so they don't have to interrupt your clients, and you'd benefit from having another business close at hand. What do you think?'

Douglas thought for a while and checked the door and where he could have a partition built. 'I have one problem. What do I do with this?' he asked, leading David out onto the pavement and going to the end of the building, where there was another smaller shop. This is also part of my property; and yes, I'd considered having a complementary business use it. It was sublet until recently, when the woman who ran it retired.'

David looked thoughtfully at the large window. 'Do you have the keys?'

Douglas handed them over and followed his friend inside. 'It was a ladies' outfitters. But the owner felt that her clientele, being on the elderly side, might not feel comfortable shopping next door to a funeral director's business. I feel I may have a similar problem whoever I sublet this shop to, and that was why I'd thought a florist might work here – but I can see that your idea to incorporate it within the main shop is much better.'

David went to the back of the shop, where he found a small workroom and another door.

'That leads outside to where we all share the facilities. Again, that may be a problem with whoever wants to rent the shop,' Douglas said.

David was now standing looking out of the large window thoughtfully as he watched busy shoppers passing by. 'I know the perfect business for this shop. Can you give me a while to convince the person she really needs to set up on her own? I can pay you some rent money to hold it?'

Douglas raised his hand. 'There's no need for that. And if I'm right, I do believe your Maisie would make a go of it as well.'

'What are you doing here, Sandy?' Sarah asked.

'I don't mean to cause you any problems, Mrs Gilbert. I just wanted to see Freda to say goodbye. I was on my way before she stopped me,' he said, glaring at where Maisie stood with her arms folded by the door.

'He made Freda cry, so I got him by the scruff of his neck and dragged 'im up here before he left the store.'

'I'm not upset, Maisie, I'm just sad about what has happened,' Freda explained. 'I know we wouldn't have made a go of things, so I'm not weeping for my lost love. Sandy is water under the bridge now.'

'But is it German water, is what I want ter know?' Maisie snarled. 'You took advantage of George, and he's a decent man; and you wheedled yer way into Freda's affections ter make yerself look good in George's eyes. I don't know where you come from, but around here we do things by the book. Whatever must yer parents think of all this?'

He looked down into his lap. 'It was a lie.'

'You mean you don't have a family in Scotland?'

'No. I was brought up in a children's home.'

Freda spun to face him. 'I know I'm over you but at the time I thought you loved me . . . but you were lying.' Her voice cracked with emotion. 'And you gave away information to the Germans about things that were being built at

Vickers? How could you sell us to the enemy? Did you want them to win the war, and no doubt kill us all in our beds?'

'No!' Sandy shouted, making them all jump. 'I wanted the war to end. In fact, I didn't want there to be a war at all. I'm a pacifist.'

'Well, you 'ad a bloody funny way of showing it. And now you've 'opped it from wherever you were being held,' Maisie said, prodding him in the back a few times to make her point. 'Were you even injured at Dunkirk?'

'I was never in the army. My leg has been like this since birth, and it's most likely why I was abandoned.'

'I lost me first 'usband at Dunkirk,' Maisie said quietly. ''Ave you got any idea 'ow painful that is? 'Ere you are telling lie after lie and 'urtin' people, and you ain't even got the guts to face what you deserve. If Woolworths sold guns I'd not think twice about holding one to yer 'ead and firing it at point blank range. I'm glad you've not got any parents – no one should live wiv the shame of 'avin' a kid like you.'

The room fell quiet as everyone digested Maisie's words. Sarah glanced at the telephone, wondering if her dad had been listening. 'How did you escape, and where were you planning to go, Sandy?'

'They weren't watching me very well, and the opportunity arose for me to slip away. My friends were arranging for me to get on a ship bound for Ireland. Before I left, I wanted to speak to Freda and say sorry.'

'You've said it now, so sod off,' Maisie spat at him.

'No,' Freda said, putting a hand on his knee as he went

to stand up. 'I want you to give yourself up, Sandy. Would you do that, please?'

Sandy took her hand. 'I'm not sure I can, Freda. You've no idea what it's like being a prisoner and knowing fellow inmates would kill me if they knew what I was in there for.'

'Wouldn't you go back for me?' she asked, giving him a pleading look.

'I'm sorry,' he said, standing up and turning towards the door. 'It was a mistake to come here. I just wanted to see you one more time, Freda. You're the only good thing to have happened in my life, but now I'd best leave before someone lets the authorities know.'

'It's too late, son,' Mike Jackson said as he pushed open the door and walked into the office, followed by three constables.

'How the hell . . . ?'

Sarah picked the telephone up and spoke softly to George. 'Thank you, Dad, I'll see you later,' she said, before replacing the receiver and turning to Mike. 'It looks as though we'll both have extra paperwork to do this afternoon?'

Mike watched as Sandy was taken away. 'On this occasion I'm happy to do it, if it means people like him are back in prison. Are you ladies all right?' he asked, looking at where Freda was sitting staring into space. 'Freda?'

'I think he did really love me,' she said, her eyes glistening.

'Tell me, Maisie – if Woolworths had sold guns, would you have used one?' Sarah asked.

'Too right I bloody would.'

*

'It's all in here, girls,' George said, leading Sarah and Maisie to the box room where his late wife's possessions were stored. 'Sarah, I have your mum's jewellery box locked away. I'll get it for you. It's yours to do with as you please. I also want you to have her mink stole, but as for the rest, you can sort out with Maisie what you wish to keep or give away.'

'As long as you're sure, Dad?' Sarah said, giving him a close look. 'Mum's things aren't doing any harm in here, are they?'

George looked uncomfortable and gave an embarrassed cough. 'The thing is, I've given notice on this house. Now that the Devon place is sold, I want to be out of here within the month and living in Erith.'

'Dad!' Sarah shrieked, and flung her arms round his neck. 'I'm so pleased you will be closer to the rest of the family. Where are you living?'

'I've just signed on a semi-detached house just off Avenue Road, behind Christ Church. I did wonder if it was a bit big for me, but Maureen said I'd have room for when Georgina and Buster come to visit.'

'Maureen?' Sarah asked with a frown. 'Why has Maureen been advising you?'

'I popped in to see Alan one day and Maureen was at the workshop. As I was off to look at the house afterwards, she accompanied me. I was glad of her company. Wandering round a strange house on your own isn't my idea of fun.'

'I'd have helped if you'd asked,' Sarah pouted.

'I can't be bothering my girl now she runs a busy shop, can I?' he said, kissing her cheek. 'Now, you get on with your sorting and I'll get the kettle on. I've even made a cake,' he grinned. 'It's one of Maureen's recipes. She told me it was easy to do, but I'll wait to see what you both think.'

'Are you sure you don't want ter come along in and help us, George?' Maisie said, giving Sarah a sideways glance. Her friend was looking quite miserable.

'No, I'll leave you to it. I have a book I want to finish, and women's fashions hold no interest for me,' he said.

'What was all that about?' Maisie asked as the two friends went into the box room.

'What was what about?' Sarah frowned as she picked up the first of the coats draped over a single bed, holding it up against herself. 'Do you think this would suit me?'

'I mean the face you pulled when yer dad mentioned Maureen. And no, it doesn't suit you. It's too ageing even fer a Woolies manager.'

'Oh, that,' Sarah said, folding the coat and placing it to one side. 'Dad and Maureen seem to be very much a couple these days. Even Nan had their names linked together on her list of wedding guests.'

'You're being daft. Why wouldn't Ruby put their names together? After all, it's yer dad and Alan's mum. It means nothing. Besides, that was months ago – why worry about something so trivial that 'appened ages ago?'

Sarah shrugged her shoulders. 'I just feel as though Maureen is starting to step in, when Mum hasn't been gone a year.'

'She was grateful to yer dad for his 'elp when her leg was still bad, and he was at her 'ouse a lot at that time; but that was because you lived there, you daft cow,' Maisie said as she picked up a full-length gown and looked thoughtful. 'I could make some lovely kiddies' party dresses out of this.'

'Perhaps you're right,' Sarah said, looking at the dress. 'What, about Maureen?'

'No, this dress. I don't think Mum ever wore it. You know, you could make some lovely things out of all these dresses. Why don't you take the lot and see what you can do with them? There's nothing I want. I have Mum's mink stole and the jewellery. She used to be so impressed with your dressmaking skills, it seems only right you have all of this.'

Maisie was thoughtful as she went through the garments. 'Do you think yer dad will give us a lift 'ome wiv 'em? Gawd knows what David will say when he gets in from work and sees it all.'

'Look at the state of you, Douglas,' Betty scolded as her husband walked in through the front door and headed to the dining room as the family was sitting down to dinner. 'You have dust all over your suit – and what is that stuck in your hair? Go and wash, and for goodness' sake take off the suit. I'll have to see about getting it cleaned tomorrow. Who would think that a funeral director could get himself into such a state?'

Clementine and Dorothy giggled as their father left the room looking suitably chastised. 'Should we wait for Daddy, do you think?' the elder girl asked.

'It would be the right thing to do. Help me carry the

dishes out to the kitchen, and I'll put them in the oven to keep warm.'

The two girls dutifully followed their stepmother to the kitchen and watched as she placed the food in the still-warm oven. 'Can we read for a little while?' the younger girl asked.

'What a good idea, Dorothy; if you fetch my bag, I have a new book for you to read. There's also something for you, Clemmie,' she added, seeing the girl's smile fade. 'I know you aren't as keen to read as your sister.'

Clemmie gave her a grin. 'You know me far too well, Betty. I do like reading, but I much prefer to be outdoors playing hockey, or perhaps going to the cinema . . . ?'

Betty laughed. She adored her two stepchildren, and after a sticky start she felt she was thought of more as their new mother than someone who had married their father. 'I thought we could go to the cinema as a family at the weekend. There's an Old Mother Riley film on at the Odeon. I know you like Arthur Lucan.'

'Oh, I do – but do you know if there's a Clive Danvers film on with it? Freda told us she'd seen his latest with her friend Molly,' Clemmie said with pleading eyes.

Betty laughed. 'We'd need to check in the local newspaper, or ask Freda.' The two girls were now firm friends with Freda, who would sometimes stay with the Billington family to look after the girls and baby Charlotte when Betty and Douglas had an engagement to attend.

Dorothy came back into the room carrying two parcels wrapped in brown paper. She passed one to her sister, and kept the one with her name written in one corner. 'Oh, thank you, Betty,' she said as she unwrapped a book. 'I've so wanted to read *Stuart Little*.' She ran her hand over the cover with a sigh before settling down in an armchair.

'Oh my,' Clemmie declared, pulling out a bundle of coloured hair ribbons and a small receipt. 'A hockey stick,' she screamed in delight before putting her hand over her mouth, knowing their baby sister was asleep in her cot upstairs.

'I wasn't able to collect the hockey stick today, so I thought a few ribbons would be acceptable,' Betty smiled as her elder stepdaughter hugged her.

'I hope there's one of those for me?' Douglas said as he came downstairs rubbing his damp hair with a towel.

'Is that a hug you're wanting, or my hair ribbons?' Clemmie giggled, moving back from Betty so that Douglas could demand his own hug.

'What's all this; have you been spoiling the girls again?' he asked, looking over Dorothy's shoulder as she read her book.

Betty shrugged her shoulders. 'They're worth spoiling, and time hangs heavy on my shoulders these days.'

Douglas had noticed that under her smiles his wife was unhappy. He'd noticed it when she thought he wasn't watching, and when she was tired. He thought he had the answer to her problem. 'Let's have dinner, and then I have a surprise for you,' he said, planting a gentle kiss on her head.

After prising Dorothy away from her new book they enjoyed a leisurely meal, with Douglas regaling them with stories of his attempts at decorating the new premises.

'You should hire a professional to take on the job,' Betty

chastised him. 'Not only are you too busy to do such things, but a decorator could do so much better.'

'I'm enjoying it,' he smiled. 'Besides, David has been coming in to help me. He's had some really good ideas for the business. I do hope he finds himself a suitable position before too long. He seems to have become rather lost since his . . . his accident,' he said, checking his words as his daughters were listening.

'Hmm . . .' Betty said thoughtfully as she cleared the table.

Bringing coffee into the living room, after saying good-night to the girls, she took Douglas's newspaper from him and folded it. 'I've been thinking about the new premises, Douglas.'

'So have I, darling, and I've had the most marvellous idea. Now, sit yourself down and listen.'

'But, Douglas, I too have had an idea . . .'

'Please listen to mine first, my love,' he said, reaching across and taking her hands in his. 'I know you've been unhappy since giving birth to Charlotte and . . .'

'No, I could never be unhappy. I'm the most fulfilled woman there can be,' she interrupted him.

'Sshh – I mean, in you no longer being a working woman. You are an admirable mother to our children. No,' he said, raising his hand as she went to speak. 'You are someone who has worked all her life and attained a level in management that many men could not achieve. It took this bumbling person to fall in love with you and whip the carpet from under your feet, and I can see that you are missing your working life.'

'Oh Douglas,' Betty said as her eyes started to shine

with excitement. Was he saying she could try again to apply for her job back at Woolworths? It would be a hard-fought battle to be able to show head office she was capable of running a home as well as a busy store, but she knew she was up for the challenge, and with her husband's support it could be done.

'Yes, I should have thought of it earlier. You would be the ideal person to run our new premises in Erith.'

Betty felt her face crumble as she listened to his plans. What a fool she was to build her hopes, only to have them dashed to the ground. 'Douglas, please, I'm sorry, but I can't do this. It would be unfair of me to go along with your plans when working in your business would make me so miserable.'

Douglas's face dropped as he listened to her explain how she was prepared to support his business, but it was his, and she'd not fit in working for the man she lived with. 'My working life has always been Woolworths, and in a way I'm mourning the loss of that life,' she explained. 'Please forgive me, my dear.'

'I can't say I'm not disappointed,' he said, 'but I respect your decision. I thought it would be fun for us to work together, but I can see how you would be unhappy working in my world. I feel somewhat responsible for taking you away from Woolworths.'

'Don't ever think you took me away from my job when I now have everything I ever wanted,' she said passionately. 'I'll find something else to fill my days. I could join the WVS or something,' she said with a false brightness in her voice.

Douglas nodded his head, not taken in by her suggestion

for one moment. 'Whatever you decide, you know you have my support. Now, what was it you wanted to tell me?'

'Douglas, I do believe you have the ideal person to run the Erith side of the business right in front of your nose. David Carlisle would make an ideal business partner, don't you think?'

Douglas thought for a moment. 'By Jove, you're right. What a fool I've been not to even think of David. But would he consider the proposition?'

Betty laughed. 'Oh, Douglas, the two of you get along very well, and to me he sounds interested in the business. This would be as good for him as it would for you and your plans to expand. Why not ring him right now and put the proposition to him?'

Douglas gave his wife a brief kiss, and hurried from the room to place a call to the Carlisle household.

Betty sighed to herself as she poured their coffee, realizing it was now lukewarm. If only her own problem could be as easily solved as Douglas's.

19

'Well, I never!' David exclaimed, returning to the front room and fighting his way through a pile of women's dresses heaped on the settee to reclaim his seat.

'Well you never what?' Maisie asked while snipping carefully at a seam, unpicking the skirt of a forest green woollen dress. 'This will make a very nice skirt fer Sarah when I've remodelled it. She's been damned good letting me 'ave all this stuff of her mum's. I'm thinking I could get a kiddies' summer coat out of what's left. D'you think I could get a stall at Dartford market to flog me bits and pieces?'

David was still astounded at how his wife could be thinking of three things at the same time. Ignoring her sewing, which seemed to have taken over the house in recent days, he concentrated on his news. 'I've been offered a partnership in a business, would you believe?'

Maisie put down her scissors and gave her full attention to her husband. 'Who would do such a thing? Not that I don't think you would be a good . . . whatever it is,' she smiled.

'It was Douglas. He somehow came to the conclusion

it would suit us both, and wanted to sound me out. He's got big plans for the business, Maisie, and I'd love to be part of it. It would mean making an investment, though, as I doubt he would take me on just for my decorating skills.'

Maisie was secretly thrilled. She'd hoped beyond hope that something would come up that would interest David enough for a new career. Helping Douglas for the past week or so had put a spring in his step and taken his mind off his damaged arm, which meant he had more of a smile on his face than the frown they'd all become used to. 'Can we afford it?' she asked, trying to be sensible.

'I need to discuss things with him properly and find out what's involved. But my parents had already said they'd back me if I wanted to set up something on my own, so we could always go to them if need be.'

Maisie saw the glint of enthusiasm in his eyes. 'You really want ter do this, don't you?'

'I really do,' he said. 'There's something else I've been thinking about.'

Maisie frowned. What could he mean?

'I want you to put everything down and come with me now,' he said, jumping to his feet and reaching for her hand.

'What about the kids?' she laughed, caught up in his enthusiasm.

'We can ask Ruby or Freda to sit with the kids for half an hour.'

'I'm not fit ter be seen in public,' she shrieked, looking down at the old smock and skirt she wore when sewing.

'No one will see you. Come on, be a devil,' he laughed.

Maisie hadn't seen him so happy in an age. 'All right, but I need ter put on me face or I'm not going anywhere. I'll be five minutes.'

By the time Freda arrived, Maisie had her coat on and was ready to leave the house. She was intrigued to know what her husband was up to and hurried to keep up with him as he marched down Alexandra Road and turned into Manor Road, which led to the High Street.

'Isn't this Douglas's new undertaker's shop?' she asked, peering through the window with cupped hands.

'No, that part's next door. This, my love, is to be "Maisie's Modes" – if you accept the challenge?' he asked, producing a key from his pocket.

'Bleedin' hell,' Maisie gasped as she stepped into the shop and David switched on the electric light. 'You kept all this a secret.'

'If I told you, you'd have blown your top and said you didn't want to run your own dress shop. Look – there's a workroom out the back, and this door leads to a small kitchen and toilet that you will have to share with next door. What do you think?' he asked tentatively.

'I think you are a crafty beggar, but I love the shop, and I love you even more, David Carlisle,' she said, putting her arms round him and giving him a kiss without caring they could be seen from outside. 'Hey, what's this?' she asked, as David put both of his arms round her.

'I've been waiting for the right moment to show you that the exercises the children have been helping me with have worked.'

'Blimey, what an evening. Yer prospects are looking

good; I 'ave a new business, and me old man's fully functioning once more.'

'Not quite yet,' David said, pulling her back into his arms while reaching to switch off the light. 'But we have all night to make sure.'

'It's a lovely house, Dad,' Sarah said as she came in from the garden and shivered. 'Although it's more than a bit nippy out there; I don't think you should be out doing the garden while you've got that chesty cough. The damp won't do you any good at all.'

'I'm fine, don't you go worrying about me,' George said as he stopped and leant on the table where he was cutting up a pile of sandwiches, as another bout of coughing racked his body. 'It's not half as bad as it was the other day.'

Sarah scowled at George. 'Mum wouldn't let you get away with being so ill and still working. You should rest up for a while. I've a good mind to come round every day to make sure you're not overdoing things.'

George chuckled. 'You sound just like Maureen. She was nagging me yesterday. I'll tell you what I told her: the womenfolk in my life don't need to worry about me. I can look after myself.'

'Dad, can I ask you something?' Sarah said, not liking that yet again Maureen seemed to be intruding into her dad's life.

'Fire away,' he said, laying out the sandwiches on one of Irene's best plates.

'First of all, those are Mum's best plates, so be careful

with them. But seriously . . . don't you think you're letting Maureen into your life too much? Mum's not been gone a year yet, and people might talk,' she said a little fearfully, not knowing how George would react.

George picked up one of the tea plates and turned it round in his hands. 'I had no idea. Perhaps it might be best if I packed them up and gave them to you. You know how clumsy I can be. I just thought they looked nice on that dresser. As for Maureen, I'd not worry what people have to say. We both know she is an old friend of the family and also your mother-in-law, don't we?' he said, giving her a quiet look. 'You trust your old dad, don't you?'

Sarah felt awful for voicing her fears. Perhaps she should have kept them to herself. 'Of course I trust you, Dad, and I'd not expect you to do anything to make people talk, but perhaps you could not be seen out with her so much so they didn't have cause to gossip?'

George banged down the plate before remembering it was one of Irene's best, and checked it for cracks. 'Ignore the gossips, Sarah. You're not bothered by any talk, are you?'

'Well, not by other people, but you've got to admit it is rather strange when we are still in mourning.'

George gave a small smile. 'Considering my own mother married six months after your mum's death, I don't think we need worry. Are you concerned, Sarah?' he asked, looking her in the eye.

Sarah squirmed in her seat. 'A little bit, but I'm more worried about you,' she said quietly.

'Then don't be,' he said, giving her a wink. 'Now eat up or you'll be late back to work, and we can't have that. I've heard that new manager at Woolworths is a right tyrant,' he laughed, before starting another fit of coughing.

Sarah hurriedly finished her food and bid goodbye to her dad. She'd have loved nothing more than to stay with him and make sure he didn't overdo things, but yet again Woolworths was demanding her attention.

Back at the store, there was a complaint by a customer that one of the new staff had been impolite and offhand in response to a question. It took nearly an hour to calm the lady down with cups of tea and promises that the incident would be investigated, whilst Maisie took the tearful staff member to the canteen and wrote out a report. Then she sent the young woman home for the day, telling her she would not be sacked, but to remember that the customer was always right – regardless of how rude she might be.

'Blimey, that was a job and a half,' Maisie sighed when they met afterwards in Sarah's office. 'That poor girl was sure she was going ter leave wiv her cards. I told her not ter be so daft, and explained that not all customers are pleasant. What do you think?'

Sarah yawned and stretched her arms above her head. 'I think you're right. She was causing trouble for the sake of it and she picked on one of the younger assistants on purpose. She was good, I'll give her that – but she started to tell me how the same thing happened at the Bexley-heath store, and how she was given compensation by way of some free goods. I told her to come back tomorrow and I'd have something for her. Meanwhile I'll ring them at Bexleyheath and find out what happened. If necessary, I'll have a word at the police station. A word from an officer might put a stop to her little games.'

Maisie laughed. 'We've seen it all 'ere, 'aven't we?'

'You can say that again; but thank you for all your help. I couldn't have handled that on my own. We make a good team, don't we?'

Maisie's face lost its broad grin. 'Ter be honest, I wanted to 'ave a word wiv you about 'anding in me notice. It won't be fer about a month, but I wanted ter be fair and tell you as soon as possible. Also because it's due ter yer mum that I'm able ter even think about what I'm going ter be doing.'

Maisie went on to explain to Sarah about the shop next door to Douglas's new premises, and David's business offer. 'I'm that excited. I want ter sell women's and kiddies' clothes as well as nearly new stuff, and making up bits and bobs from what yer dad gave me will be a really good start. Are you pleased for me?'

Sarah left her seat and rushed round the desk to hug her friend. 'How could I be anything but pleased for you? It's the perfect business idea and I intend to be one of your first customers. All the same, I'm going to miss you like mad. It won't be the same here without you. I do envy you.'

'I'll only be in the next street, so we can see each other often. And I'll be in 'ere buying up most of the haberdashery counter,' Maisie grinned.

'Will you be here for the Christmas party for the old soldiers? I was relying on you to help with the entertainment.'

'I wouldn't miss it fer the world,' Maisie said, noticing her friend looked a little pale.

'Oh good. I've begged Betty to return so she can play

the piano for the sing-song, and to see everyone again. It will be almost like the old days,' Sarah said, putting a brave face on the situation even though it seemed all her chums from Woolworths were deserting her. What with Freda cutting her hours to be with Molly after her parents' tragic accident, it seemed like Sarah would soon be the remaining musketeer at the Erith branch.

'Hello George, not at work this afternoon?' Alan asked as he looked up from sweeping the floor of the workshop. He'd been doing that a lot lately, with hardly any repair work to keep him busy.

'I've taken a few days off to settle in the new house,' his father-in-law replied, at the same time sitting down heavily on the one old seat and thumping his chest before another fit of coughing shook his body.

'Blimey, that's sounding bad. Have you seen the doctor?' Alan asked, hurrying to a tap over a chipped stone sink in the corner of the room and running cold water into a cup. 'Here, sip this.' He watched as George sipped the water and the coughing subsided.

'Thank you, it was just the brisk walk down here . . . and the cold air that did it . . . I'll be fine in a couple of minutes,' he said, breathing heavily and holding his chest with one hand.

Alan had no idea what to do, other than try and keep George calm. If he had a telephone he'd have rung someone for help, but for now he could only encourage George to take things easy. 'What made you come down here today? The weather's not so good out there, and getting more grim by the minute,' he smiled, reaching for his broom to continue cleaning up. 'I was thinking of clocking off and getting home early for once, as there's not much doing.'

'That's why I came down to see you,' George replied, clearing his throat. 'Sarah came round to see me in her lunch break, and blow me down, she'd just left when I had a phone call. I know it's been a while since I promised to help with your work, but one of my enquiries has finally come through.' He reached into his jacket pocket for a scrap of paper. 'I know things have been tough and I'm sorry it's taken a while for me to find you some work,' he added, holding out the paper, which slipped from his fingers to the floor.

Before Alan could reach George to pick up the note, George was bending over to where the note had fallen, and the action made him start to cough once more. His body shook so much that he collapsed to the stone floor before Alan could reach him, cracking his head as he landed.

'George! Bloody hell, George – are you all right?' Alan cried as he bent over his father-in-law. Rolling the older man over from where he'd landed face down, he was shocked to see that he was out cold and blood was trickling from a gash on his forehead. 'I'm going to get you some help, George,' he whispered close to the man's ear. 'If you can hear me, I'll only be gone a few minutes, so lie still and don't move.' He looked around and grabbed one of the cloths he used to cover the motorbikes. He'd laughed when his mum had insisted on laundering them, but now he silently blessed her as he folded one to place under George's head and tucked two others round him to keep him warm.

Running from the workshop, he hurried down Crayford Road to the Prince of Wales pub and asked them to call for an ambulance, explaining the problem. Without stopping, he then ran across the road to his mum's house and banged on the front door.

'Where's your key?' Maureen asked before she saw the panic in her son's eyes as he explained why he was there.

'Get back to George, and I'll be with you as soon as I can get someone to sit with the children,' she said, taking command. 'Sit and talk to him, love, even if he's still unconscious,' she added as she shooed him down the path, before leaning over the low wooden fence to bang on her next-door neighbour's front door.

'They're all up the cottage hospital, love,' Maureen's neighbour called out as Sarah put her key into the lock. 'Your kiddies are round at your nan's house,' she started to explain. Sarah took only seconds to digest what the woman had said before running as fast as she could to Ruby's house, only stopping on the way to pull off her shoes so she could run just that little bit quicker.

'Nan,' she gasped as she hammered on the door of number thirteen. 'Nan, what's going on?'

Ruby opened the door with Buster in her arms. 'Oh, love, get yourself in and calm down. You look fit to bust.'

'But what's happened? Who is in hospital – is it Alan or Maureen?'

Ruby led her through to the living room, where Myfi

was working on a puzzle with Georgina. 'Be good girls and play with Buster for a little while, will you? I want to have a word with Sarah in the front room.'

The girls sat down on a rag rug in front of the fire and Ruby propped Buster between some cushions, where he beamed at them as they waved a golliwog in front of him, much to his delight.

'They're good girls,' Ruby smiled as she closed the door behind her. They went into the front room and sat down. 'I had to tell them what's happened, as I thought they might worry.'

'Can you please tell me what's going on?' Sarah asked in exasperation.

'It's your dad. He was at Alan's workshop and had a fit of coughing, and fell and cut his head open. Alan and Maureen are with him, and Alan used the telephone to let me know what was happening. It's the first time I've been glad I've got that thing,' she added, glancing towards the telephone sitting on the sideboard.

'But why didn't you go to the hospital with Alan? Dad is your son, after all. Maureen is only related by marriage,' Sarah said with a sulky look on her face. Lunchtime seemed an age ago, and she'd already forgotten his words about not being emotionally attached to Maureen.

Ruby patted her granddaughter's hand. 'I'd rather be here waiting for news and keeping an eye on the kids. From what I can make out, Maureen rushed up to the workshop to be with Alan and her neighbour took care of the kiddies until I collected them. Alan was a little shook up, but he's fine now,' she said. 'I take it you want to go up there?'

'I would, but you should come with me. Do you think Gwyneth would take care of the children?'

'It's already arranged. Once you've had a cup of tea we can drop them off over the road and go up to the cottage hospital. David Carlisle said he will take us up there.'

'Everyone's being so kind,' Sarah said. 'But I still don't understand why Maureen is up there.'

'She thinks a lot of George. You know they were very close before your mother came on the scene, don't you?'

'I knew that Mum was Maureen's friend when she met Dad . . .' Sarah said with a questioning look.

'Let me pour you a cup of tea, then I'll tell you more. You might want to wash your feet as well,' she said, looking down at Sarah's mud-spattered feet. Sarah followed her to the kitchen and ran a bowl of water, adding some hot from the kettle. She removed her ruined stockings and quickly scrubbed her feet until they were clean. She'd have to go without stockings if she wanted to see her dad as soon as possible.

'Now, as I was saying, your dad had a group of friends from his school days and they'd go off out together hiking, dancing and the like. They were young and it was just before the last war started. Maureen was sweet on our George. I could see that from the way she followed him about. But then the lads were off to war, and things started to change. Your dad was a lucky one and came home on leave, and there with our Maureen was her friend Irene. Maureen didn't get a look in, and with your dad going back to France he and your mum had a whirlwind courtship. Before he left these shores he'd married Irene, and you arrived before the war ended.'

'And Maureen?'

'The first day George met Irene she knew it was all over, and soon after that she married one of the other lads and carried on living in Erith. I'll not speak ill of the dead, but I think Irene carting your dad off to Devon had something to do with Maureen. Irene wanted some distance between them all, in case your dad realized he'd been sweet on Maureen when they were kids.'

'And Maureen never forgot her first love?'

'I believe so, and for that reason I want you to be generous and let this run its course. Nothing bad is going to happen. The pair of them loved Irene, and they would do nothing to besmirch her memory.'

Sarah wiped her eyes when she realized tears had started to fall. 'Oh, Nan, it's all rather sad, isn't it? War has done such horrid things to couples who both expected to stay together forever. Betty and her Charlie; Maisie and her Joe . . .'

'Then they went on to love again, and with new partners who knew their first loves.'

'Just like Dad and Maureen . . . ?'

'Yes, just like George and Maureen.' And just like me and my Bob, Ruby thought to herself. 'So you'll give them a chance, eh?'

'I will, Nan, I will.'

Not an hour had passed since Sarah had arrived at number thirteen as they climbed into David's car and set off for the cottage hospital on the other side of Erith.

'I'll not come in, as I'm supposed to be looking after the children while Maisie does her sewing. She's got a lot of stock to make before the shop opens in December,' he said.

'We'll all be down to give her a hand. I'm that proud of the girl. Both of you come to that. Look at how your arm is healing – good enough to drive your car,' Ruby said, looking closely at his hands from where she sat in the front passenger seat. 'You can drive with both hands, can't you?'

David smiled wryly. 'As if I'd be carrying precious cargo if I couldn't drive safely. Now, give us a telephone call when you're ready to come home and I'll collect you all.'

Sarah hurried ahead of Ruby, who was saying goodbye to David. She was shown to a ward where Alan was sitting on a bench outside. 'Oh Alan,' she cried, hugging him close. 'Now, tell me everything before I go in to see Dad. If I thought he was as ill as all that, I wouldn't have left him at lunchtime. This bloody job at Woolworths is keeping me from those I love,' she said bitterly.

Alan explained all that had happened at the workshop and how Maureen had been a complete brick caring for George before the ambulance arrived, while he'd been beside himself with worry. 'Do you know, Mum couldn't stop crying when they took George off to have his head stitched? I suppose it was the shock.'

'No; I do believe she's a little in love with my dad – not that he's aware of it,' Sarah said.

'Blow me, I'd not noticed.' Alan grinned. 'How do you feel about it?' he said, taking her hand gently.

Sarah thought of what Ruby had told her. 'I'm all right

with it. Yes, I'm fine. Now, tell me what was it Dad was giving you when he fell?'

'I'd forgotten all about that,' he said, reaching into the pocket of his overall and pulling out the piece of paper. 'I don't believe it – look at this. No wonder George was rushing down to see me,' he said with a choked laugh as she took it from his hand.

'It says here that you have an appointment tomorrow to see the fleet manager at the GPO building in Crayford about taking on the repairs of their motorbikes. Oh, Alan, this is wonderful news,' she said, throwing herself into his arms.

'Now what's all this? Has something happened to our George?' Ruby said anxiously as she approached.

'No, Nan. It's just that Dad's arranged for Alan to apply for a motorbike repair job with the GPO. Isn't that wonderful?'

'With this under my belt, you won't have to work such long hours at Woolworths,' Alan said. 'I know you'd rather be home caring for all of us.'

Sarah's eyes sparkled. 'That would be wonderful.'

'Hold your horses,' Ruby said. 'You've got responsibilities, young lady. Managers at Woolworths can't go running off when they feel like it, so think on. Now, let's go in and see how George is, shall we?'

Sarah felt as though she'd been given a brief glimpse of happiness, only to have it snatched away. Would her dream ever come true?

20

December 1945

'I think we could start the sing-song, don't you, Betty?' Maisie said with a grin.

Betty nodded and reached for her bag, where she had stored her sheet music. She picked out a selection of Christmas carols and started to play. Soon the staff and guests were singing 'O Come, All Ye Faithful' with gusto, followed by 'O Little Town of Bethlehem'.

'It's going to be a lovely party,' Freda said as she joined Maisie. 'We have a present each for all the old soldiers, and a lovely tea thanks to Maureen putting stuff by and begging off our suppliers. Hopefully by this time next year things won't be so tight, and we can give them an even better do.'

'Yeah, that would be good, and don't forget I'm coming back ter help. You ain't getting rid of me that easily.'

Freda looped her arm through Maisie's. 'It's going to be strange not having you here every day,' she said with a wobble in her voice.

'Blimey, Freda, I live up the other end of the road and

me shop's just round the corner. You'll most likely be seeing more of me. Don't you go getting as miserable as Betty; look at her sad face. You'd think wiv her husband expanding his business and her having that beautiful baby she'd be on cloud nine. I've never seen such an unhappy face on someone at Christmas time.'

'Sarah's just as sad. Alan has that big contract with the GPO, and George is out of hospital and on the road to recovery after that horrible chest infection, but she's acting like a wet weekend in Brighton,' Freda said, looking across the room to where Sarah stood in a world of her own.

''Ave you ever been ter Brighton?' Maisie asked.

'No, but you know what I mean,' Freda laughed. 'I wish we could do something to cheer them both up. I don't like seeing my best friends so miserable. At least Vera and Ruby are having themselves a ball. I've never seen someone doing a knees-up to a Christmas carol before. They may just have shared a glass of sherry with Maureen in the kitchen.'

Maisie was thoughtful. 'I might 'ave an idea ter cheer up our Sarah. She did say that Gina Jones from head office was coming ter the party, didn't she?'

'Yes, and with the store just locking up she'd better be sharp or there'll be no one to let her in,' Freda said, glancing at the large clock on the wall of the staff canteen.

'I'm going ter pop down and keep an eye out. I want ter 'ave a word wiv her before she joins the party. Cover fer me, Freda, and don't tell Sarah where I've got ter.'

Freda shook her head, not having a clue what Maisie was up to, as her friend sidled out of the room.

Downstairs, the shop had the minimum of lights on as a couple of cleaners went about their work whilst a supervisor stood by a side door holding a bunch of keys, ready to lock up. Keeping an eye on the door, Maisie hurried over to the cleaners to remind them to come up and join in with the party. She didn't like the idea of anyone working while the rest of them were enjoying themselves upstairs in the staff canteen.

She was heading over to the side door to chat with the supervisor when she spotted Gina Jones getting out of her car. Thinking she'd like to learn to drive herself one day, so that she could cart the children about and transfer shop stock backwards and forwards, Maisie raised her hand in greeting to the inspector. After making polite chit-chat as they went upstairs, she stopped Gina entering the canteen to join in with the party. 'Do you think I could 'ave a quick chat in the office, please?'

Gina looked mystified. She was already aware that Maisie was leaving the company the next day, and was curious to what the pleasant woman had to say. In the background she could hear the staff and guests singing a medley of Vera Lynn songs as Maisie closed the door behind them.

'You've pulled out all the stops, Maureen,' Ruby said as she helped to butter bread while Vera stood the other side spreading fish paste. 'I shouldn't have had that little dance just now; I'm fair whacked and the evening has hardly started.'

'I know just how you feel. I've been up and down to

George's house checking he's doing all right. Thank goodness my bad leg has all but healed. Sarah suggested I should move in with him for a week or so, but you know how people would talk,' Maureen said, giving Ruby a dig in the ribs and nodding towards Vera.

'You shouldn't worry about what people think,' Vera said as she licked her fingers. 'There are too many gossips around for my liking. Live and let live is what I say,' she added, as the two other women burst out laughing.

Maisie emerged from the office. 'Maureen, would you do me a favour and take over at the piano while I borrow Betty?' she asked.

'Of course I would, my love. It's just the excuse I need to sit down for a while,' Maureen said, following Maisie over to the instrument. Betty was just finishing accompanying Sarah while she sang 'The White Cliffs of Dover' to appreciative cheers from the old soldiers.

'Betty, Sarah – you're wanted in the office fer a few words wiv Mrs Jones,' Maisie said. 'Hurry up; best not ter keep her waiting.'

Sarah and Betty looked at each other with puzzled expressions and followed her from the room as Maureen started to play 'Run Rabbit Run' with the guests joining in.

'Come along in and take a seat,' Gina smiled from inside the office. 'I hope you don't mind me using your office?' she asked Sarah, who just shook her head. Whatever was it that the inspector wanted? Her mind was wandering over the paperwork she'd done recently.

'Don't look so worried, Sarah. There's nothing amiss. I'm here because I want to have a word with the pair of you, and I hope we can come to some kind of arrangement that will make you both happier than you have been of late. A little bird has told me that neither of you is entirely happy with Woolworths at the moment?'

Betty frowned. 'I don't work for Woolworths anymore, Mrs Jones, so I'm not quite sure what you mean.'

'You miss it, though?'

'Oh, I do,' Betty agreed with a sad smile.

'While you, Sarah, would rather be with your young family and supporting your husband's new business?' Gina continued.

'It's my dream,' Sarah said sincerely. 'But I'd not want to let Woolworths down, as the company's been very good to both me and my husband.'

'Then it is my pleasure to invite you, Mrs Billington, back as store manager – and you to hand over the reins, Mrs Gilbert,' Gina said with a beaming smile. 'Of course, I'm not letting you off that lightly, Sarah, as Betty will need a staff supervisor who can implement the staff training plans you've devised. But in a part-time capacity, so that you still have time for your family.'

Sarah and Betty looked at each other and burst out laughing.

'You've made me a very happy woman,' Betty said, for once reaching for a white handkerchief to wipe her own eyes.

'And I don't know how to thank you,' Sarah said, leaving her seat to kiss the inspector's cheek.

'Let's just say this is a gift from Woolworths for all the hard work you've both done, carrying the store through the darkest days of war. Now, let's join the party. I know I could do with a drink, and I don't mean a cup of tea.'

21

Christmas Day 1945

'Wherever you are, serving in our wide, free Commonwealth of Nations, you will always feel at home. Though severed by the long sea miles of distance, you are still in the family circle.'

'The King,' George said, and they stood and raised their glasses as one at the end of the national anthem after the King's speech.

'It really feels like Christmas now that we've heard King George. He's seen us through some troubled times, and it's fitting we hear him again now we are no longer at war,' Bob said as he went to switch off the wireless.

George got to his feet again. 'Before you empty your glasses, I'd like to say a few more words. We've seen a fair few changes since we all gathered here for Christmas 1938, when our Sarah came to live with her nan. We've welcomed new friends and young members of the family, and we've said goodbye to others. We've seen births, a few weddings as well –' he raised his glass to Ruby and Bob

– 'and we've had illnesses and injuries, and been blessed to have people care for us.' He smiled at Maureen, who flushed slightly pink as all eyes round the table turned towards her. 'King George mentioned the family circle, and we certainly have an extended family here today. I've been thinking about that family and how it all came about. The way I see it, we have Woolworths to thank for making friends and seeing our families thrive. So please raise your glasses again, and let us all toast Woolworths.'

'Woolworths!' they all cheered.

'Blimey, I'm stuffed,' Maisie remarked as she changed the twins' nappies on Ruby's bed, helped by Freda.

'I felt quite tearful at George's splendid speech,' Betty said from where she sat on the other side, nursing Charlotte.

'Dad always makes a good speech,' Sarah agreed as she buttoned up Buster's romper suit while he dozed in her arms.

'We've travelled a long way since we all met, haven't we?' Freda said. 'Just think – if Betty hadn't taken us all on when we met at that interview back in November 1938, we most likely wouldn't be here today.'

'I can certainly say that you girls have changed my life, and all for the good,' Betty smiled at her friends.

'I wonder what the future holds for us now this war is over?' Sarah said as her son stirred in her arms.

'We will have to wait and see,' Betty smiled. 'We are stepping into a bright new future and I know I'm more than a little excited by what it will bring. As the saying goes, when one door closes another door opens – so we shall just have to wait and see what is behind that door. Whatever it brings, we will be together, and that's what counts.'

Acknowledgements

The journey to have my Woolworths books published has been quite an adventure. Although I've been a working writer for over twenty-one years, the leap to being a mainstream novelist was a momentous one. It took meeting my lovely agent, Caroline Sheldon, to see that the half-page idea had 'legs' and she signed me up to her agency with the words 'go away and write the book, and I will sell it'. Little did she know that when this rather shocked writer left her office she spent ten minutes on the street corner squealing in delight to her friends – thank goodness for mobile phones! The next step was to write the book and delve into the history of Woolworths, and Erith, so that my memories were true ones and had not been 'enhanced' by the passing of time. This is where I discovered the wonderful Woolworths Museum online along with the curator Mr Paul Seaton, himself a stalwart of Woolworths and a mine of information. For local history that had passed me by I found that the London Borough of Bexley's local archives were second to none. Yes, the Erith of my World War Two stories is now part of Greater London, and thank goodness for archivists who held on to all the historical documents. I could have spent weeks just reading about the town where I was born, which is now just a memory for locals due to the Erith we all remember being bulldozed to the ground in 1966. Talking of Erith, do you know how to pronounce the word? It is 'ear' followed by 'rith' – or 'riff' as some locals still say.

So, I started to write my book and after three chapters my new agent was true to her word and an offer was made by Pan Macmillan – the call came during a funeral, but that is another story and typical of what happens in my life. A contract for *The Woolworths Girls* plus one other book meant I joined a fabulous group of authors who write sagas for the illustrious Pan Mac. To look at all those names and how important my publisher is in the publishing world still gives me butterflies to this day. I'm a very lucky writer indeed. It was Natasha Harding, such a generous editor who has gone on to great things in the publishing world, who offered the contract and took me under her wing. After Natasha I've had the good fortune to be edited by Victoria Hughes-Williams, Caroline Hogg and now Louise Davies, with whom I'm working on the next book that's due out in May 2019: such talented and hard-working people who truly care about this author's books. However, the talent doesn't stop there as a team of copy editors and proofreaders work on my words once they are submitted, polishing a book until it shines. Linking these teams and always there to answer my questions is assistant editor Jayne Osborne. Thank you, Jayne.

My Woolies journey wouldn't be complete without a mention of the fabulous sales team who do their utmost to ensure my books reach the readers via the bookshops and supermarkets. Did you know there is quite an art to getting a book onto supermarket shelves? It's not always possible for all books to be on display, and seems to be akin to a rugby scrum as authors and publishers vie for the attention of Tesco and the like. If we aren't on view to shoppers then our books are sold on Amazon, Kobo and other online retailers – but how do we get these books seen? This is where Facebook and Twitter come into their own and you will spot your favourite authors writing about their books and sharing news about signings and talks. This is also where we call on the services of book bloggers who get book news out to readers. I've made many friends in the blogging community who read vast numbers of books and spread the word – what would we do without them? I have a wonderful public relations team – ED Public Relations who, with their contact book, can place news of my latest book with magazine editors, radio presenters and most places where books are discussed. Thank you to Bethan James and the team. You are truly fabulous!

What about friends? I've spent so many years working in the writing world as a journalist, writing short stories, non-fiction books and then my novels that I've accumulated many, many good friends who are there to support me just as I support them. We can discuss any problem and also drink Prosecco to celebrate news or to commiserate when times are bad. The Romantic Novelists' Association, The Society of Women Writers and Journalists – where I rub shoulders with colleagues and friends – online readers' groups and libraries where I meet readers and hear what they want to read in books: all of this makes up my world, so I'm never alone when sitting down at my computer to write my latest book.

To you all a great big thank you! I couldn't have done it without you xx

A Letter from Elaine

Dear Reader,

Here we are at the end of the fifth Woolworths book. When I set out to write that first book, little did I know that it would be so well received and that you would take my books, and my girls, to your heart. As you have just read, World War Two has come to an end and in many ways the story of *The Woolworths Girls* has run its course. It had always been my dream to see how my group of family and friends would survive during the war years, and I've been lucky to do just that. I have to confess to dragging my heels as I wrote the final chapters of *A Gift from Woolworths*, as I knew I was saying goodbye to my friends who I'd created over the past few years. I was saying goodbye and already mourning my mates. However, in recent weeks I've started to wonder what would happen to the girls after the war. Would Freda ever find true love? What about Maisie and her children? It would be lovely to see them grow up. Would Sarah get her dream home with roses round the door? I've started to make notes as I think about the girls from Woolworths moving into a peaceful future, a future where they have an NHS service, an Olympic Games in London, and a young queen on the English throne.

How do you see the future lives of the Woolworths Girls? Visit my author Facebook page and let me know.

Lots of love, Elaine xx

The Teashop Girls

~

It is early 1940 and World War Two has already taken hold of the country. Rose Neville works as a Lyon's Teashop Nippy on the Kent coast alongside her childhood friends, the ambitious Lily and Katie, whose fiancé is about to be posted overseas in the navy. As war creates havoc in Europe, Rose relies on the close friendship of her friends and her family.

When Capt. Benjamin Hargreaves enters the teashop one day, Rose is immediately drawn to him. But as Lyon's forbids courting between staff and customers, she tries to put the handsome officer out of her mind.

In increasingly dark and dangerous times, Rose fears there may not be time to waste. But is the dashing captain what he seems?

The Teashop Girls is a warm and moving tale of friendship and love in wartime.

Coming in May 2019 – available for pre-order